Curious George®
Cleans Up

Adaptation by Stephen Krensky
Based on the TV series teleplay
written by Joe Fallon

Houghton Mifflin Company
Boston 2007

For information about permission to reproduce selections from this book, write to Permissions, Houghton Mifflin Company, 215 Park Avenue South, New York, New York 10003.

Library of Congress Cataloging-in-Publication data
Krensky, Stephen.
Curious George cleans up / adaptation by Stephen Krensky ; based on the TV series teleplay written by Joe Fallon.
p. cm.
ISBN-13: 978-0-618-73759-8 (pbk. : alk. paper)
ISBN-10: 0-618-73759-6 (pbk. : alk. paper)
I. Fallon, Joe. II. Curious George (Television program) III. Title.
PZ7.K883Cur 2007
[Fic]—dc22
2006036477

Design by Joyce White

www.houghtonmifflinbooks.com

Manufactured in China
WKT 10 9 8 7 6 5 4 3 2 1

It was an exciting day.
A new rug had arrived.
George was curious to see
if it would fit.

It did!
George liked it.
It was the right color.

It was soft to walk on.

The rug was just perfect.

All that walking made George thirsty.
He poured himself a big glass of grape juice

Then he went back to the rug.
It felt squishy between his toes.

George thought it would
be fun to jump on the rug.
So he jumped.

George forgot about
the grape juice.
It jumped, too.

What a mess!
George had to get that juice
off the rug.

He used paper towels first.
They did not work.

George remembered soap
was good for cleaning.
If one soap was good, many
soaps would be even better.

Now all George needed was water.

Maybe he used too much.

George went to
borrow a water
pump from a
nearby farm.

It was heavy, so he had
to put it on wheels.
And he had to get help
towing it home.

He used the pump a long time.
Finally there was more water
outside than inside.

When George was done, the rug was
cleaner than ever.

The whole room was cleaner, even if it was a little wet.

But it took a while for everything
to be perfect again.

SIMPLE TOOLS AND TECHNOLOGY

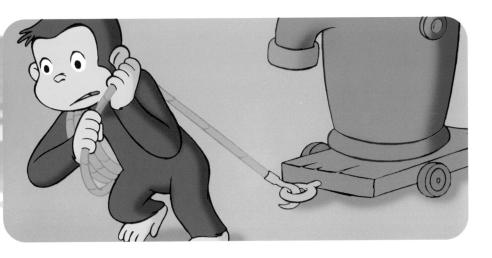

Curious George gets into trouble easily, but he always manages to find a way to fix things. In Cleans Up, he solves the problem with the help of a few simple tools. The pump was too heavy for him to lift or carry, so he used wheels and a rope for towing to help him reduce the pump's weight. What would you do in the following situation to help you solve the problem?

THINK ABOUT IT

You have a very heavy box of books that you need to move across the room without carrying it in your arms the whole way. You have the following materials: a rope, a large, flat board of plywood, several plastic logs, and a helper. How would you do it? (See possible solutions below.)

1) You put the wood on the logs, and the box on the wood. As one of you pushes the box and board over the logs, the other keeps moving the last log to the front edge of the plywood to keep your board moving. 2) You tie the the rope to the box and both of you pull it. 3) You move the books a few at a time! Are there any more solutions?

HOW IT WORKS

Curious George used a water pump to get water from one place to another. The reason the water pump worked was because the pump created an area of low air pressure inside itself. The high pressure outside the pump pushed the water up to fill the area of low air pressure. Then the pump drained the water out its other end.

HERE ARE TWO SIMPLE EXPERIMENTS WITH AIR PRESSURE

1. Stick a paper towel inside a jar and secure it with tape. Now fill your sink with water. Flip the jar upside down and plunge it into the water until it hits the bottom. Drain the sink. Did your paper towel get wet? Can you think why?

2. Insert a straw into a full glass of water. Place one finger over the top end and lift the straw out of the glass. Does the water fall out the bottom end? Now remove your finger. What happens to the water?

Explanations: 1) The air pressure inside the glass jar did not allow the water to enter the jar at all, keeping your paper towel dry. 2) When you held your finger over the straw, you lowered the air pressure on top of the straw. The higher air pressure at the bottom of the straw kept the water from falling out. Similarly, when you drink through a straw, you are not really sucking the liquid up. You are removing the air from the straw, lowering the pressure inside it. The greater air pressure outside the straw pushes water up into your mouth. It works just like George's pump!

UFOs
Over California

, 1947

TOP SECRET

During the time period between
and   The United States of
America was   by beings of
unknown   who having the form
of a   yet having an origin that
not of

CLASSIFIED

A True History of
Extraterrestrial Encounters in the Golden State
Preston Dennett

Artwork by Kesara

Schiffer Publishing Ltd®

4880 Lower Valley Road, Atglen, PA 19310 USA

Dedication

To all UFO experiencers and investigators

Designed by Mark David Bowyer
Type set in Futura Hv BT/Humanist 521 BT

ISBN: 0-7643-2149-8
Printed in China

Published by Schiffer Publishing Ltd.
4880 Lower Valley Road
Atglen, PA 19310
Phone: (610) 593-1777; Fax: (610) 593-2002
E-mail: Info@schifferbooks.com

For the largest selection of fine reference books on this and related subjects, please visit our web site at **www.schifferbooks.com**
We are always looking for people to write books on new and related subjects. If you have an idea for a book please contact us at the above address.

This book may be purchased from the publisher.
Include $3.95 for shipping.
Please try your bookstore first.
You may write for a free catalog.

In Europe, Schiffer books are distributed by
Bushwood Books
6 Marksbury Ave.
Kew Gardens
Surrey TW9 4JF England
Phone: 44 (0) 20 8392-8585; Fax: 44 (0) 20 8392-9876
E-mail: info@bushwoodbooks.co.uk
Free postage in the U.K., Europe; air mail at cost.

Contents

Acknowledgments

This book entailed a great deal of research and I am indebted to a large number of people for their assistance and contributions. Those who deserve special thanks include: George Adamski, Virginia Aronson, Gray Barker, Timothy Green Beckley, Richard Boylan Ph.D., Harold Burt, Kim Carlsberg, David Hatcher Childress, Vicki Cooper, Ellen Crystal, Peter Davenport, Richard Dolan, Anne Druffel, Idabel Epperson, Paris Flammonde, Don Ecker, Frank Edwards, Lucius Farish, Edith Fiore Ph.D., Daniel Fry, Timothy Good, David Gordon MD, John Greenwald Jr., Steven Greer MD, Michael David Hall, Richard Hall, Bill Hamilton III, James Harder Ph.D., Barbara Lamb MFCC, Roger Leir DPM, Melinda Leslie, Michael Lindemann, Coral and Jim Lorenzen, Colin Penno, Jim Peters and Tracie Austin-Peters, D. Scott Rogo, Frank Scully, Yvonne Smith, Brad Steiger, Wendelle Stevens, Whitley and Anne Strieber, Leonard Stringfield, Terrenz Sword, Jacques Vallee, Don Waldrop, Harold T. Wilkins, and all the members of the various California MUFON chapters. I would like to thank my sister-in-law, Christine Kesara Dennett for illustrating and book and assisting with my investigation and research. My family and friends also deserve mention for putting up with my obsession and sending new witnesses my way. Finally, I would like to express my gratitude to all the witnesses whose testimonies are included in this book.

Introduction

In 1542, Spain announced the discovery of a vast, fertile land that they mistakenly named the *island* of California. For nearly three centuries the Spanish lived there with the Native Americans, building numerous missions and settlements. In 1821, Mexico achieved independence from Spain, at the same time laying claim to California. This began a large Mexican emigration to California. At the same time, American pioneers also began to move westward.

During their terms, Presidents Andrew Jackson and James Polk both attempted unsuccessfully to purchase the state from the Mexican government. Then, in 1846, California enjoyed a short-lived and dubious independence when a group of settlers announced themselves as the Republic of California. President Polk then decided to take the state by force. So began the U.S.-Mexican war. After two years of hostility, Mexico finally ceded the states of California, Texas, and New Mexico for a price of 15 million, and California became a permanent member of the United States. At the same time, the California gold rush began, which led to the rapid growth of the population. In 1869, the west coast was linked to the east coast by the transcontinental railroad. California's rise to one of the most influential states in the union was assured.

The third largest state in the union, California is the most populous state at an estimated forty million, most of which is situated along coastal regions. It also boasts the nation's largest economy. It is a leader in aerospace and defense technology, computers, oil production, lumber, wine, agriculture, entertainment, and tourism. The climate is varied, the population diverse. The geography includes mountains, deserts, and the vast fertile central valley. The highest point in the state is Mount Whitney at 14,500 feet. The lowest elevation is Death Valley at 282 feet below sea level, also the hottest and driest area in the United States.

Not surprisingly, the state is also the leading producer of UFO reports in the United States. In 1977, leading investigator Dr. J. Allen Hynek, (often called the Father of Modern Ufology) conducted a study of all the cases reported to the Air Force's Project Blue Book which remained unidentified. California headed the list with fifty-one cases, or 9.9% of the total number of United States reports.[1]

In 1995, the National UFO Reporting Center (NUFORC) in Washington State was established, and began to collect reports from every state in the union. According to the center, California dominates all other states in the sheer number of calls. By 2003, they had received more than 2800 reports from California, nearly twice the number of the second leading state of Washington, and nearly three times the third leading state of Texas.[2]

California has a history of encounters stretching back to at least the 1890s and continuing to the present day. Many of the world's influential UFO encounters have taken place in the golden state. The start of the airship mystery began in California, then swept across the entire United States. In 1942, the now-famous Battle of Los Angeles took place during which a UFO was fired upon by the U.S. military. In 1947, Muroc/Edwards Air Force Base experienced a series of incredible encounters that would mark the beginning of an extensive and continuing involvement with the phenomenon.

In the 1950s, the controversial "contactee" movement began in southern California, headed by George Adamski, George Van Tassel, Orpheo Angelucci, and others. The Giant Rock contactee convention in 1954 attracted more than 5000 visitors and remains a record for the largest UFO gathering.

The 1950s was also the decade of the "flying saucer craze," during which a massive wave swept across California, producing such high profile cases as the Rio Vista wave, the Rex Heflin photos, the Red Bluff encounter, the San Fernando Valley "angel hair" case, the Tujunga Canyon abductions, and the continuing encounters at Muroc/Edwards Air Force Base and other military bases.

The 1960s brought an explosion of humanoid accounts, undersea UFOs, landings, and abductions – all of which continued strong into the seventies and eighties. Also, numerous Hollywood celebrities joined the ranks of UFO witnesses, including Sammy Davis Jr., Cliff Robertson, Jill Ireland, and Chad Everett, not to mention former President Ronald Reagan.

The 1990s brought more stunning developments – an intense wave over Topanga Canyon, the extremely well-verified Camarillo sightings, the opening of David Greenewalde Jr.'s website *Blackvault,* which has proven the UFO cover-up once and for all, and the groundbreaking research of Ventura investigator Dr. Roger Leir DPM, whose surgeries involving the removal of apparent "alien implants" have rocked the scientific community.

As can be seen, California has played a major a role in our understanding of the UFO phenomenon. I have been a southern California-based UFO investigator for nearly twenty years. In November 1988, a publicized sighting over Alaska sparked my interest in the phenomenon. I soon discovered that many of my friends, family, and co-workers were having dramatic encounters with UFOs. Stunned with disbelief, I felt compelled to conduct an investigation to find the truth. I was amazed to find that the UFO phenomenon had been recognized for fifty years. It had already been extensively documented and studied by reputable scientists, astronomers, military and governmental personnel, and other educated individuals. There were literally mountains of evidence, way too much for one person to study in a single lifetime.

This discovery changed my life. I read everything I could find about UFOs. I became an investigator for the Mutual UFO Network (MUFON.) I moved out of the armchair and into the field, interviewing witnesses, visiting UFO encounter locations, conducting on-sight investigations. I began writing articles and books, lecturing at local UFO groups, and appearing on radio and television programs. In a matter of a few years, UFOs had completely taken over my life.

Twenty years and hundreds of cases later, UFOs still remain a mystery. However, considerable progress has been made. We are much closer to understanding UFOs than we were in the late 1940s, when the subject first entered into the public consciousness. Now we know many of the patterns of UFO behavior, what the reported ETs look like, what to expect if somebody is taken onboard a craft, and so on.

UFOs are real. I am certain of it. I have seen them myself. While some people remain skeptical, UFO activity continues at a steady rate. The evidence is now strong enough to be conclusive for the reality of the phenomenon. The evidence comes in many forms including eyewitness testimonies, radar-visual cases, landing-traces, medical evidence, photographic evidence, metal-fragments, implant-removal cases, electromagnetic cases, animal reaction cases, crash/retrievals, and thousands of pages of government documents officially detailing case after case.

At least two other states have books detailing their local UFO history, including *Native Encounters* by UFO researchers Richard Seifried and Michael Carter of Oklahoma, and *West Virginia UFOs* by veteran newspaper reporter Bob Teets. I had already personally investigated more than a hundred California UFO encounters. A book presenting a history of UFOs over California seemed to be the next logical step.

This book is an attempt to compile a comprehensive history of UFO events in California. Accounts have been collected from books, articles, journals, magazines, television and radio programs, newspapers, and, most importantly, firsthand interviews. Many investigators other than myself have also contributed numerous accounts.

My first intention was to organize the book chronologically using *every recorded* account. This soon proved to be unfeasible for several reasons, the main one being that there are too many accounts to include in one book. While the book is still roughly chronological, I found it easier to group the cases according to type. Therefore, the first half of the book involves close encounters of the first and second kind, while the later chapters deal with the more extensive contact cases. These include UFO landings, ocean-going UFOs, the Edwards AFB and LAX sightings, UFO crash/retrievals, humanoid sightings, healing cases, investigator encounters, and onboard UFO experiences.

The history of UFOs over California is fascinating because it represents a microcosm of UFO activity across the world. The entire phenomenon is represented, from simple sightings of star-like objects to onboard encounters. And, of course, the California focus gives it a unique angle.

The complete story of UFOs over California has never been told, until now. As we shall see, UFOs have been visiting this state for a long time, starting in ancient times and continuing to the present day.

1. The California Airship Mystery

See color section, page 108

It is difficult to pinpoint the first actual California UFO encounters. Numerous Native American Chumash cave paintings in the Santa Monica Mountains outside of Los Angeles depict various strange big-eyed, hooded figures standing next to disk-like objects. (See photo section.) Santa Barbara resident and UFO witness, Tom X., had the opportunity to observe several of the harder-to-find petroglyphs, many of which are now on private property and inaccessible. As he says, "There are lots of very old Chumash Indian cave paintings up there, and they all depict objects in the sky. Some of these paintings date back six hundred years, and some might be over a thousand years old ... If you look at the paintings you can visualize saucer-type vehicles as well as strange-looking entities. The things that are painted on the ceilings of these caves supposedly depict things that were in the air. To get to some of the best caves you have to backpack in. It's worth the effort to go and see them. You can see that they depict some sort of vehicles in the sky ... my assumption is that this is an area that's had contact for probably thousands of years."[3]

There are a few very early accounts of mysterious objects falling from the skies of California. On August 9, 1869, Mr. J. Hudson of Los Nietos reported that his farm was showered with bits of flesh and blood. The shower lasted for three minute and covered an area of two acres. It was a perfectly clear, calm day. Scientists attempted to explain the phenomenon as being caused by vomiting buzzards. The editor of the *Los Angeles News* wrote, "That the meat fell, we cannot doubt. Even persons of the neighborhood are willing to vouch for that. Where it came from, we cannot even conjecture."

On August 20, 1878, the town of Chico experienced a large number of small fish falling out of a cloudless sky. The fish were so numerous that they covered the roof of the local store and spread out over an area of several acres.

On February 6, 1890, citizens of Montgomery County were baffled when their town was also showered by fish.[4]

It wasn't until six years later, however, that California would experience its first actual UFO wave, known today as the California Airship Mystery.

In late October 1896, San Francisco resident Mrs. Hegstrom was returning home around dusk when she observed a strange glowing light in the sky. Once home, she told her family, who didn't believe her.

Then, about one week later, on November 1, local hunter Mr. Brown told reporters that he saw a strange "airship" hovering at treetop level above nearby Bolinas Ridge. Again, however, people remained skeptical.

The first sighting to gain widespread attention occurred on November 17, 1896, when hundreds of citizens of Sacramento reported seeing a large "flying airship" move slowly over the city late at night. As reported in the *Sacramento Bee*: "Last evening between the hours of six and seven o'clock, in the year of our Lord 1896, a most startling exhibition was seen in the sky in this city of Sacramento. People standing on the sidewalks at certain points in the city between the hours stated, saw coming through the sky over the housetops what appeared to them to be merely an electric arc lamp propelled by some mysterious force. It came out of the east and sailed unevenly toward the southwest, dropping now nearer to the earth, and now suddenly rising into the air again." Among the many prominent witnesses was the daughter of the mayor of the city.

Several witnesses reported that they could hear voices coming from the strange craft. The next day, residents of Oak Park observed what may have been the same "airship" traveling overhead and leaving a trail of smoke.[5]

Five days later, on November 22, dozens of passengers on a streetcar in Oakland observed a flying object which looked like a "wingless cigar." As they watched, the object emitted a bright beam of light from one end. Shelby Yost, the driver of the streetcar, described the object as having a "blinding glow." Passenger Charles Ellis, a businessman, told reporters, "It hovered effortlessly and looked like a strange bird with four rotor wings, traveling about twenty miles an hour ... I didn't want to believe it was an airship. I had always regarded such reports as a joke. But now I have no choice but to believe them."

Another passenger, William Rodda, said, "I thought at first it was a peculiarly shaped balloon with lights. I've never seen anything so bright. Someone seemed to be controlling the machine on a downward angle."[6]

Three days later, on November 25, 1896, Colonel H. G. Shaw of Stockton, California, reported that he was nearly abducted inside an airship while horseback riding with his companion, Camille Spooner. The two of them were in the foothills outside of Lodi in the early evening "when the horse stopped and suddenly gave a snort of terror."

Shaw and his companion looked up to see three thin, seven-foot tall figures who appeared to be trying to communicate using a "warbling" sound. Shaw gives a somewhat familiar description of the apparent ETs: "They were without any sort of clothing ... their faces and heads were without hair, the ears were very small, and the nose had the appearance of polished ivory, while the eyes were large and lustrous. The mouth, however, was small and it seemed ... they were without teeth."

Shaw reached out and touched one of the beings and was surprised to find that they were nearly weightless. Two of the beings then tried to lift him, "probably with the intention of carrying me away," reported Shaw. When they were unsuccessful, the beings flashed lights at a "large airship" which hovered fifteen feet above the ground a short distance away. The beings moved to the ship in a strange hopping motion, only touching the ground once every fifteen feet. Then, says Shaw, "With a little spring they rose to the machine, opened a door in the side and disappeared." The machine took off. Shaw and Spooner returned and told their story to reporters at the *Stockton Evening Mail*.[7]

One of the strangest accounts from this particular era occurred on December 2 in the coastal town of Pacific Grove, north of San Francisco. Two fishermen, Giuseppe Valinziano and Luigi Valdivia, were in their boat offshore when they observed a small airship land on the beach. Immediately three occupants stepped out and physically carried the craft into the forest. The two fishermen attempted to approach, but were stopped by the occupants of the craft who refused to let them pass. They did allow them to observe the craft, which was described as twenty-yards long, cigar-shaped with wings that could be folded against the fuselage. The pilots refused to reveal their identity and waited for the fishermen to leave before taking off.[8]

The mysterious California airship flap lasted until December and remains unexplained to this day. Some researchers believe that the airship sightings may have been the result of early undercover experiments with human-made dirigibles. In fact, several citizens at the time made similar, though unproven, claims. Interestingly, dirigibles were invented and flown for the first time only one year later, on November 3, 1897, by timber merchant David Schwarz, of the Autro-Hungarian Empire. The first official dirigible flight in the United States also took place in California in 1904, when inventor Thomas Scott Baldwin tested his ship, the *California Arrow,* in August of that year.[9]

The many popular Native American legends of wise visitors from the sky could be the legacy of early California encounters. One of the first UFO-Bigfoot accounts occurred in 1888, and comes from the journal of a cattleman who had wintered with a tribe of Native Americans in northern California. During his stay, he saw a member of the tribe carrying a platter of raw meat into the forest. He followed the Indian to a nearby cave. Upon entering, he was amazed to see the Indian feeding the meat to a large, hairy man-like creature. The creature was totally covered with thick hair, except for its palms. Also, the creature had no neck, but was much larger than a man. The Indian tribe called him "Crazy Bear" and explained that he had come to the earth in a "small moon" which carried two other similar creatures. Inside the "small moon" were several other entities who were human-looking, only very short and they wore shiny, silver clothes. After disgorging the three creatures, the object took off into space. The Indians told the cattleman that similar incidents had happened throughout the years, but only rarely.[10]

One of the latest "mystery airship" reports came from rancher J. S. Jackson of Silsbee in 1905. Jackson was working with his livestock when a blinding flash of light enveloped the area. The cattle headed for cover and Jackson followed. Turning around, Jackson observed a seventy-foot long cigar-shaped craft with wings, one large searchlight, and small lights around the perimeter. Two of Jackson's neighbors also observed the craft before it departed. As in all cases of this kind, the identity of the pilots was never determined.[11]

2. Early Sightings

See color section, page 109

While accounts of zeppelin-like airships dominated the first UFO reports, it wasn't long before more technologically advanced-looking craft were also being seen. One very early example occurred around 3:00 p.m. one fall afternoon in 1912 in the town of Alameda. The main witness, C. F. Rowling, then fifteen years old, was with two friends when they observed three round metallic objects flying in a V-formation pass quickly overhead. The objects were totally featureless, made no noise, and left no vapor trail.[12]

For the next twenty years, there were few recorded sightings. The first wave of modern UFO reports came from the Mount Shasta area, today one of California's active hotspots. According to author Wishar Cerve, UFO activity occurred there as early as the 1930s.

What makes the Mount Shasta sightings so unusual is that the aliens responsible for the encounters allegedly live under the mountain itself. While this remains unproven, it is actually supported by several firsthand accounts.

The Mount Shasta legends began in the late 1800s when local residents reported encounters with strange individuals who would emerge from the forests to visit local towns to trade gold nuggets and gold dust for supplies. This in itself was not very unusual. However, the appearance of the people left a memorable impression. They were described as "tall, graceful and agile, with distinctive features such as large foreheads and long curly hair; the strangers wore unusual clothes, including headdresses with a special decoration that came down from the forehead to the bridge of the nose."

Visits from these strangers caused considerable interest, and local residents began to investigate the area. Several of them were surprised to come upon areas in the foothills that glowed with "powerful illuminations" with no known source. Others heard strange music. Still others claimed that they found themselves suddenly and temporarily paralyzed, or they would be accosted by a "heavily covered and concealed person who would lift him up and turn him away."

A few people claimed to have encountered very tall friendly people dressed in long flowing robes, who would hold deeply philosophical conversations about love, spirituality, and the fate of our planet.

Needless to say, these reports brought more visitors to the area. People attempted to chase down and photograph the tall strangers, but in each case, the strangers would either run away or simply vanish. Other visitors claimed to see bizarre-looking cattle "unlike anything seen in America."

Meanwhile, the strangers continued to make rare appearances in local towns. "Those who have come to stores in nearby cities, especially at Weed, have spoken English in a perfect manner with perhaps a tinge of the British accents, and have been reluctant to answer questions or give any information about themselves. The goods they have purchased for have always been paid for in gold nuggets of far greater value than the article purchased, and they have refused to accept any change, indicating that to them gold was of no value and they had no need for money of any kind."

Strange activity continued up through the 1930s, including accounts of electromagnetic effects on automobiles. Writes Cerve of one particular incident, "At an unexpected point where a light flashed before them the automobile refused to function properly, for the electric circuit seemed to lose its power and not until the passengers emerged from the car and backed it on the road for a hundred feet and turned it in the opposite direction, would the electric power give any manifestation and the engine function properly."

Most intriguing are the many early reports of UFO-like craft in the area. Writes Cerve, "There are hundred of others who have testified to having seen peculiarly shaped boats which have flown out of this region high in the air over the hills and valleys of California and have been seen by others to come on to the waters of the Pacific Ocean at the shore and then continue out on the seas as vessels ... and others have seen these boats rise again in the air and go upon the land of some of the islands of the Pacific .... Only recently a group of persons playing golf on one of the golf-links of California near the foothills of the Sierra Nevada range saw a peculiar silver-like vessel rise in the air and float over the mountaintops and disappear. It was unlike any airship that has ever been seen and there was absolutely no noise emanating from it to indicate that it was moved by a motor of any kind."

Today legends about an underground city beneath Mount Shasta continue to circulate. The area is now a magnet to the New Age community and has produced a number of impressive modern UFO reports.[13]

In the following case, while no actual UFO was observed, an unexplained event occurred in Contra Costa County, near Pittsburg, California, in the fall of 1933. The event involves unexplained light phenomenon, which was apparently *not* weather-related. It was witnessed by numerous residents across a wide area. One of the most compelling testimonies comes from an anonymous chemist: "At 11:45 p.m. I was seated at my desk facing a window with the shade down. Suddenly I heard a humming sound which seemed to come from the northeast and above. I noticed that the shade was brightly lighted, so I rose, parted the shade, and observed that the outside was lighted as bright as day but with a blue-purple light. The light was steady and did not flicker. Details of houses, streets, and hills four miles to the southwest were as sharp as observed in daytime. My wife had retired but I woke her and saw the lighted shade and heard the hum. Suddenly the light went out and ceased with a 'pow' sound. Reports in the press the next day indicated that the phenomenon had been observed all over Contra Costa County."

While it is tempting to label this sighting as meteoritic in origin, arguing against this theory are the humming sound and the steadiness of the light, which neither flickered nor varied in intensity.[14]

California officially entered modern UFO history in 1942, when a highly significant UFO event happened directly over the city of Los Angeles. Known as *the Battle of Los Angeles,* or *the Los Angeles Air Raid,* it marked the first recorded occasion in which the United States military opened fire upon a UFO.

The ordeal began on February 25, 1942, at 2:00 a.m. when air raid sirens warning of a possible Japanese attack sounded throughout Los Angeles. The citizens of the city began the familiar blacking-out process, and the military took immediate action.

The invader, however, turned out not to be Japanese, but unidentified. Several plane-like objects moved overhead, followed by a huge disk-shaped object that hovered motionless several thousand feet over Culver City. The mysterious object or objects stayed in place for a period of at least five hours. The military converged underneath, training numerous searchlights upon the main object. By order of General Marshall, 1430 rounds of ammunition were fired at the craft. Unbelievably, it sustained no damage. As a result of the attack, however, six people were killed from falling debris and heart-attacks. Damage totaling thousands of dollars was done to local structures. The unknown object was witnessed by several thousand citizens, and was photographed. The next day, the *Los Angeles Times* carried a photo of the object on its front page. (See photo section.)

After five hours, the object suddenly moved over Santa Monica and then south to Long Beach where it disappeared.

Says witness Bill Henry, "Do I think the object the searchlight caught was an airplane? I do not. Airplanes, particularly enemy airplanes, don't move that slowly or steadily, when under fire."

Says witness Raymond Angier, "When I went running outside to make sure people had doused their lights and were heading for shelters, I saw what had triggered the alarm. A formation of six to nine luminous white dots in triangular formation was visible in the northwest. The formation moved painfully slowly as if it were oblivious to the whole stampede it had created .... I ran to the roof of my home in west Los Angeles. The 'target' was 60 to 65 degrees above the horizon, coming out of the northwest from slightly off shore. Six to nine luminous, white dots were flying close together in a triangular formation, the point leading the way."

Other witnesses said that they saw "a big object, too big to be a plane."

UFO researcher Ralph Blum was only nine years old when he observed the strange craft. Says Blum, "The searchlights were converging fast. Six or more high flying objects were coming in over the ocean. The craft maintained a V-formation as they approached slowly but steadily. That was all I saw."

The military enacted an immediate cover-up of the incident, stating that that no objects were actually seen. This started the first Congressional investigation into the subject of UFOs. The military then tried to state that balloons were responsible for the reports. However, photos, witness statements, and a classified government document later released through the Freedom of Information Act (FOIA) all clearly indicate that something very strange happened over Los Angeles. The classified government document was a memorandum dated February 24, 1942 from General George Marshall to President Roosevelt, which said, in part, "...unidentified airplanes, other than American Army or Navy planes, were probably over LA, and were fired on by the elements of the 37th CA Brigade between 3:12 and 4:15 a.m. These units expended 1430 rounds of ammunition." [15]

This dramatic sighting, however, was only the beginning. One year later, on the morning of April 5, 1943, Army Air Force pilot and flight instructor Gerry Casey was teaching a student to fly a BT-13 trainer from the USAAF Ferry Command Base at Long Beach. They were cruising at 5000 feet near Santiago Mountain when Casey observed a strange-looking aircraft diving towards them. It glowed orange and appeared to be circular, about fifty feet in diameter, and had a rounded hump on the bottom and top. Casey kept his eye on the craft and prepared for evasive action.

Says Casey, "The craft coming at us appeared to be painted an international orange and was now about to pass on our left side. Unable to determine the craft's make or model, I knew it was unlike any airplane I'd ever seen. As I studied it, I was shocked to see it make a decidedly wobbly turn that quickly aligned it off our west wing in instant and perfect formation .... I'd noticed that its turn appeared totally independent of air-reaction but that when it was off our wing, the adjustment with us was held as if an iron bar had been welded between the two ... its color was radiant orange, which appeared to shimmer in the bright sunlight. As we watched, its aft end made a slight adjustment and it shot away from our position, disappearing in a climbing turn over the ocean."

Casey and his student computed the speed of the object and estimated that it departed at a rate of speed exceeding 7000 miles per hour. Later Casey became an inspector for Boeing Airplane Company and observed many of the most advanced aircraft. Never did he see anything that remotely resembled what he and his student had encountered. He remains convinced that it was extraterrestrial. As he says, "I could not reconcile its wobbling flight nor its sudden and unbelievable acceleration ... For any airman who has had a similar experience to mine, the conscious event cannot be erased. Nor can it be rationalized through comparisons with any known thing on earth."[16]

The UFOs were apparently beginning to study our aircraft and our technological and military installations. Another similar encounter occurred months later in November.

Second Lieutenant Thomas J. Duzynski was stationed east of Highway 95 at Camp Ibis with the 779th Antiaircraft Battalion. The location is about eighteen miles north of Needles, a remote small town in the middle of the vast Mojave Desert. Sometime before midnight, he got up out of his tent to take a stroll before bed. He had just exited his tent when he observed "an elliptical-shaped object" moving below the horizon, between him and the nearby mountain range, on a level trajectory at high speed. Duzynski watched as the object suddenly turned in a maneuver that defied conventional aircraft and moved upwards at the same time. It disappeared in seven seconds. Meanwhile, back inside Duzynski's tent, his pet dog exhibited signs of agitation. Coral Lorenzen calls this case "one of the early accounts of the sighting of a UFO which apparently had some effect on an animal."[17]

There is a widespread misconception that UFOs are seen only over rural areas. The truth is actually the opposite. The majority of UFOs come from areas with large population concentrations. In July of 1945, UFOs were seen directly over downtown Los Angeles. Raymond Bayless and R. McNab, two workers of the Firestone Tire and Rubber Company sighted "fireballs" darting around in the city sky. Bayless climbed to the top of the East 8th Avenue building and observed "brilliant orange darts of light" moving in strange patterns. The objects left trails of white smoke as they plunged downward. They traveled along the same path, and Bayless wondered if they might be meteors except that some of the objects would "stop in their plunge, reverse themselves, and fly back to their point of origin and disappear." Bayless watched the display for several hours, until the objects finally left. The next day, he was surprised to find no mention of the incident in local newspapers. Bayless, himself, later became a prominent paranormal investigator and the author of many books about the unexplained.[18]

One summer evening in 1945 at 1:00 a.m., thirteen-year-old boy scout, Joseph Stein woke up and exited his tent in a campground at Mt. Baden-Powell, in the Angeles National Forest. Looking up, he was shocked to see three vivid colored lights hovering over a nearby ridge. Says Stein, "They were bright enough that I knew that there were three different colors ... I remember looking at it for quite a while, and it scared me because I couldn't figure out what it was ... they weren't that far. But the thing that bothered me more than anything was the distance between the lights. In other words, it was a large something. Whatever it was, it was not small."

Stein eventually returned to his tent. The next morning, he examined the area where he saw the lights, hoping to see some sort of building or power-lines, but the sighting remained unexplained.[19]

In the middle of 1947, a UFO wave of massive proportions swept across the United States, ushering in the modern age of UFOs. The months of June and July marked a literal invasion. Interestingly, this also marked the occasion of the now-famous Roswell UFO crash. For whatever reason, the UFOs had arrived in incredible numbers.

The majority of sightings clustered around the southwestern United States, where much of the current aviation and nuclear technology was being developed. Many researchers believe there may be a connection between the atomic age and the sudden influx of sightings. In any case, the public at large became riveted by the accounts, ushering in the modern age of UFOs.

On the afternoon of June 12, pilot Richard Rankin was in his plane when he observed a formation of ten or more "disk-like" objects flying north over the town of Bakersfield. Rankin, who was a respected pilot with more than 7000 flying hours, estimated that the disks had a diameter of about one hundred feet and were flying at speeds approaching six hundred miles per hour. At first he assumed that he was observing military test vehicles. He only later concluded he had seen something more unusual.[20]

On June 28, an Air Force pilot was flying over Fairfield-Suisun AFB when he saw an unidentified object "oscillating on its lateral axis" as it moved at fantastic speed across the sky.[21]

A few days later, on July 3, a couple from Redding told reporters that they observed a shiny, silver "flying triangle" zoom silently overhead in a northerly direction.

On that same day, another sighting caused a media sensation when it was leaked to the press from a highly reputable observer. At 5:00 p.m. that evening, trained military observers at the Naval Auxiliary Station in Santa Rosa observed a twenty-foot metallic saucer hovering a mere one thousand feet above the main runway. As the anonymous source reported, "It was covered by silver material that looked like airplane aluminum. There were no marks of any sort on the surface. It was perfectly smooth ... it had no wings, no apparent projections of any sort."

The military officer assumed at first that it was a glider until he looked again and observed it more closely. Shortly thereafter, the object flew away.[22]

On July 4, two pilots encountered a UFO over Santa Monica. Duncan J. Whelan and Duncan Underhill were cruising at about 7000 feet when they saw a "disk-shaped object, not spinning, but resembling a rifle practice disk target, forty to fifty feet in diameter and traveling at about 400 to 500 miles an hour."[23]

On that same day, the Henn family of Broderick, California, was picnicking along the bank of the Sacramento River when they observed a shiny silver disk. Mrs. Henn remarked that the object must have been highly polished to reflect the sun so brightly. The object was in view for only a few moments before it suddenly vanished.[24]

The sightings continued. On July 5, Sergeant Charles Sigala of the Army Air Force said that he and three other witnesses observed a "silvery" disk circling over his San Jose home at about five thousand feet. Sigala observed the object for several moments and estimated that it was at least the size of an automobile.[25]

On July 6, the McEntire brothers of Santa Rosa observed a fast-moving metallic disk travel overhead at extremely high speed.[26]

That same day, Army Air Force Captain James H. Burniston was at Fairfield-Suisun AFB when he saw a craft move up and down across the sky. Captain Burniston estimated that the object was at least the size of a DC-3. The case was investigated by the Air Force and listed as case 36 in Project Blue Book.[27]

Also on July 6 occurred what could be the first recorded case of a UFO-caused power outage. That evening, just before the entire town of Acampo experienced a city-wide blackout, numerous residents reported seeing a "spectacular glow in the sky." Meanwhile, residents of the neighboring town of Lodi reported their observations of an unknown object flying at low altitudes.[28]

July 7 proved to be the busiest day for UFO activity recorded up to that date. While the entire United States was experiencing a wave of sightings, California in particular seemed to be the focus of an incredible flurry of activity. What makes this particular wave so interesting is that so many witnesses reported seeing large groups of craft.

It all began in the early morning hours when an anonymous woman in Palmdale called the police to report a "mother saucer" with a "bunch of little saucers playing around it."

About the same time as the above sighting, a Riverside resident went outside to investigate the reason for a strange static noise on his radio. Once outside, he observed six small metallic, flattish disks hovering over the power-lines next to his home.

At 6:21 a.m., a resident of Colton observed eight silver, metallic, "egg or disk-shaped" craft which flew silently by in single file. Only one of the craft had a flashing light on it, and all were reportedly moving much faster than jet aircraft.[29]

Four hours later, at 10:35 a.m., members of the Miramont family of San Carlos observed no less than *thirty* unidentified flying objects circling overhead at an estimated two thousand feet.

A few hours later, two farmers were harvesting barley in their fields in Glenn when they noticed a glint of light in the sky. Looking up, they noticed three "rows" of disk flying in formation overhead. As they watched, the craft maneuvered in strange motions and changed to a V-formation. The two farmers counted at least twenty-five separate objects.

That evening in Sacramento, William Smith, a photographer for the *Sacramento Bee,* observed a "round object" which appeared to tumble across the sky. Smith was a former Navy aviator and was still unable to identify the craft. He attempted to obtain a photograph but the object moved away too quickly.[30]

Meanwhile, over Los Angeles, two pilots, Vernon Baird and George Suttin, were flying a P-38 fighter at 32,400 feet over northern California for the Fairchild Photometric Engineers Company. Their mission was to map the geography of the area for the Reclamation Bureau. While conducting their surveys, a gray disk with a translucent canopy on top appeared about one hundred yards behind their plane and began to pace it. Finally the disk approached closer and Baird took evasive maneuvers. The disk appeared to split into two and the pilots lost contact after flying from California all the way to western Montana.[31]

Also on this day, Muroc/Edwards AFB experienced an incredible wave of activity. The story of Edwards is so extensive that it will be covered in a later chapter.

The final sighting for the day occurred over nearby Chino at 11:05 p.m. when witnesses described an object that moved so quickly, only a streak of light could be discerned.[32]

The wave continued strong throughout the summer of 1947. On July 29, another important sighting took place over a sensitive military installation, in this case Hamilton Field (USAF Blue Book Case #69: Unidentified). At 2:50 p.m. Lt. Ward Stewart and Assistant Operations Officer Captain William Ryherd both observed a twenty-five foot shiny whitish disk overtake a P80 jet fighter, which was coming in for preliminary approach at 6000 feet. Seconds later, both officers observed a second identical disk maneuver in a protective left to right pattern over the first disk, after which both continued south towards the city of Oakland. Lt. Stewart later told intelligence officers that the objects were unlike any conventional aircraft in his considerable experience as a B-29 pilot.[33]

While the 1947 wave subsided, sightings continued to be regularly reported throughout the next year.

Air Force Project Blue Book listed only two unidentified cases for the year of 1948. (Cases investigated by Blue Book were labeled unidentified only if officers were unable to find a prosaic explanation, for example: Venus, ball lightning, swamp gas, birds ...) The first occurred on September 23 (Blue Book Case #208) over San Pablo, and the second on December 3, over Fairfield-Suisun AFB. No other details were listed.[34]

Also in 1948, radar expert Mr. Wesley Price reported that radar scopes in a radar station in Arcata regularly registered flying objects, some of which were visible, some of which were not. They called the blips "discontinuities." On one occasion, Price was observing the scopes when three "discontinuities" appeared. The scope indicated that they were traveling at 35 miles per hour about 850 feet directly above the base. Price ran outside but was unable to see any type of craft.

His co-worker, Mr. Ehlers, reported that his radar-scope "frequently recorded signals of this kind." They flew day and night, alone or in groups of up to five. They varied in height from 800 feet to the upper stratosphere. They traveled about 35 miles per hour, in varying directions.[35]

On April 4, 1949 at 10:24 p.m., former Air Force pilot Major William Parrot was in the town of Merced when he and his dog heard a strange clicking noise. Running outside, he observed a metallic disk zoom across the sky at high speed.[36]

Four days later, on April 8, two employees of Griffith Park were outside when they observed a "silver disk flying at a high rate of speed." The disks left a white vapor trail and appeared to be about a mile high. The two employees reported their sighting to nearby Griffith Observatory, which denied seeing anything or receiving other reports.[37]

Two months later, on May 2, Marion W. Mills and Ina Monroe of Glendale saw a "silvery shining disk flying northwest." The disk had a shiny metallic appearance and flew at a "high rate of speed."

Four days later, an anonymous witness from Livermore reported his sighting of a UFO. The case made it into Project Blue Book and was listed as "unidentified."[38]

Eighteen days later, Glendale received another visit when no less than eighteen witnesses reported a mysterious object hovering in the sky. It was described as having an "odd oval shape." It remained above the stunned witnesses for several minutes, at which point "it suddenly flipped in the sky and disappeared."[39]

One afternoon in July, 1949, Mr. J. S. Stankavage reported seeing a "heart-shaped object" hovering over Los Angeles. Fearing ridicule, he told nobody what he had seen. However, a few months later his curiosity overcame his fear and he finally broke his silence. According to Stankavage, the object was definitely a craft of some kind. It had two portholes and moved with the point of the heart facing forwards. He only saw it for a few moments before it disappeared from view.[40]

The end of the 1940s marked the beginning of a mystery that would continue to plague California and the world for decades to come. It all began with simple sightings of distant objects in the sky. But the 1950s would bring a new level to the phenomenon. Not only did the number of sightings increase; for the first time, people began to report UFO landings and encounters with apparent extraterrestrial entities.

3. The Golden Age of UFOs

See color section, page 110

While the 1940s marked the beginning of the modern age of UFOs, the 1950s is often called the Golden Age. This decade produced so many high quality reports that they simply could not be ignored. For the first time, UFO reports were widely disseminated through the mainstream media. An entire UFO culture sprouted overnight, with movies, magazines, fan clubs, research organizations, and more. It was also during this decade that many of the now classic cases took place.

While the public UFO scene was spreading like wildfire, the military behind the scenes was in absolute pandemonium. All through the 1950s, UFOs conducted what amounted to a tactical survey of our military and technological installations. This, of course, caused great concern at high levels of government.

On February 9, 1950, Alameda Naval Station experienced a close-up pass by an apparent extraterrestrial craft. The headline for the *Los Angeles Herald Express* read: "Flying Cone – Check Report of Odd Craft Over San Francisco." According to the article, five residents of the town of San Leandro, including Lieutenant Commander J. L. Kraker, observed a 30-foot ice cream cone-shaped object. It was seen to fly southeastward at about 5000 feet, moving at about 85 miles per hour, leaving a vapor trail.[41]

A particularly credible report comes from astronomer Dr. C. D. Shane of the Lick Observatory on Mount Hamilton in Santa Clara. On February 16, Shane observed a "queer object" which he thought might be an asteroid except for the fact that it was "moving unusually swiftly. I call this celestial phenomenon one of the most unusual objects sighted in the sky for a long time. It happens that I saw it by chance." Dr. Shane obtained eight photographs of the strange object.[42]

Spring of 1950 marked an incredible wave of activity across all of California. On March 9, housewife Ruby Lytle of La Crescenta was outside her home in the morning when she and several other witnesses saw a "gondola-shaped object attached to a light colored hull" moving at a "slow and dignified pace" in a northerly direction over the city. Lytle called the local police and reported the sighting. Around that same time, city communications operator William E. Smith sighted a strange "revolving wheel-like object" moving quickly over Lockheed Air Terminal in Burbank.[43]

A few hours later, composer and amateur astronomer Eddie Coffer (Coffman) reported seeing a saucer-shaped object hovering 400 feet above the ground while driving to his home in Van Nuys. Once he returned home, Coffer alerted his neighbors, who also viewed the object. He was then able to observe the object through a 20-power telescope, and estimated that the UFO was at least "fifty feet in diameter."[44]

On March 12, medical assistant Bette Malles was outside her home in Hawthorne when she saw a "circular blob" emitting a "cone of light" from its underside. Seconds later, Malles saw another object emitting another cone of light. The two objects were adjacent to each other and both were surrounded in a halo of light. Malles ran inside and obtained her camera. She quickly snapped a photograph, at which point the objects promptly disappeared. Says Malles, "I saw something queer ... but I don't pretend to know what it was." Unfortunately, Malles' photograph was blurry and inconclusive.[45]

One day later, on March 13, numerous residents of Salinas called the Los Angeles Times to report an unidentified flying object over their city. While astronomers at nearby Lick Observatory speculated that the object might have been a meteor, at least one resident said that the object swooped down towards his automobile, performed loops, and hovered at a very low altitude.[46]

Around the same time as the above sighting and 150 miles further south, thousands of residents of Calexico reported seeing a "strange round object" which hovered high in the sky over the city. The object returned and was seen in the same location for three days in a row. Two pilots observed the object from their aircraft. One pilot thought the object might be a weather balloon at 20,000 feet. Another disagreed and said the object appeared to be sailing against the wind.[47]

On the same day, in the city of Monterey, government airport inspector Francisco Martinez Soto observed a "flying body" which moved in a straight line from southwest to northeast.[48]

Nine days later, on March 22, a large "metallic disk" was seen hovering at about 30,000 feet over the mountain resort town of Idyllwild. More than 100 witnesses observed the object as it moved northward.

The next day, Air Force Sergeants Robert O'Hara and William Elder swore under oath that they also observed a remarkable UFO display over Idyllwild. They both witnessed a total of eight 100-foot "elliptical" disks moving across the sky at an elevation of only 2000 feet.[49]

On March 24, several "silver" disks were seen over the northern California towns of Willows and Corning. The witnesses include Deputy Sheriff Frank Slavlicek and Police Chief Martin Dixon, who viewed the objects for a period of ten minutes.[50]

The next day, March 25, a fleet of eight flying saucers was seen over Laguna Beach, heading out towards sea. This case is particularly reputable because the primary witness, Dudley Gourley, worked for three years as an Army aircraft observer, and was therefore very familiar with unusual aircraft.[51]

That same day, at 7:00 p.m., newspaper writer Daniel Swinton was in his backyard burning garbage when he observed an unidentified object as it hovered above his home in North Hollywood. He described the object as being "elliptical in shape, brilliant and undimming, but not blinding. It flew on a due west course, then made a U-turn, sharp as a hairpin, and whirled away to the southeast ... What I saw was strange to my eyes." According to Swinton, the object moved at a speed exceeding 1000 miles per hour.[52]

On April 6, rancher Ralph Burke of Terra Bella was outside irrigating his fields when he saw several circular, silver objects flying across the sky. The objects appeared to be playing a game of cat and mouse with planes. At certain times, the disks would swoop down and emit a puff of black smoke.[53]

Later that day, scores of residents of El Centro reported seeing hundreds of objects that looked like bright lights hovering over the city in the night sky. The witnesses reported that the objects moved both slowly and quickly, and eventually disappeared.[54]

Three days later, on April 9, at least seven residents of Monterey observed a thirty-foot "chrome-like" flying saucer as it moved in a northerly direction about 4000 feet above the city. One of the witnesses was deputy sheriff Ted Cross. Says Cross, "It was definitely some kind of aircraft, but not local. In fact, nothing like anything seen in this world before."[55]

The next day, UFOs visited the city of San Francisco. Four high school students, Paul Montez, Richard Ririzary, John Garcia, and Jerry Fletcher, observed a disk fly overhead as they played in the park. Says Montez, "I'm positive it wasn't a plane. A plane that high would have left a vapor trail. It was just a gleaming object. It looked about the size of a dollar and then as it went higher it was about the size of a penny."[56]

One day later, on April 11, headlines for the Los Angeles Times read: "Chrome-like Saucer Seen Over Monterey." At least seven residents of the city observed a 30-foot metallic saucer cruising at a high rate of speed at an altitude of about 4000 feet.[57]

On June 24, the crew of a Navy transport plane flying one hundred miles northeast of Los Angeles observed an unknown object pace their plane for a distance of one hundred miles. The object was cigar-shaped, dark gray, and appeared to be at an altitude of at least 50,000 feet. What most impressed the Navy pilots, however, was its speed, which exceeded 1500 miles per hour. The object changed directions and then disappeared out of view. It remained unidentified.[58]

One day later, on June 25, at 1:35 a.m., three airmen at Hamilton Field observed a strange-looking craft pass overhead at an elevation of less than 5000 feet and a speed of about 1500 miles per hour. Corporal Garland Pryor saw the object first and alerted Staff Sergeant Ellis Lorimer, who had three years experience in control tower observation. Lorimer observed the object as it made two additional passes overhead. Staff Sergeant Virgil Cappuro also observed the mysterious visitor using binoculars. None of the airmen were able to identify the object, which eventually disappeared over the Pacific Ocean, trailing a blue flame "like an acetylene torch."[59]

On the same day, an air base at Oakland was visited by a circular disk shooting out blue flames. Three airmen observed the object, which moved at an estimated speed of 1500 miles per hour.[60]

On October 7, a pilot and copilot were flying over the San Fernando Valley at 4500 feet when they saw a strange-looking craft with "six to eight lights strung out along its length." Although they clearly observed the craft, they were unable to identify it. Fearing ridicule, the pilots at first demanded anonymity and refused to admit that they saw an actual UFO. Copilot Jack Conroy later revealed his name and said that no plane could have lights in the configuration that they observed.[61]

On March 13, 1951, military and civilian witnesses reported unusual UFO activity over McClellan Air Force Base. Blue Book investigators listed the case (#907) as unidentified.[62]

In July of 1951, a family that prefers to remain anonymous witnessed a dramatic UFO display in the daylight skies over a densely populated portion of Long Beach. The family first sighted a "gray-white sphere-shaped object" moving slowly overhead at a high altitude. The family was attempting to identify the object when it suddenly stopped in place. After ten minutes, it began to eject several small, "silvery" objects that glinted brightly in the sunlight. Shortly after the smaller objects appeared, they surrounded the larger object and entered back inside it. As soon as the last smaller object had entered the large object, the latter immediately went "straight up into the sky so fast that it was out of sight in seconds."

The entire family was astounded that more people hadn't seen the display. As one family member said, "The thing that really amazes me is that this took place over a thickly populated area. Surely hundreds of people must have seen it. It is possible that it was reported, as just about the time the small objects appeared a plane flew in that direction. It was then that we realized how very high these things were, as the plane appeared much lower."[63]

On September 6, military officers in Claremont reported their sighting of an unknown object to Air Force Blue Book personnel, who listed the case (#964) as "unidentified."[64]

Military bases continued to be the main target for UFO reconnaissance. On September 23, at March Air Force Base outside of Long Beach, two Air Force F-86 jets were scrambled to intercept an unknown object detected in orbit at fifty-five thousand feet above the base. The F-86's were forced to land due to insufficient fuel to continue the pursuit. Two additional F-86's were launched but also had to return. The pilots reported observing a metallic plane-like object, though there was some disagreement about the presence of wings. In either case, the mystery was deepened by the fact that the Air Force had no planes at that time that could fly higher than the F-86.[65]

On November 2, two forestry workers in Mojave experienced an incredible close-up encounter with a UFO. They were driving in their jeep when they observed a metallic disk-shaped object pacing their vehicle. The flying craft appeared to be thirty feet in diameter and about ten feet thick. It glowed an intense blue-green color.

The witnesses stopped their jeep and signaled the object. At that point, the disk swooped towards the witnesses, approaching within twenty feet, and then withdrew. The witnesses felt that it was playing with them. After a few moments, it disappeared "like a magician's trick."[66]

On November 21, Guy Marquand and two friends were driving through the hills of Riverside. This particular area contained a large number of orange groves. Unknown to Marquand and his friends, mysterious explosions had been occurring recently among the orange groves. Without warning, an object shape like a "cap" flew overhead, veered around their car, and flew back in the same direction. Marquand had just enough time to grab his camera and take one blurry photo of the object.

In late 1951, the United States was hit by a wave of mysterious "fireballs." While fireballs are a natural astronomical phenomenon, these particular fireballs exhibited several unusual properties such as controlled descent, lack of crater, and lack of meteoritic fragments. One of these fireballs was seen to descend and land in a field near San Jose. Investigators found a burned trail across the field, but no evidence of a crater or meteoric residue. Dr. Lincoln La Paz, an expert on meteors and an Air Force consultant, specifically pointed out the San Jose fireball as being unexplained.[67]

In December 1951, a U.S. Marine had stopped off at Palomar observatory while on his way to Camp Pendleton. While at the observatory, he overheard a conversation between two Palomar scientists involving UFOs. The conversation was so incredible that the Marine remembered it in detail. Reports the Marine, "The Palomar man said that U.S. Federal Bureau of Investigations had forbidden the publication of astrophysical photos taken at Palomar. 'Why?' asked the other. 'Well, they show things which the U.S. Government think wiser people should not know. They might cause panics. There are pictures of jet planes chasing flying saucers and disintegrating in mid-air'."

Later, further information would surface to indicate that Palomar was well aware of the UFO situation.[68]

Despite official denials, highly-placed government officials take a serious attitude towards UFOs. As reported by Blue Book chief officer Edward Ruppelt, sometime in 1951 (exact date not given), Ruppelt's superior at the ATIC, Brigadier General William Garland, told Ruppelt that he believed in UFOs. As Ruppelt wrote in his personal papers, "General Garland ... was a moderately confirmed believer. He had seen a UFO while stationed in Sacramento."[69]

On March 24, 1952, radar operators at Point Conception, just north of Santa Barbara, received unexplainable blips on their radar-scopes. No known aircraft accounted for the anomalous returns. The case found its way into Blue Book and was listed as "unidentified." (Case #1077.)[70]

A few weeks later, citizens in Santa Cruz reported UFO activity. Blue Book officers sent to investigate were unable to account for the sighting and listed it as unidentified. (Case #1115.)[71]

A particularly compelling sighting occurred at 11:00 a.m. on April 25, when two skeptical scientists from San Jose observed a "small metallic-appearing disc rotating and wobbling on its axis." Researcher and fellow scientist James McDonald later interviewed one of the witnesses, who described the sighting in more detail, saying they saw a "large black, circular object joined by two similar objects that dropped out of an overcast. The small disc accelerated upwards and one of the larger objects, perhaps one hundred feet in diameter, took off after it on a seemingly converging course; both then vanished in the overcast." The two scientists were utterly convinced that they had seen "some propulsion method not in the physic books," but for fear of ridicule, they refused to come forward with their account. They called it, "a most disturbing experience."[72]

Numerous cases have already been recounted in which UFOs show an undue interest in our military bases. The incredible amount of UFO activity around Edwards is only one example. Another is that of George Air Force Base, located just southeast of Edwards Air Force Base.

All throughout the month of May 1952, George AFB experienced what researcher Michael David Hall calls "a particularly intense series of sightings." The sightings were so dramatic, in fact, that they rival some of those at Edwards.

It all began at 10:50 a.m. on May 1 when four officers in the base Range Control Tower observed five white disks swoop down out of the sky from the direction of Apple Valley to the southeast, and then cavort directly over the base. Air Force Blue Book investigator J. Allen Hynek spoke with the witnesses (see Blue Book Case #1176, unidentified). Said Hynek, "The discs were very maneuverable, appearing almost to collide and then break away."

In an official statement to Air Force investigators, one of the control tower personnel testified, "The objects, five in number, appeared to be round and disc-shaped. The diameter of these objects seemed to be greater than the length of an F-51 fighter plane. They were of a flat, white color and gave off no glare or reflection. They moved in formation with the last two darting around in a circular motion. I estimated that the speed of the objects was about twice that of ordinary jet aircraft ... and the altitude of the objects to have been about 4,000 feet."

The witness stated that the objects were in view for about thirty seconds, after which they veered to the north and departed. Unknown to those in the control tower, there was another witness – the Wing Director of George AFB – four miles away, who also observed the entire incident. The fifth witness was actually playing golf on a course in nearby Apple Valley when he looked up and saw one of the mystery objects. As he later told investigators, "The shape of the object was round. I could not see if it was shaped as a ball or a disc. It was white in color, made no noise, had no visible exhaust and the speed appeared to be in excess of 1,000 miles per hour. The outline was very clear, like the edge of a sheet of paper. The object was not maneuvering in any way and was flying in a straight east direction. I could not estimate the altitude but thought it was very high."

Evidently, the fifth witness observed the tail-end of the sighting and saw only one of the objects as it quickly zoomed away from the base. However, the ordeal was far from over. Exactly eight days later, at 10:30 a.m. on May 9, an officer on the base sighted a "round, silver object" moving overhead. At the same time, two pilots in two F-86 aircraft also observed the same object (see Blue Book Case #1194: unidentified).

Two hours later, numerous personnel on the base observed two objects making a low, slow pass over the base. They were described as having "a silver metal color with a dark spot in the center and at certain angles to the sun gave off a bright glare."

Then, at 5:20 p.m., additional witnesses observed a "dull-colored" object in the shape of an "arrowhead" pass high overhead.

By now, the base was surely on high alert. The sightings, however, appeared to have stopped.

Then, two days later, at 12:20 p.m. on May 11, a whitish object "like a white paper plate" was seen tumbling at jet-speed over the base. At one point, the object appeared to reduce its speed, and then moved away.

Two days later, at 2:25 p.m. on May 13, the base was again put on high alert when a single, round, shiny, metallic disk hovered stationary overhead, remaining in view for more than thirty minutes. As observers watched, the disk appeared to glow or reflect a white-silver color.

The disk was back the next day, this time at 2:05 p.m., and was observed by the same officers, all of whom agreed that it was apparently the same object.

Then, one week later, on May 20, the disk returned for its final survey of George AFB. It appeared at 2:25 p.m., right on schedule, and remained for a period of five minutes hovering stationary over the base before moving away and disappearing.

This dramatic series of sightings caused a major investigation. The head of Project Blue Book, Captain Edward Ruppelt, learned of the case and arrived on May 20, the day of the last sighting. Ruppelt had high hopes of seeing one of the disks himself. He met with the Base Commander Major Vincent Walrath of the 146th Fighter Wing and convinced the commander to let him go aloft in a T-6 jet to look for the saucers himself. Major Walrath agreed and gave him a plane and pilot. Unfortunately, Ruppelt and his pilot saw only a normal balloon. For whatever reason, the sightings at George AFB had come to a sudden end.

The Blue Book investigation then focused on the possibility that the disks were actually weather balloons, but due to the strangeness of the objects, investigators eventually labeled the case "unidentified." [73]

It is well-known among investigators that UFOs are attracted to highly technological installations. On June 1, technicians for Hughes Aircraft were conducting experimental radar tests outside of Los Angeles. During the tests, the scientists picked up an unknown blip on their radar. The blip indicated a solid object at about eleven thousand feet heading over the San Gabriel Mountains. The technicians were trying to identify the mystery craft when it did something no conventional craft can do; the radar set showed that the object suddenly moved upwards at 550 miles per hour, then dived downwards, leveled out at 55,000 feet and headed southeast towards Riverside. Edwards AFB was alerted, but they denied any involvement. The case remains unidentified. [74]

On June 18, a B-25 crewed with Air Force personnel was paced by an unknown object for a period of thirty minutes while en route over southern California.[75]

Then, on June 30, world-famous columnist Walter Winchell made a stunning announcement, "Scientists at Palomar Observatory are supposed to have seen a 'space ship' land in the Mojave Desert, in May last. Four persons stepped out, took one look, and went off again. The U.S. Army may officially announce it in the fall." Needless to say, the announcement never came. However, Palomar Observatory was again indicated as having knowledge about the UFO situation.[76]

On July 15, 1952, the first of a series of sightings occurred over Los Angeles International Airport. Because of the dramatic and extensive nature of these sightings, and those that came after them, they will be covered in a later chapter.

On July 23, several aircraft-plant workers in Culver City used binoculars to observe an "elliptical-shaped" object which hovered in place. As they watched, two smaller disks emerged from it, circled around, rejoined the mother ship which then took off at high speed.[77]

On the next day, personnel at Travis Air Force observed a UFO (not described). The case was reported to Blue Book (Case #1588), and was labeled unidentified.[78]

Three days later, on July 26, a military jet reportedly chased an object over an unnamed AFB in southern California. The object easily out-maneuvered the jet and disappeared.[79]

A possible airplane crash involving a UFO occurred sometime in July. Citizens in the town of Anselmo observed a "strange silvery object" high in the sky. Five minutes later, a pilot flying over Nicasio, five miles away, crashed and was killed. No explanation for the crash was found.[80]

On August 1, citizens of Lancaster reported an unknown object over the city. The case was reported to Blue Book (Case #1771) and was labeled unidentified.[81]

Two days later, on August 3, a rare "radar-visual" sighting occurred over Hamilton AFB. Officers at the base sighted two huge silver disks, which were soon verified on radar scopes to be circling the base. Several F-86 jets were immediately scrambled to intercept the craft. Immediately, six additional disks appeared and assumed a diamond formation. Seconds later, the objects accelerated out of sight.[82]

Two other unidentified Blue Book cases occurred in mid-August. Blue Book Case #1920 occurred on August 18 and involved military witnesses in Fairfield. Blue Book Case #1928 occurred on August 19 over the town of Red Bluff, which would later experience a highly dramatic UFO wave.[83]

On August 25, UFOs again appeared over the city of Glendale. Mr. and Mrs. Edward Gray were driving through the town and had just exited their vehicle at around 7:00 p.m. when they saw a bright glowing sphere moving in a full-circle across the sky. Mrs. Gray described the object, "The front part was like an extraordinarily bright headlight of orange color and behind was a long tail of a golden red tinge like fire ... it didn't look like anything we ever had seen in our lives before." At least three other independent witnesses also reported the same observations.[84]

On September 14, military personnel in Santa Barbara reported their sighting of a UFO to Project Blue Book. The case (#2086) was labeled unidentified.[85]

On September 27, numerous residents of Inyokern reported strange objects in the sky (see Blue Book case #2128).[86]

Sergeant Robert Blazina (USAF Ret.) worked for twenty-one years as a military pilot who specialized in transporting nuclear weapons. He held a top-secret clearance and traveled all over the world.

Sometime in 1952, he had his first and last sighting of an unidentified flying object. He was on a flight from Seattle to Sacramento. It was a clear, dark night, around 11:00 p.m. On this occasion, he was the copilot. Says Blazina, "Sitting there, looking ahead, I saw this orange glow in front of us. I didn't want to ask the pilot if he saw it because I thought I was just tired. And he did the same thing. Finally, he couldn't wait any longer so he asked me if I could see anything unusual. I told him that I saw this red glow in front of us. He felt better. We watched it. Finally he said, 'Well, let's try to catch up and see what it is.'

"We added power and we kept getting closer and of course it got larger until we got up to about Redding, California. It went into a descent and we followed it. We picked up quite a bit of speed in a shallow dive and it went clear into Sacramento and across the city and right over the capital building. We were right on it. We had the aircraft red-lined, as fast as it could go. At that point, it went vertical and it disappeared in a matter of two seconds, straight up. It was just starting to take some kind of shape when it went vertical."[87]

In early November, employees of MGM studios were working on a movie production in Studio Lot #2. At around 4:00 p.m., the camera crew noticed a large disk-shaped object moving overhead. Normal shooting was interrupted as one of the crewmen quickly grabbed a camera and snapped a photograph. The photo was never released and the entire event would have remained confidential if not for researcher Wendelle Stevens (Lt. Col. USAF Ret.), who uncovered the case.[88]

On December 13, Jerrold Baker was at Palomar Gardens when he observed a "bell-shaped circular craft" that looked similar to the ships allegedly photographed by George Adamski in the same area (Adamski would later become a well-known UFO contactee, claiming to have met friendly human-looking ETs). Baker grabbed his own camera and was able to take a photograph of the craft as it descended to tree-top level.[89]

On December 28, a civilian witness from Marysville reported his sighting of a UFO to Project Blue Book, which declared his case unidentified (see Blue Book Case #2302).[90]

Sometime in 1952, Bob Jung was in his boat off the coast of Catalina Island when he observed an unidentified craft in the daylight sky. He snapped several photographs before the craft departed.[91]

By 1953, the "saucer craze" had mounted to a near-frenzy. Up until this point, there had been only a few reports of UFO landings or entities in California. UFO abductions were as of yet unheard of. Even UFO organizations were reticent to accept any accounts of humanoids. The idea that these objects were piloted by actual extraterrestrials seemed too preposterous to entertain. Nevertheless, in the mid-1950s, the cases of humanoid encounters emerged in growing numbers, and they became difficult to ignore. Like it or not, the ET's were here and they were not going away. The landing and humanoid cases will be treated in a later chapter. Meanwhile, the sightings continued all across California, most of them concentrated over military and technological installations.

On January 10, 1953, residents of Sonoma reported UFO activity. The case was referred to Blue Book personnel who declared it unidentified (see Case #2326).

On the afternoon of January 27, John Bean – an employee of the Atomic Energy Commission Research Facility in Livermore and a pilot with seventeen years' experience – drove by Oakland Municipal Airport when he observed a UFO pass over the building where he worked. Says Bean, "It began a shallow left turn and at that point I could see that it was perfectly round and had a metallic sheen somewhat similar to that of aluminum with a satin finish ... brushed aluminum."

Bean watched in amazement as the object performed tight maneuvers, easily circling around a DC-6 and a jetfighter, which were also in the sky. The object remained in view for only a few more seconds before darting away at high speed. Bean was convinced he had seen a solid, controlled, unknown craft.[92]

On January 28, Rex Hardy Jr., a retired lieutenant commander in the U.S. Navy and a test a pilot for Northrop Aircraft, was flying over Malibu with two other crewmen. At 2:20 p.m., the three men sighted four separate unknown flying objects. The UFOs were described as being "the size of a B-36, circular in shape [and] aluminum-colored." Lt. Commander Hardy estimated the speed of the objects at about 1200 miles per hour.[93]

Just under seven hours later and about fifty miles farther south, another incident occurred over the cities of Newport Beach and Long Beach. At 9:00 p.m., the control tower at El Toro Marine Base observed an unknown object in the nearby vicinity. At the same time, observers in the Long Beach Airport control tower also observed the object. Marine jet pilot Major Harvey Patton was quickly scrambled after the mysterious visitor. He was able to pursue the UFO, which was described as "a large fiery red disk-shaped object." After four minutes of pursuit, Major Patton was unable to close the distance between himself and the object, and the chase was ended.[94]

At the same time, Blue Book personnel were alerted to UFO activity occurring over Point Mugu, also located adjacent to the Santa Catalina Channel. Although they had no information about the other activity, the case was declared unidentified.[95]

A couple of days later, on February 2, an anonymous witness from Victorville was outside his home at 6:00 p.m. when he observed and photographed a UFO as it passed overhead.[96]

On February 20, a private pilot was flying over Stockton when he observed an unusual object in the sky, which he was unable to identify. He reported the sighting to Project Blue Book, whose investigation resulted in the conclusion: unidentified. (Blue Book Case #2426.)[97]

On July 13, Ethel Carson and Mr. and Mrs. Rice of Pleasant Valley were alerted at 4:00 a.m. to the presence of a disk darting over their home. The object emitted sparks "just like fireworks" and appeared "about a quarter as big as a full moon." The object hovered over the nearby foothills.[98]

Around this time in Chico, only a few miles from Pleasant Valley, "a number of civil defense sky watchers reported seeing noiseless, round, silver objects either floating or speeding around town."[99]

Following the above sighting, the town of Chico became embroiled in the middle of a massive UFO wave. On July 15, three witnesses, Joyce Battrell, Mrs. E. H. Burnight, and her son, Daniel, observed a "silver-colored disk-shaped object" hovering above the almond orchard a quarter mile from their homes.

On the other side of town, an anonymous woman observed the same object which she described as "real shiny."

On July 16, the craft returned and was observed by Hannah Stone. Says Stone, "[It] veered like it was going over the city, then it turned sharply toward the north and rose rapidly until it went out of sight. It was round and looked something like a large transparent baseball."

Five days later, Mr. and Mrs. Joe Carlos of Chico were fishing along the Feather River when they saw a "bright object, just like a flying saucer" heading out of Chico towards Oroville.

The wave then appeared to move slightly southward. From July 29 to August 1, numerous witnesses reported seeing a disk-shaped metallic object hovering over the Sequoia-Kings National Park.

It all began when park rangers observed a "large disk-shaped" object hovering over the park at treetop level. The object returned over the next two days and was seen at close range by Park Superintendent E. T. Scoyen and several of his park rangers. Fern Gray, the telephone operator at Ash Mountain, the location of the sightings, reported that her entire switchboard was knocked off-line when the object appeared. The rangers alerted the Air Force who expressed curiosity in the fact that the UFO was interested in the Sequoia area.

On the fourth day of the object's appearance, a squadron of Air Force fighters were ordered to attempt to force the object to land. As Major Donald Keyhoe wrote, "Just before midnight, the pilots saw the disc slanting down at reduced speed. When it was well below them they started down, matching the UFO's speed as they leveled out above it. To the pilots, it seemed impossible for the spacecraft to climb without hitting one or two jets and seriously damaging the ship. Rather than take this risk, it seemed likely that the aliens would give in and land at the first safe spot. But suddenly, without even slowing down, the UFO stopped in midair. The jets instantly overshot. Before the pilots could even begin to turn back, the disc soared steeply above them and was gone."[100]

Twenty days later, on August 10, Susan Perdue of Oroville told reporters that she observed no less than five saucers with green lights, flying silently and very fast, and at an extremely low altitude.

On August 16, the last sighting of the wave took place. J. R. Bowling was fishing along the Feather River when he was distracted by strange lights in the sky which reminded him of flares except that "the first one appeared round and then flat on the edges, and it was going too rapidly to attempt a description."[101]

Meanwhile, further south, activity began to flare up. On August 25, Mrs. W. A. C. of Hemet was woken up in the middle of the night by a light which lit up the entire interior of her house. Says the witness, "I at once rose, and outside found that the whole half-acre around my house was intensely illuminated. I slipped on a dressing-gown and rushed out onto the terrace. Right opposite me was a huge disc which was slowing down, and becoming stationary. As I saw it, almost as if it had seen me, it suddenly accelerated and crossed over the hills towards Winchester. The light seemed to spotlight our place, and came from a ring surrounding the disk which was then stationary. The main disc had a kind of crumpled silver surface."[102]

In late August, engineer Frederic Hehr witnessed a dramatic UFO display over Santa Monica. Says Hehr, "Twice in one day I saw saucers, and witnessed a whole squadron of them go through various maneuvers, lasting ten minutes."

Hehr observed several "brilliant white bars" dart very quickly across the sky. Suddenly, they all came together and "formed a diamond pattern around a somewhat diffuse object." As Hehr looked on, the central object disappeared and the surrounding objects darted around and also disappeared. Later that evening, Hehr returned outside and observed another UFO outside his home. He described the object as looking like "two Jupiters, closely coupled." The object hung motionless in the sky for a few moments, then disappeared.[103]

Around that same time (exact date not given), Topanga Canyon resident, Frieda X. reported seeing a "silver bar hanging in the sky, quite near, with a pendulum movement." Topanga Canyon would later become the location of an intense UFO wave.[104]

At 9:00 p.m. on August 20, a TB-29 bomber/trainer plane from Castle AFB observed an oval metallic gray object which began to make diving passing at their plane. The strange object made a total of four passes before moving away vertically at high speed. The case was investigated by the now anti-UFO biased Air Force Project Blue Book, which was nevertheless forced to declare the case unexplained.[105]

Project Blue Book is now widely believed by investigators to have been more a publicity campaign than a serious investigative body, a way for the Air Force to extricate itself from the sticky UFO problem.

On August 20, officers at Blue Book investigated another California sighting (Blue Book Case #2686) by military officers. Again, no explanation was found, and the sighting was labeled unidentified.[106]

One week later, on August 28, a trained military observer from the Ground Observer Corps (GOC) witnessed a veritable fleet of UFOs. Now released through the Freedom of Information Act (FOIA), an official report was made to the Joint Chiefs of Staff, the CIA, and the NSA. The report reads, "Fourteen cigar-shaped object without wings ... lights on them in loose V formation. About the size of a bi-motor aircraft. No sound or means of propulsion observed. One object appeared to be leading the formation at an estimated speed of 200 miles per hour ... objects were first observed heading west through break in the clouds. Then objects appeared to turn and head north, disappearing behind clouds ... observer appeared to be reliable and has been an observer on duty with GOC for several years during WWII and during postwar years." While no further information was revealed about the case, it does show again that our government takes the UFO situation very seriously.[107]

One clear summer afternoon in 1953, a family of Philippine immigrants was picking strawberries from their farm outside of Livingston, in northern California. Suddenly, they looked up to see three typical flying saucers, floating only a few feet above the ground, each only about fifteen feet in diameter. Says one of the witnesses, Sally Sanders (pseudonym), "It was all a silver-steel color ... no windows." As they watched, the three disks hovered above the field, as if surveying it. Everybody stopped picking the berries and watched the amazing sight. Says Sanders, "They all just sat there. It seemed like it was forever. We were scared. We were looking up at it ... it was really weird. It's like you don't know what to do. It was right there. It was so close."

The objects rotated slowly and emitted a soft whispering sound. They stayed there for nearly twenty minutes, hovering silently. At one point, Sanders received a telepathic message from the saucers. As she says, "I remember thinking, feeling that they had mental telepathy so we wouldn't be afraid ... It was kind of scary. I don't know if they were actually communicating to us, 'It's okay.' They might have been. I remember thinking that."

After twenty minutes, the objects suddenly departed as quickly as they had arrived. The family returned to picking the strawberries and the subject was never brought up again. It wasn't until many years later that Sanders finally decided to reveal her story.[108]

On September 4, at 3:00 a.m., Charles Rogers of Modesto observed a strange glowing object high in the morning sky. The object seemed to be stationary. Rogers was employed as a newspaper photographer, so he quickly went up onto the roof with his camera. He set it on a tripod, aimed it at the stationary object, and snapped a photograph using a very low shutter speed. The results were impressive. As published in *True Magazine*, the photo showed a well-defined elliptical-shaped yellowish light.[109]

On October 13, Mrs. E. Cortsen of Pleasant Hill was outside feeding her turkeys when the birds suddenly became "greatly excited." Looking up, she noticed four round objects, flying at a "great height" and glistening in the sunlight. Seconds later, the saucers ejected a "mysterious white substance" which drifted slowly to the ground and disintegrated.[110]

On November 3, a witness identified only as "J." observed and photographed an object (not described) as it hovered over Norton Air Force Base at around 4:00 in the morning.[111]

On November 16 of 1953, a UFO event occurred of such magnitude that today it remains a classic case in the annals of UFO literature. A "huge silvery ball" was seen hovering a few thousand feet above the west San Fernando Valley outside Los Angeles. The incident gained considerable publicity because more than three hundred people witnessed the gigantic sphere being chased by three jets across the San Fernando Valley. The mysterious object easily out-distanced the jets and returned back over the valley, flying in strange darting patterns. At one point, the object hovered and ejected a large volume of spider web-like filaments, popularly termed "angel hair." The substance thickly coated two square blocks, covering power-lines, buildings, homes, streets, sidewalks, and vehicles. One bakery truck driver reported that his car was completely buried in the stuff. Concerned residents attempted to gather samples of the mysterious substance, but it dissolved soon after it touched the ground. As one witness said, "It looked like finely shredded wool or spun glass. But held between the fingers, it dissolved into nothing." Another witness wrote that the substance "fell onto bushes and jumped out to passersby as hair does to a magnetized comb."

Three engineers from Lockheed, North American, and Douglas Aircraft came to the area to investigate and retrieve samples of the substance. However, there was no official investigation and no results were ever released.[112]

One month later, on December 16, an extremely well-verified case took place over Agoura in southern California. There were two independent groups of witnesses to the same event. All the witnesses were trained engineers and pilots employed by Lockheed.

It was 4:29 p.m. and the Lockheed Chief Flight Test Engineer, the Lockheed Chief Aerodynamics Engineer, two other test pilots, and another engineer were flying at 20,000 feet when they observed a classic "flying saucer" moving in front of their plane. For five minutes, the crew pushed their plane to its top speed of 225 miles per hour, but were unable to close in on the object. After five minutes, the object suddenly increased speed until it was only a speck in the sky, and then disappeared.

Meanwhile, down on the ground, Lockheed's Chief Engineer was at his ranch in neighboring Point Mugu. He was looking out the window when he noticed a strange object moving across the sky. Grabbing a pair of binoculars, he ran outside and observed a "solid black ellipse" heading out over the ocean. He observed the object for ninety seconds. The report was sent to ATIC and Project Blue Book. Without any investigation, Blue Book labeled the sighting as "a cloud."[113]

Finally, on December 24, two Navy pilots flying over El Cajon reported seeing ten silver, oval-shaped objects for a period of ten minutes, at which point the objects moved out of sight. Blue Book officers investigated the case (Blue Book Case #2840) but were unable to come up with an explanation.[114]

Two days later, Blue Book was called to another case in Marysville. Again, however, no explanation was found (Blue Book Case #2844).[115]

As revealed by UFO researcher Lucius Farish, sometime in 1953, a pilot from Lockheed was flying a T-33 Jet Trainer aircraft over Palmdale when he spotted a "bright round object high in the sky." The pilot aimed his gun-camera at the object and was able to take photos. Because of the high altitude, the resolution of the photo was poor.[116]

The sightings continued. At noon on January 25, 1954, the day was cloudy and overcast. Housewife Rose Sockett of Glendale stepped outside her home when she noticed a strange movement in the sky. Looking up, she saw two objects which she described as "brilliant bluish white, and their edges appeared to be saw-toothed." The two objects were rotating quickly around each other in a tight circle. Sockett observed the objects for a period of fifteen minutes, at which point they quickly departed.[117]

Less than one week later, another UFO-angel hair case took place, this time over the town of Puente. It was the first day of February when Mrs. W. F. Daily observed a "saucer" maneuvering in the sky above her home. As the saucer darted, she was surprised to see it eject long strands of a shiny substance. Daily thought it was "the saucer's exhaust." She observed thick strands of the substance float slowly down and drape itself over trees, plants, and power-lines. She rushed up and tried to determine what it was. Says Daily, "It vanished when I tried to touch it with my hands."

She rushed back inside and telephoned Mount Wilson Observatory for information on how to best collect the substance. Unfortunately, Daily reports that the scientists at the observatory scoffed at her story and provided no assistance.[118]

Two weeks later, on February 18, Roy Safire of Los Angeles saw an "elliptical cylinder accelerating at a tremendous speed" across the sky. Safire is certain that the object was not a plane because he watched it turn at sharp right angles. He estimated that it was moving at "about 1200 miles an hour."[119]

UFOs have a long history of hovering over small bodies of water. For whatever reason, lakes and reservoirs hold a special interest for UFOs. A typical California example occurred on March 14, at Puddingstone Reservoir, about fifty miles north of Los Angeles. Mr. J. W. Wasker was visiting the area when he observed a large metallic disk, somewhat resembling a gigantic hamburger bun, flying low over the reservoir. Wasker had a camera and quickly snapped a photograph.[120]

On April 14, another classic case occurred over the city of Long Beach. It was around midnight when United Airlines Flight 193 encountered a UFO while in flight at 5000 feet. Without any warning, Captain Schidel and his copilot both observed a large object looming directly in front of the cockpit. In an official statement Schidel explained what happened: "It appeared so suddenly, it was as if it was flying dark and had just turned its navigation lights on. I can remember thinking – red light on the right and coming fast. It was in sight just two seconds and made no movement to avoid me."

Captain Schidel was forced to make emergency evasive maneuvers to avoid a collision with the UFO. He instantly whipped the jet into a steep climbing turn. The emergency turn caused havoc in the passenger cabin. One passenger, Cose Barber of North Hollywood, flew out of his seat and broke his left leg, and a stewardess lost her balance and fractured her ankle. Captain Schidel radioed the Los Angeles Airport control tower which confirmed that there were no other aircraft in the area. Schidel and his copilot no longer had the object in sight. Says Schidel, "After disappearing under our nose we never saw it again."

The incident caused a media sensation when a newspaper intercepted the radio report. When Flight 193 landed, reporters were waiting. However, according to Major Keyhoe, "Reporters were kept from questioning him ... [and] Air Force Intelligence moved quickly to keep the story quiet." Today the Schidel sighting is among the most famous of airplane-UFO encounters. Schidel was convinced the object was a UFO because it appeared without any warning, either visually or from airport control towers.[121]

One week later, on April 22, servicemen stationed at San Nicholas Island reported seeing a gray cigar-shaped aircraft descend and apparently crash-landed on the island. A cloud of smoke appeared where the object had landed, however a search yielded no results.[122]

On May 10, military witnesses in Elsinore observed unusual UFO activity. Blue Book Officers were unable to provide a conventional explanation and listed the case unidentified. (Blue Book Case #2994)

On May 21, at around 9:00 p.m., the Miller family of Pasadena was outside their home when they saw what looked like "a house on fire" flying quickly across the sky. As they watched, the object stopped and hovered. Within seconds, the neighboring military base trained a powerful searchlight on it, revealing a dome and other details. The object emitted a series of flashing colored lights and departed the area.

However, the very next night the UFO returned. Then one month later, in mid-June the Miller family reported a third display involving the same object.[123]

About one month later, on July 30, the city of Los Angeles was visited by a UFO (not described). The case was referred to Blue Book, but an investigation produced no explanation. (Blue Book Case #3140)[124]

On September 18, a noisy UFO was seen and heard over the skies of Oakland. The witnesses include two deputy sheriffs and a retired Air Force officer, all of whom observed a "green object" in the sky. Moments later, a "strange explosion" was heard in the sky. The noise appeared to be linked to the appearance or disappearance of the UFO.[125]

A few days later, the desert community of Barstow was visited by an object that was witnessed by dozens of residents. Blue Book officers investigated the case and declared it unexplained. (Blue Book Case #3222)[126]

On the night of December 16, the desert communities of Victorville and Apple Valley were the location of a highly dramatic UFO encounter. The incident began around 6:00 p.m. when residents observed a large, silver, "cigar-shaped" object hovering stationary in the sky. When the strange object refused to move, the number of witnesses quickly grew to the hundreds.

As darkness fell, the craft began to glow a bright reddish-orange. Numerous photographs were reportedly taken by various witnesses. The craft was observed all night long. The next morning, it was still in the same location, and had again taken on a silvery metallic appearance. Witnesses estimated that the object was more than twice the size of a B-29 bomber. Two large portholes could be seen on one end of the object. It appeared to be at about 25,000 feet directly above the Apple Valley Inn. In the days following the incident, "local authorities" demanded and were given the photographs taken by the witnesses. No official explanation was ever provided.[127]

4. The Golden Age Continues

See color section, page 111

The second half of the 1950s brought a continuing flood of reports. The accounts included not only sightings, but reports of landings and humanoids. The first cases involving missing time-UFO encounters also began to turn up. The mid-1950s UFO scene had another unique feature – the *contactee*. At this time, dozens of people converged on southern California claiming to have had encounters with friendly human-like extraterrestrials. The contactee accounts shall be treated in a later chapter.

Meanwhile, the sightings continued. On New Years' Day 1955, a B-47 jet bomber was en route over California when an unknown object struck its wing. The plane made an emergency landing, but no cause was discovered for the damage.[128]

One month later, on February 2, Miramar Naval Air Station went on alert when military officers observed a UFO hovering over the base. Investigating Blue Book officers were unable to provide an explanation and declared the case unidentified. (Blue Book Case #3416.)[129]

On March 12, Orville H. Mitchell attended the popular flying saucer convention at Giant Rock in Yucca Valley. During the convention, he became intrigued by several curious-looking small clouds in the clear blue sky. The clouds themselves weren't particularly unusual. The strange thing was, they kept appearing and disappearing in the same place. On an impulse, Mitchell snapped two photographs.

At the time, he didn't see anything. But once the photographs were developed, he was shocked to see four self-luminous, delta-shaped objects hiding in the clouds. While they weren't visible to the naked eye at the time the photographs were taken, Mitchell's camera apparently had the proper film and filters to capture what the eye couldn't see. Mitchell used a 4" x 5" Speed Graphic camera with a Wollensak Raptar f4.7 coated lens and a Wrattan A filter. The film was Super-X. The photographs were later printed on the cover of *Saucers* magazine.[130]

On April 6, a thirteen-year-old boy from Beaumont was outside his home when he observed a "round silver object" hovering in the sky. Its apparent size was that of a silver dollar held at arm's length. He observed it for a period of time before it quickly moved away. Blue Book investigators labeled the sighting as a "probable airway beacon." J. Allen Hynek, however, wrote that Blue Book handled many reports under the policy of "It can't be, therefore it isn't." He was apparently convinced of the genuineness of the case.[131]

In 1955, engineer and Yale graduate Bryant Reeve, and his wife Helen, decided to drive 23,000 miles all over the United States to investigate the UFO phenomenon. On their "flying saucer pilgrimage," they met with numerous prominent investigators and contactees and also visited various UFO hotspots. While they expected to learn much about UFOs on their journey, they never expected that they would have their own encounter with an actual extraterrestrial craft. Not surprisingly, it occurred in California.

The Reeves were spending a few days in Joshua Tree on their way to meet contactee George Van Tassel. On the morning of April 22, they sighted their first and only UFO. Writes Reeve, "We were walking toward our car when I happened to glance northward towards a series of mountains in the distance. I stopped suddenly and grasped Helen by the arm and said, 'Do you see what I see?'

"'Yes, yes,' she exclaimed excitedly. 'It is a mother-ship, a cigar-shaped mother ship!' It seemed to be over and somewhat beyond a mountain which was some miles away. It was silvery white and was moving towards the right of the mountain top."

Helen Reeve grabbed a pair of binoculars and was just able to get the object in view before it darted away. They attempted to give chase, but were unable to locate the elusive object. The Reeves are certain that they saw an unconventional craft of enormous size. Writes Bryant Reeve, "Later I tried to estimate the length of the ship by comparing it with the mountain. It seemed to us enormous. It covered about one-third of the mountain top and was beyond it. My best guess is that it must have been well over a mile in length."

The Reeves were excited and delighted by their encounter. Says Bryant, "To us it was a never-to-be-forgotten thrill. After all, we had waited what seemed like a long time to see one."

Later the Reeves learned that several other people had also seen the same craft.[132]

On May 19, 1955, a dramatic UFO display was witnessed by more than a thousand residents of the neighboring cities of Tujunga, La Crescenta, Sunland, San Fernando, and Montrose. The sighting began when calls flooded local police stations reporting three "silver-colored objects" floating over the Tujunga canyon area. The Morris family of La Crescenta said that they observed the objects through binoculars for at least fifteen minutes.

The Montrose police station received so many calls that they sent out several cars to observe. Sergeant James Thorpe and deputies John Corbett and Anthony Machinist all observed the objects and declared them to be unidentifiable. The Montrose Sheriff's station later launched a full-scale investigation focusing on the possibility that the UFOs were actually weather balloons. To their dismay, the results of their investigation revealed that no weather balloons were launched anywhere near the area.[133]

This particular area would later produce more high quality reports. As pioneering southern California UFO researcher Ann Druffel says, "The Tujunga Canyons are themselves a hotbed of UFO activity and were so even back in the early 1950s."[134]

On November 14, two pilots experienced an incredible interactive encounter with a metallic disk. Private pilot Gene Miller was flying over the San Bernardino Mountains with his friend, Leslie Ward MD. It was late at night when they both observed a "globe of white light" maneuvering ahead of their plane. Miller assumed he was observing a commercial airplane and, as normal procedures required, he blinked his landing lights twice. To his shock, the object disappeared from view and then reappeared, twice.

Stunned, Miller and Ward realized that they were closing the distance between them and the now mysterious object. Fearing a potential collision, Miller flashed his landing lights three times in quick succession. To his amazement, the mysterious craft responded likewise, blinking three times. At that point it "suddenly backed up in mid-air and took off."

Richard Haines Ph.D. says of this case, "The UFOs light signals were obviously in response to the pilot's light signals."[135]

China Lake is the location of some of the United States most advanced aircraft testing. Throughout 1955, physicist Dr. Elmer Green worked as the chairman of the Optical Systems Working Group, whose job it was to photograph and record trajectories of rockets and other advanced aircraft. According to Green, UFOs were an everyday part of his job. As researcher Richard Thompson writes, "In his position, Green frequently heard about incidents in which UFOs flew into camera range during weapons testing and were photographed. He heard about good-quality films that had been made of UFOs, and he personally saw black and white still photos of UFOs that were made by people in his group. He was aware of some forty to fifty professional people who had some connection with UFO sightings made during weapons testing."

Green himself had a sighting with his co-worker, photographic officer Jack Clemente. While watching an AJ bomber come in for a landing at the base, they saw a sixteen-foot disk fly about 400 feet underneath it. Suddenly, the disk "flipped up" to the wing of the plane, paced it for a moment, and then darted away. The entire incident was captured on film. Later, however, when Clemente tried to obtain records of the incident, he was told that no such report existed.[136]

On June 6, a resident of Banning observed a UFO. The ordeal began at 4:30 a.m. The witness was driving when he observed a disk-shaped object with a dome on top hovering about thirty meters above and one hundred meters away from his car. As he watched, the object crossed the road in front of him and turned. He drove past the object, which then crossed the road behind his vehicle. As he watched, the object suddenly vanished. The case was referred to Air Force Blue Book investigators who declared the sighting unidentified. (Blue Book Case #4127.)[137]

At around 10:00 p.m. on July 10, Harold Huntman observed a 200-foot disk-shaped craft hovering very low over his backyard in Escondido. A slight mist surrounded the object, which was white in color and appeared to have portholes around the circumference. Huntman quickly grabbed his camera and snapped a photograph. Seconds later, the craft zoomed out of sight. The photograph shows the UFO surrounded in mist, but no portholes are visible. It was later published in the book, *UFOs: A Pictorial History*.[138]

About two weeks later, on July 22, a near-disaster occurred when a UFO apparently collided with a plane. Air Force Major Mervin Stevens was flying at 16,000 feet over the small town of Pixley. He told reporters that, at 11:00 a.m., the engine of his C-131-D suddenly staggered and the entire plane was knocked to the right by a "terrific blow ... It was as if we struck a brick wall."

The plane went into an immediate uncontrolled "vertical dive" and both Major Stevens and his copilot blacked out from the incredible gee-forces. Incredibly, Stevens regained consciousness and managed to recover control of his aircraft. He radioed to Bakersfield airport that he had been "struck by a flying saucer." He requested and received clearance for an emergency landing. Fortunately, the plane landed with only one injured crewman, Airman First Class Charles Stamper, who was hospitalized at Hamilton AFB with injuries to his face and knee.

An examination of the plane revealed that the left elevator control surface was "gone or smashed." A team from Edwards Air Force Base was dispatched to the scene to study the damage. An Air Force spokesman later told reporters that "it looked like something struck from above."

Later, Major Stevens was silenced by his superiors and refused to discuss the incident. The official Air Force explanation came when Captain Smith of Edwards AFB Information later announced the cause of the accident as mechanical malfunction.[139]

In support of the UFO explanation for the above incident is the fact that numerous residents in the area also reported seeing UFOs at the same time of the accident. Reports came in from San Joaquin Valley and from Fresno. Mrs. Ray Brown of Fresno reported that at 5:30 a.m., that morning, she observed a glowing, green, "egg-shaped object" move overhead. Further stunning confirmation came from Mr. and Mrs. Kenneth McMullins of Pixley who said they also observed an unknown object in the sky on that day. Both Brown and the McMullins reported their sightings after hearing about the mysterious airplane collision.[140]

One hotspot that consistently produces UFO reports is Yucca Valley. At 2:00 p.m. on September 18, Ray Stanford was visiting Joshua Tree National Monument when he observed a "glowing light high in the sky." As he watched, two jet aircraft appeared on the horizon and headed directly for the object. Stanford just happened to have an 8 mm film camera set up and ready to go. He aimed it at the object and shot about six feet of film showing one of the jets chasing the object. The altitude of the jets and the object were so high that the jets themselves were only visible because of their contrails. The glowing object, however, was clearly visible. Stanford concluded that it must be "many times the size" of the jet aircraft.[141]

On October 10, commercial photographer Joe Kerska had ascended Twin Peaks to take a panoramic photograph of the city of San Francisco. It was around 12:30 p.m. when he suddenly heard a strange humming noise. Looking up, he observed a large disk-shaped craft with a dome on top zoom overhead. He was so shocked, he forgot about his camera, which was already set up to go. He was disappointed that he didn't even think of getting a photo when suddenly, another identical craft moved overhead. This time he didn't hesitate and quickly snapped a photograph. The photo shows a silver, metallic saucer less than a hundred feet distant from the witness. (See photo section.)[142]

Seven hours later on that same day, another Californian, identified only as "H.," managed to snap a photograph of a mysterious object which hovered over his home in Bostonia.[143]

One month later, at 9:20 p.m. on November 7, Richard Veloz of Los Angeles noticed a brilliant, glowing object over his home. He snapped two photographs of the light before it moved away.[144]

A bizarre cat-and-mouse game involving UFOs and USAF jet fighters occurred in late 1956 over Castle AFB. The incident began when citizens from the nearby town of Modesto reported UFO activity. Two F-86 jet fighters were put on alert duty and instructed to fly over the town and attempt to intercept the "unknowns."

However, while heading towards Modesto, two control tower personnel observed a "luminous elliptical object" darting and hovering above Castle AFB, and the two interceptors were ordered to return.

Once the fighters returned to the base, they closed in on the mysterious object. At one point, they approached to within a few hundred yards of the UFO, which then eluded them by sneaking in and out of the low cloud cover.

Both pilots obtained radar-returns indicating a solid object. One of the pilots began to run low on fuel and started to descend for a landing. At that moment, the UFO maneuvered itself close behind the other jet fighter. Fearing a confrontation, the first pilot returned to protect his wing-mate. The UFO then promptly shot off into the distance and disappeared.

Following the incident, several high-ranking officers from a nearby base debriefed the witnesses and ordered the pilots to never discuss the sighting with anyone. When local citizens outside the base asked about their own observations of the disk, they were told that the sightings were actually caused by geese.[145]

Also in 1956, 15-year-old Michael Savage was outside his home in San Bernardino when he observed a metallic disk hovering above the high-tension wires. The object hovered for a period of about twenty minutes. Suddenly realizing what he was seeing, Savage ran inside and grabbed a camera. He quickly snapped a photograph before the object moved away. The photograph shows what appears to be a large craft hovering above the telephone wires. Because of the high credibility of the witness (his father was a prominent physician), the case received considerable publicity and the photograph became one of the best-known UFO photographs of its time. (See photo section.)[146]

On March 23, 1957, thousands of witnesses over Long Beach sighted four large, solid, round objects flashing brilliant red lights. The witnesses included at least three Ventura County Deputy Sheriffs. The objects were also tracked on CAA radar. At midnight, Air Force personnel at Oxnard Air Force base made first visual contact. An F-86 was sent in pursuit, at which point the objects climbed upwards and moved quickly away. The tower operator at Oxnard AFB said that the object "was moving much faster than anything I'd ever seen. About forty miles away, it came to an abrupt stop and reversed course, all within about a period of three seconds." According to the radar returns, the objects were moving a distance of thirty miles in about thirty seconds, or a speed of 3600 miles per hour!

A security lid was quickly clamped on the case and UFO investigator Major Donald Keyhoe was unable to obtain any further confirmation.[147]

Five days later, on March 28, at exactly 10:35 p.m., several witnesses in Reseda, California, observed a cigar-shaped object the size of a DC-6 aircraft, hovering at an altitude of 1500 feet. The object was surrounded by a bright halo of white light and remained in place for several minutes.[148]

Later, on August 28, Gary Kiel and R.K. Menkin of Glendale observed a dark hovering object above their neighborhood. They obtained binoculars and verified that the object was solid and definitely not a plane, helicopter or balloon. After a few minutes, the unknown object darted quickly away towards the northwest.[149]

The next day, an anonymous witness reported his observation of a "circular object" which flew from the north to the west and was in sight for four minutes. The sighting was reported to the Air Force's Project Blue Book, but was evaluated as "unreliable." J. Allen Hynek, however, who actually worked on Blue Book pointed out this case as an example of how the staff brushed aside good UFO reports without investigation.[150]

Many accounts of UFOs being chased by planes have been recorded in UFO history. Much more rare are reports of planes being chased by UFOs. On September 27 at around 4:00 p.m., a "round object with a dark center" was seen by Glendale residents chasing two jets planes.[151]

In March of 1958, Air Force Blue Book investigators were called to research a sighting which had occurred on March 14 in the town of Healdsburg. The case began at around 8:45 a.m. The two witnesses were in their backyard when they observed an unidentified "round object" about one meter in diameter swoop down out of the sky and make a controlled landing in the field behind their home. The object was an estimated fifty feet from the witnesses when it took off towards the east, then turned south and accelerated out of sight. The case was declared unexplained by the investigators. (Blue Book Case #5716.)[152]

While the majority of UFO sightings involve objects the size of a car or larger; occasionally witnesses report seeing UFOs that are much smaller. On May 20, 1958, an anonymous North Hollywood resident, then four years old, experienced a bizarre encounter with a tiny UFO. Says the witness, "I was playing in the front yard when a ball-like object slowly came down from the sky. It was the size of baseball ... in the sky it was a dot. I could barely see it. It caught my attention as it came a little closer. I still could not see it clearly. I went inside for lunch. I came back out and it was still there about 75 to 90 feet away. I sat on the driveway and stared at it. It was neat. It stayed there all day. The next day I looked up and was looking for it, interested and curious. It came back and got closer. The object came up to me only two feet from me. I tried to touch it but it would move just out of my reach ... it was clear, yet solid. It would constantly change its surface."

According to the witness, the strange ball-like object visited him repeatedly for a period of a week, leaving him forever changed. As he says, "It reacted to me and communicated with me. It was like unconditional love. It taught me and gave me great intelligence and insight. I was tested a few years ago with an I.Q. of 196. I have gifts I can't explain. I wonder if anyone has had similar experiences."

Unknown to the witness, other similar accounts involving small balls of light which communicate telepathically turn up consistently in UFO reports.[153]

On November 9, residents of Humboldt, Trinidad, Rio Dell, and several other neighboring northern California towns were "inundated" with showers of a strange web-like substance, with strands of the material up to forty feet long. While no UFO was sighted, the material sounds like the popularly-known "angel hair," which is sometimes ejected from UFOs. A biologist at Humboldt State College examined the substance and was able to rule out the explanations of mold growth or animal products.[154]

It wasn't Venus, that much was sure. But what exactly was viewed by three police officers, two Air Force Lieutenants, and a life guard on the first day of the year 1959 at 4:45 p.m. remains a mystery. Sheriff's Deputy Fred Gunzelman of Corona Del Mar had stepped outside to take down the flag for the evening, when he observed a "bright object" hovering over Newport Beach. He immediately got two more witnesses, Deputy Elmer Sandling and Sergeant Bruce Young. All three observed the object using binoculars. A nearby lifeguard station was notified. Guard Jack Bell and Lieutenants Mike Henry and Jim Richards also observed the object.

When one of the witnesses suggested that the object was Venus, the other witnesses kindly pointed out that Venus was clearly visible in a nearby portion of the sky. Using binoculars, the lighted object appeared to be "a round or disk-shaped thing with a tail that rotated around it at various intervals." The object remained for a period of fifteen minutes, at which point it suddenly broke up into four separate pieces, each of which departed in a different direction at high speed.[155]

An incredible story of UFO contact occurred on the evening of February 24 in the town of Victorville. The principal witness was an anonymous high-school student, described by the investigating Air Force intelligence officer as "an average young man of average intelligence ... liked by his schoolmates and teachers."

He was baby-sitting his younger brother and the two of them were alone in the house. He was getting into bed at around 10:00 p.m. when he observed a "bright, white, steady light" that was much too intense to be a car. At the same time, the family's pet dogs began to howl and run around in terror, begging to be let in the house.

The witness opened the front door and was shocked to see a 150-foot-long egg-shaped object. It had a dull red color, with purple tinges on the edges and was emitting an intense white light. The object was about 100 feet away and moving at tree-top level. He realized with shock that the object was heading directly for the house.

In ten seconds, the object approached until it was directly above the house, passing over the front yard at a height of ten feet. At this point, the witness could hear a sound described as "similar to the hum of a transformer, but higher in pitch."

The object passed overhead and seemed to disappear. The witness returned inside to check on his younger brother and the dogs. When he returned outside again, the object was back. It was just west of his house and was again approaching at a height of about eight feet!

Terrified, the boy dashed inside. His parents were at night-school and he felt he had to protect the family. While he retrieved the family gun, his younger brother looked out the front window and observed the object hovering in front of the house.

The main witness then took the gun and went outside. Again, he saw the object to the west of the house, but this time it was approaching him at high speed. Terrified, he dashed back into the house.

Watching from the windows, the two boys saw the object move away and then come swooping down again directly over the house. Fifteen minutes later, the object returned, coming so low that the entire house vibrated. The witnesses also noticed that each time the object passed over the house, the radio would become completely blocked by "intense static" and a strange, crackling noise came from the craft.

The two terrified boys remained inside as the craft swooped over their house a total of at least five times before it finally left. The boys' parents arrived home at 11:00 p.m., but by then the incident was over. They did notice, however, that both dogs were "whimpering and shaking and hiding under the furniture."

The sighting was reported to Blue Book officials. The interrogating intelligence officer said that the witness "was sincere, did not change his story although questioned several times on different points and seemed generally convinced that what he saw actually exists."

Further confirmation surfaced when officers separately questioned the neighbors, two of whom reported "severe radio and television interference" at "about that time." Incidentally, the home of the witnesses is located less than eight miles from George Air Force Base, itself the location of several highly dramatic encounters.[156]

Just before midnight on December 22, Kenneth Lindsley and several other witnesses in Oakdale observed an orange, glowing craft landed or hovering at ground level. The object was the shape of a bowl and covered the entire width of the road. Lindsley and the other witnesses observed "shadows that appeared to be moving." No other details were noted.[157]

The 1950s proved to be one of the busiest decades of UFO activity ever recorded. Despite this, civilian UFO investigators were few and far between. In California, the scene was dominated largely by UFO investigator Ann Druffel, a pioneer of UFO research, whose thorough investigations are responsible for several of the above reports. Druffel herself was amazed by the sheer number of accounts, particularly over the city of Los Angeles. Says Druffel, "As the years passed, UFO reports from the Los Angeles area mounted into the hundreds."[158]

Research David Hatcher Childress has also remarked upon the high concentration of sightings over LA. As he says, "What are we to make of these sightings, and why should they be focused in the Los Angeles area? The fact that major aerospace industries are located around Los Angeles might shed some light on the mystery of the saucers."[159]

Writes researcher Kenn Thomas, "The sprawling metropolis of Southern California has a unique history with the phenomenon. The famed 'Battle of Los Angeles' occurred there in February 1942 ... Clearly, ideation about aliens and spaceships now almost dominates Los Angeles and the national culture it influences so strongly ... "[160]

While southern California had recently been the focus of UFO activity, the next wave would move back up to the northern part of the state.

5. The Red Bluff UFO Wave

See color section, page 112

B y the time the 1960s arrived, the UFO situation had evolved beyond mere sightings and landings. More and more witnesses reported seeing actual alien entities or being taken onboard a craft. At the same time, more waves of sightings were reported over various towns and cities. It seemed as if the UFOs were becoming increasingly brazen, as if they were putting on displays and wanted to be seen.

Among the most prominent of the 1960s encounters is known as the Red Bluff UFO wave. Although Red Bluff is named as the location, the wave actually occurred all across northern California, encompassing the cities of Red Bluff, Willow Creek, Concord, Eureka, Pleasant Hill, Healdsburg, Santa Rosa, Roseville, Mineral, Dunsmuir, Honeydew, and Redlands. For five days, beginning on August 13, 1960, literally hundreds of sightings took place. Among the many witnesses were more than a dozen police officers from varying towns.

The first sign of the wave was actually the sighting of an unexplained red object over the southern California city of Hollywood. At 10:30 on the night of August 13, 1960, an anonymous witness reported a glowing "red object" hovering over the city.[161]

A half-hour following the Hollywood sighting, a similar, or perhaps the same, object was seen over Willow Creek. For the next two hours, reports of at least two red, glowing objects came in from nearby Red Bluff.

At 10:05 p.m., Deputy Sheriff Clarence Fry was performing his duties as jailer of Red Bluff prison when he observed an "oval pale-yellow glowing object with a flashing red light on each end and squarish white lights along the side."

Two hours later, at 11:45 p.m., Red Bluff patrol officers Stanley Scott and Charles Carson were on patrol when they encountered what was apparently the same UFO.

According to their official report of the incident, they were attempting to pull over a speeding motorcyclist when "we saw what at first appeared to be a huge airliner dropping from the sky. The object was very low and directly in front of us. We stopped and leaped from the patrol vehicle in order to get a position on what we were sure was going to be an airplane crash."

Once they were outside their car, the policemen first noticed an absolute silence. "Still assuming it was to be an aircraft with the power off, we continued to watch until the object was probably within 100 feet to 200 feet off the ground, when it suddenly reversed completely at high speed and gained approximately 500 feet altitude. There the object stopped. At this time the object was surrounded by a glow, making the round or oblong object visible. At each end, or each side of the object, there were definite red lights. At times about five white lights were visible between the red lights. As we watched, the object moved again and performed aerial feats that were actually unbelievable."

Stunned, Officers Carson and Scott alerted the neighboring sheriff's stations and also radioed the local radar base. Says Officer Carson, "The radar base confirmed the UFO – completely unidentified."

The officers continued to observe the object, which then approached their vehicle and sent down a powerful beam of red light, moving back and forth. In response, Officer Scott turned on the red siren. The object immediately responded by moving away. The officers returned the response by chasing after the craft.

Says Officer Carson, "The object began moving slowly in an easterly direction and we followed. We proceeded to the Vina Plains Fire Station, where it was approached by a similar object from the south. It moved near the first object and both stopped, remaining in that position for some time, occasionally emitting the red beam. Finally, both objects disappeared below the eastern horizon. We returned to the Tehama County Sheriff's office and met Deputy Fry and Deputy Montgomery, who had gone to Los Molinos after contacting the radar base. Both had seen the UFO clearly, and described to us what we saw. The night jailer also was able to see the object for a short time; each described the object at 2350 hours and observed it for approximately two hours and fifteen minutes. Each time the object neared us we experienced radio interference."

Officer Scott wrote in his report, "We made several attempts to follow it, or I should say get closer to it, but the object seemed aware of us. We were more successful remaining motionless and allowing it to approach us, which it did on several occasions."

While Officers Scott and Carson dealt with their encounter, a group of policemen in Mineral reported their observations of six unknown aerial objects which maneuvered at high speeds, diving, climbing, and hovering. At least three other deputies also gave chase but were easily outdistanced. At the same time, numerous motorists up and down Highway 99E reported seeing another low-flying UFO.

From midnight to 1:00 a.m. reports poured in from Concord, Pleasant Hills, Healdsburg, and Santa Rosa of a strange "red sphere" moving slowly across the sky.

Three days later, around 8:30 p.m. on August 16, citizens in the town of Corning observed two oval-shaped objects cavorting around the sky. One hour later, residents of Eureka reported at least six red, glowing objects which moved in formation. Twenty minutes after that, the town of Corning was again visited by a boomerang-shaped object.

The wave continued on August 17 when Police Captain Hughe McGuigan, Sergeant James Hall, and several other witnesses from Roseville observed two UFOs move in darting patterns overhead.

Later that evening, a "whining" object with red and white lights was seen hovering low in the skies over Folsom. Then, just after midnight, Dunsmuir residents observed the same apparent object. Meanwhile, residents in Redlands experienced a close-up sighting of the craft, which appeared to be egg-shaped with a dome and a circle of red-lights around the perimeter.

The wave finally came to a close around August 18, when the postmaster of the town of Honeydew observed a strange wing-shaped object glowing bright red move overhead and disappear off into the distance.

Among the many reputable witnesses of the Red Bluff wave are Officer Montgomery, Chief Criminal Investigator A. D. Perry, Sonoma County Sheriff's Deputies William Baker and Lou Doolittle, Plumas County Sheriff's Deputy Robert Smith, and Mount Shasta Police Officers Pete Chinka, Jack Brown, and George Kerr. UFO investigator Paris Flammonde calls this wave of activity "One of the most impressive multiple sightings."

Pioneering UFO researcher, Dr. James A Harder Ph.D., of the University of Berkeley, California, personally investigated the sightings and interviewed many of the witnesses. On July 29, 1968, Harder delivered an official paper in support of the case to the Committee on Science and Astronautics, House of Representatives, United States Congress.

Incredibly, Air Force Blue Book officials labeled the case as "atmospheric inversion" without any investigation.[162]

Dr. Harder, however, became a strong supporter of UFO reality. As he writes, "On the basis of the data and ordinary rules of evidence as would be applied to civil or criminal courts, the physical reality of UFOs has been proved beyond a reasonable doubt."[163]

Further confirmation of this wave comes from an anonymous scientist who worked with the Air Force studying early warning radar systems. Throughout 1960 and 1961, "Dr. B." was stationed at Point Arena, California, to help manage a new experimental radar system. Says Dr. B., "We had an ANF PS35 Radar. It is nine stories tall with a 466-foot antennae, and its power was five megawatts ... its range was 455 miles. That was all classified information at the time. It was what's called a search set. And we'd look out every night over northern California, and thousands of Bogies, UFOs, would come down about 20 miles from Point Arena. And they'd come down at 20,000 miles an hour. Go down just about to Baha and then they would turn left and go across Mexico where they are seen going 5,000 miles an hour. They had a vertical descent [of] 20,000 miles an hour, lateral speed of 5,000 miles an hour, almost every night ... they'd shred about half the reports. And that was really weird, you know. A lot of shit went on up there. But that was the beginning of me in the military, you know. This would have been about 1961, 1960. A thousand. We would report over to [deleted] Air Force Base, which is right inland from Novato there ... I mean all year round this went on."[164]

As the above report verifies, UFOs were seen not only in northern California, but all the way down to Mexico. On September 10, between 9:50 and 11:00 p.m., a family of four from Ridgecrest observed a luminous light gray object that was either boomerang or disk-shaped with a small pod in the front. The witnesses watched as the object whooshed back and forth across the sky at high speed. At first it appeared to be at an elevation of 6000 feet; but, by the third time the object swooped over the witnesses, it appeared to be about 500 feet away. They heard a soft "whirring or swishing" sound as the UFO accelerated into the distance. Although the object itself glowed, no actual lights were visible.

Independent anonymous witnesses also obtained film footage of the event which was forwarded to Project Blue Book.

Then, on November 27, 1961, seven people, including two amateur astronomers, observed an incredible display of UFO activity over the town of Chula Vista in southern California. The incident began at around 7:30 p.m. when the manager of a trailer court and other residents observed a reddish star-like object "with a very long antennae rod attached." The object appeared to be very high in altitude. The witnesses observed a "white light of high intensity" travel up and down the rod-like part of the object. But what most impressed the witnesses was the object's maneuverability. It moved at incredible speeds, performing huge circles, and flashing back and forth across the horizon, as far south as Mexico, out over to North Island, and back to Chula Vista in a matter of seconds. Amateur astronomers Lewis and Olive Hart wrote a report to the Air Force's Project Blue Book which states, "It was unquestionably some kind of intelligently controlled air or space vehicle." Blue Book officers evidently agreed and declared the sightings unexplained. (Blue Book Cases #6962 & #7133.)[165]

Late one evening in September 1962, dairy rancher A. T. Gray of Orland observed some strange lights in the fields near his home. He thought at first it was a car driving through his field, but as the object came close, he realized it was actually a flying vehicle. It was oblong in shape with rounded edges. It stopped, hovered about twenty feet off the ground, and was totally silent. Gray approached to within 150 feet of the object when it suddenly accelerated towards him, rose upwards, and took off towards the southwest.[166]

On February 27, 1963, seven witnesses from Modesto described a crescent-shaped craft with portholes which was seen to hover, descend to an altitude of less than 1000 feet, emit a bright beam of light for about fifteen seconds, and then dart away. The witnesses were so impressed, they reported their story to Modesto Bee, which published their account.[167]

On June 26, numerous witnesses, including a technician, observed a dramatic display involving a number of green glowing objects over the city of Pine Crest. The witnesses first observed three objects moving westwards. These were approached by another object moving from the opposite direction. The objects converged, hovered, then split formation and continued on in different directions.[168]

On September 14, 1963, UFOs were seen over the small northern California town of Susanville. Blue Book officers who investigated the case declared the case unexplained. (Blue Book Case #8548.)

6. The Rio Vista UFO Wave

See color section, page 113

In May 1964, the small, virtually unknown town of Rio Vista (then a population of about 2000 persons) experienced a two-year-long wave of sightings, as reported by hundreds of local residents. Starting early in the month, witnesses began seeing a torpedo-shaped object about five feet wide and twelve feet long. It glowed bright red and moved silently at treetop level through the town.

It appeared so regularly throughout the month of May, that residents were able to predict its appearance. As a result, one witness was able to obtain color photographs of the object, which she eventually presented to the local sheriff's office. The object usually appeared above a particular water-tower about five miles outside of town, where it would hover less than fifty feet above the ground.

One of the first dramatic sightings occurred on May 13, when an anonymous female resident reported that she saw two objects – both described as round and luminous. One of the objects came down and landed in a nearby field.

The next case involved two teenagers who took their .22 rifles and shot at the object. The witnesses are sure that the bullets found their mark as they both heard a metallic "twang" as the bullets hit, and the object flared up brightly in response.

Still, the craft continued to visit the water tower, and would do so regularly for the next two years. Later, in 1965, a remarkable encounter would involve nearly the whole town and would generate interest from Air Force officials.[169]

Meanwhile, things began to heat up in southern California. On September 15, a crew of 120 military personnel at Vandenburg AFB prepared for the launch of an Atlas F missile. The launch took place as scheduled. Dr. Robert Jacobs (then a lieutenant) was put in charge of filming the missile in flight. He used a telescopic camera hooked up with a radar display that kept the viewfinder locked on the missile. The launch was initially successful; however, at about 60 miles of altitude, the missile mysteriously lost control and plunged into the Pacific Ocean, hundreds of miles short of its target. Little did Jacobs realize, he was about to begin an ordeal that would haunt him for the rest of his life.

At the time, he didn't notice anything unusual. However, the next day, he was called into the office of his superior, Major Mansmann, where two plain-clothed men from Washington D.C. waited. Jacobs was instructed to watch the film of the missile launch and explain what he saw. Says Jacobs, "Suddenly, we saw a UFO swim into the picture. It was very distinct and clear, a round object. It flew right up to our missile and emitted a vivid flash of light. Then it altered course and hovered briefly over our missile ... and then there came a second vivid flash of light. Then the UFO flew around the missile twice and set off two more vivid flashes from different angles, and then it vanished. A few seconds later, our missile was malfunctioning and tumbling out of control."

Jacobs was instructed to study the film closely and give his professional conclusions. He did so and told Major Mansmann that he believed the object was a UFO spacecraft. Mansmann replied, "You are to say nothing about this footage. As far as you and I are concerned, it never happened. Right? ... I don't have to remind you of the seriousness of a security breach ..."

In another interview, Jacobs elaborated on the incident. "I watched the screen and there was the launch ... and into the frame came something else. It flew into the frame like and it shot a beam of light at the warhead. Now remember, all this stuff is flying at several thousand miles per hour. So this thing fires a beam of light at the warhead, hits it, and then it moves to the other side and fires another beam of light, then moves again and fires another beam of light, and then flies out the way it came in. And the warhead tumbles out of space. The object, the points of light that we saw, the warhead, and so forth were traveling through subspace about sixty miles straight up. And they were going in the neighborhood of about 11,000 to 14,000 miles an hour when this UFO caught up to them, flew around them, and flew back out. Now, I saw that! I don't give a goddamn what anybody else says about it. I saw that on film! I was there!

"Now Major Mannsman said to me after some discussion about it, you are never to speak of this again. As far as you are concerned this never happened. And he said, I don't need to emphasize the dire consequences of a security breach, do I? I said, no sir. And he said, fine. This never happened. As I started for the door, he said, wait a minute. He said, years from now if you are ever forced by someone to talk about this, you are to tell them it was laser strikes, laser tracking strikes. Well, in 1964 we didn't have any laser tracking strikes."

Stunned, Jacobs concurred and kept his silence for more than seventeen years. He finally revealed his experience, saying, "I have been afraid of what might happen to me. But the truth is too important for it to be concealed any longer. The UFOs are real. I know they're real. The Air Force knows they're real. And the U.S. government knows they're real. I reckon it's high time that the American public knows it too."

Jacobs had good reason to be afraid of reprisal. As a result of his going public, he was publicly ridiculed by arch-skeptics James O'Berg and Phillip Klass. He also received numerous anonymous phone call death-threats in the middle of the night. On one occasion, his mailbox was destroyed with skyrockets followed with another threatening phone call. He even lost his employment as a result of going public.

Investigators, however, tracked down Major Mansmann, who surprisingly confirmed Jacobs' testimony in a written letter, saying, "The events you are familiar with had to have happened as stated by both Bob Jacobs and myself because the statement made from each of us after seventeen years matched. What was on the film was seen only twice by Bob Jacobs, once in Film Quality Control and once in my office at the CIA attended showing. I saw it four times. I ordered Lieutenant Jacobs not to discuss what he saw with anyone because of the nature of the launch [and] the failure of the launch ... The object was saucer shaped."

Major Mannsman was suffering from a recurrence of cancer at the time he wrote the above letter. He refused to reveal much more detail for fear of jeopardizing his security oath. He died shortly thereafter.[170]

Meanwhile, the sightings continued. On December 28, a crew of park rangers in Santa Clara County Park in Watsonville, northern California, reported their observation of a "disc-like" thing over the Hecker Mountains.[171]

One spring evening in 1965, the Reid family of Gardena witnessed a strangely shaped multi-colored "cluster of lights" dart across the sky, performing right angle turns only a few hundred feet in altitude. At first they thought it might be a helicopter, but that theory was quickly exploded. As Adam Reid says, "The object, whatever it was, kind of scooted across the sky in a zigzag fashion ... it was like zip, zip, zip! And it zigzagged across the sky quite a bit ... it impressed me very much that it was looking for something."

After darting around for several minutes, the object hovered and took off sharply towards the east, leaving the Reid family convinced of the reality of UFOs.[172]

On August 3, 1965, some of the world's most famous and best-verified UFO photographs were taken by Los Angeles County Highway Investigator Rex Heflin. Part of Heflin's job included taking photos of car accidents. Because of this, he always carried a Polaroid camera next to him on the seat. While driving during the day along an isolated stretch of road outside Santa Ana, Heflin sighted a silent, hat-shaped UFO pacing his truck. The object sent down a beam of white light. Heflin tried to radio his supervisor, but the radio went dead (a fact later confirmed by his supervisor). He then quickly grabbed his Polaroid camera and snapped a series of four photos. The metallic disk disappeared off into the haze and Heflin immediately radioed his supervisor. The radio worked perfectly.

After the incident, Heflin sought no publicity. Reporters from United Press International in Los Angeles heard about Heflin's photos. They persuaded him to turn them over for study. He agreed and the UPI photo experts conducted an extensive analysis, even attempting to restage the whole incident at the same area. After their study, the photo experts at UPI declared them genuine.

All four photos clearly show a large metallic object hovering about twenty feet above the road. One photo shows a strange disturbance underneath the object, like a dust-devil.

Heflin, like many witnesses who have hard evidence of UFOs, received a mysterious visit a few weeks later. The visit was from a man claiming to from NORAD. The man demanded the photographs. Heflin turned them over. Denying that they ever had or studied the photos, the Air Force still denounced the pictures as a hoax. In response, NICAP photographic analyst Ralph Rankow and other scientists studied the pictures in detail and also declared them genuine. Today, the Heflin photos have been widely published. Journalist Frank Edwards calls the photos "the best UFO photographs in civilian hands." (See photo section.)[173]

Starting in May 1964, and continuing through 1965, the town of Rio Vista had experienced a series of sightings involving a mysterious red, torpedo-like object which would consistently hover near a local water-tower.

By September of 1965, events had escalated to the point of near hysteria. The UFO was attracting hundreds of witnesses. The object had been photographed and shot at. Calls and complaints flooded the local police station.

Deputy Sheriff John Cruz was initially skeptical, but when the number of calls mounted into the hundreds and a witness brought in a photograph, he was finally forced to investigate. On September 22, 1965, events mounted to a climax. Deputy Sheriff Cruz was told that a crowd was gathered on the hilltop around the infamous water-tower, in prediction of a visitation. Cruz realized that the situation had the potential to become dangerous, and he drove to the area. When he arrived, he was shocked to see nearly four hundred people standing patiently in the darkness, waiting for the object.

To his amazement, the object appeared right on schedule. All the witnesses reported seeing the same red, glowing cylindrical-shaped object which hovered at tree-top level, moving slowly back and forth and finally departing.

The incident caused a local media sensation, and worldwide attention was focused upon the formerly anonymous town. Eventually, officials from Travis Air Force Base conducted an "investigation." Incredibly, Air Force officials claimed that the case was easily solved, and that the witnesses were actually observing the planet Venus![174]

The wave, however, wasn't over yet. Late one evening on October 4, Betty Valine and her twelve-year-old son Robbie encountered a "large plate-shaped machine with a dome on top, inside which three creatures were clearly visible."[175]

Following the above report, the Rio Vista wave came to an abrupt end. Either that or the sightings were no longer publicized. The next year, however, brought more high quality reports further south. Again, it seemed the UFOs were keeping tabs on our technological development.

In April 1966, designers of the new Saturn rocket at Seal Beach experienced a dramatic sighting. One of the scientists involved, "Dr. B.," reports the incident: "The first night we are bringing the Saturn rocket out of the hanger I get a shake. I'm sitting there at the computer console, sound asleep, it's 4:00 in the morning. One of my engineers comes up and shakes me. Mr. B., come outside, there is something big happening .... They had just pulled the bird [the Saturn Rocket] out and were taking pictures. And a big disc came down. I don't have a picture of the ship hovering over it, but the disc came down and 400 hundred employees saw it at 4:00 in the morning, early spring. It was April 1966."[176]

While most UFO cases involve no physical evidence, occasional cases do turn up. One type of evidence is known as medical evidence. The following case is a good example. It was early morning on August 20 when Otto Becker, his son, and daughter-in-law woke up to find their home in Healdsburg bathed in bright light. Looking outside, they observed an object as big as a "six-story" building, hovering at treetop level less than 200 feet away. The craft gave off a rainbow array of colors, which appeared to pour off its edges "like water." The witnesses heard a "distinct engine noise." At the same time, all the domestic animals in the area reacted to the presence of the object. At that point, the UFO took off vertically. In the days that followed the incident, all three witnesses suffered from inflammation of the eyes, apparently caused by the intense light emitted by the object.[177]

On December 8, an anonymous resident from Vacaville was outside during the day when he saw a large, silver, disk-shaped craft hovering only a few hundred feet in the sky. He quickly grabbed his camera and snapped a photograph. The photograph shows a typical silvery flying saucer. The photographer sent the picture to the local newspaper, The Reporter, who published it under the pseudonym, "cautious citizen" because the witness didn't want any publicity.[178]

Despite the military denials that UFOs are hoaxes, hallucinations, and misperceptions, some of the best cases on record have occurred directly over military bases. A perfect example is the UFO incident which occurred on December 16 over the San Diego Naval Auxiliary Air Station. Witnessed by more than fourteen officers, the incident began at 9:30 p.m. when helicopter pilot Ensign John Schmitt and several other base personnel exited the main gate. Schmitt happened to look upwards and observed an incredible sight. Says Schmitt, "There were three of them. They were bright, round, yellow objects up about fifty thousand feet and flying in a triangular formation."

Accompanying Schmitt were pilots Ensign David Conklin and Ensign David Coghill. None of the men were able to identify the lights. Says Schmitt, "We don't know what they were. But none of us had ever seen anything like them. We agreed that they couldn't be meteors. They would hover, then go forward, then to one side. They were traveling at speeds from about the maximum speed of a bomber to about five times that."

As the objects cavorted about overhead, the crowd of military officers observing the objects grew. But what made this particularly sighting so memorable was what happened next. Says Schmitt, "A fourth one came over the horizon from the east at a terrific speed. It came up to the group of three, stayed near the formation for a minute, then headed east. It dropped to a lower altitude and the magnitude of its light increased. It dropped what appeared to be two spheres of light, which disappeared. Then it headed west and we lost sight of it. The other three objects suddenly disappeared. They flew in formation and moved in different directions. We had these objects in sight for about nine minutes."[179]

The very next night, on December 17, a young couple who work as antique dealers in Whittier observed a "nocturnal light" for a period of five minutes. The wife told investigator J. Allen Hynek, "I kept saying, 'What can it be?' He [her husband] just kept repeating, 'Oh, my God!'"[180]

It was late at night on July 19, 1967, when Jack Hill (age 60), nightwatchman for the Lumber Consolidated Company in Wilmington, encountered a UFO. He was patrolling the grounds when he observed a fifty-foot long metallic craft covered with lights hovering only a few hundred feet away. To his shock, the strange object zoomed straight towards him. Hill took immediate defensive action. His fight or flight instincts prevailed, and as he couldn't flee, he decided to shoot first and ask questions later. He speedily drew his service revolver and fired six shots at the object in quick succession. Says Hill, "Then the lights of the craft went out and it flew away." The craft apparently was unharmed. Hill, on the other hand, was impressed enough that he later told his story to reporters at the *Los Angeles Herald Examiner.*[181]

On October 8, 1967, Diane Swanson was in her home with two friends, Ray Riley and Michael Mord. Looking out the window, they observed a "large, elongated disk" floating slowly north of Swanson's home in North Hollywood. The three of them were so amazed that they piled into their car and chased the slow-moving UFO across the valley into the city of Sunland. At one point, the car engine mysteriously stalled. Mord elected to walk home while Swanson and Riley continued to chase the UFO on foot into a remote area. At one point, the witnesses were able to get within a distance of "two city blocks." Suddenly, the object emitted an "electrical beam" which struck the hillside. The object then quickly sped away. To their shock, the couple discovered it was already morning. They had been following the UFO all night long. Later they speculated on the possibility that there was a period of missing time.[182]

Less than one week later, three witnesses in Mendota were drawn outside of their home at 2:30 a.m. where they observed an unknown object at close range for a period of three minutes. J. Allen Hynek, who investigated the case, classified it as a "close encounter of the first kind," because there was no interaction between the UFO and the witnesses and no effect on the surrounding environment.[183]

A particularly colorful UFO was sighted by two families on the evening of August 14, 1968. One of the witnesses describes the object: "It was gray in color, cigar-shaped, with myriads of green, red, and white lights ... like sparklers along its length." Witnesses watched as a private plane approached the object. When the plane came near to the UFO, all the lights on the object winked out and the UFO disappeared from view.[184]

Around 8:00 o'clock one autumn evening, the Tanouye family of Pacoima witnessed an impressive UFO display. It all began when they sighted a star-like object while driving home. When they arrived home, the object swooped down. Says Ron Tanouye, "It was just like a bright light, but at times it would kind of lose its brightness and it would change shape at the same time .... It would make a vertical movement, I mean, almost straight up from its position, 180 degrees either way, up or down, then a 90 degree angle to the left or right. It was just so quick. I mean, this was amazing. And then it seemed like it was getting closer ... it got to the point where you could see the bright light coming out what was kind of like, maybe portholes or something, but bright light coming out of certain areas of this object."

The Tanouye family got their pair of high-powered binoculars and observed the object in detail. As they watched, it began to emit smaller objects were hovered on either side of the larger object. The Tanouyes were about to call the police when the smaller objects suddenly returned into the larger, and the UFO left.[185]

George Air Force Base is one of the many highly technological locations that seem to attract a disproportional amount of UFO activity. On the night of June 17-18, 1969, two base security policemen observed a "bright, orange-colored object" hovering over the base. They estimated that the object was at least 375 feet in diameter. The account was somehow leaked to the press and would otherwise have remained secret.[186]

7. Sightings in the 1970s and 1980s

See color section, page 114

The next two decades brought more high quality reports, many of which showed again that the U.S. military takes UFOs very seriously. For example, in 1970, USAF Air Traffic Controller Michael Smith was stationed in a radar tower in Klamath Falls, Oregon. He reports that one evening he received a call from NORAD regarding a California UFO that was heading his way. Says Smith, "I was on the radar, and NORAD called me and informed that there was a UFO coming up the California coast and would be in my area pretty soon. I said what do you want me to do? And they said, 'Nothing, just watch it, don't write it down.' We have a log book in which we are supposed to keep track of anything out of the ordinary. But they said, 'Don't log it or anything, just watch it. We are just letting you know – heads up.' NORAD was well aware, obviously, that these UFOs were around, and the action of the people when I first saw the UFO on radar was as if it happens quite often."[187]

On May 11, 1971, an encounter occurred over Yucca Valley during which the Air Force again attempted to intercept an "unknown craft." The sighting was reported by several residents of the area, including one scientist. At one point, the craft hovered low and sent a powerful beam of light which illuminated a wide area. The beam suddenly retracted and the various witnesses observed three jet interceptors racing directly towards the UFO. Before the jets could get close, the object accelerated and disappeared out of view.[188]

Also in May, Ellen Crystal was in her Hollywood apartment when her neighbor called her outside to look at "some UFOs." Although she was skeptical, her neighbor was adamant. Crystal agreed to at least look. To her incredible shock, she saw a large number of star-like objects darting around in the sky above her. Says Crystal, "At any given moment, as many as thirty objects seemed to be moving in the sky ... these objects made right angle turns, had no noise associated with them, and seemed to be going nowhere."

Crystal was so impressed by this sighting that she launched her own investigations into the phenomenon and eventually became a prominent researcher, writing a book about her discoveries.[189]

Several California cases are on record in which witnesses experienced apparent telepathy with the alleged UFO occupants. While telepathy is commonly reported during onboard UFO experiences, it also turns up in simple sightings. A typical example occurred one summer evening in 1971. Ronny Baron was in his Reseda home when he felt a powerful and strange impulse to go outside. Baron went outside with his son and immediately spotted five star-like objects performing amazing maneuvers above their home. Says Baron, "They stayed kind of still in one spot, and they came together, and they split really fast. Then they'd separate and go higher ... whatever these things are, they're in touch with each other, and they're doing things together. They obviously have some kind of heavy communication because they're all doing strategic things together. They knew how to split. They knew how to take off in an instant, like somebody said, 'Ready? Go! And *shew!*'"[190]

As we have seen, UFOs are strongly attracted to our technological installations. The following case is a particularly intriguing example of this phenomenon. Just west of Menlo Park is the Stanford linear accelerator which actually runs in an underground tunnel directly beneath the adjacent highway. The accelerator itself ends in a funnel-shaped depression not far from the road. It was from this exact location that two witnesses observed a landed UFO take off one February evening in 1972.

The witnesses were driving down the road when they heard an intense humming noise. The men stopped the car and got out. Writes UFO researcher Jacques Vallee, who investigated the case, "The hum became more distinct as the object came into view. It was glowing red. It flew in a straight line up the hill, as if following the roof of the elongated tunnel. Then it flew down again and was lost from sight in the valley. But not for long. It soon came back into view, and this time it took off, rising very high and very fast as it passed overhead. The two men below saw it very clearly: it was somewhat like looking directly at the sun, they said, although contours of the light were sharp."[191]

Many skeptics wrongly assume that UFO encounters occur to only one witness, often believed to be a kook, a liar or very gullible. However, the truth is that the vast majority of UFO reports involve two or more witnesses. In a few rare cases, the number of witnesses is even greater. In the following case, which occurred early in the year over Costa Mesa, more than a *thousand* citizens viewed a highly unusual UFO display. One witness, who prefers to remain anonymous, worked in the military for years and is familiar with all kinds of aircraft. He remains convinced the event was unexplained. As he says, "I saw something that thousands and thousands of people saw. Everyone was out on the streets looking at it. It was a big cloud that was perfectly oval-shaped, and colors moved around it. There were pinks and others, and they moved. They would scintillate like this [up and down] and move around it. People were out in the streets. Everyone was looking at it. I mean, thousands and thousands of people saw it, just staring at it, looking at it .... The thing was perfectly shaped and it was moving slowly ... there were lights in it, and they were around it – they were moving through it – colored lights ... people were just going, 'What is that?'"

Local newspapers featured the account and called it "unusual atmospheric phenomena." The story was front page news for a week, but ended up remaining a mystery.[192]

A few months later, on August 22, UFOs visited Hollywood when a pilot and several other witnesses on the ground reported seeing a bright object "with flames."[193]

On October 16, at around 11:00 p.m., Sig McGill was outside watering the lawn of his Santa Cruz home when he heard a "strange whooshing" noise. Looking up, he saw a "silvery-black" cigar-shaped craft traveling a mere 150 feet above the street. The object sprouted fire from its rear end. It traveled down the street, made a right turn and disappeared behind some trees. McGill ran inside and called the police who told him that many other people had already called to report the UFO.[194]

All through October, Santa Ana experienced an intense UFO wave of activity. On October 18, headlines for the *Santa Ana Register* read, "Skies Thicken as Reports of UFOs Rise." The next day, the *Los Angeles Herald Examiner* ran a story called "LA Joins UFO Mania."

The activity in this flap was particularly intense, but followed a familiar pattern. Writes researcher Leonard Stringfield, "The stories were the same: mischievous reconnaissance over houses and cars, light beams affecting people and electricity, and silent little elfish creatures doing 'crazy' things and again, the 'robot' wearing the crinkly metallic suit."

One of the researchers of the wave was Idabel Epperson, one of the first civilian UFO investigators and at that time, the California Mutual UFO Network State Section Director. Epperson said of the flap, "There are many sightings which may have been in the outstanding classification if we had the people to investigate them. I'm sure there must be at least fifty reports just scribbled on my clipboard sheets ... and there were many that I heard on the radio that did not give enough details to even write down."

Because of the intensity of the wave, speculations were offered as to the possible cause. As Leonard Stringfield wrote, "[The wave was] no less puzzling than any one of a hundred other repetitive acts of surveillance behavior. Perhaps, also, there was a certain attraction to the dazzling lights shining up from Disneyland, or something of great geologic importance about the San Andreas fault line, which drew UFOs into California in 1973. Whatever dictated that course of action, California came under heavy surveillance."

There are a number of sightings in the UFO literature in which UFOs hover over drive-in theaters. One dramatic example occurred in 1972 at a drive-in movie theater in Paramount. The Blacios family was preparing to view a movie along with hundreds of others when a large, silver disk, complete with portholes, hovered directly adjacent to and above the movie screen. Panic instantly ensued. Says Claudia Blacios, "All of a sudden, we see people running past us, and cars honking, and headlights turning on and off ... I heard a lady screaming ... people were walking so fast to their cars and dropping their popcorn ... we're just staring at this thing, and people are fighting to exit ... .cars are honking and a lot of people are leaving."

The Blacios family watched the object until it suddenly "went straight up" and disappeared. Says Claudia, "It was kind of long like a cigar, but it was metallic ... it was making this weird sound ... like a little droning sound, but it was very, very faint, in between all the screaming."

Claudia later received confirmation of their sighting when another witness to the same event described the encounter during a radio program.[195]

Daylight sightings of UFOs are relatively rare. When they do turn up, they are usually very impressive. In the summer of 1974 — Ronny Baron, who had seen UFOs a few years earlier with his son in Reseda — experienced this type of encounter.

Baron had gone to an afternoon party at a friend's house in Encino in the summer of 1974. He and about two dozen other people were in the backyard when they sighted several small, round, white objects darting in the sky almost directly above them. The sighting occurred in broad daylight and lasted for hours. Says Baron, "We were watching them go back and forth in these triangular motions, really fast. I mean anything that we could see would just turn on a dime, you know, be flying in one direction and all of a sudden head back in the opposite direction and go up to interlock these two lines. It would fly to a point, and then make a square in the back of the triangle. They were constantly moving, but they weren't moving *away*. They were moving in a little mile area, and they were making these triangles."

The objects were the talk of the party. Though after about an hour of observations and speculations, the guests actually grew bored. Baron reports that the objects were still in the sky when he and others left.[196]

Any denials from the military about the existence of UFOs can be easily dismissed by the numerous accounts in which military planes are sent to intercept mysterious, unidentified craft. A good example of this occurred at 8:00 p.m. on September 3. Three witnesses, Mr. & Mrs. Cromwell and Celia Bryant, were drawn outside of their Tujunga canyon home by the sound of a helicopter. Looking up, they observed a helicopter and about 1000 feet above it, a bright, glowing object. The witnesses obtained binoculars and observed that the object was blue-green on top, white in the middle, and red on the bottom. The helicopter was circling under it as if surveying it.

As they watched, the UFO changed shape. The object began to move away and two additional helicopters rushed in and surrounded it. Moments later, two military jets sped close by, again as if to investigate it. Mrs. Cromwell also noticed that the lights at the Mount Pacifico Nike Base near her home all went on – something she had seen only a few times before. She believed that the personnel at the base must have been aware of what was happening.

This cat and mouse game went on for more than three hours, at which time the disk-shaped object finally moved slowly west, still followed by the helicopters. The following day, all three witnesses reported severe eye irritation.[197]

Later that month, on September 30, a highly dramatic close encounter occurred to two employees of the Kent Plott Dairy Farm, seven miles south of Corning in northern California. It was 3:30 a.m., and Hubert Brown (22 years of age) went outside to the back lot to round up the cows. Instead, he was confronted with a large disk-shaped object with a dome on top, hovering very low over the field. A bright beam of light was emitted from the object, lighting up the whole lot "like daylight."

Brown ran back inside and returned with his co-worker, Tyrone Phillips (age 38). Both men watched as the object emitted a bright red light and made a humming sound. The object raised a huge cloud of dust and all the cows fled the scene. The two men watched the object for about five minutes when it suddenly took off "in the blink of an eye."[198]

Many witnesses report a strong telepathic rapport with the apparent occupants of a UFO. A dramatic example occurred to Southern California metaphysical researcher Peter Gutilla. It was around 1:00 a.m. on April 15, 1975. As Gutilla drove along the Santa Ana freeway, he heard a voice in his head enquiring about his cigarette. Looking to his right, he was startled to see a "ruby-red light traveling in an up/down wave-like motion."

Gutilla realized that the object was following him. He pulled off the freeway and got out of his car. The object came to a stop and hovered a few hundred feet away. Gutilla asked mentally, "What do you want?"

Suddenly, Gutilla found himself flying out of his body and into the UFO. As he says, "In the space of a few seconds, I was inside the object looking out of a bubble-like window at myself standing near my car."

A split-second later, he was back in his body. The object swayed back and forth. Gutilla mentally asked the occupants to turn on more lights. The UFO obligingly reacted. Says Gutilla, "Instantly port and starboard lights blinked on momentarily, lighting up the entire body of the object ... it gave me enough time to see its disc shape and that it was gray in color and maybe 45-50 feet in diameter."

Gutilla asked mentally for a landing, and the message came back, "No, we cannot – we are being watched. We will be back." Gutilla reports that the object then moved quickly away over the Pacific Ocean and was gone. He has not yet experienced a return visit.[199]

The week after Easter in 1975, film industry artist George Gray (pseudonym) was driving along the Santa Monica freeway at around 5:00 a.m. when he observed a helicopter-like object darting back and forth in strange motions. Realizing a helicopter couldn't move that fast, Gray kept his eye on it. As he drove up towards the beach, he was shocked to see the object zoom forward over the beach and send down a beam of light. Says Gray, "I know helicopters have spotlights, but this was an incredibly different type of light. It was like a cylinder of light being actually lowered down ... and the light was a brilliant bluish-green light. I could see the beach where the wet sand would be illuminated because of it. And within this cylinder of light, it would send smaller cylinders of light within it. And those were even more brilliant, like a yellow-lime-green and an orange cylinder also within this other cylinder."

At this point, Gray got a good look at the craft. As he says, "It was definitely completely metallic with a silver dome on the top and a silver dome on the bottom of it, like two plates put together. And they had little lights around it."

Like many witnesses, Gray felt that the craft knew he was there and was actually showing itself to him on purpose. He felt like he had a telepathic link with the occupants. After a few moments, right when the sun rose up, the craft took off.[200]

It was 9:00 o'clock one evening in 1975 when Carson resident Steve Sisneros exited his home to take out the garbage. Looking up, Sisneros observed a disc-shaped object hovering a mere 135 feet above him. He ran inside and got his mother. Both observed the disk, the bottom of which appeared to be covered with mud, as if it had just landed. Suddenly, the disk began to hum and wobble. In a split second, it darted away. According to the witnesses, it flew underneath a small plane, causing considerable turbulence to the plane before it disappeared. The next day, they discovered that their two electric clocks were both exactly five minutes slow.[201]

One early summer evening in 1976, construction worker Joel S. and a friend (now deceased) were hiking in the vacant foothills of Granada Hills when they saw a large, fiery object streak slowly across the sky. Says Joel, "It looked to me like a house on fire flying through the air. That's the only way I can describe what it looked like. It was dark red with an orange outer layer, a trail behind it, kind of yellowish-orange."

Neither of the witnesses could believe what they were seeing, but at the same time, it was impossible to ignore. Says Joel, "I'll tell you, I've never been so scared in all my life. I mean, I've been in some bad situations, but this scared the hell out of me. We stopped what we were doing and we ran."

Joel was sure that hundreds of people in the crowded San Fernando Valley must have also seen the object. He and his friend scanned the newspapers for weeks, but never found any independent confirmation of their sighting.[202]

A rare example of a miniature UFO sighting took place on August 30, 1976. Mr. Frances DeJohn of Pasadena was in his backyard smoking a cigar when he saw a translucent sphere the size of a tennis ball float towards him. Says DeJohn, "It moved in my direction very slowly. When it was about five feet past me, I walked up to it."

Examining it more closely, DeJohn was shocked to see three "things" inside the sphere. He reached out to touch it when he heard a voice in his head, "Would you harm entities from another world?"

DeJohn withdrew and watched as the small sphere darted away, never to be seen again. The case was investigated by MUFON investigator Ann Druffel, who says, "I found Mr. DeJohn to be intelligent, well-read and articulate ... in spite of the unusual nature of [his] experience, it can be accepted as coming from an honest and rational man."

Says DeJohn, "This to me is a pleasant, happy and an enjoyable experience and one that I will never forget for as long as I live."[203]

A highly credible sighting took place on February 1, 1977, when two Tujunga law enforcement officers were on routine helicopter patrol over La Crescenta. Suddenly, they both observed a bright, glowing, yellow object dart below their helicopter at speeds in excess of one hundred miles per hour. At first they assumed it was a conventional plane without proper identification lights, and they turned to better observe it. At that moment, the unidentified object ascended to their altitude and began to orbit around the helicopter at a distance of 500 feet. Both officers could clearly observe a dark, metallic-looking cylindrical shape behind the light. After a few minutes, the object moved away at unbelievable speeds. As one of the officers told UFO investigators, "It didn't disappear into the distance as if it put on speed. One minute it was plainly visible; the next instant the light and cylinder were not there."[204]

About one month later, in mid-April 1977, three teenagers, Mark Dennett, Greg Randall, and Phil Stephens, observed a metallic craft with a dome and multicolored lights hovering only a few hundred feet over Reseda. When the object started to move away, the three teenagers chased the object in their van. Stephens described the object as having "sort of like a round-like bowl on the bottom." Randall said it had "a pyramid, almost like a triangle on top – each light going to the top." Dennett was most impressed by the movement. As he says, "A helicopter can't move like that, a sharp ninety-degree turn."

As soon as the three teenagers saw the object, it darted away. Says Randall, "We immediately took off chasing this thing through Granada Hills. And as we drove around, we had at least four or five car-loads of people chasing the same thing." The chase lasted for at least twenty minutes, but in the end the UFO simply departed the area.[205]

A few months later, on a warm mid-summer night at around two a.m., three Van Nuys residents, Melissa Chappell, Adlai Fredrickson, and a friend, observed three orange, "shiny, maybe metallic" glowing spheres hovering in a triangular formation only a few thousand feet above Van Nuys Air Force Reserve station near their home. Says Chappell, "There was one really big object and two smaller ones on either side and above it, and these objects appeared to be all the way up near the mountains. You could see the outline of the mountains behind them, so they were below the level of the mountains."

Says Fredrickson, "[The] lights appeared to be moving in unison. They came and just hovered overhead for a little while and started shifting, moving around at different angles." After about twenty minutes, the objects suddenly and quickly moved away. The witnesses speculated that the objects were surveying the many technological installations in the area, including Lockheed, Hughes Aircraft, and the Van Nuys Air Base.[206]

On March 27, 1978, a UFO incident caused the destruction of three military planes and cost the life of three pilots. All three planes were stationed at naval stations near San Diego and were involved in routine flights.

While in flight, an "unknown object" appeared off the San Diego coast. Immediately, the electrical systems in all three planes went haywire. An F-14 Tomcat from Miramar Naval Air Station lost control during landing and crashed onto a crowded highway, killing one of the pilots.

Later, a twin-engine S-3A Viking antisubmarine jet lost control and plunged into the ocean six miles off the coast of North Island Naval Air Station, killing both pilots.

Meanwhile, a Navy A-4 Skyhawk fighter lost control and fell into the sea. Fortunately, that pilot ejected and was later rescued.

A Naval public relations officer officially denied the presence of a UFO saying, "The unknown object reportedly seen by witnesses off the San Diego coast was a meteor."

However, according to researcher Ron Edwards, unofficial Navy sources later admitted that the object was a UFO, and that it had rendered the planes' electrical, weapon and navigation systems completely paralyzed.[207]

Because they are often outdoors, a large number of sightings occur to police officers. Sometimes, the officers suffer severe repercussions for seeing a UFO. On May 13, 1978, Officer Manuel Amparano was patrolling the streets of Kerman at around 3:30 a.m. when he saw a "circular-type thing, about 100 feet from the ground."

Amparano realized he was seeing an actual UFO. As he says, "I just stayed in my car and looked at it for a few minutes. It just hovered there above the trees and I started to adjust my spotlight on it. But just when I got ready to turn the spotlight on, it flashed blue-white, then went up and over and flew away to the southeast."

At first, Amparano intended to keep his experience a secret. However, his fellow officers immediately asked him what was wrong with his face. It was then that he realized that the upper front half of his body was severely sunburned. When blisters formed the next day, Amparano was briefly hospitalized and treated for burns. He later learned that at least two other Kerman residents also reported seeing a UFO on the same evening.

The officer's sighting became a media sensation. Amparano learned the hard way that seeing a UFO sometimes has consequences. As he says, "There's no question I was passed over for a promotion because of it. As an officer, I can go out, see somebody shoot someone, write a report, and then send them to prison. But something like this happens and all of a sudden, I'm a nut."[208]

While Amparano was being maltreated, the sightings continued. On May 27, 1978, dozens of calls poured into the Police Department and Sheriff's Station in Chula Vista. At the same time, a magnetometer at Precision Monitoring Systems was mysteriously set off. The calls were in regard to a large object which was hovering next to the Chula Vista drive-in theater. The witnesses were put in touch with investigators; however, when the investigators arrived the witnesses were strangely unwilling to talk. Says the main investigator, Peter Schlesinger, "They wouldn't talk to us. They just stared at us blankly, like zombies."

Schlesinger talked to several others who observed the object. Most were badly frightened by its appearance. When Schlesinger heard that four police officers also observed the craft from the station roof, he arranged to interview the officers. However, when they went to meet them the next day, all four officers had been transferred and two were moved from their residences. Also, two of them were no longer employees of the Chula Vista Police. Three years later, Schlesinger tracked down one of the officers in Montana. The officer, however, still refused to acknowledge the incident. Schlesinger speculates that they were either threatened or paid off to keep silent about the encounter.[209]

In the summer of 1978, two members of the Schwindler family and a friend were camping out in the desert outside of Palmdale. It was late at night and they were watching the stars. All at once, they noticed that some of the stars were not only different colors, they appeared to be moving in strange darting patterns. Says Chris Schwindler, "We saw these different colored lights, and they circled around each other, went down and pulled apart, and went down and pulled apart. It lasted for probably a couple of minutes." The three witnesses have no idea what they saw, but are sure the explanation could not involved planes, helicopters or other conventional aircraft.[210]

Around the same time but 150 miles further south, atop the tallest building in San Diego, twelve people witnessed a gigantic V-shaped UFO. The main witness, Rick Leibert, is a leading special-effects technician. On this occasion, he set up a twenty-two watt green spectrophysics laser which would move in unison to the songs of a local radio station. However, what started as a publicity stunt ended up attracting more attention than the witnesses had bargained for.

Says Leibert, "We were looking at the [laser] beam as it took off up into the sky, or bent and shot off to the west. And as we were looking up, this huge presence that was … uh … like a huge silent bulk, glided over the top of the building. And there were soft lights that were in a regular formation, at regular intervals, forming something like a huge V. And this whole presence glided over the top of this building and continued to glide on. It was like a chevron pattern in terms of the lights, and it just continued on in that direction.

"And then off to the left side of this thing was another much smaller shape which also had lights on it in that same chevron pattern, but smaller – sort of like a baby version. There were ten of us up there, and all ten of us saw it at the same time."

The witnesses immediately called the airport control tower at nearby Lindbergh Field; however, airport officials reported no unusual radar returns. Later, Leibert and his associates would inadvertently initiate additional UFO visitations using similar methods.[211]

In late 1978, Canyon Country resident Robert Murphy, a radiologist by profession, was in his home in a rural area when he noticed bright lights landing in the corner of his yard, about twenty feet from his back door. Says Murphy, "All of a sudden, in the corner of my yard, there were red and white lights flashing, and they looked like they were on an object … and this thing was really close …. There was no sound at all so it was obviously not a helicopter." Murphy was so amazed, he staggered back and looked away. When he looked back seconds later, the object was gone.

He assumed the experience was over; however, the next night he experienced a terrifying Bigfoot encounter, which he feels was somehow linked to the UFO sighting. The area near his home has produced a number of Bigfoot reports in the past.[212]

In July 1978, an eleven-year-old boy was swimming in a pool in Palm Springs. Looking up, he observed five white, glowing disk-shaped objects, hovering in a square formation at about 3000 feet. He estimated the disks were at least 50 feet in diameter. As he watched, the objects accelerated at high speed over the horizon. Seconds later, another formation of five objects darted overhead, stopped, hovered briefly, and returned the way they had come. The witness called Edwards AFB and was told that the objects were just "helicopters on maneuvers." The witness later joined the Marines and says that he never saw any aircraft that remotely resembled what he had seen.[213]

By the time the 1980s arrived, the field of UFO research was exploding. Numerous civilian researchers entered the field, and the reported accounts became more extensive and varied.

Throughout the summer of 1980, the city of Santa Monica experienced numerous visitations of a glowing red craft. Longtime residents Donald and Bonnie X, their three children, and two neighbors all viewed a crescent-shaped glowing red object hovering above their home one summer evening around 9:00 p.m. Says Bonnie, "We saw this thing up in the sky that was absolutely quiet, and it was just hovering. It wasn't a helicopter or anything, because there was no noise … we just kept on saying, 'What on earth could it be if there's no noise and it's just hovering?'."

The family obtained their binoculars and viewed the object. They were still unable to identify it. Says Donald X, "We just don't know what it was, which I guess is what a UFO is. It appeared to be stationary … we watched it for the longest time."

Two days later, Bonnie's parents, who live in neighboring Playa Del Rey, also reported seeing a reddish disk-like object hovering over their home. They too called out the neighbors to witness the UFO.

Around that time period, pilot and flight instructor Toshi Inouye was flying over the Santa Monica mountains with a student when they both observed an unknown flying object described by Inouye as "glowing red in the shape of a cigar ... about two to three times bigger than a bus." Inouye was about to call the control tower to report the unknown craft when "all of a sudden, it disappeared. It disappeared while we were looking at it, which means that the object moved away with a very, very fast speed."

Two weeks following this incident, Inouye's student was driving through the Santa Monica mountains at night with his friends when they saw what appeared to be the same glowing red UFO. On this occasion, the object swooped down over the witnesses and chased their vehicle for several miles.

The total number of witnesses to this particular glowing red UFO is at least fifteen, but is likely much greater than that.[214]

A particular intense flurry of sightings hit the San Jose area in the early part of 1981. Richard Haines Ph.D., Irwin Wieder, Dick Henry, and Andrew Grotowksy were the lead investigators. As the thirteen page summery of their investigation reads in part: "A total of 37 eyewitnesses ranging in age from 10 to 56 years reported seeing one or more intense lights in the sky over the greater San Jose area during the period of January 9 through March 7. Most of these sightings took place between 10:00 p.m. and midnight and involved a red, round, diffusely edged luminous area of lights which would hover, quickly accelerate, change directions and disappear in various ways."

Among the witnesses were several pilots and two controllers from San Jose airport. The objects failed to appear on radar.[215]

A few months later, southern California was hit by a wave of flying triangles. As investigated by prominent southern California MUFON investigator William Hassel, the cases involve more than a dozen witnesses to five independent sightings. In each case, the witnesses observed a large triangular object, moving very slowly at low altitudes and emitting a soft humming noise. Even though the objects were of low altitude, several of the witnesses observed them through binoculars. Two of the witnesses complained of itchy, burning eyes following their encounter. Hassel had the witnesses draw what they had observed. The drawings are remarkably similar, each showing a triangular craft covered with about five bright lights.[216]

One week after New Year's Day in 1983 medical biller, Robert X., and five of his friends – all men in their early twenties – were driving through the Lake Naciemiento area outside Paso Robles in northern California. It was a still night, perfectly clear at around 8:00 p.m., when one of the six witnesses spotted a ring of star-like lights rotating and moving across the sky. Says Robert, "They started moving! It was like, wow! It was like a central light, and there were these other ones that would fly around it. It was really weird. I've never seen anything like it before ... they just looked like a cluster of stars at first. There was one real bright one in the middle, and a bunch of little ones around it. And we were watching, just looking around, and you'd see them move. They would dart across the sky, dart back, but they'd go right back to the same place which was kind of weird."

The men pulled the car over and watched the display for several minutes. Finally somebody mentioned the word "UFO." Everyone looked at each other and was surprised to find that they all agreed. There was simply no other explanation.

They drove around and observed the objects from other locations. Says Robert, "It was really weird. We went driving up to the lake, and there were other people standing around looking up. There were other people who pulled over, looking up, watching. So we weren't the only idiots who saw it."

The witnesses watched the object for about four hours before driving away and losing sight of them.[217]

On May 19, 1983, art designer Arni Whyler was helping to throw a party for NBC studios. The party was held outside the La Brea Tar Pits in Santa Monica, and involved a dramatic light display. Whyler and others, including leading fireworks expert Rick Leibert, were putting together a display of computer-controlled pitchel lights in the shape of a peacock's tail. The display was completed and then turned on.

Shortly after the bright lights had been turned on, three UFOs came swooping down from above as if to investigate the strange scene. Says Whyler, "We looked off to the south .... Off in the distance there were three lights – and they were rather large. They looked like the illumination of the top of a building, but there were no buildings down there! We looked at these things and they seemed to get a little larger as if they were coming towards us. And they just stopped in one area ... then what happened is, as we looked at them all three of them just went off. They just shot off. They went west towards the ocean."

This, of course, is not the first case of its kind. Says Whyler, "I mentioned it to Rick, and he said, 'Oh, yeah, I've seen those things before.' Rick said that every time he has set up these pitchel lights in regular patterns, he's experienced this type of thing."

Amazingly, several UFO groups have now used similar methods involving powerful lights to successfully initiate their own encounters.[218]

Late at night in mid-1983, contractor Robert Hale and his lady friend, Lisa Hamilton, were driving along the isolated Highway 40 between Needles and Barstow, in the middle of the remote Mojave desert. The Mojave is the largest and most isolated desert in the United States so it is not too surprising that it has generated a number of reports. As the couple drove, they observed a bright "green light" emitted from behind a nearby mountain. That in itself wasn't very strange. The only thing that bothered the witnesses was that there was supposed to be nothing out there. Says Hale, "There was nothing out there. I mean, it was in an area that is totally remote."

As they watched, the light suddenly extinguished. Neither of them could come up with any logical explanation except perhaps a secret military exercise. The only thing was, there were no roads out to the area. Says Hamilton, "It was unexplained."[219]

In the summer of 1983, eight climbers from *Wilderness Challenge* (a group of people who have successfully overcome addictions) ascended to the peak of Mount San Gorgonio to celebrate their achievement. It took three days to reach the top. Fifteen minutes after they set up their camp, a large glowing sphere of light descended above the group. One of the climbers, Mark Grant, describes the encounter, "There was a light that kind of hovered overhead. I don't know – it looked like it could have been a helicopter, but none of us thought that it could be way up on the top of a mountain like that. There was no noise whatsoever with this. And the light just kind of hovered overhead .... It was very uncomfortable to look at because the light was so intense ... it was about three or four hundred feet above us. I mean, it was very close and the whole area around us lit up ... it was very apparent to everyone that there was something there. You know, it's just something that's just not really explainable."

Later, Grant would experience an even more dramatic missing time encounter in Topanga Canyon.[220]

It was late 1983 at Mission Bay when Whitney Wright and his brother decided to take their father's boat for a midnight trip into the bay. The two teenagers were discussing the Bible when one of them saw a "small, little white dot cruising across the sky."

Wright watched as the light swooped down beneath the cloud bank. He was immediately impressed by the way it moved and pointed out the object to his brother. As if in response, the object went crazy. Says Wright, "It was too small to be a plane or anything ... when he started crawling out and looking at it, it went radical. It went in straight lines, but every which way, in all different directions, in like a little pattern. It was weird ... the clouds were like coastal fog, they were really low. That's what freaked me out, because when it was up against the black sky, it looked like it was small and far away. But when it came underneath the clouds, I knew it was small and close ... and the minute I started telling my brother, it went crazy. It went back and forth, up and down, just like a little scribble. Then it took off."[221]

Electromagnetic effect cases are relatively rare. Even more rare are cases involving multiple vehicles. One evening, sometime in 1984, two vehicles carrying a baseball team from Washington State were heading south down the coast of California. It was around 10:00 p.m., when one of the passengers noticed an "oblong object" that was pacing their vehicles. Suddenly, the object approached close. Says one of the witnesses, "All our lights, radio, EVERYTHING on the van in front of us and in our car went out. I looked at the object and it looked closer still and looked to be hovering. We pulled over to the side of the road as quickly and as safely as we could when you have no lights or any guidance, and stopped."

No sooner had they exited their vehicles when the object disappeared, and the carlights came back on. Says the main witness, "I wouldn't have believed this if I hadn't seen it with my own eyes."[222]

Topanga Canyon is one of California's leading producers of UFO reports. Around 11:00 p.m., one summer evening in 1986, three teenagers, Gabe Aldort, Vadja Potenza, and A.W., were playing outside their homes when they saw two star-like objects approach each other from opposite ends of the sky, rotate around each other, and depart. All three witnesses were left speechless by the maneuver. Says Aldort, "It was really weird because I knew planes couldn't do that. They just stopped, like they looked at each other, and then they circled around each other, and then they just split ... I've never seen anything like that before."

Potenza was equally impressed. "I didn't think it was a plane because I'd never seen a plane that could do that."[223]

Also in 1986, Ronny Baron was driving with friends through the southern California desert outside Fresno. It was midday. Baron was in the front passenger seat and his friend was driving. Suddenly, they both observed a large aircraft swoop down in front of them over the freeway. Says Baron, "It happened so quickly ... it looked like it was a big airplane ... it had lights on it like landing gear on an airplane, very similar. It looked like lights coming down over the road, coming right at us. And I looked at the driver of the car, and he looked at me. He didn't say anything, and I didn't say anything. We saw these two things up there, and nobody said anything. And all of a sudden, these lights came straight at us and disappeared into the ground on the side of the car ... it went right down into the ground, no smoke or anything. No sound."

Baron had seen UFOs on several previous occasions, however, he was still deeply impressed. As he says, "We were both very puzzled. Still, nobody said anything about it. Just such a mind-blow. There was no explanation for it. It scared me because it reaffirmed that there's some kind of life and intelligence happening up there. To see it actually up close like that, you know that we're not here by ourselves. You know what I mean? That kind of shakes you up because we don't know who they are and what they're about."[224]

On September 6, 1987, two residents of Long Beach reported seeing a "gray metallic box about 10 feet long, 5 feet high" zoom across the sky. One of the witnesses is a United States Marshall, and described the object as a "flying boxcar."[225]

In 1987, four teenagers, Gabe Aldort, John Heldman, and brothers Ivan and Leif Eason, all became witnesses to a dramatic UFO display over Topanga Canyon. They were sitting on their back deck in the evening when they saw a small metallic object with a "weird-looking sports car shape" fly slowly overhead. Heldman described the object as "kind of circular with one big light on top of it."

The first object was immediately followed by two other identical objects which flew side by side over the witnesses. This was followed by an enormous metallic craft which hovered low over the house and sent down a beam of light next to the shocked witnesses. It was totally silent except for a soft buzzing noise. Says Aldort, "It came right over his house, really, really close ... and the beam, it came down and it moved across this particular part of the house."

Heldman reports that the object "had little lights on the outside of it, all the way around. And then it shined a beam down on the house ... we all kind of freaked out and hid under the side of the house."

All of them were in a state of total awe. Says Leif Eason, "We were just looking at it, going, wow, that's a spaceship!"

The beam from the large object retracted, then the object moved away. Seconds later, another small UFO flew overhead. The witnesses had sighted a total of five UFOs in a span of about five minutes.[226]

On May 20, Andy Anderson and Frank Mulholland of Simi Valley were working on a car-engine in their backyard when they heard a "low hum" getting louder and louder. Looking up, they observed an object that was "rectangular, with one light on each corner. It was bigger than an airplane and wider."

Anderson is positive the object wasn't a plane, not only because it made a strange noise and was a perfect rectangle, it was flying at an elevation of only 300 feet. Says Anderson, "It was too big and going too slow. There's no way a jet could do that."

Says Mulholland, "I don't know what it was. It was making some weird sounds."

The two men called out several other witnesses, all of who observed the strange object move slowly southeast towards the San Fernando Valley. Inquiries with the Simi Valley police revealed no other callers.[227]

On May 27, 1988, Diego Mazzoleni and his friend Zoltan Bukovacz were drawn outside of their home in Burbank when they saw a glowing object hurtling downwards out of the sky. Says Mazzoleni, "I really panicked because I thought it was coming for our house." Mazzoleni phoned his aunt, Bonnie Bunyik, who was also able to observe the object. They all three watched it hover for several minutes and then drift away. They called up Burbank Airport and the Federal Aviation Administration, but were unable to receive confirmation.[228]

On August 4, Kay Stricker was driving her van through the desert community of Lancaster. It was 11:15 in the morning when she noticed a shiny, oval-shaped object hovering low in the sky. Intrigued, she watched it for a few moments after which it "just evaporated. It disappeared, became invisible." Stricker called up the local newspaper, which hadn't received any other calls. But because Lancaster had a history of UFO encounters, Stricker's account made the newspapers the next day.[229]

The desert area of Anza in southern California has generated a number of reports, most notably in late 1988. From October to December 1988, numerous residents observed UFOs hovering over the town. One witness observed a "large cigar-shaped vessel." Another described a "craft" that would dart across the sky for hours.

Yet another witness, an elderly lady, was driving when she observed a craft descend and hover above the power lines. As she watched, about six "beings" exited the craft, checked the outside and quickly re-entered. Seconds later, the craft zoomed away. At the same time, neighboring people reported television and radio interference, including airstrip alarms being mysteriously set off.[230]

In the following case, a man and his wife encountered a gigantic UFO on a lonely mountain road in December 1988. As the main witness wrote in an emotional letter to newspaper columnist Richard Barbour Ph.D., "I write to you reluctantly, because you may decide I am crazy. My wife and I were driving home from Las Vegas. It was near midnight, on a clear moonlit night. We topped Cajon Pass, near San Bernardino. Above us we saw what looked like a huge flying wing. It was longer than a football field and quite wide. It moved slowly and silently from east to west. On the side was a long row of dim lights. It was bigger than any plane ever built. We stopped to watch. It moved steadily in the direction of Los Angeles .... Dr. Barbour, we were not drinking. Our eyesight is good. We were wide awake. We don't have hallucinations. We have concluded that we really saw something from out of this world. Can you explain it?" Dr. Barbour offered that perhaps they had seen the stealth bomber, "except for the size of the object you saw." He concludes saying, "I wish that just for once I could see a UFO myself!"[231]

The year of 1989 brought more high-quality sightings. On June 19, more than a dozen people called the Los Angeles Times to report the sighting of a UFO over Encino. One caller described, "Two large bright orange lights, right next to each other. They moved away for a few seconds, then came back."[232]

Autumn brought a huge wave of sightings. House-painter Joe Clower was on the job, painting a home in Los Angeles, when he saw a large metallic saucer hovering and gliding just a few hundred feet above the suburbs. He quickly grabbed a small plastic Polaroid camera and snapped five clear photographs. (See photo section.) As the sun set, the object finally darted away. Clower had seen UFOs on several previous occasions, and finally decided to carry a camera. Like some witnesses, he reports that he feels a strange electrical feeling before the UFOs appear.[233]

In October 1989, at least a dozen people (including a doctor, a border patrol agent, and a newspaper columnist) independently observed a very bright white sphere of light emitting a cone of light beneath it, just off the coast of Del Mar. The object appeared suddenly and remained stationary in the sky for a period of about three minutes, at which point it suddenly winked out. The object was so bright, it generated reports from neighboring counties. Said one witness, "I thought it was odd that it wasn't moving. I was driving so I couldn't stare at it. The next time I looked up, it was gone."[234]

Also in October 1989, Arni Whyler, an art director for NBC and other major studios, was in his home in rural Pasadena when he received an overwhelming impulse to look out his window. Says Whyler, "I looked out the window, and a spot of light appeared over the house ... it was a perfectly round disk, a little oval." As Whyler watched, the light darted from east to west, shrank in size, and disappeared. Seconds later, "a wave of light" swept across the house. Whyler's ears popped in response. Meanwhile, he noticed that a distinct after-image of the UFO had been burned into his retina. He ran outside to see if the UFO was anywhere near. To his shock, the entire environment was enveloped in a strange muffled silence. Unknown to Whyler, this was another common detail of UFO encounters known by researchers as the "oz factor." Says Whyler, "It was absolutely silent."[235]

On October 15, two separate families in San Marcos observed a gigantic W-shaped craft fly low over their homes and head out over the Pacific. Both groups of witnesses said that the craft was at least as big as a football field. The first family, the Retas, told investigators that the enormous object actually tilted and flipped over, at which point it flashed a multitude of colored lights. They immediately called the police.

The other family, the Clarks, saw the object from their back deck. They watched as it suddenly turned off all its lights and glided silently towards the ocean. About twenty minutes later, another triangular object passed quickly overhead with six military jets in pursuit.[236]

October 1989 proved to be particularly active. A few days before Halloween, Mary Bennett and Irene Evans were driving through the city of Inglewood when they sighted a "pair of huge lights" hanging low in the sky. As they watched, the lights suddenly swooped towards them and then either disappeared or moved very quickly away.[237]

Around the same time, another UFO was sighted by two young ladies from North Hollywood. The witnesses, who prefer to remain anonymous, were in their apartment when they heard what they thought was a plane about to crash into their building. They rushed outside and were shocked to see a huge string of bright lights in an upward U-shape, hovering only a few hundred feet above their heads. Says one witness, "We saw weird lights, that's all, and it went really fast. It stayed in one area in the sky, and then it went off really fast. And the lights were really weird. It wasn't a plane light ... it was big. I knew it wasn't a plane because a plane has a certain amount of lights. The noise we heard was so weird; it was so loud."[238]

On December 8, 1989, two ladies were driving home from a party outside of Coronado. Looking up, they saw four red lights suspended in a row in the sky. They were trying to determine what the lights could be. Suddenly, the objects began to dart away. They realized they were seeing actual UFOs, and followed them in their car to a remote parking lot. They pulled over and watched as the four objects moved back and forth, in an apparent display. Says one witness, "They were skimming across the sky, but not going very fast. It's like they were cruising."

At first the display was fascinating. But the ladies became instantly frightened when one of the objects swooped straight at them and buzzed their car within a few feet. They then saw that the objects were actually octagonal with a triangular shape on the back and three pulsating lights. Each was about the size of a Greyhound bus and made no noise.

Says one of the ladies, "By then we were kind of nervous, so we left." They went home to get more witnesses, but when they returned, the objects were gone.[239]

8. The Topanga Canyon UFO Wave

See color section, page 115

Of all the decades in UFO history, the nineties seem to be designed to prove to everybody that UFOs are real. All across California, UFO activity increased dramatically. The most-populated state was about to face its biggest challenge. There were waves of activity over major population centers. The number of abduction cases increased. Furthermore, *conclusive* evidence was obtained proving the reality of the UFO phenomenon once and for all.

On the morning of February 8, 1990, Anna Ciborowski was woken up by the frantic shouts of her husband. She ran outside and, with her husband, observed a veritable fleet of UFOs hovering over the Marine Corps Air Ground Combat Base near their home in Twentynine Palms. Also present were her child and several construction workers who were helping to renovate their home.

The witnesses watched as what looked like three "glowing clouds" descended over the nearby Marine base. Suddenly, the clouds moved away and revealed an incredible sight. Says Ciborowski, "I couldn't believe my eyes as we stood watching the three craft approach. As the increasing winds blew away more of the clouds surrounding the ships, we could see their shapes distinctly against the morning's blue sky. The rising sun glinted brilliantly across their smooth metal skins."

The witnesses saw that the craft were different sizes, the largest of which was shaped like a cigar and had portholes around its perimeter. They watched the craft for twenty minutes. Ciborowski returned inside and noticed that the radios were giving off a strange static noise. More shouts from her husband drew her outside. Says Ciborowski, "Running out the door with shoes in my hand, I looked up where the three ships had been. There, we witnessed the first of what were to be fifteen more unusual craft arriving. Hanging in formation, they appeared in groups according to types and/or sizes. Swooping down towards the base at high speeds from a westerly direction, each group of craft stopped at an apparently pre-designated place, as they rotated in distant formations. For the next hour, these incredible machines arrived in groups of three."

Ciborowski's husband grabbed his camera and managed to snap several pictures, which unfortunately are not impressive. Two hours and twenty minutes passed when, suddenly, the fleet of UFOs departed in a period of three minutes, at exactly 8:40 a.m. Ciborowski had friends who worked at the nearby base and she later asked them for information. She learned that at the time of the incident, the entire base became paralyzed by, as one employee told her, "the meanest sandstorm I've ever seen come through this area." Another employee of the base told her that visibility was down to zero, and all field exercises were cancelled. Ciborowski called the Public Information Officer on the base and was impolitely rebuffed. She and the other witnesses, however, remain convinced that they saw a total of eighteen ET craft. As she says, "No other experience can match the sense of awe and wonder that remains within every one of us who saw it."[240]

A few months later, in June of 1990, a Palomar airport employee had just left work and was driving home when he observed a strange triangular craft hovering nearby. He could hear a low humming noise, and watched as the craft shot down three bright beams of light on the ground. After about ninety seconds, the craft shot straight up and disappeared.[241]

On November 19, 1991, Canyon Country resident Robert Murphy was in his home in the rural foothills when he saw a strange, kite-like object as big as a car floating a mere fifty feet above the fields behind his home. He ran inside and retrieved his binoculars. He was able to view the object closely and described it as "reddish-orange, and it was shaped like a rectangle with all four corners kind of pointed ... it wasn't swaying or moving or anything like that. It was just a solid piece of something right there."

As Murphy watched, the object darted instantaneously from one point in the sky to another. Murphy was certain that the object was definitely not a kite, balloon or conventional vehicle. After about fifteen minutes, the object darted out of view and never returned. Afterwards, he inspected the area where the object had hovered and found strange depressions in the grass. He also reported strange plant growth in the area following the encounter.[242]

House-painter Joe Clower had already seen and photographed a UFO over Los Angeles in 1989. Like many people who see a UFO once, he began to see UFOs again and again. Some people appear to attract UFOs. It was only after he had seen UFOs on a few occasions that he began to carry a camera at all times. In 1991, he had just exited a restaurant in Pacific Palisades where he had eaten lunch. As he walked towards he car, he saw a bright, silvery disk moving slowly over the parking lot. He instinctively grabbed his Polaroid camera and snapped a photograph. The object moved slowly away, so he jumped in his car and followed it as it moved overhead. He took two more photos of the object through his windshield. As the object started to hover again, he got out and prepared to take another photo. At this point, the craft turned and zoomed southwards. Clower snapped a final photo of the craft as it moved towards the Santa Monica Pier. (See photo section.)

One of the most intense UFO waves in California history began on June 14, 1992, and continued at a feverish pace for more than two years. The location was Topanga Canyon, a rural community of about 8000 residents outside of Los Angeles. On that evening, numerous residents called the local police station to report UFOs.

The first police report came from a gentleman and his girlfriend who were driving through the canyon around midnight. The man told the police an incredible story. "We are very shaken up and somewhat disoriented ... we are almost ashamed to tell you what we saw. You'll think I'm crazy, but I don't know who to tell."

The caller assured the officer that he didn't drink or take drugs. "Officer, we were driving through the canyon, where the canyon gets deep, and we noticed a bright light in the sky. And we had a very uneasy feeling because it was moving and we both felt it was following us. All of a sudden, on top of us was this extremely bright object. We could hear it wasn't a helicopter – it had a high-pitched sound. And we lost control of the car and it lifted us up into the sky. It lifted us up off the ground. Now, I'm telling you, I've never been more frightened in my life."

By now the caller was near tears, and the deputy did his best to reassure the frightened witness. The caller concluded his report, "We were put down. We lost our memory for I don't know how long, maybe a couple of minutes. And it wasn't there anymore. I don't believe in these things. I'm telling you, I'm a normal human being. I have a job, a good job. My girlfriend has a good job – she's a nurse. We are very disoriented. We got home by the grace of God. My girlfriend was near hysterical. I don't know what to do ... we are very nauseous and we feel very weak and disoriented."

The officer recommended seeking medical help and gently terminated the call.

A few minutes later, the second call came in. The caller gave his name and asked, "Did anyone call in and report anything strange happening in Topanga?"

The officer on duty denied any unusual activity and asked what the caller saw. The caller replied, "My girlfriend and I saw three very strange – God, who does one report UFOs to? ... We saw three UFOs – disks, flying disks – in the canyon. They were saucers. And they were following us above our car. And we got out and we saw them. We watched them. And within three seconds, like a bat out of hell, they just went *whoosh!* And they were gone ... They didn't do anything to us ... we thought there was a possibility they were helicopters except they didn't make any noise."

The officer asked a few questions and then recommended that the caller contact the Air Force if he wished to pursue the matter.

Shortly thereafter, a third call came in. A man who identified himself as a college professor said, "I live up in the canyon, and my wife and I were woken up – there was a very, very bright light coming above our home, into the windows. And we went out to look at it. We could see an extremely bright light hovering above us, but we couldn't hear anything .... It was awfully strange ... the damn thing didn't make any noise .... To tell you the truth, it was the strangest thing I've ever seen. The only sort of noise we did hear was sort of a high-pitched hum."

The officer asked for more details. The caller then said, "It really quite scared us. The light was very intense. And in fact, it lit up the whole house inside ... my wife is a bit shaken up right now."

The officer mentioned UFOs, but the caller replied that he "didn't believe in such things." The officer then offered another possibility, such as illegal activities by humans. The caller replied, "If someone is doing something illegal, they have a hell of a lot of wattage ... damnedest thing I've ever seen in my life," he concluded and hung up.

The final call came from a man who was driving southbound through the canyon on the night in question. Like all the callers, he inquired about aircraft activity and said, "About an hour ago, I was going down Topanga Canyon, and I think they were helicopters, because they were shining damn bright lights on me, but they kind of chased me down the road a bit ... I think they were helicopters, but I sure couldn't hear any sound ... it sure put out a powerful bright light, very bright. It was kind of like tailgating me from above. I couldn't see it. I couldn't see anything actually because it was so damn bright ... it sure was strange."

While the police station was fielding the above calls, the office of the local Topanga newspaper, *Messenger,* also received reports. One call came from Topanga resident, Dr. Murray Clarke, who observed an intensely bright star-like object zoom over his home sometime after midnight. "I looked through my view window ... it was traveling south-to-north very fast in a horizontal path, an intense yellow-white light. As it sped away from me, about over the last ridge, it just vanished."

Another call came from a lady who lives along the boulevard. "I saw a brilliant ray of light outside through my window ... I saw it and I'll never forget it. I'm telling you this now, but, well, I'm a professional person and I can't afford the risk of ridicule."

The caller insisted that the beam was not a car headlight. "I've lived here for years and because of the hills around, I can tell you no headlights can pass around by the house."

Nor did the caller believe that the beams were from helicopters. "I've seen those lights over and over ... this light was so focused, so intense, like nothing I've ever seen." The witness apparently viewed the actual beams of light that were tailgating or lifting cars and being emitted over homes.

At around 10:00 p.m., another car filled with three occupants was heading south-bound into Topanga Canyon. Bill Boshears and two friends had just entered the canyon when they noticed a strange darting light. Says Boshears, "All of a sudden I saw a streak of light. Then I saw another streak of light to the north. It went up over the mountains, very high up. And at first I thought it was a rocket launch. It was very bright, and it literally lit up the sky to the point that it might be a firestorm or something. So I stopped, got out, and it got brighter. By that, I mean you could literally see the shadow of the car on the ground as this thing played and moved over the canyon. It was almost like daylight."

Looking straight up, Boshears was amazed to see what looked like a gigantic bar of light hovering at about 3000 feet of elevation, ejecting smaller glowing football-shaped objects which darted across the sky. "I was not the only person to see this. There were several people that saw it. I thought it might have been a dirigible because earlier I had seen a *Fuji* blimp that was moving around over the ocean. Then I thought, 'Oh, maybe Hollywood is making a movie.' You have to think that to maintain stability. And for the next twenty minutes, I was looking straight up to the point that my neck started aching. I literally laid down on the hood of my car and watched it for twenty minutes."

Boshears and his two passengers watched the long glowing object eject numerous small craft continuously. "First [there was] the light, then the object and the lights going in and out of the object and around it. Silvery disk-shaped objects, lights changing colors – and it began to play in that area. And I say play, not that I could orchestrate it – the thing that I can relate it to most is a fireworks display ... you can see everything as bright as if it were day. The people who were with me, we just couldn't talk."

Boshears' friends stayed in the car and finally begged him to leave. He reluctantly agreed. The activity was still going on as they exited the canyon.

Also on that evening around midnight, Phillip and Mandy (pseudonyms), a middle-aged couple, were driving through the canyon after a dinner party. Says Mandy, "We were coming home. And just a few minutes after we pulled onto Topanga Canyon, all of a sudden, there were several of them. I can't remember the numbers now, but it was like five. Five or six huge bright lights moving at all different angles."

At first Mandy assumed the objects were helicopters tracking illegal activity. But she and her husband soon realized the objects moved at right angles, made no noise and were saucer-shaped. Says Mandy, "We were followed – definitely followed, halfway down the mountain, the whole drive down, until we got to the very bottom. I thought they were helicopters except they were totally silent. These brilliant lights were just all over us as we were driving down the mountain. I thought that there was a drug bust or something like that. The lights were incredibly bright, pure white lights. But they made absolutely no sound."

Mandy's husband saw the lights but paid little attention until they approached closely. Says Phillip, "I saw three craft coming over the hill. There appeared to be some lights on them and I jokingly turned to Mandy and said, 'Oh, look, Mandy! There are flying saucers!' And she thought I was kidding. You know, I wasn't really sure, but it did look like it. And they appeared to be silently floating, just moving over the hills .... My first impression was that they were flying saucers in that they appeared to be easily floating and moving over the hills, reminiscent somewhat of what we see in the movies .... They were definable. They were craft. As a matter of fact, there seemed to be lighting on the craft, which is why, after I made my joke and I wasn't really sure, I just discarded it because I didn't really expect to see a flying saucer that close in such a highly inhabited area. It just didn't make any sense. So I said, 'Oh, it must be some kind of craft.' But it did appear to have some kind of lights on it ... there appeared to be a dark body behind the lights. It wasn't just like a little spot of light in the sky. It was odd. It was clearly odd. It was not a craft I could readily identify. I couldn't."

With so many people reporting objects at the same time, it is clear that there were multiple UFOs. But if so many people saw the objects, exactly how many were there? Where were they coming from? Where were they going?

The answers to most of these questions was provided by another couple, Daniel and Katherine, who reside on one of the highest points of Topanga with a panoramic view of the entire canyon. At around 8:30 that evening, they sat down to watch a video. Almost immediately, their attention was drawn outside by flashes of light. Katherine assumed it was lightning even though there were no clouds in the sky. A few minutes later, she looked out the window and saw a strange glowing bar of light. Again, she sort of shrugged off the experience. "It looked like a perfectly straight line of light came out horizontally, which I thought was very strange. I said, 'Well, that's not lightning, you know.' But I sort of dismissed it. I just thought, 'Oh, that's weird.'"

A few minutes later, their dog began to bark. Looking outside, they both observed a "white oval shape, like a white glow, just sitting there" hovering over the nearby ridge. The object then disappeared and reappeared above and to the right of the original location. Seconds later, another object appeared. "It disappeared and appeared again," explained Daniel. "It was here, and then it disappeared, went *poof!* It was there instantaneously. And then it sat there for awhile. And then another one appeared right where that one had disappeared."

The couple could now see two objects hovering over the nearby Santa Ynez Ridge. Almost instantly, the first object took off and headed straight for them. Says Katherine, "It was as if this one moved up there to where the horizontal bar was that I had seen earlier, and another oval glow came to this location. Then the one that had moved up there would suddenly flash over our heads, lighting up the whole sky in almost a triangle shape."

The couple watched in disbelief as one object after another rose from behind the ridge and headed in various directions throughout the canyon. Says Daniel, "There was a number of them. This went on for quite awhile in kind of a rhythmic way. They would go directly overhead, right overhead .... Twice, one started out, it would stop, change at a ninety-degree angle, *zoom, zoom, shew!* And it moved so fast ... they would accelerate really fast. And every now and then, just a few times though, they'd start off in one direction, and then suddenly go make a right angle turn and go in the other way."

After fifteen minutes, the activity stopped. Daniel and Katherine had counted about twenty objects. They returned inside and tried to relax. Fifteen minutes later, another series of bright flashes brought them outside. To their shock, the same thing was happening again. Quickly, one after another, more than ten objects appeared and zipped overhead. Says Katherine, "Sometimes one would wait there, like it would start to leave and then it would wait there, and you'd think, 'Well, what's it waiting for?' And then it would go *shoot!* And then other one, *shoot!* And then *shoot!* And then the other one would wait."

Finally, the activity stopped and they returned inside. Shortly later, however, more UFOs appeared. As Daniel says, "Clusters, four or five, sometimes ten, a little more, twenty I guess, in clusters. Then it would stop. Then they would suddenly go, *whoosh, whoosh, whoosh, whoosh!*"

The UFO activity continued on and off for more than two hours. After about the fourth wave, Katherine began to count the objects. "There were so many of them. We were so caught up in the excitement of it. We were so amazed. We kept thinking it would end. I was trying to keep count, though I'm sure it wasn't an exact count. It was like, 'Okay, that was about forty. Okay, that was about forty.' And I said that at least five times. So my estimation of how many lights, or how many flashes of these oval things we saw, was about two hundred .... Now that was very frightening to me that there was so many ... Daniel doesn't like me to say that there were two hundred of them because he says that's too wild. Well, that's exactly why it was so upsetting to me. I don't know if it makes it any more wild seeing a hundred as opposed to two hundred, but it was a lot."

Says Daniel, "She was really frightened by how many. She said, 'Where are they all coming from? Where are they going?' It was frightening to her."

After about two hours, the objects left for good. By then, the couple was so upset, they went straight to bed and stopped looking outside. Says Katherine, "I didn't want to see it anymore .... It was not good news. I didn't sleep that night and I was upset for weeks after that. I always thought that if I saw an alien spaceship, that would be exciting and I would be happy. And if there were aliens from another planet, that I would want to meet them or experience them. But I have to say, that was not my actual reaction. Maybe if it had been three or four, I would have thought, 'Oh, that's fascinating.' But because there was so many, I was very intimidated."

Daniel agreed. "If one of those stopped, I would hate that. The feeling is, what can you do. They'll do whatever they're going to do."

So closes the evening of July 14, 1992. However, that day marked the beginning of a wave of activity which continued strong for two years. On July 15, 1992, two NBC employees were working at nearby Burbank Studios on the program "Unsolved Mysteries." At 7:15 p.m., one of the employees, Eric Weisman, stepped out of the building to return home. Says Weisman, "I got about three steps out of the building and immediately my head turned up towards the north, almost as if this thing were calling me ... it was an object that just sat there, and it looked like a dark square. There were tinges of orange and reds to it."

Weisman estimated that it was about three thousand feet up and less than a quarter mile distant. As a kite-collector, he knew instantly it wasn't a kite or a balloon. He rushed back inside and got his co-worker, John Dunn.

Says Dunn, "I walked out there, and I looked up in the sky and I said, 'Wow, what is that?' It looked like a pen-top and it just sat there. And I'm the kind of person who's not going to believe in UFOs until I see something myself, basically .... I just sat there and stared at it. I must have stared at it for maybe two minutes, and it was just a really weird feeling because I couldn't identify it. I couldn't identify it at all, and it was just hovering, just sitting there."

As the two men watched, the object began to change shape, from rectangular, to triangular, and other odd shapes. After several minutes, Dunn returned inside and Weisman went to drive underneath the object. However, as soon as he turned his gaze to his car keys, the object disappeared. Weisman called the local airport and police to report his sighting, but was unable to get any other information.

Says Dunn, "It was just a really weird experience for me. It's unidentified as far as I'm concerned. I have no idea what it was. I'm not saying it was a UFO. All I know is that it wasn't anything I've ever seen, and it was just sitting there."[243]

At 1:45 a.m. on August 5, 1992, a UFO narrowly missed striking a jumbo jet carrying 300 passengers. The Boeing 747 had just taken off from Los Angeles International Airport and reached a cruising altitude of 23,000 feet and an airspeed of 600 miles per hour. Suddenly, without any warning, the pilot and crew members spotted an unidentified craft in front of their windshield. Instead of avoiding a collision, the UFO seemed to be heading directly for the nose of the airliner. When the object was right up against the windshield and collision seemed inevitable, the mysterious object suddenly dropped in elevation and narrowly missed the jet. The object moved at an estimated speed of 1800 miles per hour, and was in view for only a few seconds.

News of the sighting quickly reached officials at Edwards and George Air Force bases who denied having any information about the sighting.[244]

Two weeks later, on August 16, two men driving along the Pacific Coast Highway in Malibu observed a formation of six black, diamond-shaped objects moving at high speeds over the nearby mountains. One of the witnesses, Adam, says, "There were five or six objects – actually five in a circle with the sixth one in back of it, and they were black, diamond disk-shaped objects ... they were very futuristic-looking ... it was definitely no ordinary aircraft."

The other witness, Mario, says, "... they moved at an incredible, incredible speed .... I've been in the military seven years and I've never seen anything move that rapidly, that fast."

The two men actually chased the objects in their car until they lost sight of them driving through the canyons. As they drove, they passed a group of people sitting in lawn chairs along the road, apparently looking for UFOs.[245]

On September 22, Topanga Canyon resident Ethan Holtzman observed a "huge, red ball of fire" shoot straight down next to him on the road. Says Holtzman, "I don't know what it was ... I saw a solid mass. I saw it. It fell. It just fell out of the sky. And it looked about the size of the sun. It was a deep red. I didn't hear any noise."

Holtzman was driving at the time, and didn't pull over to observe the object. As he says, "I was freaked out because I thought the aliens were abducting me."[246]

Many accounts exist of UFOs effecting electromagnetic machinery. A unique and dramatic example occurred sometime in 1992 (exact date not given), when hundreds of residents in San Diego and the surrounding counties woke up to find their lights and appliances turning on and off by themselves. Some residents looked outside and also observed a large "glowing light" hovering over the city. The light was reportedly *pulsating in time* to the appliances going on and off. Local utility companies were contacted but were unable to offer any explanation for the bizarre effect.[247]

Meanwhile, north of San Diego, in the city of Oceanside, several people observed a glowing cigar-shaped craft hovering over a water-treatment plant. The main witness, an employee of the plant, observed the craft drop out of the sky to an altitude of a few thousand feet, where it hovered for a few moments and then took off at high speeds. The case was investigated by Orion, a private group of San Diego County Ufologists. Orion was formed in the late 1980s by Eric Herr and is responsible for investigating dozens of local cases.[248]

Throughout 1992, prominent researcher Bill Hamilton received numerous reports of sightings in southern Antelope Valley, and all along the San Gabriel Mountain range. Most of the sightings involved a "dark, triangular, silent object." Hamilton astutely remarked that the sightings had something to do with the many technological installations in the area. He speculates that some of the sightings may be the result of reverse-engineering of UFO technology by human beings.[249]

At the same time of the above sightings, the San Diego based UFO research group Orion recorded more local high-profile cases. On January 29, 1993, two teenagers observed an oval object emanating laser-like lights as it hovered over their home in Oceanside. One of the boys was deeply traumatized by the incident and experienced severe insomnia for a period of days following the sighting.[250]

On March 7, 1993, Topanga Canyon resident Valerie Dennett observed a star-like object with red and blue lights hovering outside her home for a period of hours. The object returned for three days in a row. Dennett had the distinct impression it was interested in her newborn baby, who was less than a week old. Says Dennett, "I got nervous because I thought it was watching me .... I thought that maybe it was going to come down and take me away, or my baby or something, because I just had [the] baby five days before that. It sure did make me nervous. I mean, I started getting really nervous. It was kind of weird."[251]

In May of 1993, Malibu resident Judy X. was in her home one evening when she observed nearly a dozen oval objects moving across the night sky. She quickly grabbed her camera and snapped four photographs. Says Judy, "At the time, these weird lights were not a big deal. I just took the picture because I had been seeing these lights, off and on for a long time, but this was the most I had ever seen in one group and I thought it was pretty phenomenal .... Some of them would become fainter and even disappear and then suddenly blink back into sight. A couple of them piggy-backed each other. I remember that after I finished taking the photographs, they all blinked out at once. I just sat there and said, 'Wow, that was so neat.' And then I just forgot about the photos."[252]

A rare case of a UFO-caused injury occurred in Oakdale to an anonymous woman. As investigated by MUFON researcher Allen Dunkin, the witness was driving alone late at night when she observed a large object shaped like a hockey puck hovering above her car. The craft emitted a powerful light, too bright to look at. The craft moved slowly enough that the witness was able to follow it for several miles. At one point, the craft stopped and hovered. The witness raised her arms to shield her eyes from the glare, and the object quickly took off. When the witness returned home, she was distressed to find that her arms and neck were "pockmarked with what seemed like cigarette burns."[253]

In the early morning hours of September 5, 1993, a group of twelve UFO researchers, all members of the group CSETI, gathered in a semi-remote location in the Chatsworth foothills on the edge of the San Fernando Valley. The group used various techniques in the hopes of attracting a UFO sighting. These techniques include sending telepathic messages, the use of powerful lights, and playing tones recorded from other actual encounters.

The group had no success and was leaving the site at 1:45 a.m. when "two powerful lights" appeared on a nearby ridge top. Using their own flashlights, the group flashed back at the objects. On several occasions, the lights flashed back, perfectly mimicking the original flashes. This went on for about fifteen minutes. At one point the lights moved back and forth and a powerful red light appeared and winked out.

Among the witnesses were two medical doctors, two professional psychologists, and others, including the author of this book. This was one of several similar sightings that I had after joining the group CSETI. We all found it extremely exciting to have interactive encounters with what appeared to be genuine UFOs. Our LA group would later have even more incredible encounters.[254]

Two weeks later, one of the most incredible Topanga Canyon encounters took place. This particular encounter confirmed again that the U.S. military is very interested in UFO activity. The main witness is Dr. David Phillips, a professor at Santa Monica College and a Topanga resident. He woke up one evening to observe three military helicopters circling above Topanga Canyon State Park, sending down powerful search-lights. He wondered what the helicopters were looking for when he saw it: a bright, silvery, saucer-shaped craft. Says Dr. Phillips, "It was kind of disk-shaped with sort of a little bubble on top ... the helicopters were behind it. And this thing just scooted down the canyon ... it was absolutely silent. It just went down the creek over the highway, with the hill in the background."

Phillips is convinced that the helicopters were attempting to locate the unknown saucer-shaped craft.[255]

Sometime in 1993, an anonymous gentleman from Rohnert Park stepped outside his home one evening to smoke a cigarette. Looking up, he was shocked to see a "very large black rectangle" move silently above him at an apparent altitude of less than 50 feet. The object moved leisurely southward until it was out of sight.

The witness was amazed, but like many people who have a close encounter, he didn't react the way he thought he would. Says the witness, "I am the kind of person who would be the first to call others over to look at some interesting thing, but I never did. In fact, I forgot about it until recently, which is weird because normally something that unusual I would recall."

While it may seem difficult to believe that somebody could actually forget a UFO sighting, this may be fairly common. Missing time is a consistent feature of onboard UFO encounters, and even simple sightings are sometimes shrouded in this same bizarre amnesia.[256]

Meanwhile, the Topanga Canyon wave continued with numerous residents reporting disk-like objects hovering low in the canyon. In July of 1994, the television program "Encounters" sent a crew into Topanga and successfully captured a UFO on video.

The following interesting case was reported to the National UFO Reporting Center in Washington state by a resident of Michigan Bar, California. Says the witness, "In late '94, my brother took me to show me some lights he sees. When he showed me one though, I saw something different. We stopped on the side of the road, and a large saucer with teardrop-shaped windows with staggered lights around them with seats and cabinets visible in them, was hovering fifteen feet off the ground, right on the side of the road. I walked under it and saw it was saucer-shaped. My brother could only see an orange light, so we left. Later that night, down the road he saw a light and walked towards it. I clicked the CB and said 'radio check,' and the power meter went off the scale and back to zero. My brother became frightened and insisted we leave. He told me later that he saw a blinding light, which I did not see. Many other UFOs have been seen in the area."[257]

By the end of 1994, the Topanga Canyon UFO wave was over. Instead the activity moved south to Orange county. On February 9, 1995, dozens of residents from Santa Ana, from varying locations, observed a large, strangely-shaped object cruising slowly across the sky. One witness said, "To me it looked like a Model-T that got hit by a freight train .... It was like a piece of junk hanging from an invisible balloon."

Another witness said, "It was all different shapes; it wasn't just one shape. It wasn't really round, it wasn't really square."

Yet another said, "It was like a cylinder, black, turning, rotating in the sky."

Nearby military bases, the police department, the weather service, and Disneyland were all contacted. None had any information about the sighting.[258]

The town of Vista, just north of San Diego, became the next target of the UFOs. As investigated by MUFON investigators Marie Jones and Laura Miller, a wave of sightings hit the town starting in October of 1994 and continuing into 1995. More than a dozen residents reported seeing various objects described as "fireballs," "orbs," "metallic, disk-shaped," "misshapen lumps," and "diamond-shaped."

The objects were viewed through binoculars and even videotaped. One witness reported physiological effects: "a solid ring of burnt skin around each eye, which peeled away within four to five days." Also reported were numerous instances of "sky-quakes" or mysterious "compression waves" of sound which roared through the southern California sky without explanation. The activity continued until as late as March 1995.[259]

December of 1995 marked an intense UFO flap over the eastern Sierra Mountains. Jeffrey Nelson, co-founder of the Unexplained Phenomena Investigations (UPI), says that his organization received more than 100 calls from residents reporting UFOs in the last month. Says Nelson, "There are some pretty dramatic cases from this area. We're getting more calls than we anticipated. They're still coming in."[260]

The year 1996 brought a new wave of activity. Los Angeles MUFON investigator Don Waldrop investigated two sightings which occurred in May over the town of San Gabriel. Says Waldrop, "We had two sightings within hours of each other of a triangle-type craft running up San Gabriel Boulevard. There have been numerous such sightings throughout the years in the area."[261]

One clear evening in July, a man in Buena Park went outside and observed an object "three times the size of a star." He was able to discern a dome-shape on top. The object also emitted powerful rays of light "as bright as the sun." When the object left and returned two more times, the witness finally called local UFO investigators to report his account.[262]

In September 1996, house-painter Joe Clower and his friend Steve Thomsen were walking near the beach during the day when they both observed a large metallic craft hovering overhead. Each of them had seen this craft or similar ones on numerous occasions, and had also managed to photograph it. As they watched, the familiar craft moved only about fifty feet overhead. Clower had recently traded his Polaroid for a new 35 mm camera. He managed to take four photographs of the UFO before it moved south and then turned west over the Pacific Ocean. (See photo section.)

A particularly close-up sighting of an apparent ET craft occurred in early October 1996 to the Fonseca family while driving at 11:00 p.m. through a rural part of Camarillo. Her two children were with her. Suddenly, they noticed a bright light zooming out of the sky towards them. Says Fonseca, "At first I thought it was an airplane. Then it got bigger. It was huge and I started getting scared."

In seconds, the object was directly over the car, less than twelve feet above them. Fonseca reports that the object was the shape of a sting-ray, and covered with colored lights. It appeared to be the size of a large building. Her two children began screaming. Fonseca couldn't believe her eyes. As she says, "I was in shock."

Instantly, the object spiraled upwards at high speed and vanished. She reported her sighting to local investigators who told her that they had received a number of recent reports. Checks with the FAA, nearby Point Mugu Naval Base, and the local sheriff's office failed to yield any additional information.[263]

While most UFO witnesses are unable to obtain any evidence of their encounter, this is not always the case. In early December 1996, a UFO appeared over the city of Camarillo for six consecutive days. On the second day of the visitations, witnesses were able to obtain photographic proof of the sighting. Author Whitley Strieber calls the incident "one of the best documented sightings in recent United States history."

The first sighting actually occurred on November 28 when John Epperson sighted an orange-yellow object landed on a hillside off the Ventura freeway. Epperson and numerous other vehicles stopped to observe the object. Epperson eventually left.

The next case occurred on November 29, when a family noticed a bright light hovering in the daylight sky. The object moved away, but returned for the next three days in a row. On each occasion, the object would change shape and eject smaller objects.

The next case occurred at 4:55 p.m. on December 2, when an anonymous witness observed an object emitting a pure white light, high up in the sky. Ten minutes later, the object turned red in the setting sun. It then ejected two smaller objects which moved in tandem and then seemed to disappear. The sighting ended at 5:12 p.m.

Alice Leavy, a UFO Investigator and a witness, heard about the sighting. Knowing that UFOs often visit the same location on several days in a row, Leavy organized a team of MUFON researchers. The next day they arrived with a video camera and still cameras with telephoto lenses.

To their amazement, the UFO showed up right on schedule. On December 2 at 4:46 p.m., witnesses observed a "spherical object" floating high in the sky. The video camera was trained on the object, while others observed through binoculars or took still photographs. At 5:09 the object turned reddish and a smaller object was ejected from the top of the larger object. The larger object then broke up into a string of smaller objects, all of which disappeared.

Throughout the entire ordeal, the witnesses continued to maintain photographic records. While the video camera didn't have the resolution to register the smaller object, the telephoto still photos did.

Whitley Strieber took an interest in the case because of the credibility of the witnesses and the quality of the photographs. As he says, "I have seen some of the still photographs and can verify their remarkable combination of clarity and impossibility. Being that the object's actions were witnessed by half a dozen witnesses, both through binoculars and with the naked eye, and recorded on video and photographed at the same time, it is hard to maintain a case that they are anything but unexplained."

Meanwhile the sightings continued. On December 6, a resident of the Santa Monica mountains observed a black triangular object "as big as two football fields." The object had colored lights around its perimeter.

On December 12, a resident of Simi Valley observed a bright object zoom overhead at very high speed. The next day, a couple from Carpinteria observed a "large, thick black triangle outlined with dim white lights around the edges." They also said the object was totally silent.

Later that evening, another Carpinteria resident observed a "manta ray-shaped" object pass silently overhead. On December 18, a Santa Barbara couple reported their sighting of a bright glowing UFO very high in the sky.

And so ended the intense wave of sightings, involving dozens of witnesses and photographic evidence. Later, Jerry Barber of Sunland Video Productions analyzed the video of December 3 and concluded that the objects were not actually disappearing, but were actually *accelerating* at an estimated 5000 miles per hour.[264]

More sightings continued into the next millennium, but now it is time to examine some of the more extensive aspects of the baffling phenomenon of extraterrestrial contact.

9. The Contactee Movement

See color section, page 116

One of the most controversial aspects of the UFO phenomenon is the contactee movement. A contactee can be defined as a person claiming repeated interactive contact with friendly human-looking extraterrestrials. The movement began in southern California and was spearheaded by a storeowner/metaphysical student and amateur astronomer, George Adamski.

On October 9, 1946, Adamski was observing a meteor shower outside his home in Palomar Gardens when he saw his first UFO. Says Adamski, "I actually saw with my naked eyes a gigantic spacecraft hovering high above the mountain ridge to the south of Mount Palomar, toward San Diego. Yet I did not realize at the time what I was seeing ... suddenly, after the most intense part of the shower was over and we were about to go indoors, we all noticed high in the sky a large black object, similar in shape to a gigantic dirigible, and apparently motionless."

Adamski and the others assumed that it was a United State's craft launched to study the meteor showers. However, the next day's front page news told that the craft had been seen by hundreds of observers and remained unexplained.

In August of 1947, George Adamski reported his second sighting of a "bright light object" which scooted across the sky. Adamski watched as this was followed by another, then another. He called out more witnesses and together they observed a total of 184 objects. Adamski's interest in UFOs became very strong. In early March 1950, he began to photograph UFOs hovering over the Mount Palomar area. He eventually obtained two clear photographs, which were published on April 4 in the San Diego *Tribune-Sun*. Around this time, he was asked to lecture for a number of different groups about his sightings. Little did Adamski know, his career as a UFO contactee was about to begin.

Throughout 1951 and into 1952, George Adamski claims to have taken more than 500 photographs of UFOs over Mount Palomar. As he says, "But barely a dozen of them turned out good enough to preserve as proof that these craft were different from recognized Earth craft."

On November 20, 1952, seven people drove out to the isolated high desert outside of Desert Center near the Arizona border and into UFO history. The five people included George Adamski, Alice Wells, Lucy McGinnis, Al and Betty Bailey, and George and

Betty Williamson. They had traveled to the same location on several previous occasions in the hopes of seeing a UFO. On this particular day, they were not to be disappointed.

After several hours of watching and waiting, a "gigantic cigar-shaped silvery ship without wings or appendages of any kind" appeared overhead. All the witnesses were awestruck and watched the object through two pairs of binoculars. When the ship began to move away, the witnesses piled into their car and followed.

After a few minutes, the object stopped and everyone exited the car. Adamski walked about a half mile into the desert and waited. Minutes later, a number of planes arrived and chased the object away. Disappointed, Adamski waited and was delighted to see a smaller craft swoop down and hover about a half mile away. Adamski snapped several photographs and stared at the craft.

At this point, he noticed a figure standing near him. Says Adamski, "He was motioning me to come to him, and I wondered who he was and where he had come from ... the man looked like any other man, and I could see he was somewhat smaller than I and considerably younger. There were only two outstanding differences that I noticed as I neared him. His trousers were not like mine. They were, in style, much like ski trousers and with a passing thought, I wondered why he wore such out here in the desert. His hair was long, reaching to his shoulders ... the beauty of his form surpassed anything I had ever seen. And the pleasantness of his face freed me of all thought of my personal self."

Adamski realized he was in the presence of an extraterrestrial. Adamski asked several questions and was made to understand that the extraterrestrials were concerned about atomic testing. Then followed a long telepathic conversation about the extraterrestrials, their activities, and reasons for coming here.

After several minutes, the visit ended. The ET returned to his craft and the craft left. Meanwhile, the other witnesses observed the entire event from a distance of a half-mile. While Adamski would later make much more controversial claims of being taken onboard, this experience in the desert appears to be valid. Years later, the six additional witnesses have all stuck with their story, claiming that the visitation did, in fact, take place.

On February 18, 1953, George Adamski received a powerful telepathic impulse to visit a particular Los Angeles hotel where he had stayed on previous occasions. While there, Adamski was approached by two human-looking gentleman who said that they were actually extraterrestrials from Mars and Saturn. The three of them drove out into the local desert where they boarded a spacecraft. So began a fantastic adventure during which Adamski was taken to the moon and shown many incredible things. Later on, in mid-April, Adamski again met his ET friends in the same hotel and was taken onboard for another adventure.

While these particular claims have been seriously questioned, his initial experience, and several of his photographs and moving films have never been proven a hoax.[265]

While Adamski is probably the most famous contactee, he is certainly not the only one.

On May 20, 1952, three days following a rash of sightings over George AFB, Los Angeles contactee Orpheo Angelucci had his first onboard face-to-face UFO contact. Six years earlier, while living in New Jersey, he and his family experienced a dramatic sighting after releasing a "navy-type" balloon. Angelucci was conducting a scientific experiment at the time, and shortly after launching the balloon, the entire family witnessed a saucer-shaped craft following the balloon. After investigating the balloon, the saucer scooted off into the distance.

Then, six years later, at 12:30 a.m. on May 23, 1952, Angelucci was returning home from Lockheed in Los Angeles, where he worked, when he saw a red, luminous "oval-shaped object" moving ahead of him in the air. He followed it to a park area where it hovered in place. Angelucci exited his car. At that time, the object ascended to a higher altitude and emitted two smaller objects, both which swooped down towards Angelucci, stopping only a few feet from him. Between the two objects, a "screen" was projected. Then proceeded a lengthy telepathic communication between Angelucci and the alleged ETs. The ETs explained that they were contacting various people across the planet in order to make humanity gradually aware of the ET presence. They explained about their technology and told Angelucci that they would meet again.

On July 24, 1952, Los Angeles contactee Orpheo Angelucci experienced his third contact. He was drawn to an isolated area along the dry river bed of the Los Angeles river, only a few blocks from his home when he saw a translucent thirty-foot craft resembling an "Eskimo Igloo."

A door opened and he boarded the craft, which was instantly taken to an elevation of 1000 miles. While he didn't see any beings, he observed an incredible view of outer space and several other saucers through a transparent section of the ship's wall. He heard heavenly music and was given spiritual information and ecological warnings. He was then marked with a strange symbol on his body and was returned to the area from which he had been taken.

Orpheo Angelucci's fourth and most dramatic encounter occurred on August 2, 1952. He was outside his home when he was confronted by a tall, well-built man dressed in a strange, tight-fitting, seamless uniform. The man claimed to be the occupant of the saucer on which Angelucci had been taken, and proceeded to warn him of upcoming ecological disaster. He called Earth "the home of sorrows."

In late October 1952, Angelucci experienced his fifth and final contact. On this occasion, the human-looking ET, dressed in a business suit, met him at a Greyhound Bus Station in order to prove to him, they said, that ETs can and do function in public society undetected as being extraterrestrials. Angelucci later wrote his experiences in his 1955 book, *The Secret of the Saucers*. Like most of the contactees from the 1950s, his story continues to generate controversy.[266]

One of the most unusual contactee accounts occurred in March of 1953 when a tall, strange-looking gentleman entered a Los Angeles newspaper office and told a newspaper reporter that he was actually an extraterrestrial. The story was told to popular UFO researcher Harold Wilkins by a correspondent who insisted upon anonymity, but felt compelled to tell the story.

The reporter said that the alleged ET was human-looking, but there were several strange things about his appearance. He was very tall, dressed in shoddy clothes, and had bluish skin and pointed ears. The ET told the reporter, "I am a man who has recently landed in your state from what you call a flying saucer. We set it down on the floor of the Mojave Desert. I wish to have some publicity in your newspaper, for it would help both me and your Earth."

The reporter was shocked by the man's appearance and called up his editor. The editor assigned reporter Jim Phelan to the story.

The next day, the alleged extraterrestrial returned with his friend, another human-looking ET. According to Wilkins' correspondent, "The two were as much like each other as peas in a pod. Both were 6 foot 6 in height. Their skin had the bluish tinge one often sees in cardiac cases ... both were emaciated. The clothes they wore looked as if they had come out of a sailors' slop shop. Very loose in fit and shoddy. When the reporter looked closely at their heads, he was struck by their ears which were pricked, like those of a breed of Asiatic dogs. They hands too, were queer – seemed to be jointless."

The two strange gentleman repeated that they had landed their saucer in the desert. They claimed to be extraterrestrials from the planet Venus. Their mission was to study the minds of humanity and their level of scientific knowledge. They claimed to have learned the language by listening to radio and television broadcasts. They again asked for publicity, but changed their minds when Phelan explained what would happen if they went public with their claims.

Phelan then asked them to prove to him that they were actually ETs. One of the men walked over to a hard-wood desk, and with his fingernail he scored a quarter-inch-deep furrow into the wood.

Phelan was apparently so impressed that he offered them a job. For the next two weeks, the mysterious men were employed in a Los Angeles city attorney's office where they worked locating missing persons. Reportedly, they were so good at their job that they were able to locate people in a matter of hours – something which normally took weeks. During this time, one of the men gave another demonstration of his powers by scratching a deep furrow into a bar of steel.

This apparently caused their coworkers (who didn't know of their alleged extraterrestrial ancestry) to become suspicious. The FBI was alerted. An investigator was sent; but, when he arrived, the two men mysteriously disappeared, never to be seen again. Wilkins, himself, remains ambivalent in his endorsement regarding the veracity of the account.[267]

Interestingly, Wilkins later heard a similar story which seemed to support the above account. Wilkins says that he was sent a letter from a gentleman who claimed to have met a human-looking extraterrestrial in mid-1953. The alleged ET appeared "out of the blue" next to the witness at a bus-stop. According to the witness, the ET was human-looking, but stood about six feet six inches, had a strange whitish-blue complexion, high cheekbones, and Oriental-looking eyes. The ET told the witness the reason for the contact: he wanted the witness to contact other people who were also having contact and help them tell their stories. The witness reports that he fulfilled the strange man's requests, which included meeting with contactee Orpheo Angelucci and reporter Jim Phelan.[268]

Next to George Adamski, one of the most influential California contactees is former test pilot and car mechanic George Van Tassel. In 1947, Van Tassel leased a piece of property in Yucca Valley known as Giant Rock. It was there that Van Tassel meditated and made contact with human-looking ETs. His first encounter occurred on August 24, 1953. He awakened at 1:50 a.m. to see a human-looking figure standing at the foot of his bed. The man said his name was Solgonda and he was an extraterrestrial from the planet Venus. Van Tassel claims he was taken onboard a craft where the ETs warned of the dangers of war and the abuse of atomic weapons.

The ETs then instructed Van Tassel to build a machine called the Integratron, a small-domed building with special properties that would supposedly provide a rejuvenating force allowing humans to significantly increase their life spans.

To get the funds needed to build the Integratron, Van Tassel single-handedly organized the most popular UFO convention of all times. The 1954 Giant Rock convention attracted more than 5000 people and would continue annually for sixteen years. Each year, Van Tassel channeled messages from the ETs about peace and goodwill. He managed a small store and airport there until his death on February 9, 1978. At that time, the Integratron was eighty-five percent complete. Unfortunately, it was never able to be used for its original purpose of rejuvenation.[269]

For some reason, California has been a nexus for UFO contactees, or people claiming contact with friendly, often human-looking ETs. Among this group is the highly prominent contactee, Daniel Fry. In 1954, Fry had three separate contacts outside of White Sands, New Mexico. Following his contacts, he moved to Puente, California, just east of Los Angeles. It was there that Fry claims to have had his fourth and final contact. And on this occasion, he has photographic evidence to support his encounter.

On September 18, Fry was driving along Garvey Boulevard when he received a telepathic message to obtain a camera in order to photograph an actual ET craft. Fry pulled over and bought a Brownie Holiday camera at a convenience store. Continuing his drive, he was between Baldwin Hills and Azusa when he saw "the saucer." Fry said that the saucer "posed" for him while he took the photograph. The photograph shows a dark, metallic-looking, disk-shaped craft hovering a few hundred feet above someone's home.[270]

In 1952, Robert Short was experimenting with automatic writing when he heard about contactee George Van Tassel. Intrigued, Short arranged a meeting. While with Van Tassel, Short himself began to "channel" alien intelligences. So began Short's lifelong career as a contactee. He didn't have any physical contact, however, until six years later, in October 1958. Short was walking outside his Joshua Tree home when a bright light suddenly approached from above. Says Short, "There was this orange-bluish light coming at me from up over the hills and my first impression was to run fast and get the hell out of there. I was sure the thing was going to hit me."

Instead the light veered to the left and landed. A large, metallic, saucer-shaped craft became visible. Out stepped a human-looking male who gestured towards Short, telepathically told him that they would meet on a later date, smiled enigmatically, and then returned to the craft. This turned out to be Short's only such visitation; however, he later experienced several other UFO sightings in the presence of numerous witnesses. One of the best-verified occurred during a UFO convention on October 14. A group of seventy-five people had gathered to listen to Short channel. As soon as he began to speak, two saucer-like craft moved slowly over the amazed group at a height of only 1000 feet. The crowd was suitably impressed. Short also claimed to channel messages from extraterrestrials for more than twenty years.[271]

Sometime in 1963, band conductor and school teacher Hal Wilcox experienced a face-to-face contact with a human-looking extraterrestrial. Wilcox was working at Paramount Studios when a strangely-dressed man walked into his office. The man introduced himself as Zemkla from the planet Selo in the Bernard star system. To prove his assertions, Zemkla took Wilcox outside and showed him his craft, which was hovering over the building.

Wilcox, who already had degrees in music, architecture, and science, said his real education began with Zemkla. Says Wilcox, "[Zemkla] made available to me all the science, all the research, not only from Planet Selo, but the interplanetary culture exchanged between 50 principal planets."

Wilcox's fantastic claims include being taken to the planet Selos, which he described as being near-Utopian, with no crime, no pollution, and no disease.

Like most contactees, Wilcox was given a mission to spread the word about his contacts, which he continues to do. He also claims to have continuing contacts.[272]

On 2:00 a.m. on January 30, 1965, radio and television technician Sid Padrick walked along the beach outside of Watsonville. He had not heard of recent sightings in the area, so when he heard a loud roar and looked up to see a huge disc-shaped craft, he was understandably shocked. He turned to run when a telepathic voice told him to have no fear. Padrick was then invited onboard the craft. The ETs appeared to be human, although they looked different, having pointed chins and noses and long fingers. There were seven men and one woman. Only one of the occupants claimed to be able to speak English and was the only person to whom he spoke. Padrick described the interior of the craft in familiar terms: "The walls, floors, and ceiling were all the same shade of pale bluish-white. There were no square corners anyplace. Everything was rounded, corners, doorways, seats, anything movable or even fixed. Corners of rooms were all rounded. The light seemed to come right through the walls. There was no direct lighting whatever. In other words, the whole wall was lit."

Padrick was shown the ETs mother ship and was told of their near-Utopian society. The ET told him, "As you know it, we have no sickness; we have no crime; we have no vice; we have no police force. We have no schools – our young are taught at an early age to do a job, which they do very well. Because of our long life expectancy, we have very strict birth control. We have no money. We live as one."

The ETs told Padrick that they believed in God and also explained to him some of their advanced technology.

The story told by Padrick was incredible; however, he was able to provide numerous character witnesses who vouched for his integrity. The recent sighting by several park rangers in the area also gave credence to his account. Further stunning verification came from a highly reputable source – none other than George M. Clemens, the mayor of the neighboring city of Monterey, who observed a "bright object" hovering over Monterey Bay on the evening of January 29.

Padrick was encouraged to report his account to the Air Force, which he did. Padrick was questioned by Major D. B. Reeder of Hamilton Air Force Base, who grilled him for three hours on every detail of his experience. They then asked him not to talk publicly about his encounter. As Padrick says, "There were certain details they asked me not to talk about publicly, but I think in telling it that everything should be disclosed."[273]

On April 21, 1973 inventor and scientist Fred Bell, of Laguna, experienced a close-up contact with what he believes is a craft from the Pleiades. For several months, Bell and a small group of friends had formed a group to try and make telepathic contact with ETs. They had no success until April 21, when Bell felt a sudden, strong impulse to go outside his home. He followed the impulse and, to his shock, saw a large craft hovering 20 feet off the edge of the cliff behind his home. Bell's friends were too afraid to approach any closer, but Bell claims that a door opened and a human-looking woman appeared. The woman told Bell that they would meet again when conditions were better.

Bell later learned that the woman was named Semjase, the same ET with whom Swiss contactee Billy Meier made contact. Bell's story contains many of the same elements as that of Meier, including long discussions with Semjase on future Earth changes, spirituality, science, and a number of other subjects. Bell is only one of a number of people who claim to have had contact with human-like ETs from the Pleiades.[274]

On December 24, 1981, Pleiadian contactee Fred Bell demonstrated the proof of his contact to a number of friends. He had been told telepathically to bring a small group of friends to a certain location near his Laguna home, so that they could witness one of the Pleiadian craft.

Shortly after the group arrived, a large metallic saucer appeared, swooped low over the witnesses, and sent down a shower of sparks. The craft made three passes overhead, thoroughly convincing the witnesses of the reality of Bell's contacts.[275]

The contactee accounts remain an enigma, often dividing investigators as to their authenticity. Yet they remain an important and influential chapter in California UFO history.

10. Celebrity Sightings

See color section, page 117

Because so many celebrities make their homes in California, it was only a matter of time before one of them had the guts to reveal their encounter. The first celebrity to come out of the UFO closet was none other than world-famous entertainer Sammy Davis, Junior. In August of 1952, the actor/entertainer visited the southern California desert community of Palm Springs. He had heard of a number of sightings in the area and was keenly interested. Says Davis, Jr., "I wasn't to be left out."

The actor was not disappointed. During his stay, he was outside with a large group of people when a number of small silver disks appeared and "floated overhead." The disks then began to perform incredible maneuvers, proving beyond any doubt that they were actual spacecraft. Says Sammy Davis, Jr., "First they would stand still and then they would take off and stop again, before finally shooting away in a flash."

The actor is convinced that the UFOs are friendly. As he says, "I feel quite strongly that if they wanted to harm the human race, they could have done so a long while ago."[276]

In early December 1955, world famous aeronautical engineer and inventor William Lear and pilot Hal Herman were flying at 12,000 feet over Palm Springs when they observed a "flying disc." Lear reported that the disk hovered motionless, giving off a green glow, and then quickly darted away. Lear immediately radioed his sighting to an airway radio station. Immediately after Lear's report, two other pilots in the vicinity also reported their observations of the glowing disk. Two months following his sighting, Lear gave a press conference detailing the sighting, and was from that point a strong public supporter of UFO reality.[277]

Yet another celebrity who has gone on record as a UFO witness is Cliff Robertson, who won an Academy Award for his performance in the motion picture *Charley*. In July of 1963, at exactly 3:00 p.m., Robertson was standing on the observation deck of his Pacifica Park home that overlooks the southern California coast. Says Robertson, "Suddenly, my eyes were diverted toward an object high in the sky. Whatever it was, was traveling from south to north and sparkling like a diamond as it reflected the rays of the mid-afternoon sun."

At first Robertson thought it was a plane, helicopter or balloon, except that it moved strangely and looked even stranger. He grabbed a pair of binoculars. Says Robertson, "By no means was I prepared for what I saw through the binoculars. Instead of supplying me with a rational explanation, it only convinced me that no identification was possible. I've been a pilot for years and I have to be honest and say, never before have I encountered anything remotely like this during my experience as an aviator. There, in front of me, was a weird, alien contraption, a cylindrical-shaped craft made of highly polished metal."

The stunned actor watched the craft for ten minutes, when it finally moved away. Says Robertson, "It just hovered out there, high up over the water, then – boom! – all of sudden it was gone. It disappeared in the twinkling on an eye ... it was definitely a UFO, like so many other people have seen around the world. I was awed by its sleek design, its trim appearance, and the fact that one minute it could hover on a dime and the next blast off into space at a fantastic speed. I don't know of anything built on this planet that could maneuver in such a fashion."[278]

Another famous UFO witness is actress Jill Ireland, wife of Charles Bronson. One warm mid-August day, Ireland was on the veranda of her Bel Air estate when she and her nanny saw a "round object [with] perhaps a dome or tower on top." The object was so highly polished that "the sun was striking the body of the craft as if it were a mirror." As Ireland watched, the object moved straight up very quickly, as if under intelligent control.

Ireland told her husband, who is firmly convinced of his wife's sincerity. Says Charles Bronson, "There's got to be something to it. If Jill says there was something strange in the sky, I see no reason not to take her at her word. I remember she talked about it for quite a while afterwards, and besides, I know she wouldn't make the whole thing up! Why would she?"[279]

One of the most famous UFO witnesses of all times is former President Ronald Reagan. The sighting occurred when he was governor of California during a routine night-time flight. Pilot Bill Paynter revealed the details in an interview. "I was the pilot of the plane when we saw the UFO. Also on board were Governor Reagan and a couple of his security people .... We were near Bakersfield when Governor Reagan and the others called my attention to a big light flying a bit behind my plane. It appeared to be several hundred yards away. It was a fairly steady light until it began to accelerate, then it appeared to elongate. Then the light took off. It went up at a 45-degree angle, from a normal cruise speed to a fantastic speed instantly."

Although the sighting is not very well-known, Reagan himself confirmed the details to Norman Miller, then Washington bureau chief for The Wall Street Journal. Reagan told Miller that after sighting the object, he ordered Paynter to follow it. Says Ronald Reagan, "We followed it for several minutes. All of a sudden, to our utter amazement it went straight up into the heavens. When I got off the plane I told Nancy all about it. And we read up on the long history of UFOs."

Miller was surprised that the Governor was so candid and asked Reagan if he actually believed in UFOs. Says Miller, "When I asked him that question, a look of horror came over his face. It suddenly dawned on him what he was saying – the implications, and that he was talking to a reporter. He snapped back to reality and said, 'Let's just say that on the subject of UFOs I'm an agnostic.'"

Although Reagan never gave further interviews regarding his sighting, when he was President, he made several statements that revealed his belief in extraterrestrials.

In 1985, President Reagan made the following enigmatic statement: "If suddenly there was a threat to this world from some other species from another planet, we'd forget all the little local differences that we have between our two countries, and we would find out once and for all that we really are all human beings on the Earth together."

Two years later, in 1987, President Reagan again discussed the extraterrestrial presence: "In our obsession with antagonisms of the moment, we often forget how much unites all the members of humanity. Perhaps we need some outside, universal threat to make us recognize this common bond. I occasionally think how quickly our differences worldwide would vanish if we were facing an alien threat from outside the world."[280]

A third comment from President Reagan was revealed by Fred Barnes, the senior editor of the *New Republic*. Barnes overhead President Reagan speaking with Russian Foreign Minister Eduard Sheyardnadze. President Reagan reportedly asked Minister Sheyardnazdze, "What would happen if the world faced an 'alien threat' from outer space. Don't you think the United States and the Soviet Union would join together?'" Sheyardnadze replied, "Absolutely, yes."[281]

Yet another celebrity to reveal his encounter is actor Chad Everett, the star of countless feature films and television movies. In October 1993, he appeared on the daytime talk show "Vicki." On the program, Everett revealed his own encounter, which took place at his home in Beverly Hills.

Says Everett, "There were three of us. And we were looking out from the Beverly Hills location, over Malibu. We faced that way; we could see that way. Now, at a distance which we measured to be about a yard by our arms – how many miles that would be that far away from the beach, lots right? We tracked a light that was going bump-bump-bump-bump [Everett moved his hand side to side to illustrate the movement] and you could track it. It was making turns like that ... nothing I know of moves like that. We called and we were told, 'There's some helicopters on maneuvers.'"

Everett is certain, however, that the object was not a helicopter. The host of the show asked him, "A helicopter doesn't move that fast?"

"No, of course not! Of course not! No craft that we have could track that fast at that time, and make turns like that."

Many other celebrities have revealed similar sightings. Actor Charlie Sheen recently revealed that he had a sighting from his southern California home. Likely there are hundreds more well-known personalities who have had encounters but are afraid to link their names with the subject matter.

11. UFOs in the Ocean

See color section, page 118

The year of 1947 marked a massive wave across the United States and the modern age of Ufology. That year also marked the first accounts of underwater UFOs, many of which occurred off the coast of California. On July 7, 1947, at 3:10 p.m., two teenagers in San Raphael saw a "flat glistening object" emerge from the ocean, fly through the sky, and then dive back into the water four hundred yards from the shore. The impact caused a tall column of water. The witnesses then observed the craft to slowly sink beneath the waves.[282]

Throughout August and September, 1947, the Coast Guard and Navy up and down the California coast detected strange underwater masses that would appear and disappear in various locations. The ordeal began when the U.S. Coast Guard received reports of a "strange flaming object" which fell into the sea.

Following this incident, steamers going in and out of San Francisco Bay encountered an "undersea mountain" that would appear and disappear in various locations in the bay. Several ships reported the mysterious mass, calling it a "reef" or "submarine mountain" that had appeared seemingly overnight. Another ship then reported "a large mass under water, off the Golden Gate." Following that, the mass disappeared.

However, at that same time, the Navy survey ship, *Maury*, and several other craft were sent to investigate another report of a "phantom reef" that had appeared about 400 miles off the coast of southern California.

No charts listed any such mass in the area. And when Captain Hambling of the *Maury* arrived, the strange "mass" seemed to have disappeared. The ship immediately surveyed the surrounding area. To their shock, they found that the "mass" had moved again. Says Captain Hambling, "Our echo sounders did pick up a strange echo, when we were about three-quarters of a mile off the reported locations of the 'reef.' It seemed that the sounders had got an echo from a mass about 1,600 yards away. We changed course, and started right towards it. Four hundred yards away from it, we found it had vanished, and we got no other echo. We tracked and re-tracked the area, using fathometers and echo-sounders. We covered five square miles very carefully, and another five miles round the outside of that area."

Needless to say, the strange undersea mass had disappeared.[283]

The next report occurred on November 21, 1951, when, according to researcher Harold Wilkins, "an unidentified burning object fell into the Pacific, off the coast of California."[284]

On August 8, 1954, another USO (unidentified submersible object) was seen off the coast of Long Beach, California. The witnesses were the crew of the steamship, *Aliki,* voyaging to California from Honduras. The United States' Coast Guard intercepted a radio message from the steamship. An insider later leaked the message to investigator Harold Wilkins. The message recounted the UFO sighting and read: "SAW FIREBALL MOVE IN AND OUT OF SEA WITHOUT BEING DOUSED. LEFT WAKE OF WHITE SMOKE; COURSE ERRATIC; VANISHED FROM SIGHT."[285]

A large number of "USOs" have been seen in the Santa Monica Bay and Santa Catalina Channel. A particularly compelling case occurred on July 10, 1955, and involved numerous independent witnesses.

It was a bright, sunny day at around 11:00 a.m. when fishermen off the coast of Newport Beach reported seeing a cigar-shaped object which was blue on top and silver on the bottom. As they watched, the object flew overhead at a "moderate speed and medium altitude."

Later that afternoon at around 2:30 p.m., Mr. & Mrs. George Washington and their eleven-year-old daughter were thirteen miles off the coast of Newport Beach on their way to Catalina Island on their yacht when Mrs. Washington spotted the strange object hovering at about 2,500 feet.

Mr. Washington stopped the boat so they could better observe the object. Using binoculars they saw a "perfectly round, gray-white" craft. It appeared to be rotating and was surrounded by a strange "haze." After about six minutes of observation, the Washingtons restarted their boat and continued their journey. To their amazement, the object maintained its position directly over their boat. Mr. Washington radioed the Coast Guard and explained their situation. The officials at the Coast Guard told Washington to keep the object in sight, and they would launch a plane to investigate.

Suddenly, the object rose upward in a zigzag maneuver and disappeared into the clouds. By the time the Coast Guard plane arrived, the object was long gone.[286]

Also in the summer of 1955, multiple residents from the coastal town of Santa Maria in northern California observed a "long silvery object" emerge from the ocean near the shore and take off into space.[287]

The mid-1950s marked the beginning of an intense wave of underwater UFOs seen off the California coast, particularly the area of the Santa Catalina Channel. Writes pioneering southern California UFO investigator Ann Druffel, "This body of water lies between the coastlines of southern California and Santa Catalina Island, twenty miles offshore to the southwest. The area has for at least thirty years been the scene of UFO reports of all kinds – surface sightings of hazy craft which cruise leisurely in full view of military installations, aerial spheres bobbing in oscillating flight, gigantic cloud-cigars, and at least one report of an underwater UFO with uniformed occupants."[288]

A dramatic case of an underwater UFO in this area took place on January 15, 1956, in Redondo Beach. It turned out to be a particularly well-verified and dramatic case involving dozens of witnesses, including many local residents, a nightwatchman, Redondo Beach lifeguards, and neighboring Hermosa Beach police officers. It all began when residents reported seeing a large, glowing object glide down out of the sky and float on the surface of the ocean about seventy-five yards offshore of Redondo Beach. As the crowd of witnesses gathered and watched, the water seemed to "froth," at which point the UFO sank beneath the surface. The glow of the object was so intense that it could still be seen. The police officers radioed in for help, and divers were brought out to investigate.

Unfortunately, by the time the divers arrived, the glowing light was gone. A Geiger counter was brought to the scene by a police officer, but it did not register any radiation. A search the next morning also yielded no results.[289]

Less than one month later, on February 9, another oceangoing fireball was sighted off the coast of Redondo Beach by military personnel. One year following the incident, UFO investigator Leonard Stringfield obtained an official report of the incident which said only: "FIREBALL HITS WATER. SUBMERGES."[290]

Sometime in December, 1957, the British steamship, the *S. S. Ramsey*, was off the coast of San Pedro. It was during the day, when officers on the bridge sighted a large, gray-metallic disk moving overhead. The disk had strange antennae-like projections around its circumference. One of the men on the bridge, Radio Officer T. Fogel, quickly grabbed a camera and snapped a photograph of the strange object. The photo clearly shows the object, in focus, hovering only a few hundred feet away. It appears to be a typical flying saucer with a small cupola on top.[291]

Just before dawn on the morning of July 28, 1962, a chartered fishing boat was fishing in the Santa Catalina Channel when the skipper noticed some lights that appeared to be floating stationary in the water about six miles southeast of Avalon Harbor on Catalina Island. The captain headed his boat towards the mysterious lights and trained his binoculars on them. He was amazed to see a definite structure of some kind. As the anonymous captain said, "It appeared to be the stern of a submarine. We could see five men, two in all-white garb, two in dark trousers and white shirts, and one in a sky-blue jump-suit. We passed abeam at about a quarter mile and I was certain it was a submarine low in the water, steel gray, no markings, decks almost awash, with only its tail and an odd aft-structure showing."

At this point, the captain assumed that it was a Russian submarine, though it seemed unusual for it to be so close to the shore and remain in view. Then suddenly it performed a maneuver which left the captain amazed. The mystery submarine moved forward towards his boat, as if to ram it. The captain had to turn to avoid the sub which moved past them at high speeds, emitting no noise, and leaving no wake except for a "good-sized swell."

Concerned about what he had seen, the Captain contacted the Navy, who took detailed statements and attempted to identify the sub with various photographic comparisons. Marvin Miles, an aerospace editor for the *Los Angeles Times* heard of the incident and called to verify the incident with the Navy. He was told, "There's nothing to it." Miles wrote up the story in a column about "Soviet subs." UFO researchers Jim and Coral Lorenzen, however, speculate that the object might have had extraterrestrial origins. They cite numerous other similar examples of ocean-going objects and say, "The high surface speed, lack of wake and sound, and the huge swell makes this object suspect." One might also mention the odd shape of the submarine itself and its lack of fear of observation.[292]

On February 5, 1964, eleven survivors were rescued by the Coast Guard from their emergency raft following the sinking of their yacht, the *Hattie D.*, off the coast of Mendocino. What makes their story particularly unusual is that all eleven survivors insist that they were sunk by an unidentified undersea object. The boat had set sail from Seattle, Washington, and was making its way down the coast of California when tragedy struck. Without any warning, the yacht either struck or was rammed by an unidentified "metal object." The boat sank shortly later, without any evidence of what had struck their boat remaining.

Crewman Carl Jansen elaborated on the event, saying, "I don't care how deep it was ... what holed us was steel, and a long piece. There was no give to it at all."

Whatever sunk the *Hattie D.* remains unidentified.[293]

One evening in June of 1980, therapist Linda Susan Young and a friend were driving along the Pacific Coast Highway adjacent to Santa Monica Beach. As Young's friend drove, Young noticed a lighted object, a brilliant white light, floating perfectly stationary several miles out to sea, in the center of the Santa Catalina Channel. Says Young, "It was just a light. It was a white light and that was all. I didn't see any definition of anything else. For the size of the light, I should have been able to see some sort of definition ... I couldn't figure out what this would be. And I said to the guy with me, 'What do you suppose this is?' And he turned around and looked at it. And he saw it only for a second when it just shot straight up in the air and blinked out. It didn't look like it went far enough to disappear from view, like from a distance. It just sort of stopped. It just stopped being there."

Both the witnesses were amazed. They are certain the object wasn't a flare or anything conventional. Says Young, "I have always assumed it was a UFO."[294]

On May 5, 1992, two friends were on Malibu Beach when they observed a "sort of light/ fireball" descend from the sky over the ocean. Says the witness, "It was going at an incredible speed and it was less than a mile away. It looked like it hit the ocean .... Once the object made its way to the ocean's surface, it disappeared, so my guess is that it went underwater."[295]

The area off the southern California coast has produced a huge number of reports. An intriguing report comes from a surfer who, on May 4, 1990, observed a metallic disk off the coast of Malibu. Says the witness, "I was surfing with another guy when it came out of the fog bank just offshore. The stranger and I were focused on the horizon, awaiting another wave. We didn't know each other, but it's wise to buddy-up when you're in the drink. So there we were, silent, sitting on our boards .... It was a good morning of waves coming in sets about 7-10 minutes apart. At exactly 12:20, what looked to me like a brushed aluminum saucer with a bump in the middle (both top and bottom alike), approached the shoreline from out of the fog bank sitting about a mile offshore. [It] stopped its lateral approach to the shoreline just inside the fog bank, where it was clear and sunny ... so it comes into the sun, settles at about 300 feet over the ocean surface, and begins an oscillating descent, much like a flat rock in water, or a leaf towards terra. Side to side it drops, for about three times. On the fourth, it slowed, tilted towards the shore (us), tilted away, and then in a blink of an eye, took off at a 60 degree climb into and through the fog bank out to sea .... We looked over at each other. 'You see that?' 'Yep.' ... Silence returned as we realized deep in the core of our consciousness that life was deeper than the ocean we surf. We didn't talk anymore."[296]

One evening in early 1991, Tony X. woke up and looked out of his Malibu oceanfront home. To his surprise, he observed a brilliantly lit object floating on the ocean's surface about two miles away. Says Tony, "It looked like a big prism, kind of various colors out there. I got a telescope out there and looked at it, and although it's a thirty-power telescope, when I looked at it, it even seemed more like a prism, just different colors."

After a few hours, the light winked out and Tony didn't think anything of it. However, two years later, in January 1993, the glowing prism returned. The vivid colors made Tony speculate that a boat might be on fire.

Says Tony, "I got the telescope and looked at it, and it was the same kind of thing ... the colors seemed so ... pure, for lack of a better word. They seemed real coherent."

Tony called up the Coast Guard, who denied that any boats were on fire and suggested that the lights could be caused by a fishing boat. Tony, however, has lived along the coast for years and never observed anything quite like that. Today he remains undecided about what he observed.[297]

While ocean-going UFOs are relatively rare, the above reports show that UFOs have the ability to travel in our oceans with ease.

12. UFOs Over Los Angeles International Airport

See color section, page 119

The Los Angeles International Airport (LAX) is one of the largest airports in the world, shuttling millions of people every year to various locations throughout the world. It is located in the heart of the huge, sprawling metropolis of Los Angeles. It covers several city blocks and is always crowded with thousands of people. It has a state-of-the-art air traffic control tower, complete with sophisticated radar. It is surrounded by busy freeways, gas stations, restaurants, several large hotels, and countless residential homes. On the south side lies the Chevron Oil Fields. On the west side lies the Pacific Ocean. Within a few miles are several aerospace, defense, and military bases.

Amazingly, this highly populated area has been visited numerous times by UFOs. One of the first incidents occurred on July 15, 1952. For four consecutive nights, dozens of witnesses observed unidentified craft directly over Los Angeles International Airport. The objects would brazenly approach within a quarter mile of the control towers and hover in place for minutes at a time.

As one witness (a major Los Angeles aircraft company's principal who insisted upon anonymity) wrote to the *Los Angeles Examiner*, "I am amazed at the increasing audacity of the strange disk-like objects seen in the sky over the Los Angeles Airport Control Tower. For four nights running, they've been seen at the same time (between 7 and 8 p.m.), and the same place. On the last occasion, three of them hung poised for five minutes by the clock."[298]

This particular sighting was only the first of many sightings that would later occur over this location. On April 3, 1966, several witnesses, including a helicopter pilot, observed an "oblong object with several pairs of lights" hovering almost directly over the airport at a few thousand feet of altitude. The object moved away after a few minutes.[299]

On April 1, 1973, at around dawn, several Hollywood residents reported seeing a "disk-like" object, which was glowing, spinning, and moving like a "cork bobbing on the ocean." The object seemed to be on a course directly towards Los Angeles International Airport. Although this sighting took place on April Fools' Day, it appears to be a serious report.[300]

In 1995, an anonymous air-traffic controller at LAX revealed that during his six years of employment as a leading controller handling restricted air-space, he heard numerous accounts of UFO sightings and received several reports from pilots firsthand.

The air-traffic controller describes one such incident which occurred on August 5, 1992: "Northeast of LAX, a UAL 747 on climbout, about 24,000 feet suddenly said, 'Do you show something went right under us?' We didn't; there was absolutely nothing on radar. The pilot said it 'went right under us, opposite direction, about three times the normal closure rate,' which normally is 900 knots .... We pulled up the primary radar (raw radar returns) and there was absolutely nothing. The pilot said it was 'kind of like a rocket, but with something on the top,' and it was 'about the size of an F-16.' I got on the landline to the lower controller to warn him for subsequent aircraft. The only nearby restricted (military) area had no activity at those altitudes, and there were no military aircraft in the area. We told the supe, and he just said, 'huh.' We just shook our heads, and mostly forgot about it, though the pilot did make a report on it and it appeared in *Aviation Week and Space Technology*."[301]

The magazine article described the sighting: "The pilot and copilot of United flight 934, with a heavy passenger load from Los Angeles to London, said they saw an unusual aircraft coming directly at them and pass under the 747 by an estimated 500-1000 feet. The incident occurred near George AFB at about 1:45 pm on August 5. The 747 was at 23,000 feet departing from Los Angeles International Airport on a heading of about 40 degrees magnetic ... the several second sighting gave the crew the impression that the other aircraft was a lifting-body configuration, and they described it as looking like the forward fuselage of a Lockheed SR-71 – without wings but with a tail of sorts. They estimated the size as similar to an F-16 .... Defense Department and Air Force officials said last week that it was not one of their secret projects."

At 2:48 p.m. on February 17, 1995, municipal park worker, Brian Forrest, was outside on his normal route when he looked up and observed a large black object hovering over Imperial Highway about two hundred feet up in the air, practically right over Los Angeles Airport. It was less than a mile distant and it was very obvious to Forrest that something very strange was hovering there.

Says Forrest, "It was about two to three hundred feet in the air. I know the distance because I drove it in a car. The way I was able to tell it was approximately over there is a jet was taking off behind it. The pilot had to see this thing. I figured the people in the air control tower had to see it. It was shaped along the lines of a dark cylinder – not a cylinder, more of a cone with a rounded top and bottom. Not pointed, but rounded, the bigger part being at the top where you might think of it as an acorn-type shape. I would say it was approximately the size of a single car garage turned on end.

"It did not move. It just stayed there ... it was the strangest thing because I've never seen anything like that. Your mind immediately goes, 'It's a helicopter. It's a balloon ... it's a ... it's a ... it's a ... no, it's not that. And I just kept staring at it. It did not move. This jet was taking off behind it."

Forrest noticed another strange detail. "The strangest thing is – I think about it now in retrospect – is, it's as though it was in focus but almost slightly out of focus. Everything else was clear as a bell, but – imagine a canvas with fresh paint on it and you went up and just slightly smudged just a bit of it ... it was in focus, but almost slightly out."

Forrest also remarked other details that UFO investigators look for, including immobility and lack of reflection. "You just don't see things there in the sky without some apparent reason, something holding it up, or it's drifting or moving in some way. But just to see it there and not move at all. It was like a rock. It didn't move. It was like a part of the sky. It was the strangest thing ... there were no details. This object was completely black, no reflection on its surface."

After deciding that the object was definitely unidentified, Forrest rushed back inside to get another witness. By the time he returned, the object was gone. He is convinced he saw a genuine UFO. Says Forrest, "It was like looking at a piece of the 'Twilight Zone'. It was a real weird moment."

One week later, the *Orange County Register* printed an article, "Neighbors Encounter Unidentifiable Object," detailing the sighting of a dark, strangely-shaped object hovering in the sky just south of LAX. Various descriptions include "dark, oblong objects," "a Model T hit by a freight train," and "a piece of junk hanging from an invisible balloon." One witness gave a description very similar to Brian Forrest's, saying, "It was like a cylinder, black, turning, rotating in the sky."

Two months later, Pat Brown, a massage therapist from Panorama City, was driving along the freeway directly next to the LA Airport at around 3:00 p.m., when she saw something so strange and unusual that it was instantly obvious that it was a UFO. It was an enormous golden sphere gliding silently downwards over the airport.

Says Brown, "I was driving down the 405, and I got off the freeway at that New Howard Hughes exit. And I was looking up at the sky, and the sky was crystal clear blue. And then, all of a sudden, there was a big gold ship. And it was obvious it was a ship. It was gold and it was circular. It was like an airplane that was coming in for a landing at LAX, not as large as Southwest Airlines – that's one of the smaller planes. It was maybe two-thirds the size of a Southwest Airline.

"It was just seconds that I was able to see it. It was obvious to me because I saw it. And really, on this exit there aren't a lot of cars. So there was no one to my right and no one in front of me that I was aware of, and I didn't check behind me. It was just there, and then it wasn't there. And it was really interesting because it was on a forty-five degree angle, like it was coming in for something."

Pat Brown has had other sightings and has also experienced firsthand contact with gray-type aliens.[302]

Probably the granddaddy of all Los Angeles Airport encounters occurred in mid-April of 1997 when dozens of witnesses reporting seeing "red lights" over the airport. Numerous witnesses called the local news stations. That evening, the sightings were given only brief coverage. Locals described "red lights" and "strange lights" that "hovered." The objects had also reportedly been caught on radar. The news coverage was tongue-in-cheek and incomplete, but they did verify the incident.

One gentleman who didn't appear on the news and declined to be formally interviewed reported that the red lights weren't bright, but that they were very obvious. He said that they appeared close – maybe a few thousand feet high. He observed them to hover in place for several minutes before disappearing.

The sightings continued. Just after midnight on March 31, 1999, a police helicopter pilot and crewman were flying, immediately adjacent to LAX, over the city of Carson. They were circling their target location at 500 feet of altitude when the pilot shouted out that an "orange ball of light" was an estimated two miles ahead of them and approaching fast. The ball of light raced towards the observers, changed direction, moving at right angles. The helicopter pilot aimed the helicopter so that the two of them could continue to view the approach of the object. Says the crewman, "The object then changed direction again, accelerated, and headed directly at the door of the helicopter."

The crewman admitted that he was so startled that he pressed both the radio and the intercom and shouted out an expletive. Says the crewman, "The object got within 200 feet of the aircraft and then changed direction again, flying to the north at a very high rate of speed and out of view."

The crewman insists that they viewed a genuine UFO. As he says, "I hope you don't think I'm a nut, but I've been around/involved in aviation for a long time. I've never seen anything like this. The texture, the shape, the movement, the speed changes and the drastic angles all add up to it NOT being anything that I have ever seen."

The crewman called the National UFO Reporting Center shortly afterwards, but requested complete anonymity.[303]

With UFOs appearing so regularly over LAX, it was only a matter of time before somebody got photographic evidence. This exact event occurred just after 10:00 p.m., on July 23, 2002, when more than a dozen witnesses, including MUFON State Section director for Los Angeles, Mark Hunziker, observed a large triangular-shaped UFO with red lights move directly over the south-western end of Los Angeles International Airport and out over the Santa Catalina Channel.

Mark Hunziker was in Marina Del Rey, just north of LAX, when his neighbor alerted him to the object. Hunziker looked overhead and observed a "brightly-lit array of lights which looked like they were configured to what appeared to be a central jet aircraft." However, when he looked closer, he realized the shape was wrong and the object was covered with bright red lights.

At the same time, more than a dozen witnesses from neighboring communities observed the same object. One witness captured the object on videotape, an analysis of which showed it be a large triangular-shaped craft. This event will be discussed further in the final chapter.[304]

A final recent sighting occurred on November 27, 2003. An anonymous Los Angeles resident was driving along the 110 freeway directly north of LAX. He was watching the incoming planes line up when he saw "an anomalous craft crossing over the approach path to LAX." The craft appeared to be a very large triangle with several lights underneath it. The witness carefully observed the craft as it moved northeast over the airport. He later investigated all the flights that took place on that day at that time, and was unable to find a corresponding match. He remains convinced he saw a genuine UFO, and reported his sighting in detail to NUFORC.[305]

While it may seem hard to believe that such a highly-populated area as Los Angeles Airport could attract UFOs, there are now nearly a dozen such sightings on record. And the fact is that numerous other airports, military bases, and highly technological bases attract UFO activity. And LAX being one of the largest and most advanced airports in the world, it is surprising that it doesn't attract more attention.

13. The Invasion of Edwards AFB

See color section, page 120

The events which have taken place at Edwards Air Force Base in the Mojave Desert of southern California rank among the most important in UFO history, perhaps rivaling even those of the UFO Roswell crash. The witnesses to the events now number in the hundreds, and many are of unimpeachable credibility. Despite this, there has been almost no serious investigation into the UFO events at the base. These events go way beyond simple sightings and would better be described as an *invasion*.

Several of the UFO events that have occurred at Edwards AFB are among the best-verified in history. Some of the events are also among the best covered up. Definitely they are among the most controversial.

We have already examined several cases in which UFOs exhibited a strong interest in military bases. The book *Clear Intent*, by Fawcett and Greenwood, focuses exclusively on these types of cases across the United States. In terms of the most visited bases, Edwards, as we shall see, is at the top of the list.

Edwards was originally called Muroc Field and was established in 1933. It was later renamed Edwards Air Force Base in honor of Captain Glen W. Edwards, a test pilot who lost his life there in 1948.

Edwards is where the United States military conducts its aviation experimentation and development. Many of our most advanced aircraft have their origins at Edwards. On October 14, 1947, test pilot Chuck Yeager broke the sound barrier as he flew his X-1 plane over Edwards. Because of secrecy concerns, nine months elapsed before an official announcement was made.

Also in 1947, the record for the highest elevation of a human being was made at Edwards. The base is arguably one of the most technologically advanced places on Earth. Therefore, it is not too surprising that it has been a powerful magnet for intense UFO activity.

Located north of Victorville in the southwestern section of the vast Mojave Desert, Edwards experienced its first recorded visitation at the dawn of the modern age of UFOs, only a few days after the Roswell UFO crash. It is important to note that some of the Roswell wreckage may have been taken to Muroc at this time.

It all began on July 7, 1947. Test pilot Major J.C. Wise was preparing for takeoff when he saw a yellow-white spherical object heading east over Muroc Air Force Base. The event marked the beginning of one of the most important events in UFO history.

The next day, on July 8, a series of incredible sightings took place over Muroc. The sightings were of such magnitude, involving so many reliable observers, that it would forever change the way the Air Force handled UFO reports. Finally, the military was finally forced to take UFOs seriously.

Listed as case number 50 (unidentified) in the Air Force Blue Book files, the saga began at 10:00 a.m. when the base billeting officer, Lieutenant Joseph C. McHenry was outside his office. Only minutes earlier, McHenry and other officers had been talking at the base's Post Exchange about the recent sighting at the base and the other sightings that "had been headlining the local newspapers for the past week." McHenry was skeptical of all the reports and joked with his fellow officers, "Somebody will have to show me one of those discs before I will believe it."

Little did Lieutenant McHenry know, his wish was about to come true. As he walked outside his office, he heard a plane coming in for a landing. He observed the plane, but then he also observed something else. Says McHenry, "Looking up, as I always do, I observed two silver objects of either a spherical or disc-like shape, moving about 300 miles an hour."

The objects appeared to be at about 8000 feet altitude and were heading northwest. McHenry dashed inside and called out three other officers. Says McHenry, "[The officers] immediately came to where I was standing. I pointed in the direction of the objects and asked them the question, 'Tell me what you see up there?' Whereupon, all the three, with sundry comments, stated, 'They are flying discs.'"

McHenry and the others carefully observed the objects to make sure that they weren't the result of an optical illusion. All of them concluded that the objects couldn't be weather balloons as they were "traveling against the prevailing wind."

At this point, a third object appeared. Says McHenry, "Two of us at the same time sighted another object of a silver spherical or disc-like nature at approximately 8,000 feet traveling in circles over the north end ... from my actual observance the object circled in too tight a circle and too severe a plane to be any aircraft that I know of."

Lieutenant McHenry and the other witnesses signed affidavits attesting to the truth of the events. Said McHenry, "This statement has been given freely and voluntarily without any threat or promises under duress."

Another one of the officers stated, "I have been flying in and have been around all types of aircraft since 1943 and never in my life have I ever seen anything such as this."

That, however, was only the beginning. Two hours later, an Air Force test pilot observed a yellowish-white sphere traveling against the wind over the base. Two hours after that, a group of technicians, including a Major, also observed an object and made the following report: "We observed a round object, white aluminum color, which at first resembled a parachute canopy ... as this object descended through a low enough level to permit observation of its lateral silhouette, it presented a distinct oval-shaped outline, with two projections on the upper surface which might have been thick fins or knobs. These crossed each other at intervals, suggesting either rotation or oscillation of slow type ... no smoke, flames, propeller arcs, engine noise or other plausible or visible means of propulsion were noted."

The above sighting was also witnessed by yet another observer, a Captain at nearby Rodgers Lake, who said that at one point the object actually appeared to land on the ground.

Events, however, were still in progress. A few hours later, at 3:50 p.m., another pilot flying at 20,000 feet forty miles south of Muroc observed a "flat object of a light reflecting nature." He attempted more than once to pursue the object, but it easily evaded him.

The rash of sightings put the base on high alert and the Technical Intelligence Division of the Air Material Command was immediately informed. Intelligence reports indicated that the craft were probably neither Soviet nor German. Officials at the base, however, were convinced that the objects represented solid craft of some kind.

At 9:20 that evening, the disks made a final pass over the base at an altitude of about 8000 feet.

This cluster of sightings directly over one of the most sensitive military installations in the United States had an enormous effect on how the military would handle future UFO reports.

To handle the publicity end, professor J. Allen Hynek, then the Air Force Astronomy consultant for Project Sign (the predecessor to Blue Book), was called in on the case. Says Hynek, "I was impressed with this case, one of the very first that came to my attention when I became Astronomical Consultant to Project Sign. I remember wondering why the Air Force had not paid much greater attention to it and to a similar sighting that occurred at Muroc AFB just two hours later. The witnesses were certainly excellent, independent military men describing the most unusual sighting on a clear sunny day. What more could the Air Force want?"

Hynek apparently did not know the full extent of the sightings, nor the waves that they were making at higher levels. He would later learn that his job as a consultant was basically to downplay the sightings and provide a possible astronomical explanation. Normally very skeptical, Hynek nevertheless gave this case high merit. As his report for Project Sign reads: "No astronomical explanation for this incident is possible. It is tempting to explain the objects as ordinary aircraft observed under unusual light conditions, but the evidence of the 'tight circle' maneuvers, if maintained, is strongly contradictory."

Hynek was unable to take any further investigative action. As he says, "As an astronomical consultant, my official responsibility ended there."

Meanwhile, officials at much higher levels were realizing the seriousness of the situation. Pioneering UFO investigator and Blue Book insider Captain Edward Ruppelt called the case "the first sighting that really made the Air Force take a deep interest in UFOs."

Researcher Michael David Hall agrees, and writes that the Muroc sightings had far-reaching effects: "Those disk sightings over Muroc on the seventh and eighth really shook up the Pentagon [and] were the pivotal event which sprung the United States military into serious action on the saucer mystery ... the incidents led the United States Army Air Force to issue classified orders requiring reports of any 'saucer-like' objects to be given to the Technical Intelligence Division of the Air Material Command at Wright Field in Dayton, Ohio .... The Muroc incidents threw matters into high gear and motivated the Pentagon to ask for a maximum intelligence effort from intelligence units around the world. Orders were then sent to all United States Army air bases requiring sightings near their area to be investigated ..."

Writes researcher Richard Dolan, "The Muroc incident continues to provide evidence for military knowledge, interest and secrecy regarding UFOs."[306]

The above dramatic series of sightings marked the beginning of a long history of UFO activity that would eventually escalate to incredible proportions. Just over two years later, Muroc/Edwards Air Force Base was visited again by UFOs. It was 12:15 a.m. on August 31, 1949. Private pilot Bob Hanley, described as "a steady and reliable pilot," was flying over Mint Canyon when he observed an object "trailing a blue flame [of] exhaust nearly a mile long." He estimated the object had an elevation of about 50,000 feet and was located directly above Muroc. Hanley's two passengers also witnessed the incredible display. The stunned witnesses reported their observations when they landed at Lockheed Air Terminal in Palmdale and at Long Beach Airport.[307]

On September 30, 1952, Edwards AFB again went on alert when several witnesses sighted two disks hovering and darting over the base.[308]

One of the most incredible and potentially important stories in UFO history occurred from February 17 to 20, 1954, when President Eisenhower was visiting southern California. It was at this time that the President of the United States allegedly had a face-to-face diplomatic meeting with extraterrestrials at Edwards Air Force Base. This story has circulated within the UFO community for years, with accounts beginning at the time of the incident, with new witnesses and evidence being revealed even today.

It all began when researcher Harold Wilkins heard from an inside source that the actual purpose of the visit was not a golf tournament. Rather, it was arranged so that the President could view the alien bodies and UFO craft that were being held at Edwards' AFB and to host a diplomatic meeting between humans and one or more extraterrestrial races.

As incredible as these rumors may seem at first glance, they have a surprising amount of confirmation. Even the normally skeptical UFO investigator Jenny Randles wrote, "The stories about this are surprisingly consistent."[309]

Writes William Moore, "No doubt one of the reasons that this particular rumor has continued to circulate for such a long time is that there are a number of verifiable facts associated with it – some of them rather curious .... Clearly something unusual involving the president did occur on the evening of February 20, 1954."[310]

When President Eisenhower came to visit Palm Springs, he suddenly disappeared from public view. This much is fact. The press, who had been following his every move, was unable to locate the President during this period. Speculation about Eisenhower's whereabouts ran wild, with some accounts suggesting that he had died or been assassinated. That evening, the Associated Press actually released an official statement saying, "President Eisenhower died tonight of a heart attack in Palm Springs." Two minutes later, the AP retracted the statement. Later an impromptu press conference was called and the press was told that the President had actually had an emergency dental visit.

Later, researchers attempted to confirm the dental appointment with the dentist's widow, who was unable to recall any details about the fixing of the president's tooth, but recalled in detail the dinner with the President the following evening. Other inconsistencies with the dental explanation is that the Eisenhower Presidential Library which maintains a comprehensive record of Eisenhower's activities shows no record of any such visit. When one considers the fact that every move of the President was pre-scripted, constantly observed, and fully recorded, the absence of the dental records seems conspicuous. Writes researcher William Moore, "This would appear to suggest a cover-story."

Another early researcher to claim that some sort of meeting between the President and aliens took place was British researcher Desmond Leslie. Shortly after the event, Leslie claimed that he interviewed an Air Force officer who was present during the incident, which actually involved a landing at the base. According to the officer, he observed a metallic disk one hundred feet in diameter land in full view on the base runway. The entire base was locked down, put on high alert, and all personnel returning to the base were not allowed to reenter, nor was anyone allowed to exit.

It was researcher and author Harold T. Wilkins, however, who broke the story wide open. As he wrote one year following the incident, "In April 1954, I received an air-mail letter from a friend [Mead Layne] in California reporting a startling event in the flying-saucer drama. 'An unconfirmable report that President Eisenhower, in a recent visit to the Edwards Air Force Base, California, was informed that a recent investigation of five types of flying saucers by experts and technicians there, has thrown them all into confusion and consternation. It is alleged that the experts have reported on the materialization and subsequent dematerialization, into a fourth-dimension of invisibility, of some type of the mysterious aeroforms, or unidentified flying objects.'"

Meade Layne was then the national director of the Borderland Sciences Research Associates. Later Meade Layne revealed his own source, a fellow scientist by the name of Gerald Light.

Gerald Light was a UFO researcher and scientist who had connections in high places. In his letter to Layne, Light claimed to have visited Muroc base with an elite group of persons, including Franklin Allen of the Hearst Papers, Edwin Nourse of the Brookings Institute (and financial advisor to Truman), and Bishop MacIntyre of Los Angeles. The letter was the first solid evidence that the diplomatic meeting between the President and Extraterrestrials did in fact take place.

Writes Light,

My dear friend: I have just returned from Muroc. The report is true – devastatingly true .... When we were allowed to enter the restricted section (after about six hours in which we were checked on every possible item, event, incident and aspect of our personal and public lives) I had the distinct feeling that the world had come to an end with fantastic realism. For I have never seen so many human beings in a state of complete collapse and confusion as they realized that their own world had indeed ended with such finality as to beggar description. The reality of 'otherplane' aeroforms is now and forever removed from the realms of speculation and made a rather painful part of the consciousness of every responsible scientific and political group.

During my two day visit I saw five separate and distinct types of aircraft being studied and handled by our air force officials – with the assistance and permission of the Etherians [ETs]. I have no words to express my reaction. It has finally happened. It is now a matter of history.

President Eisenhower, as you may already know, was spirited over to Muroc one night during his visit to Palm Springs recently. And it is my conviction that he will ignore the terrific conflict between the various "authorities" and go directly to the people via radio and television – if the impasse continues much longer. From what I could gather, an official statement to the country is being prepared for delivery about the middle of May.

I will leave it to your own excellent powers of deduction to construct a fitting picture of the mental and emotional pandemonium that is now shattering the consciousness of the hundreds of our scientific "authorities" and all the pundits of the various specialized knowledges that make up our current physics. In some instances I could not stifle a wave of pity that arose in my own being as I watched the pathetic bewilderment of rather brilliant brains struggling to make some sort of rational explanation which would enable them to retain their familiar theories and concepts .... I shall never forget those forty-eight hours at Muroc![311]

After the letter was later released, it caused a sensation in the UFO community. Numerous investigators later attempted to contact Layne and Light, neither of who would respond. Both are now deceased.

Wilkins' friend, Mead Layne, was the recipient of the above letter, and it was he who contacted Wilkins. As Wilkins writes, "From a reliable source in southern California, I am assured that these five saucers did land *voluntarily* at this Edwards Air Force base. They were discs of five types and their entities invited the technicians and scientists to inspect their aeroforms and witness a demonstration of their powers."

Mead wrote to Wilkins: "I can positively assure you that a friend of mine visited Edwards Air Force base, soon after this demonstration. He was accompanied by (1): a man prominent in the Hearst news syndicate; (2): a bishop of either the Methodist or the Episcopal Church; (3): a former confidential adviser of ex-President Truman. I cannot release to you're their names at this moment.

"I have also confirmatory reports by two other persons, but these would not carry weight by themselves. The story has gotten out all over the U.S., but NOT in public prints or newspapers. It was, of course, given the horse-laugh by the Pentagon and the Air Command at Washington, DC. But the basic facts are that some of our technicians and scientists have actually 'gone off the deep end' mentally, when the saucer entities confronted them with new, and to them, inexplicable physical data. The entities demonstrated before their eyes that they could dematerialize and materialize themselves – become alternately visible and invisible. All this for our bright boys – now you see it and now you don't!"[312]

Yet another independent testimony was leaked to researcher Brinsley Le Poer Trench by a test pilot, now a retired Colonel, who was present when Eisenhower made his visit. Says Trench, "The pilot was one of six people at the meeting. Five alien craft landed at the base. Two were cigar-shaped and three were saucer-shaped. The aliens looked human-like, but not exactly."

The ETs reportedly spoke fluent English and informed the President that they wanted to start an "educational program" for the people of Earth. They then displayed their technological prowess by making their ships invisible.

The Earl of Clancarty, a member of the British House of Lords also claims to have spoken to another or the same British pilot who was present. According to the pilot, the aliens wanted to announce their presence officially, but Eisenhower felt that this would cause a panic. The ETs agreed, but stated that they would continue a limited campaign of contact so that humanity would gradually become aware of their presence. The ETs also expressed concern about the use of nuclear technology. They then made an offer: get rid of all nuclear weapons and they [the ETs] would give them spiritual wisdom and some limited technology.

In another version, President Eisenhower and his companion, Robert Saunders, were both invited onboard one of the craft. They were given a tour of the interior and then were taken on a flight into space. Eisenhower was then told that the aliens wanted to begin an education program. Eisenhower and his top aides discussed the plan and expressed their fears that such a disclosure would upset the economy and that there would be a severe backlash from the religious community. Eisenhower reportedly insisted that humanity was not prepared for official disclosure. He also declined to give up the U.S. nuclear program in exchange for other technology or knowledge. And there the meeting ended.

In 1974, Professor Robert S. Carr from the University of Florida reported that he spoke with firsthand witnesses of a UFO crash/retrieval in Aztec, New Mexico. Accord-

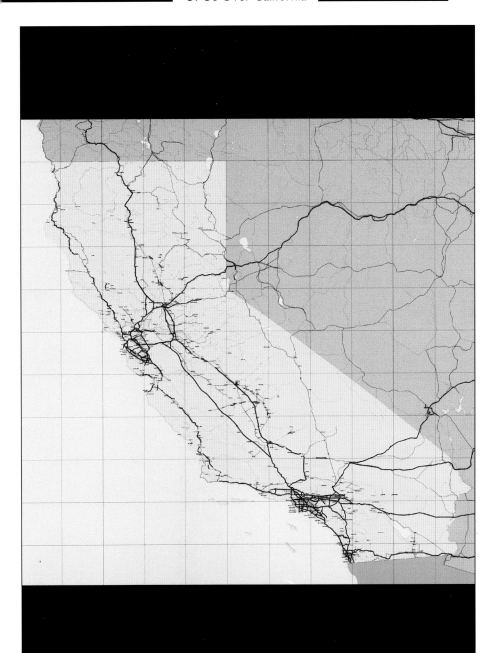

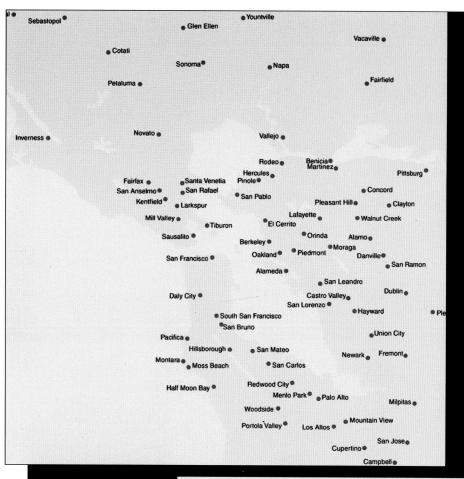

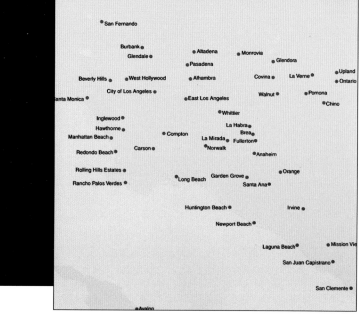

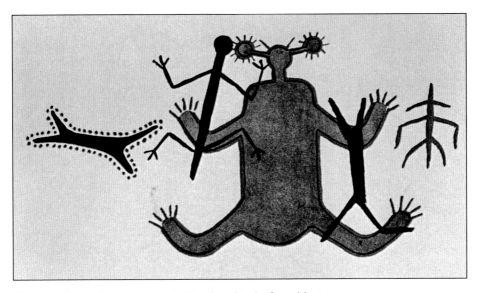

Chumash Native American cave paintings found in the Santa Monica Mountain range, the location of heavy UFO activity. Is this evidence of early visitations by extraterrestrials? *Courtesy: Colin Penno.*

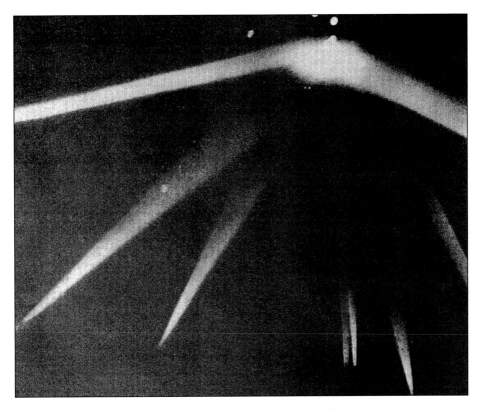

Photo of unknown object hovering over Los Angeles on February 25, 1942, during the so-called "Battle of Los Angeles." *Courtesy: LA Times.*

Photo taken by Michael Savage of saucer-shaped craft hovering over telephone wires in San Bernardino in August 1952. *Courtesy: LA Times.*

Photo taken by Joe Kerska on October 10, 1956, of metallic
saucer hovering over San Francisco. *Courtesy: Joe Kerska.*

First of four photos taken by highway accident inspector Rex Heflin of metallic disk
hovering over a highway in Santa Ana on August 3, 1965. *Courtesy: Santa Ana Register.*

Second photo by Rex Heflin. *Courtesy: Santa Ana Register.*

Third photo by Rex Heflin. *Courtesy: Santa Ana Register.*

Fourth photo by Rex Heflin. *Courtesy: Santa Ana Register.*

Photo by Joe Clower of metallic disk over Los Angeles in
Autumn of 1991. *Courtesy: Wendelle Stevens of the UFO Photo Archives.*

Photo by Joe Clower and Steve Thomsen of metallic disk hovering over Pacific
Palisades in September 1996. *Courtesy: Wendelle Stevens of the UFO Photo Archives.*

Photo by Joe Clower of metallic disk hovering off the coast of Pacific
Palisades in 1991. *Courtesy: Wendelle Stevens of the UFO Photo Archives.*

Photo by Michael Davey of metallic saucer hovering over two radar towers in Titus Canyon in 1998. *Courtesy: Wendelle Stevens of the UFO Photo Archives.*

Photo by Steve Thomsen of metallic saucer hovering over Topanga
State Park in 1998. *Courtesy: Wendelle Stevens of the UFO Photo Archives.*

Photo taken by Young Chyren of a saucer-shaped craft hovering off the
coast of Santa Monica on January 3, 2004. *Courtesy: UFOEvidence.org.*

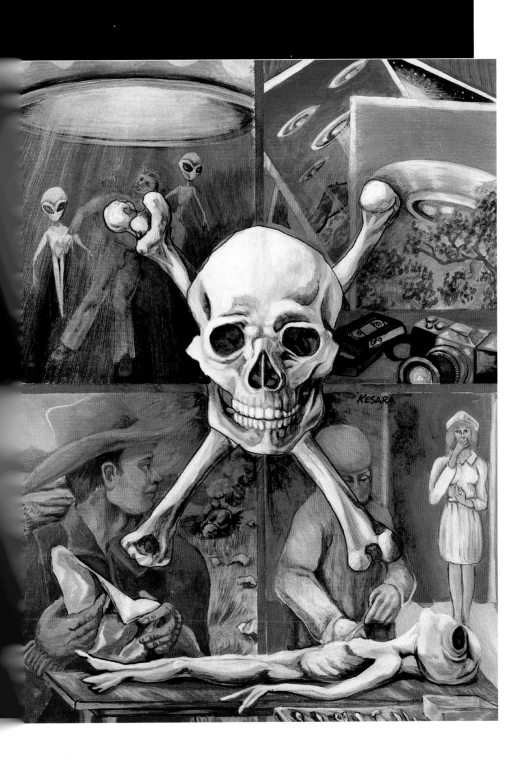

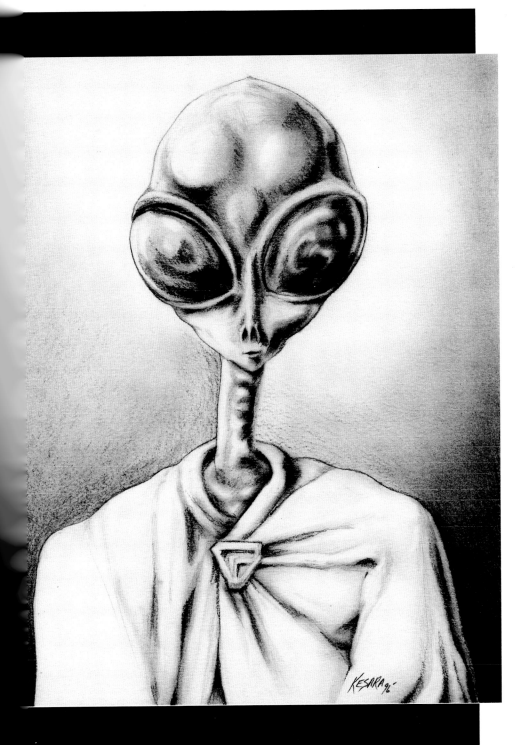

ing to Carr, his firsthand witness was also at Edwards when Eisenhower visited to view the captive craft from Aztec. Carr's announcements caused a media frenzy, though Carr remained firm in his statements and refused to reveal his sources.

Recently, in 1993, the highly-respected Dr. Hank Krastman of Encino revealed to researchers that although he didn't view the meeting, he was actually present at Edwards AFB on the day of the historic meeting between ETs and humans. At the time, he was a sailor in the Royal Dutch Navy. Krastman recalled that on February 19, his commander was briefed about a highly important meeting to take place at Edwards on the next day. At 10:00 a.m. on February 20, Krastman accompanied his commander to the Base. Once they arrived, Krastman was shocked to see President Eisenhower, not to mention Albert Einstein, Werner Von Braun, Victor Schauberger, and Howard Hughes.

Krastman overheard his commander being told that there were five ET craft in the hanger, and that some of the ETs were going to demonstrate the capabilities of their craft. At that point, Krastman's commander left and went into the hangar in question.

When his commander later returned, Krastman says that he appeared pale and shaken, and he refused to give any details of what had just transpired. The next day, they left the base, never to return.[313]

Further stunning confirmation of the diplomatic meeting surfaced in December 2000 when researcher Steven Greer MD obtained an interview with Don Phillips who worked for the United States Air Force, Lockheed Skunkworks, and the CIA to develop aircraft construction and design. Early in his career, Phillips worked on highly secret projects and was an insider to many top-secret events involving UFOs, including the now-famous Edwards' meeting.

Says Phillips in his first public interview, "We have records from 1954 that were meetings between our leaders of this country and ETs here in California. And, as I understand it from the written documentation, we were asked if we would allow them to be here and do research. I have read that our reply was, well how can we stop you? You are so advanced. And I will say by this camera and this sound, that it was President Eisenhower that had this meeting. And it was on film, sort of like what we are doing now."[314]

Even more confirmation of extraterrestrial activity at Edwards Air Force Base and Eisenhower's interest in UFOs comes from Brigadier General Steven Lovekin, Esquire. Lovekin was a member of the White House Army Signaling Agency and served under Presidents Eisenhower and Kennedy with an above top-secret clearance. He claims to have been involved in a number of high-level secret projects involving UFOs. He attended several above top-secret meetings in which UFO sightings, radar evidence, films, and actual recovered alien artifacts were reviewed and studied.

Says Brigadier General Lovekin, "There were stories about radar lock on. Several of those stories came out of Ohio at Wright Patterson Air Force Base but several others came from California, Texas and Washington from what I can recall ... Edwards Air Force base was mentioned as an experimental station. When I say mentioned, in that context I mean Edwards was involved in testing whatever ET materials they found. It was said that was what was being done. Radar lock-ons had come from Edwards Air Force Base."

According to General Lovekin, President Eisenhower expressed strong interest in everything concerning UFOs. Says Lovekin, "He [Eisenhower] would take to doodling and one of the things that he did doodle was various forms of UFOs. I never saw Kennedy do this but President Eisenhower did it, and he did it in my presence as well as several other people who were attached to the White House Army Signaling Agency where I was assigned .... I got an opportunity to travel a little bit with the President .... Well, on some of those occasions he had just been given messages or had been given information pertaining to sightings or information about UFOs and I know that for a fact because I was in the COM Center and I saw that information. When he would get these reports it would excite him .... He was very interested in the shapes and sizes of the UFOs and what made them go .... Very, very much interest. In fact, I would say that this subject was probably among his highest interests at that time. Yes, indeed."[315]

Still more confirmation of the Eisenhower-ET meeting comes from well-known Spanish researcher Antonio Ribera. In a letter to Milwaukee researcher, Richard Heiden, Ribera revealed that his friend, publisher Mendizabal Fizalde, had attended a gathering at which Miguel Aleman, former President of Mexico, was present. When the subject of UFOs came up, Fizalde and others at the gathering heard President Aleman say that he met President Eisenhower, and that Eisenhower "told him that he once visited an air base in the Southwest United States, where they showed him a flying disc and the cadavers of several of its crew members."[316]

Former university professor Michael E. Salla has researched some of the above accounts for his book, *Exopolitics: Political Implications of the Extraterrestrial Presence*. After his investigations, Salla has concluded that the meeting between President Eisenhower and the "Nordic" ETs took place as described. Says Salla, "There was telepathic communication. They [the ETs] were afraid we might blow up some of our nuclear technology, and apparently that does something to time and space, and it impacts extraterrestrial races on other planets."

Archivist Jim Leyerzapf at the Eisenhower Library remains skeptical. Nevertheless, he admits that the rumors have persisted for years. As he says, "We've had so many requests on that subject that we have a person specializing in this."[317]

As can be seen, the alleged meeting is more than just a rumor. Instead of becoming weaker, the story has instead grown stronger, with more details, new witnesses, and independent confirmation coming from an increasing number of sources.

Probably the best confirmation of the event is what happened at Edwards following this meeting. While repeated sightings, landings, captive UFOs, and alien bodies might seem incredible enough, the Edwards story doesn't end here. For the next fifty years, the base continued to be a magnet for all kinds of UFO encounters.

Not surprisingly, there were more sightings. Says one anonymous resident in 1954, "Saucer sightings have been there. Visibility there is usually 150 miles plus .... The few people there are outdoorsmen and outdoorswomen, and very observant. Here are located Edwards and Muroc air and naval bases, where all the latest devices are tested. The base atom bomb testing ground lies just over the northern rim of the desert. No wonder, then, that plenty of flying saucers have come over the area to give the flyboy competition the raspberry, and thumb them with the freemason sign! Also, to keep an eye on what is going on around there."[318]

Edwards AFB has played a powerful role in influencing UFOs over California. While the above events may sound fantastic, they are corroborated by yet another compelling testimony.

One of the most incredible UFO incidents to occur at Edwards (or anywhere for that matter!) was revealed by none other than Apollo astronaut Gordon Cooper. In an interview with journalist Lee Spiegel, Cooper said that when he was project manager of the Flight Test Center at Edwards in 1958, a large, metallic flying disk actually landed at the base. Several Air Force personnel observed the landing and were able to take motion pictures.

Says Gordon Cooper, "[The disk was] hovering above the ground, and then it slowly came down and sat on the lake bed for a few minutes. There were various estimates by the cameramen on what the actual size of the object was, but they all agreed it was at least the size of a vehicle that would carry normal-size people in it. It was a typical circular-shaped UFO. Not too many people saw it, because it took off at quite a sharp angle and just climbed out of sight ... I think it was definitely a UFO."

Although Gordon didn't witness the actual craft, he did view the film, which he found totally convincing. As per orders, he sent the film to Washington D.C., and never heard from it again.

On a later occasion, Steven Greer MD conducted a follow-up interview and confirmed the details of this incredible encounter. Says astronaut Gordon Cooper, "At Edwards Air Force Base I was having some of the cameramen film precision landings and we were right on the edge of a dry lake. A saucer flew over them, put down three landing gears, and landed out on the dry lakebed. They went out there with their cameras ... towards the UFO. It lifted off, put the gear back in the well, and flew off at a very high rate of speed and disappeared. So while I was going through all of the regulation books and finding out the number to call in Washington to report this, I had the cameraman go over and develop the film. By the time they got back with the developed film I had higher and higher and higher level officers talking with me. Finally a Colonel told me that when the film arrived on my desk to put it in a courier file. There would be a courier there at my office and they would arrange for him to fly in our base airplane back to Washington with these films. [The Colonel said] to not run the prints. So we stuck them in the courier packets."

Cooper examined the film firsthand. As he says, "Good close-up shots. Nothing like I had ever seen ... double inverted saucer shape. It didn't have wings on it or anything. It was pretty much the same [saucer] shape ... at that point in time there was no doubt in my mind that it was made someplace other than here on Earth."[319]

Although the encounter was amazing, Cooper admitted that it wasn't unique. As he told Spiegel, "There were always strange things flying around in the air over Edwards."

Incredibly, the Edwards story becomes only more complicated. Further dramatic developments would soon occur.[320]

Evidently, there is something about the base that is highly attractive to UFOs. Yet another encounter occurred on October 7, 1965. Researcher Steven Greer MD not only interviewed one of the witnesses, but was also able to obtain an audiotape of the conversations between the pilots, air traffic controllers, and other officers. Says Greer, "This extremely important case involves a seasoned Air Force Air Traffic Controller, an official 'UFO officer,' four separate radar stations, lock-on from onboard radar on a jet interceptor, many hours, and many objects over several hours. The debunkers and those who would ridicule the UFO matter need to be able to explain away all of these elements – and the voice tape of the actual event."

The incident would probably never have been publicly revealed if not for USAF Sergeant Chuck Sorrells (retired). In an interview with Greer, Sergeant Sorrells revealed the details of the entire ordeal.

Says Sorrells, "This event happened on October the 7th of 1965 at Edwards Air Force Base. It was on a midnight shift and I was the Air Traffic Controller on duty in the tower. At about 1:30 or so in the morning, I noticed this real bright light to the east of my tower. It was a light green and it had a red light underneath it. The red light was a pulsating type of light, and it had a white light on top that just glowed. It was very bright and quite large. I observed it for quite a while, because there wasn't any aircraft in the area at the time. I called the dispatcher down at the base operations and the weatherman that was on duty that night (the forecaster), and got them all to go outside and take a look. I had one of the guys from the interceptor detachment that was on the base look also, and I had the captain down there look ...

"We called it down to the Air Defense people at Los Angeles defense sector. The director down there called around to his sites, and at one point in time they had at least four different radar sites that were getting radar returns on it. [The UFOs] were getting seen at a couple of other towers, like George Tower, and there were a couple of other places that were seeing them. So, there were several people on the ground looking at these UFOs, and about four radar sites. This [went] back and forth and back and forth for two or three hours. They finally decided to scramble an aircraft on it, to go up and take a look at it. This was coordinated with the other, higher headquarters, and I think NORAD was involved."

Sergeant Sorrells states that he was first observing the one bright light when suddenly three more objects appeared, flew in formation to the south, and hovered in place. A little later three more appeared. Says Sorrells, "They would fly individually around and go north, south, east, west – a lot of maneuvers. At this point I had seven of them at one time. This is when they decided to scramble the jet interceptor."

As Air Traffic Controller, it was Sorrells' job to help guide the pilots to intercept the UFOs. Says Sorrells, "They were having no luck intercepting these UFOs. They kept asking me, in the tower, where was this object in relation to the plane ... about three different times, he'd say 'contact,' and that contact means he had contact with something on his radar in the cockpit of the aircraft. What it was, we don't know to this day. But they were real."

The various objects easily eluded the jet interceptor, rising in altitude from 2000 to 100,000 feet in a matter of seconds. Says Sorrells, "They could move real fast. They could be to the east of my field, and then in just a short period of time they could be to the west. They could probably go 30-40 miles in the time you could snap your fingers. I mean, just fast! And they could rise – just go straight up. It seemed like they could do that instantaneously. At some points they would hover and just sit for a long period of time – then they would move. The smaller three individual ones had a lot more movement than the other ones. The original very large UFO didn't move all that much. After a couple of hours, though, it moved a little bit ... but it didn't make any sudden, fast movements until they tried to run an intercept on it, and then it went straight up."

Three of the objects continued to dart back and forth over the base, swooping down to a few thousand feet, and then darting upwards at "thousands of miles per hour." Sorrells noticed that the UFOs seemed to hover mostly over the base's rocket test-site, which had recently been used for fuel-mixture experiments.

But each time a plane was sent to intercept, the objects darted away. And when the plane left, the objects would return. Says Sorrells, "The radar people were having a hard time determining speed because they'd be in one place and they'd sit for a little while, and then they'd move real fast. By the time the radar screen got around to finding them, the UFO was already at another location ... they could make quick turns and had all sorts of maneuverability that we didn't know anything about at the time. It was a very strange evening."

Sergeant Sorrells kept quiet about his experience for many years, until 1993, when Steven Greer MD brought together numerous other military and government UFO witnesses like Sorrell and had them testify before Congress. Sorrells then revealed his encounter, which again is supported by an audio-tape of the radio communications during the hours-long event. A verbatim copy of the transcripts is presented in Greer's very important book, *Disclosure*.[321]

On September 1, 1967, yet another dramatic sighting occurred over Edwards Air Force Base in the Mojave Desert. The account was actually leaked by a civilian employee of the base who accidentally saw the report. According to the account, an X-15 came in for a landing with the pilot claiming that he had been chased by six UFOs. The University of Colorado funded the Robertson Panel study of UFOs, which tried unsuccessfully to obtain official data on the case. The Air Force base officials refused to cooperate.[322]

While the Air Force attempted to cover-up UFO events, with so many people involved in UFO projects, information continued to leak out. In 1973, Kent Sellen worked at Edwards Air Force Base as a crew chief for experimental aircraft. One evening, Sellen's supervisor told him to drive out to the North Base to pick up a defective "ground power unit." This was not unusual. However, Sellen hoped to save time. Instead of taking the longer perimeter road to the North Base facility, he drove straight across the dry lake bed.

He came up from the other side and drove up to several rows of Quonset huts. The door to the first hut was cracked open so he stopped and looked inside. To his shock, he saw a typical flying saucer hovering above the ground. "This thing was flat on the bottom, sloping sides ... I wasn't there for fifteen seconds [when] I heard footsteps running up to me, and before I could even turn around and look, there was a machine gun barrel at my throat. A gruff voice said, 'Close your eyes and get on the ground, or we're going to blow you're head off.'"

Sellen reports that he was blindfolded, a hood was placed over his head, and he was taken into a room where he was debriefed for a period of eighteen hours. During the debriefing, he was told that the craft was in fact extraterrestrial and operated using anti-gravity.[323]

A rare report of a miniature probe-like UFO occurred on July 1, 1978 in Mojave, near Edwards AFB. The main witness was working on a construction project for the local police when a small object descended from the sky and hovered over his head. Says the anonymous witness, "I observed a very small object at one meter from me, hovering. Alone, I watched it. It was almost transparent. I couldn't see through it, but it was as though it was liquid. It was the size of a small orange, silver in color. When I finally yelled to the others, who were on the other side of the building to check this thing out, it moved away. Of course the others didn't see it. It headed towards the Edwards AFB ... I guess since it was so small and no one else saw it, I don't get many believers."[324]

The events at Edwards AFB have already been examined in detail. These events include sightings, landings, and even face-to-face encounters with actual ETs. Later, accounts of human beings studying alien craft were revealed. While this may seem to be as strange as things can get, it is actually only the tip of the iceberg.

What is really happening at Edwards Air Force Base may be considerably more extensive than most people could even imagine.

In April 1991, three separate witnesses phoned a call-in radio program on KPFA-FM in Berkley to reveal their experiences the past year while working at Edwards Air Force Base and the nearby China Lake Naval Weapons facility.

All of the witnesses insisted upon complete anonymity. One of them identified himself as a former member of the Green Beret and a veteran of the Vietnam war. Later he worked on Top Secret military projects as a general contractor at numerous sensitive installations at Nellis, Scott, Andrews, and other Air Force Bases. In 1990 he was contracted to work at Edwards Air Force Base where he and his co-worker had an experience that left a very memorable impression.

The witness reported that the projects he worked on were "mostly underground." He said they were very large constructions, electronically-controlled, four foot-thick concrete walls; what he called, "definitely not military structures." According to the witness, Edwards is a vast underground base reaching an estimated thirty-stories down into the Earth. An elevator trip down to this site took more than five minutes.

While working in this deep underground area, the witness made the startling discovery that extraterrestrials were working along with humans, side-by-side. He entered his work-site one day and was walking past a room with an open door. He looked in and got the shock of his life. Several men were working in the room along with an actual extraterrestrial. As the witness reported, "He was – I'd say between eight and nine-to-ten feet tall. He was wearing a lab jacket and talking to two engineers. This [being's] arms were almost down to his knees. It threw me into shock."

The radio interviewer asked if perhaps he had seen a deformed human being. The witness replied, "Definitely not. He had big slanted eyes. A big head. Greenish skin. And his fingers were extremely long."

No sooner had he seen the ET than a security guard saw the witness and quickly ordered him to leave. The experience was so unnerving, that the witness says he walked off the job the next day.

However, later, he was contracted for a job at nearby China Lake. On this occasion, he was working late to finish a particular job when one of his co-workers said to follow him – that he had found something they needed to see.

Unknown to the witness, he was about to have his first experience corroborated by another. According to the witness, "We looked in the window and there were these four little gray guys about three feet tall. Right then security saw us and they told us, 'We thought you guys left.' And they escorted us and said, 'You're not allowed around this hanger. This hanger is off-limits to everybody. You'll get yourselves shot'."

The threat was obvious and the witness decided to keep his distance. However, the witness states that his co-worker's mind had been "messed" with by the encounter and that, on several subsequent occasions, he sneaked into the hangar for another look. It turned out to be the biggest mistake of his life. According to the witness, "He finally got caught and was kicked off the base. About three months later they found him mysteriously dead in Orange County."

The witness is totally serious about his account. He realized how serious things were after his friend was killed. The event "kind of put a scare" into him.

The anonymous witness still felt like the truth had to be told. As he says, "I know what's going on at Edwards is real …. Somebody's playing games with us."[325]

In April of 1992, UFO investigator Richard Boylan Ph.D. toured the United States, visiting various highly technological research and development installations, such as Area 51. One of his visits included the Tejon Ranch in the Tehachapi Mountains, sixty miles north of Los Angeles, and immediately east of Edwards AFB. Boylan Ph.D. had learned that the Northrop Aircraft Corporation was allegedly using the site to test and reverse engineer captured extraterrestrial spacecraft. Southern California researcher William Hamilton III had also visited the site and interviewed insiders who revealed the purpose of the location is the reverse-engineering of ET craft.

On April 15, Boylan staked out the area between 3:00 and 5:00 a.m. Using a pair of binoculars, he observed what he believes to be humans using and testing extraterrestrial technology.

From his location, he could see the Northrop installation. Parked on the ground in front of one of the hangars, he observed several fifty-foot wide craft. One after another, the craft would slowly begin to glow and then rise up and perform incredible maneuvers before returning to the base and landing. Says Boylan, "I saw the same intensely burning bright orange-gold craft being test flown there that I had seen above Areas 51 and S-4. As I watched, four ultra-bright orange-gold orbs rose and traversed a brief one-and-a-half mile test loop. At intervals of about a half-hour, each orb took off and plied its course. The first three took off from what appeared to be the southwest hangar area of the Northrop complex."

Boylan observed the display for a few hours, fully convincing himself of the reality of Hamilton's claims. Boylan calls the location "California's Black Budget Palmdale-Lancaster region."[326]

Boylan's claims are supported by another independent inside source, an anonymous employee of the B-2 bomber facility out at Plant 42, in Palmdale, who, in the summer of 1992, saw exactly what Boylan also observed. The gentleman reported that because he worked the late shift, he was outside at around 10:00 p.m. smoking a cigarette when he noticed that all the streets around Plant 42 were being blocked. The employee had actually seen this before. As he says, "They do that anytime there is a classified aircraft that is coming in to land or is departing from Plant 42."

However, he became intrigued when he noticed that several tractors had formed a circle and blocked off a particular area with an enormous black curtain. Suddenly, the employee looked above the curtain and saw a "big, black lens-shaped flying saucer, just sitting there above the vehicles."

Someone on the ground flashed a light at the saucer which slowly lowered down behind the curtains and onto the tractors. The object was covered with the curtains and promptly driven into the hangar."

The employee was amazed, and he increased the number of his smoke-breaks in the hopes of a repeat performance. One week later, his patience was rewarded when he observed the covered craft removed from the hangar and uncovered. It then rose 500 feet above the group of tractors, at which point, someone on the ground flashed a light three times. Immediately the craft took off at supersonic speeds, disappearing off the horizon in less than two seconds. There was no noise or shockwave associated with its incredible movement.[327]

The Edwards AFB-UFO connection should be clear by now. Yet another sighting occurred on the morning of July 25, 1995. A civilian witness was driving by the base and saw a disk-shaped UFO hovering about a hundred feet away. "It was shaped like a saucer and it was rotating above a power line tower. It was silver in color." The witness reports that the object emitted no sound or exhaust. It traveled too quickly to follow with the eye. Says the witness, "I live near Edwards AFB .... I have seen everything that can fly from that base. I have never seen anything like what I saw that Sunday morning."[328]

Sometime in December 1998, an aerospace contracting consultant was on his back porch in Victorville when he observed a large "silvery disk" high in the sky, surrounded by several smaller "orbs." The object was stationary, but appeared to wobble. The witness observed the object through binoculars and estimated that it was hovering at an altitude of 75,000 feet. The witness then grabbed a camera and snapped a few photos. Says the witness, "Often we see strange craft coming out of Edwards AFB nearby. Incidentally, the craft would have been just south of the Edwards AFB southern boundary."

The witness observed a passenger jet pass beneath the object. He says, "Therefore, the main object must have been much larger than a large airliner, and the smaller orbs about the size of the airliner. Keep in mind, I viewed with binoculars. I have 30 hours flight training and my wife is a private pilot ... I am not mistaking this sighting for conventional or any kind of typical experimental aircraft."[329]

As can be seen, Edwards contains virtually the entire range of UFO phenomenon. The complete truth of what is actually happening at the base may never be known. But judging from the history of the area, it won't be long before another UFO encounter occurs. And if trends continue as they are, eventually one of these encounters will be of such a magnitude that it will be impossible to cover-up.

14. California UFO Crash/Retrievals

See color section, page 121

Today there are many accounts of UFO crash/retrievals such as Roswell, New Mexico; Kecksberg, Pennsylvania; and Aztec, New Mexico, to name a few. However, back in the 1950s, firsthand accounts were much more rare.

While most people assume that the UFO crash at Roswell in 1947 was the first account of a crash of a flying saucer, the fact is that there are several accounts that pre-date Roswell. In 1952, Mr. Joe Rorher of Pike's Peak Radio Company told researcher Harold Wilkins that he had spoken with an air pilot who had actually been inside a recovered saucer that was being held in a California military base way back in 1942.

Says Rohrer, "A little man from a saucer is being tenderly cared for in the 'incubator room' at San Diego, while cadavers of two saucer pilots are being dissected by surgeons of the U.S. Army-Air Force Medical Division. A California air pilot told me that, in 1942, he had been right inside a giant saucer, and seen giant fly-wheels sheathed in metal-skins, and found that the motive force came from electrostatic turbines whose fly-wheels create an electromagnetic field of force, creating tremendous speeds. The little saucer men have a smaller bony structure than earth men, but the bones are proportionally heavier, and their stomachs smaller."[330]

While the Roswell case was widely publicized, dozens of other UFO crashes have occurred with little or no publicity. One such case was uncovered by MUFON Western Regional Director Paul F. Cerny. The case took place in a carrot patch outside of Salinas on a summer morning in 1947, about the same time as Roswell. The main witness, today a successful businessman, was nineteen years old at the time of the accident. He and his fellow worker were cutting hay when the ranch foreman told them that a strange object had come down in the field and was still there. The witness told Cerny that the object was a large disk, nine feet in diameter, four feet high, and made of a dull gray metal. There were small rectangular portholes around the rim of the craft. Otherwise there were no markings or evidence of damage.

The witnesses walked around the object and finally stepped up and kicked it. There was no reaction other than a hollow metallic clang. Around that time the U.S. military showed up. Writes Cerny, "They instructed the two men to 'get lost' and warned them not to breathe a word about what they had seen. From a distance the witness and his companion observed the military group proceed to struggle the vehicle onto the truck bed, cover it with a tarp, secure it, and drive off. That was the last they saw or heard of it. Inquiring of the foreman later, they learned the ranch owners had informed the military authorities of the object's presence."[331]

Another early mysterious incident occurred to Leon Crice and his wife, both of whom observed a television news story about a crashed UFO. Says Crice, "It was about 1948, maybe later, when my wife and I were watching the news on our new TV set, that a disc-shaped object was shown stuck, slightly tilted, in a sand dune. It had a dome at the top and no windows."

According to Crice, the narrator said that the object had crashed on the Mexican border, near the Rio Grande. The narrator also said that bodies had been recovered and that the craft had been shipped to an *air base in California*. At that point, the sound was cut off and the screen went black. Crice and his wife never heard another word about the incident.[332]

Another very early reference to UFO crashes comes from Roy Dimmick, a sales manager for an explosives company in Los Angeles and well-known amateur golfer. On March 9, 1950, Dimmick told the *LA Times* that he was on a business trip into Mexico when he observed a crashed saucer, 46 feet in diameter. The wreckage contained the body of at least one 23-inch tall midget humanoid with "a big head and a small body." The story caused a newspaper sensation. Dimmick, however, refused to give further details. While the case was eventually dismissed as a hoax, several researchers have raised serious questions concerning the possible validity of the case. Two days following his revelation, Dimmick suddenly denied ever having seen the saucer and said he only saw a "piece" of it. He said that two of his "business associates" saw the craft.[333]

Interestingly, that same year, another gentleman, Buddy Haak, a CPO Radar Observer stationed at a Naval Air Station in Sunnyvale reports that while he was stationed at the base, he observed an actual recovered ET craft. Writes Leonard Stringfield, "Buddy Haak, according to testimony received from members of his family, had accidentally entered a door of a large hangar, temporarily unguarded, and saw a huge, round saucer-shaped craft with a row of windows. A guard shut the door in his face and ordered him to forget what he had seen, or else."

Two years later, Haak was killed when his plane mysteriously disappeared without a trace outside of San Diego. Researchers confirmed his story with Haak's family members. Haak's mother recalls her son often saying, "It was certainly no aircraft of ours."[334]

In July 1952, researcher Harold Wilkins received the following letter from a correspondent in Oklahoma: "On a business trip to San Francisco, last week, I met a nice reliable fellow who has heard from a pal in the U.S. Air Force that they have captured a little fellow, three feet tall, from a force-down saucer, and are keeping him alive in a pressure chamber somewhere in California. He comes from another planet, and was one of three others killed in a crash caused by radar, in an Arizona desert, in 1950. They are showing him pictures and teaching him to read and write and understand."[335]

We have already seen that Edwards Air Force Base is apparently working on reverse-engineering saucers, and is alleged to contain dead and live aliens on the base. While this may sound incredible, it is no more unbelievable than sightings, landings or abductions. Take the following case, which was uncovered by highly respected researcher Leonard Stringfield. Writes Stringfield, "My information for one known UFO crash incident comes from a professional employee in a technical position at a large General Electric plant. His brother, who wishes to be unnamed, was on duty as a radar specialist at Edwards Air Force Base, in 1952, when he saw a UFO descending toward Earth at great speed across his radar screen. When the UFO was confirmed to have crashed, the Captain on duty gave him instructions, 'You didn't see anything!' The specialist learned a short time later from base officials that an unidentified craft did crash in a nearby remote desert area. The retrieved craft was more than 50 feet in diameter with a row of windows around its equator. Its metallic surface was in a burned-blackened condition. He also had heard that the craft was occupied by humanoid bodies approximately 4-1/2 feet tall."

According to Stringfield's source, the craft was held only temporarily at Edwards before being shipped off to Wright-Patterson Air Force Base in Ohio.[336]

In 1967, a Marine officer from the Canine Corps assigned to Camp Pendleton reports that he and his team were flown to an undetermined and remote location somewhere in the California desert. His team was put on guard duty. The officer, R. C., became curious about the contents of the hangar that they were guarding. On his fourth day at the location, he decided to peek inside the hangar. To his shock, he observed a thirty-foot-diameter metallic saucer with a dome on top. The craft was surrounded by people working on the craft with instruments.

At that moment, R. C. was grabbed by a security officer and escorted to the headquarters tent. He was reminded of his security oath, (he had an Alpha Red TS Crypto Clearance) and was sent back to Camp Pendleton for reassignment.

When R. C. went public with his story in 1980, he suffered a series of harassments and threats from apparent government agents. When his fiancé was killed in a mysterious hit and run accident, R. C. severed all connections with researchers and refused to share any further UFO information.[337]

Numerous other military bases also have been named as conducting UFO studies utilizing the hard evidence obtained from retrieved crashed UFOs. One name which comes up again and again is Norton Air Force Base.

One account was uncovered by investigator John Lear and involves an Air Force photographer known only as "Mike." In 1973, Mike told John Lear that his security clearance was suddenly upgraded and he was flown to Norton AFB for a temporary assignment. Upon landing at the base, Mike was put inside a bus with blackened windows and driven to an undisclosed location. Mike was told he was going to photograph a UFO and the autopsy of three dead ETs. He was issued a white smock and boots and was escorted into an underground installation where he observed a metallic disk-shaped craft, thirty feet in diameter, suspended in a net from a large crane.

Mike was taken inside the craft and told to photograph control panels and other fixtures. Later he was taken outside the craft and told to photograph it from various angles. Finally, he was taken to another room where he photographed three dead aliens. Mike described them as being almost human-looking, except their eyes were larger, the skin was very white and they were all five feet tall and dressed in blue uniforms. Mike reports that, afterwards, he was driven back to Norton AFB and then sent out of state for reassignment.[338]

On November 12, 1988, aircraft patent specialist Brad Sorenson was with his client (a former Secretary of Defense) attending an Air Show at Norton Air Force Base in southern California when he was invited into the inner sanctum of the privileged few who have seen the captured ET craft.

During the air show, Sorenson's client invited him to view several extraterrestrial spacecraft that were being held in secret at the base. The Defense Secretary told Sorensen, "There are a lot of things in here that I didn't expect they were going to have on display – stuff you probably shouldn't be seeing. So, don't talk to anybody, don't ask any questions, just keep your mouth shut, smile and nod, but don't say anything – just enjoy the show. We're going to get out of here as soon as we can."

Sorensen agreed and followed his client. Sorenson later told his associate, Mark McCandlish (also an aerospace design expert), what he saw. Says McCandlish, "They go in and they turn the lights on, and here are three flying saucers floating off the floor – no cables suspended from the ceiling holding them up, no landing gear underneath – just floating, hovering above the floor. They had little exhibits with a videotape running, showing the smallest of the three vehicles sitting in the desert, presumably over a dry lakebed, someplace like Area 51 ... so he listened intently and collected as much information as he could, and when he came back, he told me how he had seen these three flying saucers in this hangar at Norton Air Force Base on November 12, 1988 ... . Brad said that in this exhibit at Norton Air Force Base, a three star general said that these vehicles were capable of doing light speed or better."[339]

It is not difficult to attain firsthand accounts of the government cover-up of crashed UFOs. Further evidence supporting the UFO connection to Norton Air Force Base comes from Lieutenant Colonel John Williams. In 1964, Lieutenant Colonel Williams entered the Air Force. He later became a helicopter rescue pilot in Vietnam, then obtained a degree in electrical engineering and was put in charge of major construction projects for the Military Air Command. Lt. Col. Williams reports that his "need-to-know" status allowed his access to numerous highly secure facilities, including Norton AFB.

He has apparently been given official permission to reveal his story. Says Lt. Col. John Williams, "I can discuss Norton Air Force Base .... There was one facility at Norton Air Force Base that was close hold – not even the wing commander there could know what was going on. During that time period it was always rumored by the pilots that that was a cover for in fact the location of one UFO craft. The reason for that location was that folks could come out, land at Norton, play golf, be part of a golf tournament and so forth and during that process could go by the facility and actually see the UFO. But I was never allowed in that area when I was there at Norton Base .... I heard this during my Vietnam career where I was a rescue helicopter pilot .... It was there that I heard several stories along that line from different pilots. All that was known, because it was so close hold, was the fact that this facility did contain a UFO. The time period would have been in 1969 to 1970 when I heard that first. And I validated that the facility did in fact exist in the 1982 time period ... because I was responsible for that base's facilities from 1981-1982."

Colonel John Williams reports that many highly placed officials often visited the off-limits facility. Says Williams, "It's my understanding that Bob Dole was at the facility. It's also possible that back in the early '50s that Eisenhower actually visited that facility."[340]

Researcher Bill Hamilton has received many reports of UFOs directly over military bases. The early 1990s brought a flood of such reports. He interviewed a group of witnesses who were at Northrop when they observed a "disc hovering directly over the facility in broad daylight, streaking off towards the mountains."

Hamilton describes another sighting over the same Northrop facility: "Back in October 26, 1988, witnesses saw two large boomerangs escorted by seventeen disks in formation, at very slow speed, that flew over the Northrop facility and was seen that night in Fresno. A friend who saw one of the boomerang-shaped craft pass directly overhead estimated it was twice the width of his property, which was 330 feet wide."[341]

As can be seen, hard proof of UFOs does exist, only most of it appears to be controlled by highly placed officials in the military-industrial complex.

15. Landings and Humanoids

See color section, page 122

While UFO sightings are interesting, more compelling are cases in which UFOs land and humanoids exit the craft. In these types of cases, explanations of misperceptions are virtually impossible. The witnesses are viewing some type of solid craft, close-up, and not a distant unexplained light in the night sky. It is important to note that these cases do not involve hypnosis, missing time or abductions. These are all fully conscious experiences. And again, California has a huge number of these types of reports.

One of the first UFO landings in California left actual physical evidence of its existence. These types of cases are exceedingly rare and are called landing-trace cases. On October 18, 1927, Richard Sweed, a schoolteacher, was driving alone in the outskirts of Bakersfield when he had an experience that he kept secret for thirty-two years. As he drove, he suddenly observed a strange saucer-shaped object landed directly along the side of the road ahead of him. Sweed was able to get a close look at the object as he sped closer towards it. The object was metallic-looking, bluish-gray in color, about sixty feet in diameter with a row of round windows around the perimeter. When he got close, it suddenly emitted a loud "whining, humming, wheezing, swooshing" sound. It then rose steadily at an angle of forty-five degrees and accelerated up into the sky. Sweed kept his eyes on the landing location and pulled over to investigate. Upon examination, he was shocked to see that the sand on the ground where the object had been was "fused like grass crystals."[342]

On August 19, 1949, the first modern occupant case in California took place in Death Valley. Two prospectors reportedly witnessed the landing of a disk-shaped metallic object. Two "small men" exited the craft, and the prospectors gave chase. The two ETs easily out-distanced the prospectors and disappeared among the dunes. The prospectors rushed back to the location of the landing, but by then the disk was gone.[343]

In 1953, one of the world's most famous encounters took place outside a small isolated northern California town called Brush Creek. Today it remains a classic case in the UFO literature. The entire ordeal revolves around two titanium miners, John Black and John Van Allen, who had a series of encounters while working at their mine.

In early 1953, both Black and Van Allen observed a "metallic saucer" hovering over the area of the mine. Over the next few weeks, the object returned on four separate occasions. On April 20, their concern mounted when Black saw the craft from a distance of a quarter mile. It was obvious to the witnesses that the UFO had a strong interest in their mine.

Exactly one month later, at 6:30 p.m. on May 20, Black was returning to the mine when he saw the now familiar saucer hovering only a few hundred feet above the sandbar at the junction of Marble and Jordan creeks. The craft quickly took off towards the east and disappeared. On inspecting the area, Black found several small five-inch footprints.

Then, exactly one month later again, on June 20, Black approached the junction of the two creeks when he saw what he thought was a small child with a bucket. At that point, he saw the large saucer landed nearby on the sandbar. Black examined the figure which he said appeared to be a small man wearing green pants, unusual shoes, a jacket and a green cap. He was very pale and had black hair. Says Black, "He looked like someone who had never been out in the sun much."

Black watched as the man scooped up water with an unusual cone-shaped-bucket. Black had approached to about forty feet when the little man heard him and quickly entered a small metallic saucer that was landed on a sandbar. At that point, the craft took off quickly and in total silence, leaving Black amazed.

Somewhat concerned, Black contacted Brush Creek sheriff Fred Preston. Black jokingly asked the sheriff if it was "open season on space men." The sheriff, however, remained serious. "I told them they'd better grab it next time so they'll have something to back up their story," Preston then told them he couldn't give them permission to shoot. He did, however, contact the Air Force.

The story was then leaked to the press and so began one of the strangest events in UFO history. Because the saucer had appeared on April 20, May 20, and June 20, everyone was predicting a July 20ᵗʰ landing. More than two hundred people arrived on the scene with cameras waiting. Residents of Brush Creek, newspaper reporters, cameramen, and saucer enthusiasts all converged on the scene. Snack bars and chairs were set up as if people were going to watch a circus performance.

Unfortunately, it was a total bust. The expected UFO did not arrive and the Brush Creek ordeal came to a sudden close. However, the case has never been solved. The miners were well respected and their testimony was backed up by Vi Belcher, owner of the local store who said they were "not drinking men." The account was investigated in depth by researchers Gray Barker and Paul Spade, both of whom were actually jailed by the Brush Creek sheriff's station when they tried to conduct a stake-out for the saucer. Both came away convinced of the veracity of the case. Says Barker, "Spade made what I considered an objective investigation and reported that the story was evidently not a hoax …. Whatever Black saw, the story sounds almost too good for someone to think up, especially when such a story is credited to an isolated miner who is not likely to be at all well-read on science-fiction."[344]

A few months later, a rare landing trace case took place in Morningside on October 10, 1953, when local residents observed a "red-blue burning thing" descend from the sky. An examination of the landing site revealed only a patch of burned pavement.[345]

Because children are often outside, they comprise a significant portion of UFO witnesses. It was around 2:00 p.m. on August 22, 1955, when a group of children—ranging in age from four to fourteen years—were playing in the backyard of Mr. and Mrs. Douglas of Riverside. One of the boys had climbed onto the roof when he noticed a spinning silver disk hovering overhead. As he and the other children watched, the disk disappeared and reappeared several times. Then suddenly, the children noticed that there were now several metallic-flying saucers hovering low overhead.

At this point, one of the saucers swooped down and landed in the field next to the home. Seconds later, a "little man" with a "big red mouth, big red eyes and four diamond-shaped things where his nose should be" got out of the craft and walked towards the boys. The being was the size of a four-year-old child and wore a belt with a bright disk. The spaceman pointed at the boy on the roof and the boy felt himself begin to levitate. As he says, "I just floated off into space from a housetop."

The boy's playmates saw their friend float down off the rooftop and land on the ground. They came running. At this point, the figure pointed a gun-like device at two of the witnesses, rendering them temporarily paralyzed. Other children said they felt as if they were being mentally beckoned to go inside the craft. Finally, the "little man" scurried back into the saucer, which promptly took off and went away.[346]

An amazing series of contacts with tall human-like ETs took place in the summer of 1955, directly in the heart of the San Fernando Valley. Sometime in mid-June, 1955, Ted Kittredge, a young electrician from Van Nuys, told reporters that he was awakened in the middle of the night by the barking of his dogs. Exiting his home, he was amazed to see a gigantic gold-colored sphere landed in his front yard. Standing next to it were three seven-foot-tall human-looking figures. They appeared friendly, had long flowing hair, and spoke flawless English "as if they had memorized thousands of conversations and were repeating the words on tape."

Says Kettridge, "[The] three men approached me without hesitation and told me not to be frightened." The visitors then imparted a few brief messages and left. Says Kettridge, "I was really scared. In fact the whole thing seemed like a dream, only I know it wasn't. Several other people in the valley had seen the same thing, even talked with the men. I just hope I never see it again, that's all."[347]

One month later, on July 20, 1955, three separate, independent witnesses reported seeing a UFO and its occupants. The event occurred in a rural area of Panorama City, which neighbors Van Nuys, and appears to be connected to Kettridge's encounter. According to the report, a "huge ball-shaped object" landed in a field near the witnesses' homes. The witnesses observed "three beings approximately 6 feet 8 inches in height, with long blond hair, and clothed in tight green suits." Two of the witnesses reported that the beings made "gestures of friendship."[348]

On November 6, 1957, a very dramatic UFO incident occurred along the Pacific Coast Highway in Playa Del Rey. The story was picked up by the local media and as a result was fully investigated and verified. Today, it remains a classic in the UFO literature.

At 5:40 that morning, General Telephone Company employee Richard Keyhoe was driving when his engine mysteriously stalled. As he got out of his car, he noticed that the engines of three other vehicles had also stopped and their passengers were getting out. At that point, Keyhoe and two of the other drivers, Ronald Burke of Redondo Beach and Joe Thomas of Torrance, observed an "egg-shaped" object surrounded in a "blue haze" landed on the beach only a few yards away. The object was "tan or cream in color with two metal rings around it, upon which the object apparently rested."

As they watched, two men with "yellowish-green skin" and wearing "black leather pants, white belts and light colored jerseys" exited the object and began asking questions of the stunned witnesses. Keyhoe and the others were unable to understand the occupants, who appeared to be speaking a foreign language. The figures returned back into the craft which took off moments later and disappeared. When the UFO left, the car engines started running by themselves. Joe Thomas was so unnerved by the incident that he reported it to the local police, which eventually led to a media frenzy, forever establishing the case as a classic in UFO history.[349]

Strengthening the credibility of the above account are several sightings which occurred on the same day in the same location. About ten hours later, at 3:50 p.m., and less than fifty miles to the south, a commanding officer and twelve airmen from an Air Force weather detachment at Long Beach sighted six saucer-shaped objects zoom across the sky, just under a 7000 foot cloud cover. About two hours later, between 6:05 p.m. and 7:25 p.m., additional officers at the Los Alamitos Naval Air Station reported seeing "numerous" objects zooming overhead. At the same time, local police stations in Long Beach received more than one hundred calls from concerned Long Beach citizens reporting UFOs.[350]

One month later, in December of 1957, Edmund Rucker of El Cajon had an experience he will not soon forget. As he later told investigators, he was awakened one evening by a loud roaring noise coming from outside his home. Looking outside, he was shocked to see a "strange object" landing right next to his home. Says Rucker, "Its windows were lighted, and I saw strange-looking heads in there."

Rucker watched as an opening appeared in the craft and four beings emerged. They appeared to have bulging eyes and large dome-like foreheads. They spoke to Rucker, saying that their intentions were scientific and philanthropic.[351]

On Christmas morning of 1957, a seven-year-old child from San Gabriel had an experience with what he thought was an elf. As the witness wrote in a letter to author/experiencer Whitley Strieber: "It must've been between two or three a.m., and I was lying in bed in my bedroom .... I remember I awakened rather suddenly and was quite unable to move; seemingly frozen in bed."

The witness, although unable to move, could see out the bedroom, across the living room, and onto the front porch. That's when things became strange. "On the porch, seemingly peering into the living room was a smallish creature I remember thinking to be one of 'Santa's Elves.' I was naturally excited and wanted to get up to meet or see this elf much closer. I remember being wide-awake and desperately wanting to get up, but patently unable to accomplish this seemingly simple task. He seemed to be about three or four feet tall and was cream in color. I saw more of a three-quarter profile, and could not make much of any other distinguishing features. I was not that fearful, just excited, and burning with curiosity. My frustration was building with my seeming inability to rise from my bed. I then had a firm sense of 'It's okay now, just go back to sleep.' It had a parental tone to it, loving yet directive, however, not either of my parents' voices."

The witness fell back asleep. However, the experience was not forgotten. "On Christmas morning, as my sister was going nuts, I was relatively disinterested in all the stuff around the tree. Instead, I was determined to go out onto the front porch and check for evidence of what I knew was there."

Unfortunately, there was no evidence. Nevertheless, the witness still remembers that "my parents were rather dumbfounded at my spurning Christmas presents in favor of running outside ...." Later, the witness had further UFO experiences which seemed to confirm the validity of the Christmas day visitation.[352]

On Labor day weekend in 1964, a now classic UFO case took place in the wilderness outside Cisco Grove, near Truckee, California. Three hunters were using the long weekend to do some bow-and-arrow hunting. On September 4, the three men separated from each other and began the hunt. One of the hunters, Donald Smythe, had no idea that he was about to become the hunted. After a long day of hunting, Smythe had become lost and was having trouble finding his way back to camp. When he saw a light darting back and forth above him, he assumed a helicopter had been sent to rescue him. Instead, the object came overhead and hovered silently above him. When the object suddenly landed, Smythe realized that it was something outside of his experience. He became frightened and climbed up a nearby tree.

Smythe then saw three figures exit the craft and come towards him. Two of the figures were about five feet tall and dressed from head to toe in silvery-gray material. The third figure appeared to be robotic, with two reddish-orange "eyes" and a rectangular opening for a mouth. The three figures approached the tree and appeared to try and climb it. The robotic figure opened its rectangular mouth and belched out clouds of foul-smelling gas which made Smythe choke and lose consciousness. He climbed further up into the tree as the three figures continued to taunt him. The three figures stayed for hours, despite Smythe's attempts to dissuade them by dropping burning bits of paper and clothing. He then shot at the robot with his arrows. Although the robot was knocked down, the arrows bounced off the metallic surface.

This went on all night. When dawn broke, the figures were still there. Suddenly, a fourth figure exited the craft and Smythe saw that it was another robotic figure, identical to the first. The two robots emitted a huge cloud of smoke which enveloped Smythe, causing him to lose consciousness. When he awoke, the figures and "dome-shaped" craft were gone.

Smythe hurriedly returned to camp, where he found his friends looking for him. Upon hearing his account, one of the hunters reported that he also saw a "bright, glowing, large light" swoop down and travel at low altitude across the sky. Both companions also remarked that the incident undoubtedly had something to do with the fact that the government was already in the area looking for a "meteorite."

Smythe's wife saw him after the incident and provided additional details. "I knew something was wrong with him when I saw him. He was as white as a sheet and his eyes were dazed looking. He spoke to me in a very shaky voice. He had dark circles under his eyes. He looked terrible ... he had scratches all over his arms. He came in and didn't even say hi, hello or anything ... he then proceeded to tell me about his Cisco Grove experience. His hands shook and his voice was subdued ... he was on the verge of crying [and] was so badly shaken that he took a week off from work."

Smythe was badly traumatized by the incident and reported it to the Air Force. While the Air Force suggested he was perhaps the victim of a prank, pioneering UFO investigator Coral Lorenzen calls the case "the most spectacular report I have ever examined" and believes "it is an authentic incident and important to the documentation of 'occupant' incidents."

UFO investigators Ted Bloecher and Paul Cerny also conducted an in-depth, onsite investigation and came away totally convinced. Writes Cerny, "Having just reviewed the case files on this fascinating and unusual encounter, there is absolutely no doubt in my mind that this incident is factual and authentic. I have spent considerable time and many visits with the main witness, and along with the testimony of the other witnesses, I can rule out the possibility of any hoax."[353]

On April 14, 1964, an anonymous truck driver was driving at night outside of Chico when a "domed disk" hovered about 1,000 feet above his truck, which immediately stalled. The witness reported a strong feeling of static electricity, causing his hair to stand on end. The domed disk then lowered to the ground and landed next to the road. Amazed, the truck driver exited his truck and approached the disk. He actually reached out and touched the craft, which felt warm to the touch and caused a small electrical-like shock. The witness says he also heard what sounded like voices.[354]

The next day, witnesses in Yosemite National Park observed UFOs. The Air Force's Project Blue Book was alerted. Investigators declared the case (Case #9049) unexplained.[355]

Two weeks later, a UFO landed outside the desert town of Baker. The witnesses include Gloria Biggs, her husband, and mother, all of who observed a "brown dome-shaped object" landed along the highway ahead of them. They lost sight of it due to the path of the road. When they reached the site of the landing, the object was gone. However, they were able to see a "depression in the ground" where the object had been.[356]

A rare account of a UFO landing with humanoids occurred around 6:00 a.m. on March 31, 1966. The ordeal began when two women were passing by a construction site outside of San Francisco. They both observed a strange vehicle parked in the lot. It was described as "a large object with a pulsating bluish light on top, an orange light below, windows, and an antennae." The witnesses were even more alarmed by the fact that they could see "silhouettes" moving around inside the craft, gesturing. Seconds later, the craft took off and accelerated out of sight.[357]

For most people, seeing a UFO is a once-in-a-lifetime experience. For others, however, it is a regular part of life. A good example are Clint and Jane Chapin (pseudonyms) of the small town of French Gulch, outside of Redding. The Chapins reside in a trailer in a remote area. They make their living from their gold mine, which is on their property. The French Gulch case is particularly interesting because it involves considerable physical evidence.

The first of several encounters occurred on October 30, 1969, at 10:30 a.m. The Chapins were outside their home when they observed an oval-shaped object the size of a small car landed among the trees. Seconds later, the object lifted up, hovered briefly, and then accelerated away.

The Chapins checked the area where the object had landed and found a strange pile of sand and metal. Later, investigator Jacques Vallee arranged for the material to be analyzed. While the material was composed of substances that are found on Earth, there were several inexplicable and unusual properties. The analysts told Vallee, "The problem with your sand is that it's not sand .... Perhaps it looks like sand to you, but it's not alluvial sand or stream sand or beach sand or mine-tailing sand or any kind of naturally formed sand .... Here is some siltstone. Here is volcanic material; here, sulfide-bearing rock; green crystals; feldspar or porcelain; pyrite cubes. No quartz and no mica. All the fragments are very angular. All the components are common, but they don't belong together. This is a composite of rock fragments and manufactured materials .... It's as if somebody had taken minerals from very different areas and had ground them together until it looked like sand."

The analysis of the above sample didn't take place until decades after the event. The Chapins stored the material and only offered it for study after they experienced further encounters. Their next encounter would occur seven years later.

On December 27, 1976, at 11:00 a.m., the Chapins (now in their seventies) were driving along the road near their home when they came across a patch of ice. Clint exited the truck and walked ahead to investigate the size of the ice patch. Just around the corner of the road, he observed a car-sized object the shape of half an egg, landed on the road ahead of him. He shouted to his wife to bring the gun.

Jane jumped out of the truck and started to run. At that moment, several things happened. The object took off. Jane reports that she ran into an invisible and impassible barrier, fell to the ground, and lost consciousness. Clint reports that his left arm was pinned behind his back and he was thrown to the side of the road where he lost consciousness. Both woke up about fifteen minutes later. Both had urinated in their pants. Both felt sick and cold.

Afterwards, Jane suffered from a strange buzzing noise in her head, deteriorating vision, and pains in her arms and legs. Clint also felt unwell, and suffered from chronic pain in his left arm. Doctor's were unable to diagnose Jane's condition and called it "old age nervousness."

One year later, the Chapins would experience another bizarre encounter involving medical injuries. It was October 13, 1977. The couple were working at their gold mine when both felt a sudden wave of heat. Both instantly became ill, exhibiting symptoms similar to radiation sickness, including vomiting violently. While they didn't see any actual object or entity, they both feel that the experience is related to the UFO that had been harassing them around their mine. Following this incident, Clint's health deteriorated dramatically. He felt constantly weak, experienced heart trouble, and as Jane says, "Clint sweats when sitting on a chair, and at night he turns real red in the face."

On January 14, 1978, Jane Chapin of French Gulch finally encountered the occupant of the UFO that had been harassing her and her husband as they worked on their privately owned gold mine. The encounter occurred inside their trailer when Jane saw a figure suddenly appear. According to investigator Jacques Vallee, "The head was flat, with large eyes and a big nose."

One month later, in August, another witness corroborated the Chapin's story. An anonymous twelve-year-old boy, the son of a local doctor, observed an "unusual humanoid creature" near the area of the mine. The boy was reportedly "deeply upset" by the encounter.

A few months later on April 4, 1980, the Chapins would have their final and most dramatic encounter. Now in their mid-eighties, they were examining a road that had been cut through their property. Says Jane Chapin, "We turned to go down the road, and there was a skinny *thing* in the road …. He was four foot tall and skinny, maybe ninety pounds … and his egg [the UFO] was not 25 feet from us …. He [the humanoid] took four steps toward us and my hand fell on my gun, and he turned around and walked back. He was in a gray suit, and he left no prints or prints of the egg. Clint could not move either … the thing vanished, then the egg went up in the air and turned west."

Two months later, Clint died of an apparent heart attack. Jane Chapin has revealed no further encounters. Jacques Vallee was particularly impressed by the Chapins' story and calls it his "favorite case." Writes Vallee, "The Chapins, I was convinced, were not lying …. I did believe them, and I still do."[358]

A unique and bizarre encounter occurred in 1971 to two young students in Los Angeles. Whether or not it is ET related is hard to say. As one of the witnesses wrote to author and experiencer Whitley Strieber, "A friend and I had decided to stay up all night in an attempt to complete some studying we were doing. We were working away intensely, hoping to finish up as soon as possible. At around four o'clock in the morning, I looked over at her sitting in her chair when I saw a little being about two and a half to three feet tall appear right beside her. Although I could not make out any details, the best way I could describe it is as though it were in a kind of grayish translucent cloak of light. It was only there for a moment when I saw an extension come out of it, like a pointed finger, that pushed my friend. At that very instant, she fell off her chair in the direction in which she had been pushed! After this, we both started laughing nonstop. She had not seen anything, but she told me she had felt something push against her shoulder that made her fall off the chair. Neither one of us experienced fear. We both found it funny and I felt as if the being was just having fun with us, probably thinking how silly we were staying up all night like that."[359]

A large number of UFOs have been sighted landing along highways and freeways. On October 4, 1973, Simi Valley resident Gary Chopic drove along the 118 Simi Freeway when he saw a "triangular object" landed along the roadside. The object had a transparent bubble on top, through which Chopic could see a "humanoid" figure moving about inside. Suddenly, the figure seemed to notice Chopic and scrambled out of sight. Seconds later, the bubble retracted into the triangular object and a strange mist enveloped the craft. A moment later, the ship was gone.[360]

Thirty miles away and two weeks later, on October 16, two young children and their dog were playing in the backyard of their Burbank home when a "buzzing" object landed nearby. Two or more beings tried to get the older boy to enter the craft, but he later said that he was too afraid. The dog also reacted by barking. The figures returned inside the craft, which took off when the children's father came outside to investigate the reason that his dog was barking.[361]

On November 16, 1973, two 11-year-old boys witnessed a landed UFO. This case also provides compelling and rare landing trace evidence. It was around 6:00 p.m. when the two anonymous boys were exploring the neighborhood around their home in Lemon Grove. They discovered a vacant property surrounded by a chain-link fence. Trespassing into the area, they walked into a field and got the shock of their life. As the report on the case reads: "After passing a clump of bamboo, they came out into the open and saw an object sitting in a darkened field. They slowly approached it and, after about five minutes, one boy, who had a flashlight in his hand, walked up to it and rapped on it three or four times with the flashlight. The object, which the boys described as a dull gray, immediately came to life. The rapping had produced a metallic sound. A dome on top of the object, about as high as its diameter, became illuminated with intense red light which irradiated the entire area, including the boys. At the same time, the object, which had been about eighteen inches off the ground, rose up to about three or four feet. A row of green lights around the peripheral rim of the object started to blink in sequence and the object started to rotate making a not very high-pitch sound .... The rate of rotation became very high with the red light blinking on and off. Then the red light went off momentarily, came back on, and the object rose into the air, still making the same sound.

"The boys started to run, felt chills, tingly and weak. They agreed that they felt as if they were going to black out and that they were running in slow motion. They said the object took off toward the southwest and, as they got up to the street, they saw it disappear into the clouds."

The above case was investigated by Epperson and Donald R. Carr. Following the incident, Carr interviewed the boys and their mothers. All appeared to be very sincere. He then checked the field for landing traces. Carr discovered three holes forming a perfect equilateral triangle. In the same area, dead grass was swirled in a counter-clockwise circular pattern.

Carr then asked the neighbors if they had experienced anything strange. At least five neighbors reported intense and bizarre interference with their televisions sets. Later there was some speculation of possible missing time, though this was never confirmed.[362]

On December 14, 1973, platoon Sergeant Lance Mathias and computer programmer Mike Andrews were driving at 9:40 p.m. through Paso Robles when they saw an "amber-colored sphere" hovering at about 800 feet. A black cone on the bottom of the sphere was emitting a bright red beam of light, causing a "great disturbance" in the field below. Said Mathias, "The beam shot out, stopped, then shot again in intermittent spurts. When this was done, the cone was drawn into the sphere and a cloud of vapor became visible where the cone had been."

After a few seconds, the object darted away. Mathias and Andrews ran into the field and examined the area where the beam had hit. They found a strange ring of crushed grass, and the ground itself appeared to glow. After fifteen minutes, the glow faded.

Mathias and Andrews turned on their flashlights and prepared to return to their car. Suddenly, their flashlight beams lit up two six-foot humanoid figures in metallic suits. Says Mathias, "The two were side by side. They startled me. I know I saw them."

The humanoids waved their arms in a strange way, but Andrews and Mathias were too frightened and departed the area in a panic. Later, when shown pictures of the humanoids seen by Charles Hickson and Calvin Parker in Pascagoula, Mississippi, Mathias replied, "That's it! They looked just like that!"[363]

A highly dramatic UFO landing took place one afternoon in 1974 outside the city of Ramona, north of San Diego. The Overfelt family was drawn outside by a bright object that had swooped out of the sky and landed on a hill near their home. The object was the size of a small house, appeared to be perfectly round and was changing in color from red to white. While the craft was on the hill, the horses started bucking, the dog slammed around in his doghouse, the goats were jumping up and down, and the cat ran into the side of the house, stunning itself.

When the object remained, one of the family members called local UFO investigators. The investigators instructed them to check for electromagnetic effects. The witnesses then learned that the radio in the house wouldn't work at all, and the television screen showed strange blue spots and vertical bands. The witnesses then obtained a compass. They were amazed to see the needle oscillating rapidly back and forth between north and northeast, the direction of the object.

The UFO investigators headed out to the scene. But after about twenty minutes, the UFO suddenly hovered and took off. Immediately, several military jets appeared in hot pursuit. As the UFO took off, the compass needle flew off its glass pivot and lodged against the glass cover. The main investigator, Eric Herr, calls the case "a classic."[364]

Landing trace cases are relatively rare in the UFO literature. Much more rare are cases in which plant life experiences accelerated growth as a result of close exposure to UFO beams of light. One such apparent case took place in Project City, just north of Redding. At 7:50 p.m. on April 23, 1976, Jean Kirk was watching television when the screen became filled with intense static. She went outside to determine the cause and was amazed to see a very strange-looking "cloud" three hundred feet away, moving towards her. Kirk described the cloud as "solid white with sharp edges" – in other words, not really a cloud at all. The dogs in the neighborhood barked furiously as the cloud-like thing approached, hovered in place, and moved overhead. Kirk experienced a strong spell of dizziness, and the trees in the area bent as if subjected to furious winds, though Kirk felt none.

As the "cloud" passed overhead, it disappeared and all the commotion stopped. Where the cloud had been, Kirk observed a large red and green light, moving silently northward.

Kirk's sighting was over, but the after-effects would last for years. In the months following the sighting, the field below where the object had hovered exhibited "abnormal fast growth of the grass and weeds." In a matter of three months, the weeds had reached a height of eight feet, more than twice their normal height. Kirk chopped the weeds down, but the accelerated growth continued for three additional years. By August of 1979, the weeds had returned to normal.[365]

A high proportion of UFO witnesses are police officers, pilots, night watchmen or other people whose profession involves being outside. This is true in the following case.

On March 6, 1977, private security guard Douglas Kriese was at his station outside a factory in Sylmar when he saw a "reddish, glowing light" come from the east, fly over his head, and land behind a nearby building. Kriese went to investigate and, to his amazement, observed a landed craft shaped like a "tuna can with a high transparent dome." The object was deep red and emitted a low hum.

As Kriese approached within 300 feet, he could feel an intense heat coming from the object. He retreated and called the Van Nuys Police. The police referred him to Ann Druffel, then southern California's leading UFO investigator, who was able to interview the witness directly after the incident.[366]

A very unusual case of contact took place over a period of a few years, starting around 1977. The main witnesses are two brothers, both Native Americans from the Cortina tribe. They live in a small, isolated ranch house, with no water or electricity, outside of Colusa. The case came to the attention of investigators after the brothers told their neighbor that a "strange plane" kept landing in their fields. A short humanoid figure would then exit and harass the two brothers. As the brothers told their neighbor, the object actually showed up and then darted quickly away.

One of the brothers, Amos, told his neighbor that he disliked the visitations because the "little stranger" made all his horses go wild, and hunting the next day was difficult because all the animals would go into hiding. According to Amos, the figure didn't walk but floated a few feet above the ground. He was three and a half feet tall, wore a strange one-piece brown uniform, had long hair, a large nose, and gave off a bad smell. Amos reports that the figure would enter through the walls of his cabin and then dart away when Amos approached.

When investigators arrived later, Amos showed them where the object had often landed. Investigators found strange circles of crushed and swirled grass. During one visit, on October 18, one of the investigators observed the UFO approach close up and then dart away. When the investigators finally left, the visitations were still continuing.[367]

While reports of gray-type aliens are relatively common in the UFO literature, there are also many reports of human-looking aliens. A particularly compelling report comes from an anonymous woman and her husband from Los Angeles. The couple was driving together on a motorcycle in the late afternoon through downtown Los Angeles when their encounter occurred. Says the main witness, "I saw what appeared to be a metallic-colored disc-shaped object shoot up from behind the taller buildings nearby. It got to a height of 100 feet in the air ... we turned left ... and then the sun shined on it and I could see inside the ship because it turned transparent. I could see three or four people inside .... Two were looking out at me and were leaning over a console/platform. They looked like two handsome, ordinary human men. I gave them a peace sign because it seemed fun to do. They didn't respond and showed no emotion other than curiosity .... I don't tell many people because of my fear of ridicule. My husband saw them too but not as clearly as me .... It reminded us of a soap bubble where the setting sun shone on it. Where the sun didn't hit it, the craft remained a steel-gray opaque color. My husband doesn't think it's a good idea to tell anyone, but I've been keeping quiet too long."[368]

One of the most detailed descriptions of a face-to-face extraterrestrial encounter on record comes from commercial artist Melissa Chappelle. Then a college student, Melissa was walking down the street late at night near her Van Nuys home in the summer of 1982 when she saw two children standing in front of the local elementary school. As she walked past them, she got the shock of her life – they were not children at all.

Says Chappelle, "As I looked at them I started to notice that they looked kind of strange. They had on these dark green jumpsuits. They had really big heads, and they weren't very tall ... but I wasn't really impacted with their presence until they turned to look at me ... they just sort of hovered and turned."

Chappelle was shocked to see the now commonly-described gray-type extraterrestrials. She further described the figures as having "really, really big eyes" and skin that was "all pale, really, really white." They had a very small nose and mouth.

Says Chappelle, "Their jumpsuits were this dark olive-green color, and they came up in like a Mandarin collar around their necks. It was just very plain."

Chappelle was so shocked that she just walked away as quickly as she could without panicking. At the time, she had no idea what she had seen. It wasn't until later, when accounts of gray-type aliens surfaced in the media, that she realized what she had seen. Says Chappelle, "I realized that they weren't normal, and probably weren't human. They didn't move like humans. They didn't look like humans. They were identical."[369]

Extraterrestrials encounters can happen in places you would least expect. In the following case, clerical worker Traci Stoor experienced an encounter in a hotel room. Stoor reports that she was staying in the Marriott Hotel in Woodland Hills when she was suddenly woken up out of a sound sleep to find a short, skinny figure standing on the foot of her bed with a blazing red light coming from behind it. Stoor describes what happened, "I remember seeing something standing there with a foot on me, standing towards my feet with a foot on my leg. Imagine somebody in the dark in front of you with a bright red light behind them so all you see is the glow of the red light and the silhouette ... it was the shape of a person, but not a big person – a small person, maybe five feet tall. It was a skinny person."

What frightened Stoor most was her inability to move or cry out. "I remember trying to lift my head and move my arms. It was like something was on top of me, holding me down. I tried to yell, and I couldn't yell. My mouth was open and nothing was coming out. I was trying so hard to either wake up, or get up, or snap out of it, and it felt like something was stopping me from doing it."

After a few moments, the figure disappeared, leaving Stoor frightened but still wide-awake. She felt uncertain whether the experience was attributable to a sleep-paralysis dream, a ghost, a demon or an alien. She admits to a long history of similar experiences, though only on this occasion did she see a figure. Later, however, further experiences would prove to Stoor and her friends (who became involuntarily involved) that she was having genuine UFO encounters.[370]

On September 14, sometime after midnight, Diane X. and her four children experienced a face-to-face encounter with short gray-type ETs in their home in Hercules.

Diane also reports that this was only one of "numerous nighttime visits" in her home, and that she has experienced visitations by "several short aliens" for a period of years. Whenever Diane experienced a visitation, one or more of her children would invariably also report an experience.

Richard Haines Ph.D., who investigated this case, writes, "I have several drawings made by these children on the morning after an alleged visit. They show a disk-shaped object and several beings with detailed pear-shaped heads with large, dark wrap-around eyes. According to Diane, they had never drawn such picture before and told her that these were the 'friends who came to play with us last night.'" Diane later went under hypnosis and recalled an onboard experience.[371]

Maria X. (age 42) of Sherman Oaks is a divorced mother of two boys. She lives alone with her younger eight-year-old son. Her older son moved out because Maria was experiencing repeated visitations by gray-type ETs. At around 2:00 a.m. of November 29, 1988, Maria woke up again to find an alien in her bedroom. Says Maria, "There was a being evidently assigned to keep me absolutely frozen to the spot ... he seemed most unhappy with this task .... He was standing like a sentry."

Maria was particularly upset because her eight-year-old son was also in the room and each time she tried to open her eyes to see him, she was forced by the "sentry" ET to close them again.

After a long mental struggle, Maria gave in. Her next memory was waking up the next morning. During breakfast, she asked her son if he had a good night's sleep. He replied, "Yes, and you know what? My aliens came back!" Like Maria, her son was unable to recall any onboard sequence, however, he vividly recounted how it felt to be taken *through* the closed front door. As he told his mother, "Well, you see, once you get half way through it, it's not wood anymore ... it's really neat. It changes into lots of little colored balls. And that's the most fun part and the only time the aliens ever get mad at me is because I like to stay in the middle and look at the balls for a really long time. But they tell me its dangerous to say in the middle. I have to come out the other side."

Says Maria, "He was disappointed about that. But he was very emphatic and then he went on to ask what was for lunch later ... and he dropped the whole subject. It was just as matter of fact as could be."

Writes Richard Haines Ph.D., the primary investigator to this case, "I worked with Maria over an eighteen-month period. She claimed to have had over fifty separate visits, one every eleven days on the average. This event took place during the middle of this sequence."[372]

On December 26, 1988, physical therapist Teri Smith of Chatsworth was staying with her boyfriend and three other people in a four bedroom condominium. She and her boyfriend slept in the same bed in one room. They were alone. In the middle of the night, Smith woke up to find herself paralyzed and unable to see or cry out. She felt a sharp pain in her ankle, as if it was being held by a metal clamp.

After an intense struggle, Smith sat up and saw a light move out of her room through a closed window. Outside the window, she saw the light transform into a foggy mist which then entered inside a large white egg-shaped object which was landed in the alley-way behind the condo. The object immediately took off straight up and moved out of view. Says Smith, "I just saw this bright light leave the room, and then – which really sounds stupid but it's what I saw unless I'm crazy or dreaming – I saw this, I don't know, a spaceship or something. It was round, and it just took off. It looked like a round-like space-ship, I have no idea, like a flying saucer. It just went shew!!! ... and up and gone." The next day, Smith experienced severe pains in her ankle, however, no marks were visible.

She called up her best friend, Traci Stoor, and told her the incident. To her shock, Stoor revealed a long history of similar encounters (see above.) And not only that, Stoor's boyfriend was staying with Stoor, and he also reported a visitation identical to Smith's on the same night, only a few miles away. As happens in some cases, encounters can apparently spread like a contagion.[373]

People experience ET contact in many different ways. A rare case of telepathic contact occurred to Maryann X., a waitress from Carpinteria. Maryann had seen a UFO before and therefore knew that they were real. This knowledge, however, did not prepare her for her dramatic encounter, which occurred four years later in October of 1992. She was in her home watching television when she became overwhelmed by the feeling of a presence in her home.

Suddenly an image filled her mind. She saw the typical gray-type alien. As she says, "He's hairless. He's pale. He's short. He's very thin. [His eyes are] almond shaped and they're dark, and there are no pupils …. He doesn't wear anything, but it's kind of an asexual body. You can't tell who the male or the female is."

Maryann felt the impulse to perform what is known as automatic writing. Placing a pencil in her left hand, she began to write messages coming from the ET, who called himself Kevin!

Says Maryann, "He's very interested in our interest in him and his race. He calls it a race … [and] that they've been here for a long, long, long time. Longer than we have, from what I understand … they're vastly interested in us. They're almost more interested in us than we are in them. They're fascinated by us. They don't think the same way we do."

Maryann was given considerably more information. The ET told her that their population numbered in the billions, that they've been around for centuries, that they inhabit the oceans, they are a benign race and are just here to observe. He warned of upcoming tragedies, and expressed concern that Maryann was not overly scared by the encounter.

Maryann reports that she later experienced several episodes of contact during which further messages came through.[374]

On January 16, 1994, the night before the powerful Northridge earthquake, Marcellina X. and her boyfriend observed a large unidentified object hovering over their home in Topanga Canyon. Says Marcellina, "It came flying over the water tower. It was so big … the thing was huge … it was shaped like a crystal, like a rectangular-shaped thing, but it was pointed at the front. The whole thing had red flickering lights."

The large object appeared to be towing a smaller object with a beam of light. Marcellina and Lewis watched the objects as they moved low overhead and disappeared. Both heard a low buzzing noise emitted from the object.

A few hours later, the devastating Northridge quake struck. Marcellina couldn't help but think that the UFO sighting was somehow related. Then, a few weeks later, Marcellina experienced a face-to-face visitation with an extraterrestrial in her living room. She was sitting on her couch when a figure suddenly materialized in front of her. Says Marcellina, "It kind of looked like it was a cat face without any hair, and a combination of a skeleton face."

Marcellina attempted to rise up and get her boyfriend, but she was suddenly unable to move. The figure began to speak to her telepathically. Says Marcellina, "It was telling me that they were trying to invent ways of intercourse. They needed babies. They were just telling me a bunch of things telepathically. There would be more earthquakes."

The being told Marcellina several other things, describing the nature of his planet, and that Marcellina had psychic healing abilities. Following this experience, Marcellina realized she was pregnant. Says Marcellina, "Then about four months later, I had a miscarriage and there was nothing in the sack."

She later went under hypnosis, but was unable to recall any new details. She also says that as a result of her encounter, she has become deeply spiritual and profoundly psychic.[375]

The above cases represent only a small sample of the total number of landings in California. And, as intense as these cases are, the next chapter focuses on cases of UFO abductions, during which people are actually taken onboard the alien craft.

16. UFO Abductions in California

See color section, page 123

One of the most controversial aspects of the UFO mystery is the abduction phenomenon. Today, thousands of people claim to have been taken on board UFOs where they undergo a variety of experiences, and there are good indications that the experience actually occurs to millions.

While UFO abductions weren't reported until the 1960s, according to the witnesses, many of the cases actually happened considerably earlier. In some cases, the memories of the onboard experiences were retrieved through the technique of hypnotic regression. In other more rare cases, the witnesses retained full conscious recall of the onboard events. In either case, it is essential to remember that, virtually without exception, abductees have varying degrees of conscious recall of unusual UFO/ET events.

The earliest California cases began way back in the 1930s. In 1988, Victoria X. of San Bernardino decided she wanted to lose some weight. She decided to try hypnosis, and was delighted to find it very effective. She began losing weight immediately, so she continued the sessions. To her shock, during one of her hypnosis sessions, she spontaneously recalled being taken onboard a UFO, at around age five, sometime in the early to mid-1930s.

She recalled that she was looking out the window one evening at a peculiar-looking star. Suddenly the star began to move. "It just comes down. It just gets bigger and it comes down." The next thing Victoria knew, she was pulled up into the light and into a craft. She found herself surrounded by tall, thin figures with large, roundish, bald heads. They told her, "You don't have to be afraid. You'll just think it was a dream."

Victoria didn't recall much else about the encounter other than the aliens staring intently at her. Her next memory was waking in bed, thinking it was just a dream. She quickly forgot about the incident. Starting from this day, however, Victoria would experience regular visitations throughout her life.

For Victoria, each onboard experience followed the same basic pattern: she was laid out on a table and eggs were removed, and then one of the ETs would drain her mind of information. For her the experiences were extremely unpleasant, and each encounter involved a battle of wills between her and the aliens. While Victoria fought to remember the encounters and protect her thoughts, the ETs seemed bent on exploring her mind at their leisure.

Says Victoria under hypnosis, "There's the table again. It's always the table you lie on .... 'You're going to give us everything.' But I don't. That's why they get so angry at me. I keep part of me, and they get real angry at me. He tried to penetrate all of it. With his eyes."

Victoria asked them why they were trying to pull information out of her brain. They replied, "You don't have to know. Only we know. You wouldn't understand."

She asked them when they would stop. They replied, "You don't ask questions. You aren't here to ask questions. You're here to do what we say."

Victoria, however, refused to give in or cooperate, particularly when the ETs removed her eggs. "I don't want them to have any part of me. I really feel robbed because they took it! They take my eggs! They knew how to probe and get them. And that's mine, not theirs .... They took me back. When I ovulated, they took me back and took the egg."

To her shock, Victoria saw another human person also in the same room. Says Victoria, "A male. They take his sperm. I don't know what it is they have ... it's like a suction they have on him ... on his penis .... He fought too. That was the other yelling I heard .... I'm just lying there. I'm cold all over."

Victoria's next memory was "just going fast. Real fast. And then the machine opens and I'm out in my backyard in San Bernardino. They had my daughter. They had Susie. She came out with me. We're sitting on the patio, and she's telling me about the little blue man."

Once she came out of hypnosis, Victoria was shocked. She recalled that, at that time, her daughter talked constantly about her encounter with a little blue man. "That's where she got the little blue man! She's always telling me that she was talking to a little blue man, and I just thought it was her imagination."

Victoria recalled several other encounters and believes she's been abducted on about ten occasions. Often she has seen many other people of different ethnicities also lying paralyzed, subject to strange examinations. "I'm just sort of elevated there. The other people are in the same position. We're all just kind of at this angle ... there's a row of us. I can't see the end. We're from all over, I know that. I know we're just not all from our country. We're from all over the world. That's what we were doing. We were hovering and picking up people from all over the world .... I feel like they're taking something, but I don't know what. They're not letting us know. We're afraid and at the same time, we're calm ... they're putting different rays on us. I don't know what they are, but they're zooming to different parts of our body. It hurts when they do this ... they've put something in us that makes us glow. They can see everything and all of our functions inside .... It's like a glowing substance."

Victoria recalled her eggs being removed several times. "They're just taking what I have. They want to try to reproduce us ... there. And become them, so they can mingle here and not be noticed. They told me. They can reproduce us on their ships."

Victoria feels violated by her encounters, and blames her weight problem on self-esteem issues caused by the trauma of her UFO encounters.[376]

In 1952, 14-year-old Monty X. was riding his bike when he saw a bright reflection moving across the sky. Says Monty, "I realized this light was very, very high, and the fastest thing I ever saw. It was directly above Mount Wilson, about one thousand feet and following the main ridgeline heading southeast over Monrovia, Azusa, and Montclair. It was huge. Disk, oblong, white, orange and as big as two Pasadena Rose Bowls put together. It traveled that distance, approximately fifty to sixty miles in about eight seconds, then shot straight up and out of sight."

Monty told his family, who were skeptical until the next day when the *Pasadena Star News* published an article about the sighting with direct quotes from other witnesses.

Twenty-one years later, in 1974, Monty was employed by the U.S. Forestry Service, had a wife and four young children. It was about 11:00 p.m. and the entire family was driving through the San Bernardino mountains between Lake Arrowhead and Crestline. Suddenly, the entire family experienced an extremely disorienting period of missing time. They all found themselves waking up simultaneously with the car parked by the side of the road, only twelve miles from home.

The incident wasn't discussed for twenty-two years, at which point Monty spontaneously recalled the period of missing time. Monty describes what he remembers, "I saw lights in my rear-view mirror. The lights were approximately one mile behind, very bright, and catching up with me .... The lights were almost behind us, very quickly, when I realized that the lights were above the road. I thought it must be a helicopter but there was no noise. Our kids began to yell ... the car was losing power, not missing, just slowing down. Diana was now screaming. David was crying ... the car stopped. It felt like the car was dragged to the side of the road. I couldn't move. I could see straight ahead but could not move my neck. It was like a blue fog. I heard the right door sliding open with a loud bang. I heard the driver and passenger doors open ... I saw movement. I was out of the car. The next thing I remember is waking up, parked on the side of Old Waterman Canyon Road."

Monty's son, however, had retained full conscious recall, and later told his father, "I could see them through the open side door. They looked like giant bugs, long spindly arms and huge bug eyes. Like a praying mantis. Dad, they take you and mom first. Mom was still screaming. Then Dave, Diana, and Scott. I'm last, but they couldn't release my grip from around the seat. The bugs tell me to relax. I can't, nor would I voluntarily. My body becomes relaxed and they release my grip. I'm terrified and again, paralyzed. It was like I just floated out and up. Bright, bluish light. I'm inside a dark place, and then I wake up in the car, parked on the side of the road, wondering if I had a bad dream."

According to Monty, everyone else in the car also remembers the event about as much as he does. While this was the most intense encounter he has ever experienced, Monty would soon experience other dramatic sightings.

In 1975 he and his family purchased a home in Twin Peaks, in the heart of the isolated San Bernardino mountains. The family of six was staying in their home one April evening when suddenly the entire house was engulfed in light coming from above. There was absolutely no noise. Says Monty, "The kids began screaming their heads off, yelling and crying. An extremely bright, bluish light from outside completely enveloped our home, inside and out."

Monty ran outside. "This very bright light had just moved to the north, below the ridge top. And light was radiating through the pine trees. This event lasted no more than ten seconds."

Monty scanned the newspapers for information about the event, but found no verification. However, a few months later, another family vacationing nearby experienced a similar event.

It was an early Fall evening in 1993 when Monty stepped outside his Hemet home. He was about to have his latest encounter. "While looking towards the mountains I noticed a very small bright light that began to move extremely fast in one direction, then quickly shoot in another direction. No human could survive G-forces of that type of movement. I estimated this light would move ten miles in one second, then instantly go in the reverse direction. This went on for about thirty seconds and the light shot out of sight."

Again, Monty scanned the newspapers in the following days but received no verification. He has reported no further encounters.[377]

While there are a few scattered abduction reports from the 1930s and 1940s, it wasn't until the 1950s that the cases occurred in large numbers.

One late afternoon in the fall of 1952, six year-old Ron X. and his family were in their home in Redding. Suddenly, the entire family observed a gigantic silver craft, "oval in shape and as big as a city block" hovering over the treetops outside their home. Says Ron, "We all just stood there staring at the strange object, not saying a word to each other. Beneath the craft we could see an orange light coming out, which covered a large area below it ... .We could not take our eyes off this strange craft. We could see nearly every detail on its bottom side as it moved slowly over the house. It made no sound as it passed over us."

The disk continued on and disappeared over the horizon. Ron and his siblings wanted to chase the object, but their mother refused to let them outside. While the disk was no longer visible, events were still in progress. Later that evening, when going to bed, Ron was shocked to see that the room was glowing with blue light and his twin brother was staring at a strange figure at the foot of his bed. Looking over, Ron observed a gray-type ET. Says Ron, "His head was large and he had no hair. He had large black eyes, and his skin was very pale. He was also tall and very thin. He was wearing a black cape that wrapped around his shoulders and hung down to his knees."

Ron turned to yell for help, but found his path blocked by another identical figure. All fear strangely left him as he felt himself taken out of the house and into a nearby floating craft. Says Ron, "As we walked in, I noticed there were no corners to the walls – no corners at all – and the walls seemed to be somewhat bowed ... there were corridors going off in all different directions. Halfway down the hall on the left were some symbols, and in the middle there was a large window or screen. I could see planets and solar systems, and I had the sensation that we were moving past them."

Ron was escorted into a room and placed in a chair such as in a dentist's office. A device was placed over his head and he saw "pictures of my life and who would be involved in it."

One of the beings spoke with Ron, telling them about their activities. Ron was then medically examined. At the end of the experience, he was told that they would return and that he would later speak publicly about his experiences.

One week later, Ron reports that his entire family was taken onboard, although most were left with only very sketchy memories of the experience. Ron, himself, recalled being placed in a room with other children he did not know.

Many years later, in 1992, Ron coincidentally met one of these children that he saw onboard the craft. The lady reports that she lived in nearby Mount Shasta, which is sixty-five miles distant from Redding. Says Ron, "She remembered being picked up by a spacecraft and placed in a room with other children."

Years later in 1963, at age seventeen, Ron experienced his second major encounter. His family had just moved to a rural ranch outside Corning. On several occasions, while driving to the house from nearby Orland, Ron and his grandfather observed unexplained lights in the sky. At the same time, the local newspapers reported UFOs in the area. Then, one evening as the family was preparing to watch TV, "a light engulfed the house and a 50-yard circle around it. It was so bright it seemed light daylight," said Ron. "We all ran into the kitchen and peered out the screen door. It was so quiet you could have heard a pin drop. But no one dared to go outside to find out what was happening. After only a few minutes, the light went out."

Everyone returned to watch the program as if nothing had happened. That night, Ron was visited again. "I awakened to see a little guy beside my bed. He was about three feet tall. His head was quite large, and he had large black eyes. His skin was grayish in color. The room was filled with the same bluish light I remember from 1952. Another alien was standing silently in the corner, but it did not approach me."

The purpose of the visit suddenly became clear. The figures told Ron telepathically that they were there to warn him of an impending tractor accident which might befall his twin brother. The next morning, Ron warned his brother about the accident. His brother, however, remained skeptical and operated the tractor. Unfortunately, the accident occurred as predicted, badly injuring his brother.

Two years later, in 1965, Ron X. and his twin brother were working for a power-line company in Storey, just north of Oroville, the location of a number of encounters. After retiring one evening, just before the holidays, Ron and his brother were woken by the now-familiar blue light invading their room. The room filled with gray-type aliens who quickly escorted the brothers out of their room to a nearby field and into a landed craft. Says Ron, "When we entered the ship, the aliens took us to a very bright room and placed us on reclining chairs. The tall ET came closer, and I could see his face more clearly. His skin was very pale, with a texture like snake skin or fish scales, but very smooth and defined. There was a small slit for a mouth and a flat surface that did not protrude outward for a nose. As he placed his hand on my arm, I noticed his fingers were quite long and had no joints."

Ron and his brother were placed on tables and given a thorough medical examination. Afterwards, Ron asked for a tour of the craft. "I went off alone with the tall alien at my side. We entered a small room with a large screen, and he showed me different star charts in our galaxy and told me where they were from ... he took me into another room where the walls were covered with unfamiliar symbols. He began to explain how the craft was able to move from one planet to another, and how it could move in different atmospheres."

Because he was an electrical worker, Ron was amazed when the ETs told him that the craft had been storing energy by hovering over the very power lines he was working on. Says Ron, "The spacecraft just flies over a high tension-line and collects the excess voltage released from the power lines."

Ron reports that his twin brother also recalls the encounter, although he was not very comfortable with the experience. However, Ron says, "As I look back on this visitation and the others I have had, I feel a sense of serenity deep inside me. I know the ETs are here to help us to look at each other in a much different way, to find love and peace within ourselves and with the rest of the world. This is the best hope for mankind."[378]

On March 23, 1953, one of California's most famous UFO abductions took place. Sara Shaw and Jan Whitley (pseudonyms) were staying in their isolated cabin in the Tujunga Canyon area. At around 2:00 a.m., the two women awoke to find an eerie blue light filling their cabin. They were planning to get up and investigate when they experienced about two hours of missing time. Confused and afraid, they left the cabin in a panic. Years later, under hypnosis, they recalled that they were apparently abducted by the now-familiar gray-type ETs, out of their home and into a landed UFO.

Sara Shaw describes one of the entities as being "not ugly to look at, or funny looking, but they're kind of funny in a way ... his head is elongated. It's like an egg, but one that isn't really wider at the top or the bottom." Sara noticed that the entities were tall, thin, and hairless. "If there's any hair, it's underneath this skin-tight – it's like a ski mask, but it's almost part of the skin."

The two ladies were taken aboard the craft via a beam of light. Says Shaw, "I'm on the beam of light. I'm standing on it and it's angled .... It's about the same angle as an escalator would be, except it doesn't have ridges or steps. It's just a very smooth, solid beam, and you just kind of stand on it."

Once inside, the witnesses were amazed by the enormous size of the craft. Says Shaw, "The inside of the ship is like one giant room, and there's a second level above us. It has circular balconies ... the balcony goes all the way around the entire inside."

The two ladies were taken into another room, laid out on tables, and given a thorough medical examination. The ETs seemed particularly interested in Jan Whitley's surgical scar. Shaw was then given a few messages concerning a possible cure for cancer, and other technical details which she was unable to retain.

Afterwards they were returned to their cabin with only partial memories of the event. Later on, both would experience subsequent encounters, which also spread like a contagion among their close friends. The entire story is told in the book *The Tujunga Canyon Contacts,* and is too long to recount here. However, this case was the first publicly revealed California abduction and marked a new phase in the investigation of UFO encounters.[379]

The story continued in June of 1956, when Jan Whitley, her friend Emily Cronin, and Cronin's young son were driving through the isolated Tujunga Canyon area late at night. At one point, they decided to pull into a rest stop and wait for traffic to thin. While they waited, the car suddenly became enveloped in a light which paralyzed the occupants. Says Whitley, "I couldn't turn or move anything. It seemed to go on forever. I felt the car swaying back and forth."

Says Cronin, "I was paralyzed too. But from where I was lying, I could see some of the light flooding in the car and illuminating the floorboards. I couldn't turn my head to find out what was causing it."

After a few moments, the paralysis broke, the light winked out, and the witnesses looked at each other in speechless confusion. They immediately drove home. Later, they tried to find the rest stop and were shocked to find that it didn't exist. Says Whitley, "The rest stop should have been unmistakable. It was really big, wide enough for three or four huge trucks to park in. But we couldn't find it, or anything to indicate it had ever existed."

This was just the beginning of the Tujunga Canyon abduction contagion. In the months and years that followed, Whitley, Cronin, and Shaw each reported nighttime visitations by large bald-headed entities. Later, another of Whitley's friends would also experience bizarre nighttime visitations by entities with large, bald heads.[380]

In May of 1957, Emily Cronin of the Tujunga Canyon group, experienced a missing-time abduction while driving through Kern county. The incident was recalled under hypnotic regression. Cronin remembered pulling her car over impulsively to look at the sky. At that point she saw a glowing sphere-shaped object hovering at tree-top level. The craft came in for a landing, and Cronin heard the telepathic message, "Do not be frightened." At the same time, she could make out the shadowy forms of two figures in the semi-translucent craft. At this point, the encounter likely continued, but Cronin's memory ended. No further details were ever recovered.[381]

In 1970, at the age of sixteen, Lori Briggs, a friend of the Tujunga Canyon group of abductees, lived in Redondo Beach. She awoke one evening to find strange figures in her room. Says Briggs, "I was frozen when I awoke. I couldn't move. I was very aware that there were beings in the room, and I really didn't know what they were .... They hadn't allowed me to open my eyes yet. I was frozen, totally frozen. And then my whole body was turned."

Later, Briggs was able to open her eyes. She immediately saw a strange-looking pair of hands. "They were very thin, and they were long. And then my eyes went up to its eyes. That's the only thing I was conscious of. I don't even know the power those eyes had, but they were extremely intense."

After gazing into her eyes for an undetermined period of time, the beings suddenly left. Briggs recalled that the beings were also very short.

She would soon learn that her group of close friends was also experiencing similar events. Five years later, she would have another dramatic encounter.[382]

One summer evening in 1974, Lori Briggs awoke in the middle of the night to hear a strange whining noise permeating her Panorama City apartment. At the same time, an eerie white light filled the entire apartment. Briggs' roommate, Jo Maine, also awoke to hear the noise and see the strange light. Seconds later, several figures entered through the closed door and into the apartment. Under hypnosis, Briggs recalled what happened next.

"One of them is right next to me .... Short! Really short, three feet, maybe four. I don't know anybody that short .... It doesn't have any hair .... It's so thin. I've never seen anything like him. Big head .... The eyes are so powerful .... It's just so different, so strange. And there's others, but they're just standing by the door."

Briggs watched in amazement as the figures floated about one foot above the floor. One of them pointed at her, and she felt herself promptly levitated. Encased in the strange light, she was floated out of the apartment and into an egg-shaped craft landed in the field next to their apartment. She recalled being placed above a stone-like table, where she remained floating a few inches above the surface. A powerful pink light, like an x-ray, shone down upon her. Says Briggs, "It's almost as if my veins and arteries are tubes in which the blood almost seems as if it's light going through them .... I think I'm being studied ... they do so many things with light."

As in virtually all such cases, the beings conversed with Briggs using telepathy. As she says, "They let me know some things ... once in a while they'll explain a couple of things to me. It's not as if they explain it in my language. But suddenly I know it ... inside your head."

After the examination, Briggs was floated back into her bedroom. Her roommate, Jo Maine, recalled only the light coming into the apartment, and a vague sense of being transported to another place.[383]

In the summer of 1953, Melissa MacLeod was a newlywed. She and her husband had just moved in together in their Los Angeles apartment. One night, MacLeod was awakened by a loud "whirring" sound. She crept around the house, looking vainly for the source. Her next memory was of waking up the next morning. She had experienced an episode of missing time. At the time, she didn't know what to think of it. Unfortunately, this was only the beginning. One year later, she would experience another missing time encounter, this time in conjunction with a close-up UFO sighting. And still later, in the 1970s and '80s, she would experience regular nighttime visitation by unwelcome entities.

MacLeod's next episode occurred in 1957 in the San Gabriel Valley. At the time, she had two infant children. She and her neighbor were together in her yard with the children when they all observed a large, silver "blimp-shaped" object flying overhead towards the East. It was so low above the ground that both women ducked their heads, thinking it would crash. At that point, her memory ends, and she is unable to recall what happened next. All she can recall is that she and her neighbor never discussed the incident.

Following this occasion, MacLeod began to experience nighttime visitations by hooded entities that would enter her room and render her paralyzed. MacLeod eventually learned how to successfully defend herself by mentally struggling against the entities, or by using intense prayer. By using these methods, MacLeod was able to end her encounters as they began.[384]

One interesting case of contact took place on May 10, 1957, to Shirley McBride, a resident of Tujunga. On the evening in question, McBride was driving alone through Kern County when she saw a small, glowing, translucent sphere descending towards her. As it approached, it expanded to a large oval sphere containing two figures which spoke to McBride, saying, "Do not be afraid."

An onboard encounter apparently took place, which instantly became shrouded in amnesia. Years later, McBride underwent hypnosis and recalled a long telepathic conversation. Interestingly, however, she refused to reveal the contents, saying only it was "a secret" and was deeply personal. She placed her loyalties with the apparent ETs and when asked what they said, would only reply, "All life is one."[385]

Around nine o'clock on a summer night in 1958, two teenaged girls, Dorothy Hudson and Carol Serrano, spotted a metallic saucer-shaped object hovering above the Pio-Pico Library in Koreatown. Says Hudson, "We saw this light in the sky. Whatever it was kept getting bigger and bigger and bigger until, all of a sudden, it came down and it was hovering above the street over the library …. We looked up and it, and it had a lot of lights on it. And it was still. There was no noise coming from it. It was still, but the lights were moving around it." Hudson reports that the disk was metallic and was easily "as big as a house, but perfectly round."

At that point, Hudson's mother arrived to pick up the girls. She also observed the object, which she described as a "flat light, like a plate that was all lit up – it was shining from the top and the bottom, but it just stayed in place like it was hovering."

The three witnesses began the five-minute drive to their home. To their surprise, the object followed them directly over their car. As Carol Serrano says, "We went home and it followed us home …. I was kind of scared … it seemed kind of weird that it picked on us."

Once they arrived home, they watched the object for a few minutes until it quickly moved away. It was then that they noticed a strange time discrepancy. It was already ten o'clock when they arrived home, although they had left the library at nine o'clock, shortly after it closed. Since the ride home only takes about five minutes, there is nearly an hour of missing time. As all UFO investigators know, missing time can be indicative of a hidden UFO abduction scenario, which can sometimes be recovered through hypnotic regression. To date, the witnesses have declined to undergo hypnosis and have reported no further encounters.[386]

On June 26, 1959, Andy Reiss of Los Angeles was in his bedroom when strange images began to appear on his television set. When the same thing occurred the next night, Reiss became highly intrigued. At that time, he received a telepathic message and was then somehow beamed onboard a craft. Says Reiss, "I became aware of a new and different environment, and saw a huge egg-shaped object. I was escorted inside the spaceship and met several of the crew, composed of ten men and two women. They seemed to be operating computers and electronic equipment."

Reiss reports that the crew members were all human-looking and very friendly. He was floated through the craft and taken to a large room with a glowing emerald-green map. The beings told Reiss that the earth is going to experience massive environmental changes, and that human beings must learn to raise their spiritual vibrations."

Reiss was returned to his room. A few days later, he experienced a dramatic sighting of "a huge orange-red fireball climbing at a 45 degree angle above Ocean Park, California."

Since then Reiss has had numerous sightings, including one in the presence of the author of this book (see Chapter 17).[387]

In 1962, a mother and her two young children experienced a dramatic missing time encounter in Topanga Canyon. The ordeal began when Beverly Smith (pseudonym) decided to drive to the local store. On the way home, Smith and her two daughters (aged seven and five) encountered three shiny, metallic silver disks hovering about a quarter mile away. Says Smith, "You could see them really clearly, and it was just really strange."

The three witnesses exited the car to better observe the objects. They watched the objects for about fifteen minutes, at which point they decided to return home to retrieve a camera and binoculars. That was the last thing they remembered. They returned home two hours later than they should have. Says Smith, "None of us remember coming home, and we didn't think about it until the next day .... It was really strange."

Says her daughter, "It seemed to me there was a fight about how long we were gone, between my parents."[388]

In 1963, the Sanz family moved into their brand new home in the suburbs of Arleta. Throughout that year and for several years afterwards, the two youngest daughters, Karen and Susan, experienced repeated weekly visitations by a figure that they termed the "muddy man." Although both children saw the same thing, neither told the other. However, not only do their descriptions of what they saw match, the description is typical of gray-type ETs, which were becoming increasingly reported.

Both sisters agree that the figure was interested only in Susan and it was often seen by them standing near her bed. Says Karen, "[It was] three or four feet tall, bald ... it had a very tall forehead ... his eyes were big and went around the side of his head. He had a neck and it was bony. He floated off the ground ... and he always went over to my little sister's bed. Every time I saw him, he would come over and he would look over at me, and then he would go to the foot of the bed of my little sister. I was always afraid that he was going to take her away. I would just try to stay awake because I thought he was going to hurt her."

Despite her efforts, Karen was never able to remain awake. She says that she saw the entity more than a hundred times on a weekly basis for a period of five years. Whenever it entered their room, both girls would unaccountably fall asleep.

Susan also remembered seeing the figure. As she says, "I do remember the shape of him very clearly. It was dark, but he was shaped ... like those aliens you see. That's the only way to describe it. I could tell it was a short little person .... He had a thin body. There was no way he was a regular person. His head was bigger than his body."

Although she didn't know why, Susan felt that the aliens were intensely interested in her. As she says, "I really feel that there was a curiosity about them when I was a child. There was a definite awe when they were looking at me, like, 'Wow, check this out. Isn't it interesting?' All that I remember is being frightened, but I had the distinct feeling that there was a curiousness there."

The visitations continued until around 1968, then suddenly stopped. The sisters grew up and moved out. Twenty-five years passed. Susan now had a little child. It was then that the visitations began again.

It was around 5:00 a.m., on a February morning in 1993, when a UFO landed in the backyard of the home of Susan Sanz of North Hollywood. On this particular morning, she woke up to go to the bathroom. She returned to her bedroom to sleep but became unaccountably anxious. She suddenly felt herself falling unconscious. Her next memory was being in the living room, watching a "cylindrical" shaped object land in her backyard. Says Susan, "These aliens start to get out of the ship, about four or five of them. And they were wearing what looks like trench coats, and they were carrying something. I don't know if it's a briefcase, if it's a box, something, I'm not sure."

Susan remembers becoming panicked with terror and then blacking out. She woke up to find her cat "very close to my face, growling with hair standing on end and his eyes wide open, looking at the door."

While she can't be completely sure, Susan does believe that the experience was real. As she says, "I feel like there was actual contact."

Susan's experiences continued and would eventually involve her daughter and husband. Around this time, her daughter complained that a "little man" had come into her room. Susan didn't think anything of it until she saw a strange scar on her daughter's leg. She was amazed, because she carried an identical scar in the same place, and she didn't know how she got it.

Then, one month later, in March, Susan's husband, Hector woke up to see a strange light hovering outside their bedroom. Sometimes helicopters would hover over their home, but this was totally silent. Says Hector, "It was weird because I wasn't really sure what it was ... the light was shining through the mini-blinds and through the curtains on the window. It seemed like somebody was looking in, but it wasn't a bright light. It was bright, but it wasn't real bright."

As soon as he saw it, Hector instantly thought, "Oh, it's Susan's aliens." He did his best to ignore it and just go back to sleep. "I felt like I knew who it was, and basically being scared I guess, I didn't want to see what was going to happen."

This case is very complex and still ongoing.[389]

In 1967, UFO researchers Brad Steiger and Joan Whitenour announced that they were working with a young California woman, described as "highly distraught," who claimed to have been "raped by an occupant of a UFO." Today, many others have made similar claims, but at the time, only a few such cases existed. Today, claims of genetic hybridization between humans and aliens is a dominant theme among onboard UFO accounts. The so-called "missing-fetus" syndrome is a typical example.

In this particular case, Steiger and Whitenour were able to speak with the abductee's doctor who confirmed that the witness did, in fact, experience a bizarre pregnancy. The doctor told them that he "treated the young woman for a premature delivery of a still-born baby that seemed to have been the product of highly dubious mixed breeding." Unfortunately, the fetus was not saved, and possible conclusive proof of UFO reality was lost.[390]

In 1967, twelve-year-old Paul Nelson (pseudonym) and his friend were in Paul's parents' boat in Avalon Harbor in Catalina when they both experienced an episode of missing time. Says Nelson, "It was just after dark, far away from sleep time. We sat down, got our comic books open, and then instantly we were unconscious. The next thing we realized, it was morning."

Paul and his friend were certain that they had experienced something unusual, though Paul's parents felt that the boys had just fallen asleep. Then, about three weeks later, Paul was alone in his bedroom in Sherman Oaks when he experienced another strange episode. As he says, "The door was rattling as if there was somebody at the door. And I could hear footsteps outside the door. I thought there was an intruder."

He flung open the door and was surprised to see that shadow of "a small little being" on the wall. The figure ran away and disappeared. Paul checked all the windows and doors and couldn't find any opening. Nobody else was present in the house. After searching the house for the intruder, he returned to his room and didn't think much more about it. Twenty-five years later, Paul was a doctor, married with children. In 1992, he observed a glowing star-like object maneuvering in the night skies in the deserts outside of Los Angeles. He developed a sudden interest in UFOs and then recalled his earlier anomalous experiences.

A few years later, he found himself in the office of a well-known southern California researcher undergoing hypnotic regression to see if he was actually abducted. Under hypnosis, he recalled that he was, in fact, abducted on both occasions. Interestingly, on the first occasion, he was taken to an apparent underground area.

Says Nelson, "I was taken into a round-walled room. It seemed to me more underground than it did onboard a ship. The walls had kind of rock-like facet to them. And I was on a table ... there were some machines on the walls. The beings weren't the typical grays, they were more the 'Praying Mantis' type ... the eyes were slightly bigger than what is seen in the typical small gray, and a little more insectoid-like .... They wear tight fitting uniforms ... jumpsuit-like things. I think there was one in that bunch that had a tunic-type thing, more looser fitting over it."

Nelson recalled being examined and told to wait while they examined his friend. He was unable to recall many more details, nor how he was transported to and from the boat. He reports feeling no fear and was, in fact, intensely interested and curious.

The second encounter was also recalled using the technique of hypnosis, although not many details were retrieved. Says Nelson, "I remember them being in the room, and then I'm onboard the ship, and then they're back in the room making sure I'm okay, and then exiting out the door, after which I chased them."

Today, Paul feels a little ambiguous about his recall and wonders if it was just his imagination. At the same time, he is unable to explain the initial missing time event or the intruder in his home. Like most abductees, he has insisted upon total anonymity.[391]

While some people enjoy their encounters with UFOs, some people are not so lucky. Bill X. is today a medical professional, married with two children. Back in 1967, when he was a teenager, he went camping with his friends in the Los Padres National Forest near Santa Barbara. It was there that he experienced a terrifying ordeal. He woke up to find himself out of his sleeping bag and away from the campsite. Looking up, he observed a bright globe of light hovering above him. His shouting woke up one of his friends and they both observed the UFO zoom away.

Years later, Bill sought out prominent southern California UFO researcher and hypnotherapist, Yvonne Smith. Under hypnosis, he investigated that incident and recalled being taken into the craft by four gray-type ETs. He was placed in a glass-like canopy. He was unable to move as his rectum was painfully probed and semen was then removed. Bill has no delusions about friendly space brothers, and reports that he was treated with the respect of a rabbit in a research lab. As he says, "I know what it feels like for a woman to be raped .... I didn't like it at all."[392]

A rare feature of some onboard UFO encounters is that people are sometimes given information on how to build an anti-gravity device or energy-free engine. One such example occurred one summer evening in 1968 to Helen X. and three friends while driving the freeways between Lompoc and Los Angeles. Suddenly, the four travelers were approached by a UFO.

Says Helen, "Out of these hills came a white light, and it moved up and began to come in our direction. An airplane couldn't have turned the way it did, so we figured it was a helicopter. Then it began to do very erratic things and twists, go very far out and come closer very quickly ... all four of us were very aware of it .... Dave and Barbara were afraid of it. George and I were encouraging the whole thing; we enjoyed this."

Then the object came very close. Says Helen, "It came up over the car in front of us, maybe 100 to 200 feet above the ground, and it was, I would say, about six lanes of the freeway in width. It was white, and it showed a very beautiful kind of glow. I seem to remember some kind of windows, but I really couldn't be sure. It didn't make any noise. The thing was big."

Without warning, the object hovered directly over the car. Says Helen, "Four white lights, funnel-shaped, extended from the perimeter of the vehicle and down around each of our bodies."

Helen's next memory was of being pulled *out of her body* along with her friends and into the craft. Then there was a time-lapse and "the next thing I remember I was coming back into the car. I looked around and saw the light shimmer around Barbara and Dave, and we slowly dissipated back into our bodies."

Following this incident, Helen became obsessed with building an energy-free machine. Later she underwent hypnotic regression in the hopes of retrieving more information. During the session, she recalled being taken onboard the craft. She was greeted by a human-looking person dressed in white who showed her the propulsion mechanism of the craft.

The account was researched by investigator Jacques Vallee, who contacted two of the other witnesses, both of whom corroborated Helen's story. As of yet, Helen has not constructed her "energy-free" engine.[393]

Also in 1968, an anonymous family in a small northern California town experienced a bizarre encounter. At the time, the main witness, Mike X., then eleven years old, recalled being drawn outside by something, coupled with a profound anxiety about UFOs. Years later, under hypnosis, he recalled what happened.

While the family inside appeared to be put into a trance-state, Mike and his mother were both drawn outside to observe a "lead-colored cylinder" swoop down out of the sky and land behind a hill next to their home. Four robot-like beings emerged and converged on his now-panicked mother and floated her out of view behind the garage. Says Mike, "During this time, I remained frozen in a corner of the front of our house. I looked to my left and saw a praying mantis figure heading towards me. It had a long head, moderate-size torso and long, skinny limbs. Its fingers were long and thin and had a gentle appearance. As it came closer, I turned, buried my head in the corner of the house and wet my pants. I was frightened beyond description."

The being then grabbed Mike's arm, at which point all fear left him. He was led into the craft, which had low rounded ceilings and was lit with a violet light. A table slid out from the wall and Mike was laid down, examined and then injected with a strange fluid. At one point he was shown a strange book. Says Mike, "The book had four rows of three 'Chinese-type' bright orange letters .... I believe the contents were about the balance in the universe, love of all living things, the peril of Earth, and coming changes."

Mike was taken into another room and told that on a later date he would remember all that had occurred. The beings placed a strange device upon his head and Mike found himself shooting back homewards. He found himself, disoriented, in his backyard. He returned only with the memory that something very unusual had happened.

Years later, he and his brother would both experience another dramatic face-to-face encounter. In late 1992, Mike X. and his brother both simultaneously dreamed that if they went to the foothills of the Sierra Mountains in northern California, they would have a UFO encounter. They felt strange about planning a trip because of a couple of dreams, but knowing that they had a history of UFO encounters, they decided to just go.

They drove to the foothills and were surprised to find the scenery that matched their dreams. They parked, and walked into a clearing by the road. Around sunset, Mike and his brother suddenly found themselves surrounded by "a dozen deer, all looking directly at us." They experienced a period of missing time and found themselves alone and dazed.

Later, under hypnosis, Mike recalled that the deer were actually "several beings of small stature – less than four feet tall – and dressed in hooded black robes." Mike reports that the beings placed their hands on his body and all of them were instantly elevated into the sky and into a craft, where he was given various messages about himself and humanity.

When asked why he was contacted, the beings told him that it was his destiny to help create a world government for all people on Earth. Amazingly, today Mike is very politically active and influential. As he says, "My political business now includes consulting in the former Soviet Union and in the newly formed European community. We have been asked to run elections in support of democracy-minded candidates in the Russian Federation and have consulted with European Parliament on the creation of a European referendum process."

Mike attributes his profession to the influence of his encounters, which he feels have been mostly positive. As he says, "I do not have any negative feelings or memories of bad experiences."[394]

So closes the California abductions from the 1900s up to the 1970s. We now move to another mystifying aspect of UFO encounters: accounts in which UFO investigators have their own encounters.

17. UFO Investigator's Disease

See color section, page 124

There is a dark secret within the UFO community. It's rarely discussed for the simple reason that UFO investigators prefer to remain objective in order not to contaminate their research. However, as many researchers have discovered, objectivity becomes shattered when the investigator becomes the investigated. It is a clear-cut case of the hunter becoming the hunted. When professional mainstream journalist Ed Conroy began his investigation into the abduction experiences of horror writer Whitley Strieber, he found himself a target of numerous kinds of UFO phenomenon, including a possible abduction. A surprising number of prominent investigators have now revealed that they themselves have had extensive UFO experiences. Conroy calls this condition, "UFO Investigator's Disease."

Ann Druffel is one of southern California's most influential UFO investigators. Like many investigators, her interest was sparked by an early childhood encounter. It was 1945 and she was living in Long Beach. Says Druffel, "I saw an object or greasy blob of golden light in the clear blue sky ... little tiny bits came out of the craft, but didn't fall to the earth. It frightened me."[395]

One of the first California investigator-abduction cases occurred on August 31, 1971, at around 2:00 a.m. Two young men were driving near their home on Dapple Gray Lane in Palos Verdes when they experienced a missing-time encounter with a UFO. While the witnesses have considerable conscious recall of the encounter, especially the beginning, under hypnosis a unique and bizarre onboard encounter was also remembered.

One of the men, John Hodges (pseudonym), had been interested in UFOs for years, and was an active southern California UFO investigator. He describes what he recalled consciously: "We got into the car, turned on the lights, and directly in front of us were two 'extraterrestrial beings.' Pete only remembers the larger one to the right, but I remember both of them."

Hodges went on to describe what looked to him like two giant floating brains. "They were both the shape of brains with the dura matter still intact – kind of a filmy bluish."

Says Hodges' friend, Pete Rodriguez, "The shape wasn't perfectly round – the edges were lumpy or like deflated. It was about the size of a basketball."

At that moment, Hodges and Rodriguez became frightened and confused. They drove home, only to find that they had had two hours of missing time.

Later, under hypnosis, Hodges recalled that after they first saw the beings, he became engaged in a telepathic conversation with the floating *thing*. Says Hodges, "It is talking to us, not with words, but with something in our mind ... telling us we must be careful, that there are many things we do not understand. If we do not take the time to understand ourselves, we will be the instruments of our own fate ... that there are many like us and we will come to know our place in the world."

Suddenly, Hodges felt himself enveloped by a strange force. He then found himself in "some kind of large room. There are people there, but they're not like people ... they are tall, skin gray, yellow eyes, very thin eyes ... mouths, but no lips. Funny flat noses. Their hands have long thin fingers, six fingers and a thumb. They're webbed more or less from the palm to the first knuckle. Their feet are much the same. They're barefoot but not naked, wearing gray vests and gray pants, looks like a kind of plastic or vinyl, with a spongy cuff ... something like a donut around their ankle. No belt, but a line seems to separate the pants from the vest. They're about seven feet tall."

Hodges described the room as being gray in color with computer-like instruments along the edges. He was told by the ETs that humans were abusing atomic energy and that we're in danger of destroying ourselves. He was shown a television-like screen which showed various atomic explosions that would take place unless humanity changed.

He was then told that he would not remember the events until much later, and that they would meet again. At that point, he felt a strange "buzzing" force envelope him and he found himself back in the car. He and Rodriguez drove home with no conscious memory of the onboard segment.

Rodriguez also underwent hypnosis but did not recall being taken onboard. Today, Hodges has mixed feelings about his encounter. He feels like the whole experience was almost like a "display," and might not be what it appears to be. He also felt that the warnings about atomic proliferation might have the purpose of persuading humans to dismantle their weapons so that the aliens can take over more easily. Hodges speculates that the encounter may even have been demonic in origin.

Ann Druffel, who investigated the case, says, "The Dapple Gray encounter is possibly the first land sighting of occupants around this area."[396]

In 1975, county mental health director Richard Boylan was hiking with a friend in the foothills north of San Francisco when they saw a typical flying saucer fly only a few thousand feet overhead. Says Boylan, "If I were to guess, it was maybe thirty feet wide. It was very clearly not a manmade object, no fuselage, no wings, no tail, no helicopter rotor, exhaust, noise, or anything else ... it was a round, dull gray metallic object – flattish round, not an orb, more like a disk. My friend saw it too. We didn't know what to make of it."

They watched the disk move against the wind and off into the distance. Boylan turned to his friend and said, "What do you know! I bet we've just seen a flying saucer."

Boylan kept thinking about the sighting and, as a result, joined the Mutual UFO Network as a field investigator. He later earned his Ph.D. and today is a prominent northern California investigator, investigating more than fifty firsthand accounts of UFO abductions. In 1992, while driving through Arizona, he experienced his own missing-time abduction.[397]

In 1979, in Saratoga, northern California psychologist Edith Fiore Ph.D. was given a UFO book by a family friend. She immediately became "intensely interested" in the subject. She soon joined UFO groups and studied the various accounts. Intrigued about the possibility of making contact, she started to send out mental "messages" and "pleas," hoping for a sighting or message. Around this time, Fiore had a dream in which she was taken onboard a UFO. "My hosts treated me as an honored guest and colleague. I sensed that they were humanoid, not the least bit frightening or strange."

Fiore only recalled a few segments and assumed it was just a dream. However, later she went under hypnosis by famed northern California researcher James Harder Ph.D. Under hypnotic regression, a different story was revealed. Says Fiore, "We quickly discovered that indeed I had been contacted. I had been floated out of the bedroom in my condominium in Los Gatos into a spaceship. Once there, I was treated with respect and kindness and much was explained to me that I was not to remember until later. Then it would filter into my mind, more as memories than as knowledge, and would be very helpful to me. Jim got a description of the aliens and the room."

While Fiore still feels some ambivalence about her recall, a month later, she started treating UFO abductees professionally as a psychologist. In the next few years, she would soon counsel nearly fifty people who had onboard experiences, making her one of California's leading investigators. Although equally famous for her work on dealing with patients suffering from "possession," Fiore would also become the first person with a Ph.D. to author a book on UFO abductions.[398]

On May 28, 1991, prominent southern California MUFON field investigator Bill Hamilton and several others observed UFOs over the desert city of Lancaster. A trained observer, Hamilton describes his sighting vividly. He said the object was "boomerang-shaped with several strobe lights dancing around its perimeter .... [It] was white with an amber tinge. It moved west above the mountain ridge, reached a certain point, then started strobing fluorescent red and white lights. As it continued to move west, and then northwest, it began to jump and dance in erratic movements."

UFOs often visit the same area on consecutive nights. For that reason, Hamilton and thirteen others returned to the same location the next evening. To their amazement, they observed nearly thirty distant star-like objects several thousand feet high that "danced and zigzagged at all compass directions." Incidentally, Hamilton had previously experienced an onboard encounter while in the desert near Area 51, outside Las Vegas.[399]

In 1996, Dr. Roger Leir DPM, best-known for his implant removal surgeries, reported having a strange dream which he hints might have been an actual contact experience. In his dream, he found himself standing in a "court-like setting" in a room with wood chairs and wood tables, and diffuse lighting.

He was shocked to see several figures file into the room and seat themselves in the chairs. "I couldn't make out much detail other than they were all about the same size, under four-feet tall, and were wearing shiny silk-like garments which seemed to wrap around their bodies. Each had a sash belted about the waist and a hood thrown over the head and draped over the shoulders."

One of the taller figures stood behind a levitating lectern and began to command to Leir, "So, you want to know the secrets. Who do you think you are to ask this of us? Why do you persist in your quest?"

Further bizarre conversation ensued, much of which was unintelligible, when a loud whirring sound enveloped Leir and he found himself waking up in bed. He assumed that he had just had a dream but then he was given reason to wonder if the experience was more than just a dream. As Leir says, "My next conscious thought was that of being back in my room, in bed and lying next to my wife. My daughter had climbed into bed with us and was sitting straight up staring at me. I must have had a surprised expression on my face. She leaned over and whispered in my ear, 'Daddy, where were you?' I thought I was going to have an instant heart-attack. What in the world did she mean?"

Leir vowed to ask her the next morning, but never did. To this day, he remains undecided if any actual contact occurred. However, he did receive further confirmation when he discovered that he had unexplained marks on his body that would fluoresce under ultraviolet light, a condition that turns up occasionally with other abductees.[400]

An astonishing case of contact took place in May 1997 to an anonymous UFO researcher under the name Bonnie X. That evening, Bonnie had attended a UFO lecture in Ventura and was returning home on the Pacific Coast Highway when she noticed unusual flashes of light coming from above. As she was passing a strange-looking vehicle parked by the side of road, her car suddenly became encased in a powerful light beam. The windshield instantly cracked. Considerably alarmed, Bonnie continued driving with the cracked windshield and returned home.

She wasn't sure if she had missing time, but the obvious anomalous nature of her experience persuaded her to explore it further. Under hypnotic regression, she recalled a powerful and friendly onboard experience. She recalled that when the light hit her car, the car engine died and the vehicle was lifted upwards and into a craft.

Says Bonnie, "It's a great big room. All around me, a circular room with hallways and doors going off it. And there's a lot of light too, but not as bright as the light I was in. But now there's a whole swarm of – I want to say people, but they're not really people. They're all around the car ... they've got these big liquidy eyes and bald heads. I mean, they're not threatening at all. They're curious and childlike and friendly. And they're just peering in, and tilting their heads now to get a better look ... they are very thin. I guess we could call them bony."

The beings unlocked the doors of the car and floated Bonnie into another room. Says Bonnie, "In the middle of the room there's a chair that has arms. It has a headrest, and a footrest and a foot place ... like a dentist's chair .... They're putting me in it .... They're putting something over my head from behind, that is part of this chair thing. It must be adjustable, and it fits right around my head."

The beings told Bonnie to relax. They then began to scan her mind for information. According to Bonnie, they seemed especially excited to have found an actual UFO researcher. For Bonnie the experience was in no way frightening. Instead, she felt excited, awed, and honored. After recording her memories, the beings thanked her and explained that they were only borrowing her memories and not stealing them. They also told her that they were contacting many people and trying to learn about humanity. Bonnie learned much other information during her onboard experience, which she feels was a benevolent encounter. Today, she continues to do important research in the UFO field.[401]

I personally know of several other California-based UFO researchers who have had sightings or abductions, but are not willing to come forward. As for me, I must admit that I have contracted UFO investigator's disease. I have had about a dozen sightings, with some interaction between me and the UFOs. Most of these have occurred in the presence of other witnesses. None occurred until I began to investigate the phenomenon.

My first sightings involved anomalous lights. In the summer of 1989 I was with a group of about twenty UFO enthusiasts, including psychic Andy Reiss (whose onboard encounter is described above) when we all observed a star-like object dart over the city of Santa Monica. Reiss actually called the UFO down and it appeared exactly when and where he said it would.

Around that period of time, I left my brother's home one evening and was driving to my home when a sphere of light the size of a golf-ball swooped down from the sky, hovered in front of my windshield, and then took off. I have since had that experience a couple of times.

During my investigation into the Topanga Canyon UFO wave, I experienced several sightings of anomalous lights. The most impressive occurred on the evening of July 16, 1994. I was in Topanga leading a group of UFO watchers and attempting to make contact. I suddenly had the impulse to look up. When I did, I observed a small pinprick of light which quickly expanded in size until it covered a good portion of the sky. Seconds later, it winked out.

I later received independent confirmation of my sighting when two witnesses called me to report their sighting, which occurred at the same time and less than two miles away. In their case, they observed a solid metallic craft, covered with multi-colored lights. I had several sightings of this type as a member of the group CSETI (Center for the Study of Extraterrestrial Intelligence).

One of my most impressive sightings occurred around 1994. I was working closely with a UFO abductee/contactee who claimed to have encounters regularly with friendly gray-type ETs. I told her I would like to see a UFO and she agreed to try and arrange it. I was amazed when she called me back and said that she had received a telepathic message to be at an appointed place at a certain time and a UFO would show up.

Needless to say, we piled into the car and traveled to the location, a dirt road heading directly off the 210 freeway in Pasadena. The instant we had hiked to the end of the dirt road, I was amazed to see an incredible sight: a golden sphere covered with sparkly lights rose up from the canyon right next to us. It was about the size of a house and less than fifty feet away, maybe about twenty feet above the ground. It was breathtakingly beautiful. It moved swiftly parallel to us and then darted ahead, around the side of the mountain and out of sight. We took off chasing it but were unable to follow. It didn't appear to be a solid object, rather a dense spherical concentration of gold, sparkly lights. In any case, it was definitely unexplained.

The witness is named Elise. She says of the sighting: "We looked up and there was that thing, that gold ship that was shooting through. And we ran after it, chasing it. It was so close I thought we could jump high enough to touch it …. It sparkled, with gold sparkles shooting off of it all over the place … it was awesome. It was pretty spectacular. I mean, it was gold."

Elise later arranged another successful sighting for me, convincing me of the genuineness of her case.

In July of 1995, after closely associating with another abductee, I had a close-up daylight sighting of a massive triangular-shaped metallic craft which moved overhead at an apparent altitude of about one thousand feet. It was obviously a solid craft and had three circular impressions on the bottom of it. It appeared to be almost translucent, as if it was somehow cloaked. I observed it from the parking lot where I work as an accountant in Canoga Park.

Around that same time, I observed another metallic triangular-shaped craft which scooted across the sky. On this occasion, there were five other witnesses. My sister-in-law, Christine Kesara Dennett, was there. She describes the sighting: "This spaceship came down … it was the shape of a boomerang except a little bit thicker and more V-like … it had the appearance of being transparent. It probably had a highly reflective surface … and it just flew right over us, slowly. And it was lower than a jet aircraft unless it was huge … it was in broad daylight, and we had six witnesses. I know the two neighbor girls were there. They were like, 'Wow, we just saw a UFO.'"

18. The California UFO Healing Cases

See color section, page 125

A UFO healing can be defined as an encounter that results in the physiological improvement of the witness. There are approximately 150 cases of UFO healings on record from across the world. Not surprisingly, California is the leading producer of such accounts, generating over ten percent of the total number.

In 1945, Ted X. of Santa Clara was about three years old when he experienced a fully conscious encounter with extraterrestrials. Says Ted, "I woke up from a nightmare and looked up and there was a person next to my bed." It was a strange figure, short, bald, a large head, dark wrap-around eyes.

Ted also had other clues that something strange had happened to him. At the time, he suffered from angioma, a medical condition involving a malformation of the blood vessels in his brain. As a result, he became paralyzed, lost his ability to speak, and stopped growing. Doctor's gave him six months to live.

It was at this time that Ted had his encounter. Immediately, Ted's condition began to improve. Ted told his parents that "doctors had cut the top of my head off." He had other memories of figures that look like the "Pillsbury Doughboy" who would communicate with him telepathically.

Amazed by the change in his condition, Ted's parents placed him in a hospital in San Francisco where doctors performed exploratory surgery. To their amazement, Ted's condition had reversed itself and he was perfectly healthy.

However, ever since that time, Ted became "obsessed" with UFOs, spaceships, astronomy, and aliens. The obsession remained with him throughout his life, and when he reached his mid-forties, he began to seriously question the source of this obsession. By this time, he was an accomplished artist and had drawn scores of highly detailed pen-and-ink drawings of various spacecraft. He finally sought out Edith Fiore Ph.D. to explore the extent of his experiences with UFOs.

Not surprisingly, Ted recalled a complex abduction at around age three. Under hypnosis, he recalled that the beings had large, bald heads, large eyes, and pale white-green skin. He also saw another type of being which looked "more like insects ... kind of like a grasshopper."

Says Ted, "I'm in a room in some kind of craft. And the room is round and there's lights and dials along the walls ... it's very clean, very smooth, and it domes. There's almost no furniture in it except for the panels of lights and this table that contours around the room."

At one point, Ted reports that he was probed by a metal pencil-like instrument. "They take this probe and they touch different parts of my body .... They press it up against the skin in different parts. This probe registers information on the dials that are on the wall."

Ted was next told that there were "enlarged tissues" in his head, and that he needed an operation. He was laid out on a table and laser-like instruments were used to open up his head. "They took an instrument and they cut open the top of the head, all the way around. And they were able to remove that part of the skull and look at the brain .... They've taken a laser device and they've cut around the skull ... they're taking an instrument, it's like a laser ... to heal something. They probe around the brain, they touch all over and find the enlargement. And with the laser light, they're able to shrink it."

Ted reports that the aliens were fascinated with him, and told him telepathically, "We are here to help you." They told him that they were currently on a space-station distant from Earth. They told him that he was healed because he was needed as a contact, and that they would return to him for another contact when he was older.

At that point, he was "transported" back home. As he says, "I see these apparatuses coming down from the sides, and they're like laser instruments. They point these down at me, and there are four of them, and they beam energy down. And my body changes into a different kind of matter, into light particles. And I travel back to the place where I began, and at that point, I materialize. I'm inside of the house. I'm back in bed now. And I wake up, and this person is standing in front of me."

Ted was left only with the memory of the strange figure standing at his bedside and the feeling that doctor's had cut off the top of his head.

Seven years later, in mid-1952, ten-year-old Ted X. of Santa Clara had his second onboard UFO experience. Later, in his mid-forties, he recalled what occurred using regressive hypnosis. Says Ted, "I'm sitting in a chair in a room in a craft. It's run by a group of mechanical beings. Metal robots. They're checking my body. The room is filled with different kinds of instruments and dials and lights. I'm in a chair that's similar to a dentist's chair, with contoured arms on each side. There's another robot behind me. I'm being studied, but I don't know why."

Ted was unable to recall much more about the encounter other than the strange appearance of the robotic beings. Later, in 1980, while in his mid-forties, he experienced his third and latest encounter.

On this occasion, he was abducted from his apartment. Says Ted, "A beam of light came down through the apartment, surrounded me and changed me into a different molecular structure, and then it took me back into the small spaceship. And from there I was taken out ... into space, away from Earth. And we came to this colony where all these different spaceships were. I was taken onboard a larger spaceship or space station. I'm in the chair. I'm being examined by the robots."

Ted recalled that several sensing devices were passed up and down his body. A blood sample was taken from his arm. He was then taken to another room and laid down. His next memory was waking up in his apartment.

Since that incident, Ted has reported no further contacts.[402]

James X. is today a successful southern California physician. He occasionally sought therapy from a psychologist because he found it useful when confronting various life issues.

During one of his sessions, he underwent hypnosis and spontaneously recalled a complex UFO abduction scenario which occurred around age eight, sometime in 1959. He recalled "being transported up on a kind of pallet. I don't understand how it happens, but I'm moving .... Maybe I'm in a bubble. I'm going right inside this big thing. Just right up. It looks like your usual depiction of a spaceship, but it's going right up inside this opening."

James recalled being taken inside a strange room and laid out on a table. He was unable to move as various instruments were placed in his nose and ears. A dome-like contraption was placed over the top of his head. He began to feel an electrical zapping sensation and experienced some fear.

They then injected his chest with two needles. "They're putting needles in both sides of my chest! I don't know what they're doing. I don't know why, but they've got these things in both sides. It's really strange .... It feels like a clamp on my heart." Sperm samples were taken.

James was then moved through the craft on the floating pallet, and was surprised to see numerous other people encased in bubbles, floating on pallets like his.

He was then floated back into his bedroom. He reports that as a result of his encounter, he was healed of severe headaches that had been caused by a recent concussion. Many years later, as an adult, James would have further encounters.

In his mid-thirties, James experienced an incredible shock when he realized that the aliens had come back for him. Just after buying his new home, he began to have bizarre recollections of strange figures in his bedroom. He discounted them until hypnosis revealed a history of encounters. Says James, "They look gray and they're maybe five feet tall. They have oval heads ... "

Fiore agreed to place him under hypnosis to explore the memory. James recalled waking up to find several gray-type ETs in his bedroom. He was unable to move as he was placed on a strange "pallet" which floated him up and through the wall "... and into that big ship that's sitting out over the trees. I don't understand why people can't see that."

James was taken up a ramp and into the craft. The aliens were talking about the dangers of announcing their presence in a physical way to humanity and were interested in James' reaction. It was his job "to explain the way people think .... I feel like a negotiator ... I feel like I'm being interrogated."

James reports that other people were also questioned in a similar manner. He was shown some of the alien technology, such as an x-ray device that allowed them to view the inside of a body. "They're demonstrating it on somebody. First an alien and now a human ... on the television screen, you can see the different energy channels, just like they're interspersed with the arteries and veins. It's like our MRI, except it shows not only tissues, it shows the energy channels."

He was shown other people being operated upon and was given considerable information about the various causes of disease. They told James that he had part of their genetic material and they expressed surprise that he had survived a childhood inoculation. He was given further information and then was returned home in "a small, round-shaped craft of some kind. It's got a clear canopy in front. It's not very big ... it lands in the backyard. And I am kind of led because I'm in a semi-awake state. I'm led back to my door. The doors open and they wait there while I get into bed."[403]

Sometime in the 1950s, a four-year-old girl from southern California experienced an episode of sexual abuse by a family member. Years later, under hypnotic regression, she recalled a visitation by aliens in which they healed her of the injuries received during the abuse. As researcher Barbara Lamb MFCC says, " ... this lady was taken by her 'little people,' the little gray extraterrestrials, and taken aboard a spacecraft. And they did a sort of whole medical procedure on her, the little gray guys did. And there was a female [ET] too, who was a little bit larger. And the female was standing by her side on the medical table on the craft. And the female was explaining that something was done here that should not have been done, and that the other ones – the little ones – were needed to fix this, to repair this. Because they wanted to be sure that everything would be fine in later years for having babies."[404]

Another rare case of a UFO-affected healing took place sometime in 1986 to a gentleman from La Jolla. As reported to researcher Brad Steiger, the main witness, Richard T., was wheelchair bound due an undescribed condition. While enjoying an evening alone on a nearby beach, Richard T. was shocked to see a 100-foot-long torpedo-shaped UFO hovering above him. The next thing he knew, he was put into a kind of trance. He then felt himself lifted up into the craft, still in his wheelchair.

Richard experienced no fear as he was examined by "smallish humanoids with large heads and enormously large slanted eyes." The next thing he knew, he found himself seated in the front seat of his van with his wheelchair tucked away in the back.

The most fantastic part of the whole experience, however, was the after-effect. According to Steiger, "Amazingly, over the next few weeks, his condition began to reverse itself – until he was finally able to walk again with the help of a cane."[405]

Licea Davidson of Los Angeles has been having UFO contacts since early childhood. Then, in 1989, she was diagnosed with terminal cancer. Doctors were unable to operate because the disease had metastasized throughout her colon. She was given three month to live.

She then experienced an abduction, during which ETs placed her on a table in a small rounded room and gave her an extensive operation to cure her cancer. Says Davidson, "I was abducted. They told me I had cancer. They said, 'Relax.' And they did a cure. It was excruciating."

Davidson was then returned to her home. She made an appointment with her doctor, and was not surprised to discover that all traces of her cancer were gone. She has recovered her medical records and reports that her cure has been verified by a major medical university. She also states that she fears the United States government (who has harassed her extensively) more than she does the aliens.[406]

Another family whose lives were changed by the UFO phenomenon are the Van Klausens (pseudonym) of Burbank, California. The case is well-known among southern California UFO investigators and is very well-verified. The Van Klausens have not only seen UFOs, they have received regular visitations starting in December 1986 and continuing through the 1990s. The main witnesses are Morgana Van Klausen and her son. The husband remained skeptical until he too experienced a visitation. Both Morgana and her son experienced regular visitations by a short, gray-skinned, bald-headed, large-eyed figure. Whenever it would visit, both would experience total paralysis. On a few occasions, she was able to end the visitations by mounting a physical struggle against the paralysis. By breaking the paralysis, the bizarre figures would dematerialize. While skeptics may say that this sounds like sleep paralysis, the Van Klausen case also involves several close-up UFO sightings, missing-time encounters, landing traces, and medical proof of extraterrestrial intervention.

On December 4, 1994, Van Klausen went to the doctor and was diagnosed with a tumor in her breast. The chief investigator to the case, Bill Hamilton, says, "An x-ray found a peculiarity in the axillary segment of the right breast. This was followed by ultrasonography over the same area. A small non-cystic mass measuring 1.6 x .6 cm was found in the problem area."

Surgery was scheduled for December 14 so that Van Klausen would have time to recover from a slight fever. On the day before the surgery, she was driving with her son when they observed a "white, triangular-shaped craft" hovering nearby. They watched it for a moment until it suddenly darted away. Her son became very excited and said, "Mom, look! Wow, this is a good sign – they are protecting us. We are protected. You wait and see, you'll have no more problems."

That evening, Van Klausen was overcome by intense pain in the area of the noncystic mass. She tried to get up out of bed, but was unable to move. She sensed strange figures in her room. At that point, she lost consciousness. She woke up the next morning and went straight to the doctor to have her surgery. That's when both she and her doctor got a huge surprise.

The doctor inserted a needle into the mass and took another x-ray. To everyone's shock, the new x-ray showed that there was no mass. Another ultrasound was ordered, which confirmed that the mass had disappeared. Says Hamilton, "Both the radiologist and the surgeon confirmed that the previous diagnostic had revealed a solid mass and that solid masses don't just disappear."

Hamilton has obtained the medical records, which confirm the disappearance of the mass. He speculates that the aliens may have been removing an implant, but as he says, "The explanation is only speculative." Whatever the case, Hamilton reports that "Morgana reported that she felt an unusual sense of well-being after the mass was gone."[407]

Linda and Sherry X. of northern California are sisters who have shared amazingly positive onboard UFO experiences throughout the 1980s. While neither of them had any conscious memory of this, Linda sought help from psychiatrist Edith Fiore Ph.D. to deal with depression. Fiore placed her under hypnosis and a complex contact scenario emerged.

Linda recalled being inside a strange room and lying on a table. She next recalled that strange beings were operating upon her. "They're opening me up here, my stomach. I don't understand what they're doing. There's no blood. They just open me up ... they're cleaning this black junk out of my stomach region. They said I had cancer! They were trying to help me."

Linda then recalled that the beings placed various instruments on her body. "It's like glass, little round pieces of glass ... they're round and smooth and they had little lights on them. And they placed them all over my body."

Linda describes the aliens as, "very, very small, very small heads, kind of pointed .... They've got big eyes."

She recalled undergoing several other strange procedures. The beings communicated with her, warning about upcoming Earth changes and teaching her alternative healing methods. They implored her to meditate daily, exercise, and eat correctly. "They're telling us we have to learn these things, it's for our survival. The world will come to an end if we don't learn these things ... "

The aliens told her, "You should understand that we mean no harm. We are here to change the world ... to keep it from disaster. Which is imminent, if people keep living the way they do .... There will be changes so powerful that only the strong will survive. We are here to give knowledge and understanding to the world of light and the world of children of God."

Linda recalled many other remarkably positive events. She saw several members of her family onboard. She recalled seeing many other people healed of various ailments including bursitis, intestinal worms, tumors, and more.

She also recalled how the beings return her to her home. "They put us in smaller vehicles. They're full of light. There's lots of lights going ... there's a driver. They take off. We're going over some trees. Aha ... I'm home. I'm back in bed."

Sometime in 1988, Linda and her sister, Sherri, were both miraculously cured of their yeast infections. It occurred overnight, at which time Sherri had a vivid dream that she was taken onboard and healed.

Both Sherri and Linda underwent hypnosis to recall the incident. On this occasion, Linda recalled how the aliens came to take her. "They take me out the front door. There's some kind of a vehicle. It looks about the size of a car and has lots of lights, and it almost looks like glass with a bubble roof over the top. The three of us get in. They put me in the back part and we go real fast. And pretty soon we're landing in a large, large, large spaceship. It's huge! I can't believe the size. It's just huge."

Linda recalled being laid out on a table and cured. "They use an instrument of some kind. It looks like a big cotton ball on a stick. You know how when they take a throat culture? It's kind of like that, and they're swabbing me inside ... they're cleaning it out somehow, swabbing it out. They have this jellylike substance that looks like aquamarine blue, and it's clear, it's transparent .... I told them it feels cold. They say that's to help freeze the bacteria. And then they take it out."

Linda was then given more spiritual information and was shown several other people being healed, including her sister, Sherri.

Under hypnosis, Sherri recalled many details that confirmed Linda's memory of events. Says Sherri, "I was lying on a table or some flat surface that seemed like it was stainless steel. I don't remember any faces, but there was a doctor, or someone I perceived as a doctor, and there was some kind of machine that, I was told by mental telepathy, could analyze if there was anything wrong in my body and could also kill bacteria that wasn't good .... I was being examined vaginally ... some kind of cream was being put inside of me ... it was a little cold and really messy ... they said it would take care of the yeast."

Like her sister, Sherri also saw many other people being operated upon. "I can see there's a machine over somebody, and I can see all the bones in their body through the top. It's like an x-ray, but it's fluorescent green."

She also agrees that the beings are "very loving" and totally benevolent. While both sisters did experience some fear during their recall, especially when being operated upon, both insist that the experiences are, overall, very positive. They both feel that they have been physically healed and given much spiritual insight by the beings. Their encounters continue.[408]

Ann DeSoto of Watsonville was driving with her boyfriend near their home one afternoon in December 1988 when their car was suddenly enveloped in fog. A short time later, they saw a bright, orange globe of light hovering over a nearby field. Desoto had seen UFOs before and was very interested in them, so they turned the car and headed towards the light.

At that point, they experienced a period of missing time. Their next memory is walking into DeSoto's boyfriend's house nearly five hours later. They both went inside and fell into a deep sleep.

The next morning, they both found that the bed sheets had blood stains. DeSoto also had a strange-looking mark on her hip. Even more incredible is the healing that took place. As the report on her case says, " ... the arthritis she carried for years in that hip, disappeared."[409]

Connie Isele of Sacramento, California, had experienced a number of unusual events, but never attributed them to UFOs until 1989. Around that time, she began to be woken up by strange figures coming into her bedroom at night. Although she didn't realize it at first, she was encountering extraterrestrials. Says Isele, "The ETs are not too pretty to look at, though. One being I see frequently has a hideous head he hides behind a bright glow, and a long thin torso that moves like an insect's body. He reminds me of a praying mantis. This being seems to be an advisor or teacher, whereas the 'doctors' are short little beings. Being examined or operated on by a human doctor is not exactly fun, so being examined or operated on by nonhuman doctors with big bald heads and big black eyes can be even more uncomfortable. Yet I have no complaints, ... for example, in 1989, I received an ET 'health checkup' during which they injected me with a clear gel, similar to white grape jelly. I was informed that this was for my benefit, that this was for healing. There were also lights involved in the procedure."

Isele reports that when she awoke the next morning, the jelly-like substance still clung to her skin and had to be washed off in the shower. Isele is convinced that ETs cured her of severe uterine cramping, a problem she had been suffering from for several weeks prior to the experience. Following the visitation, all symptoms disappeared.

In 1992, Isele reported her second UFO-related healing experience. She awoke one morning to find three evenly-spaced bruises on her knee. Since the discovery, she also noticed that the arthritis that she carried in the knee completely disappeared. She has had no pain since.

Then, in November of 1995, Connie Isele and her friend were in a tragic automobile accident which left Isele gravely injured. At the hospital, her doctors told her that her right leg would have to be amputated. Isele, however, believed that the ETs could heal her. In desperation, she prayed to the ETs for help. Isele is convinced that they responded. Says Isele, "It was an extraordinary feeling to wake up, alive. Out of the corner of my eye, I saw an ET, a very tall being with whom I was familiar. When I turned to look at him directly, he was no longer there." To everyone's amazement, Isele recovered quickly and her leg was saved. The doctors were so stunned, they gave her the nick-name "miracle legs."[410]

Late one evening in 1991, a twenty-one-year-old anonymous female was driving with her sister through the outskirts of Claremont. For years she had suffered from intense chronic back pain. As they drove, the sisters spotted a disk-shaped craft hovering above them, sending down a beam of light. Researcher Barbara Lamb describes what happened next, "The car stopped. So they got out of the car and started running across the field. And they were followed by a beam of blue light. And the beam suddenly struck her in her lower back and she felt it radiating right through her, and felt a very, very powerful energy."

The witness was running in terror from what she thought was going to harm her. Ironically, it had the opposite effect. As Lamb says, "As a result of that, she felt that she had been healed of whatever the difficulty was, and was actually quite grateful to them."[411]

One night in early 1995, Jean Moncrief of Los Angeles was wakened out of a sound sleep by three bluish-looking entities who came into her bedroom through the closet wall. The visits continued semi-regularly, and Moncrief became increasingly concerned. She had recently been diagnosed with a lump in her breast and, not having medical insurance, was afraid to go to the doctor. Around this time, she had another experience with the entities, only on this occasion she recalls being taken away to some other location. Her recall was limited only to "being floated back to the bedroom." However, the next morning, the lump in her breast was gone. Instead, she had a perfectly circular mark of lighter skin where the lump had been. Despite her healing, Moncrief still feels violated. As she says, "The things don't give a damn about humans."[412]

As can be seen, UFO encounters are sometimes transforming experiences, leaving the witness profoundly changed in ways both spiritual and physical. Another such case took place in October 1997 to David Perez of West Covina. It was only a few weeks after the mass suicide in San Diego of forty-nine "Heaven's Gate" UFO cult members.

Perez stepped out of his apartment to smoke a cigarette when he observed an unidentified craft hovering a few hundred feet away. Says Perez, "It looked like a ship .... All I saw at first were the lights all the way around it. I never saw lights like that around a helicopter or an airplane." As he watched, the object started to flash lights at him. Perez's cousin and girlfriend came outside and also observed the object, as did his neighbor. At one point, the object sent down a beam of light which apparently struck Perez. As he says, "This red bright light went on, and it seemed like it kind of penetrated my pupils, and my vision turned red. Everything that I saw was tinted red ... that's when I got kind of scared. I thought it had screwed up my vision ... I couldn't talk, and I couldn't move or anything. I don't know if it was the fear or what, but I just couldn't move anything."

A few minutes later, Perez had an argument with his girlfriend, got into his car, and drove off. He reports that the object followed him from West Covina to Canoga Park, where it suddenly appeared again over his car. A strange feeling of comfort passed over him and he realized that the encounter was affecting him physically. Says Perez, "I was kind of stressed. I've always had problems with my back. I used to cough up blood once and a while. I was kind of sick. I had pains in my chest and on my side. Ever since that night, I haven't had any pain at all. And I was also suicidal. Ever since that night, I haven't been. I've been good. I've been feeling really good, really healthy."

Perez also started to experience premonitions and developed in interest in meditation and psychic development. He believes that the UFO is responsible for his spiritual awakening. As he says, "I kind of feel for some strange reason that they have something to do with God. Ever since then I've started talking about God."[413]

19. More Onboard Encounters

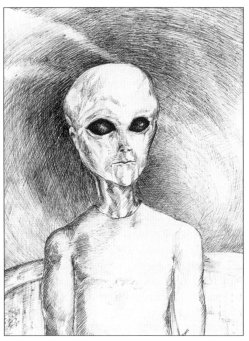

See color section, page 126

We have examined the California onboard encounters starting from early history to the end of the 1960s. We now examine the modern accounts. The biggest controversy over onboard encounters today is not their reality. As we shall see, investigators have uncovered conclusive physical evidence proving the reality of abductions. Instead, the controversy is, are these encounters harmful, neutral or beneficial? What are the long-term effects of these experiences? What are the ETs hoping to accomplish?

While the accounts are surprisingly consistent, it remains unclear whether the ETs are benevolent, hostile or somewhere in-between. An examination of the cases shows a fairly regular bell-curve, with some reports that are comforting and others that are disturbing. Some accounts are neutral. Whereas many may have both positive and negative elements, as in the following case.

Tom X. is a married professional from Santa Barbara. From an early age, he had numerous bizarre experiences with nighttime entities. Most of these experiences, however, were vague and ambiguous. But as he grew up, Tom experienced a series of dramatic UFO encounters. He eventually contacted researcher Michael Lindemann because he wanted to share his experiences in the hopes of helping others.

Tom has not undergone regressive hypnosis, and the encounters he describes are from waking consciousness. And as Lindemann writes, "Tom's case is inherently strong in the sense that there are additional witnesses to nearly every event he describes."

In June of 1971, Tom and his former wife were in their coastal Santa Barbara home, which overlooks the Channel Islands twenty-four miles out to sea. It was about dusk when the couple's attention was drawn to a very dramatic display of bright lights over the ocean. Says Tom, "At first I saw one object, and then there were three objects. I think the two additional objects may have come from the one original object, or they may have just appeared ... they appeared similar in size. From my vantage pointed they looked huge ... they had extremely bright lights that were shining down on the ocean, the brightest lights I've ever seen ... with the Channel Islands as a reference, I'd say they were probably the size of a football field. I'm not sure if all three went behind the islands, or just one or two of them, but I could see the islands back-lit by these extremely bright lights. I don't know of anything that could back-light the islands – not anything we know about, that's for sure. It was very difficult to believe ... they operated in an erratic manner. They'd stay motionless over an area with the light shining down, and then all of a sudden they would go to another area and the light would shine down again ... they appeared for about twenty minutes and then left. When they left, they went straight up at a speed that was beyond my comprehension. I'd never seen anything move that fast. It was like a streak of light just going almost straight up, and they were totally gone."

Tom learned later that there were several other witnesses to the event. At the time, he hadn't thought much about UFOs. Shortly following this sighting, he had a series of encounters which eventually led to the realization that he was a UFO abductee. Says Tom, "I've documented missing time on at least twenty-two occasions where there were UFO sightings or related activities."

Four years following his first sighting in 1971, Tom had one of the closest and most bizarre encounters of his entire life. At the time of his encounter, he was with a girlfriend, driving late at night through the Santa Barbara mountains. They were driving on east Camino Cielo ("sky road" in Spanish) and Painted Cave Road, the location of many Chumash cave paintings depicting possible UFOs and ETs.

As he drove, his headlights briefly lit up a metallic tower-looking object that was parked along a dirt firebreak road. Intrigued, Tom turned onto the firebreak to investigate. Says Tom, "What I found was a giant object that had three legs sticking out of it. My immediate thought was that it was a fire tower, because throughout the mountains up there they have large concrete structures that collect water for use in fighting fires. I thought this was a new type of structure. But on closer examination, it was an object that was made out of a material that I had never encountered before. It didn't have any seams or rivets. I drove up to the object and got out of the car. I walked around and underneath the object. Basically, it was saucer-shaped, probably 35 to 40 feet in diameter. It stood about six or seven feet off the ground, with three legs extended to keep it perfectly level. There were no markings of any kind on it.

"I parked my car just a little way away from it and allowed the lights to shine underneath it. I could not see the top very easily, but it looked to be about fifteen feet high. The material kind of looked like one piece, as if it were made in a mold or something. It was a sort of dull silvery-gray color, but it did not appear to be metal. I don't know what it was."

Tom later recalled that he felt a strong tingling sensation as he walked under the craft, but as he says, "at the time there was no noise, no lights, no sign of any activity whatsoever."

At this point, Tom realized that his date was "kind of freaking out and wanted to leave." Tom reluctantly returned to the car and they drove away. However, the encounter was not over. Says Tom, "I drove a very short distance back to the main road and encountered what looked like a rock on the road. It turned out to be an owl that all of a sudden flew straight at my windshield and over the car. This is a situation that has happened to me a dozen times in that area. And that was the point where there was missing time. From that particular moment in my trip, there's three or four miles that I couldn't account for. I couldn't account for driving it at all, although I know I had to have driven it. But the next recollection I have is of driving down the pass and arriving in Santa Barbara probably an hour or more later than I thought it was supposed to be."

Amazed by his encounter, Tom returned to the landing site the next day. He was easily able to locate it, and as he expected, there was no water tank. Nor was he able to find any landing traces.

He had already asked his date about her recollection of the event. Says Tom, "We discussed it very briefly, as to 'What the heck was that?' " Basically she became very jumpy and wanted to leave the area as quickly as possible. She did not want to get out of the car. She didn't want to talk about it later, and she never went out with me again. I think that the incident was probably very upsetting to her, and I don't think she wanted to be around anybody who had incidents like this happening."

Tom's recall of an owl in the road is a red flag to abduction researchers. In countless cases, abductees experience "screen memories" of an actual abduction event. Animals such as owls or deer with large dark eyes take the place of the ETs. Says Tom, "The fact that owls seem to have been a common occurrence when I've had segment of missing time or a UFO sighting is something I never believed to have any significance until I got into researching and found that owls are one of the things that may be involved in screen memories. There were numerous times over the years that I had been on that same stretch of road and had seen an owl suddenly fly at me. Quite often I would find myself three, four or five miles away from where I thought I was as a result. I would not remember driving the distance. And this used to concern me a lot. I thought that there was something wrong, but I always charged it off that the owl had distracted me and I didn't realize where I was."

In 1990, Tom finally elected to undergo hypnotic regression. He met with Budd Hopkins and was regressed to the above incident. Under hypnosis, he recalled that he was about to touch the landed UFO when a strong telepathic voice commanded, "Don't touch it."

Tom also recalled feeling a strong tingling sensation. The missing time incident was not explored. Tom, however, continues to experience numerous UFO encounters on a fairly regular basis. Tom also feels that his encounters have been basically positive. "The encounters that I've had have not been of the scary types. Seeing something that's unexplainable is kind of scary at times, but I've never really felt that I was in any danger. I have a strong feeling that there has been some communication that may have directed what I'm doing in my life, as a result of my encounters ... I think a lot of people tend to fear the unknown. In my case, I'm curious about the unknown, and I pursue answers. I've never had any real fear of the encounters that I've had. I think there has been some communication to me that there's no need to fear, and I've taken that as being truthful. Many of the places where I do work are remote locations where UFO activity does occur. I've never thought of the UFO activity as being related to these choices, but it may well be. So, my feeling is not negative at all ... in my case, it's been positive."[414]

Almost every abductee is given some sort of clue that an unusual event has occurred. For some this clue is more obvious than others. On the Saturday before Easter 1973, Thomas X. [not to be confused with Tom X.] was driving late at night through Grass Valley when his car was enveloped by a strange fog. He remembers losing consciousness and waking up in front of his home, pulling into his driveway. Confused, he checked the mileage and was surprised to see that the odometer registered only thirty-seven miles, a physical impossibility and much too short for the trip back to his home. He knew that something strange had occurred, but sort of shelved the event in his mind.

Years later, under hypnosis, he recalled what happened. After the fog enveloped his car, a large craft appeared above him and lifted his entire car up inside. Says Thomas, "I vividly recalled taking my hands from the steering wheel as a voice spoke, assuring me I was safe. The engine stopped running as the car left the road and lifted upwards ... through the golden, orange glow of the underside of the craft, I saw an opening appear. The car entered and settled on some sort of ramp. A small pasty-white being opened the car door, gently took my arm and helped me from the car. I noticed how thin he was and wondered how such a thin neck could support such a large head. His height was less than five feet, and he had very dark, large eyes."

Thomas next recalled being taken through a "small elevator-like tube" into a "do-nut-shaped room." He was then met by another gray-type being who placed him into a chair and asked Tom if he would be willing to undergo a "treatment."

Says Thomas, "I trustfully agreed and climbed onto the hard surface of the chair. A large headpiece came down across the reclining chair and covered my head to my nose. Once the equipment was in place, my only sensations were an initial disorientation and drowsiness." Thomas was told by the being that the treatment would improve the performance of the chemical neurotransmitters in his brain. Afterwards, he was questioned on several topics and was returned back to his car, which was now parked, still running, next to his home.[415]

In 1971, in Oakland, 16-year-old Kurt X. experienced a missing time encounter in his family home. Awakened by the howling of his neighbor's cats, he went outside and encountered a "glowing being" standing next to a "pyramid-like object" landed in his backyard. Kurt was taken into the object and was shown "a large planet getting closer and closer. It was rusty gray-orange. I called it my home."

Kurt asked why he was contacted, and the being telepathically replied that Kurt "had a gift and was needed on Earth." Kurt recalled being examined and then later returned to his room with only partial recall of the event. Later he went under hypnosis and recalled the above onboard segment and also being taken onboard again where he was shown hybrid babies. "In the middle of the room are tall cylindrical units in a circle. They contain a very rich, red fluid. There are bubbles going up the units, and in each one is a baby. I was told these were hybrids, a combination of earthlings and otherlings. I was also told that I have a son, whom I shall meet one day."[416]

The 1970s provided a large number of abduction reports. In 1973, at the age of thirty-eight, Fred X. was asleep in his home in the city of Mountain View. In the middle of the night he was mysteriously awakened to find himself floating off his bed, through the closed window, and up into the sky. He was floated over the local House of Pancakes™, the Payless Shoe Store™, the Chevy™ dealer, and upwards. He suddenly found himself inside a strange room. As he says, "It was round, and you couldn't see any light, like a light bulb or a lamp ... it had sort of like this backdrop all the way around, with fluorescent-type tubes or something on the other side. That's where the light in the room emanated from. And it was in gray tones. You're seeing color, but everything looked like tones of gray and black, like a very soft black-and-white photograph. And they put me on a table."

Fred protested, but the aliens told him telepathically, "We're not going to hurt you ... we have to do this. We have to take care of this first .... You haven't got the choice."

Fred felt embarrassed as they poked and prodded at his teeth, his genitals, and other parts of his body. During the examination, Fred experienced considerable fear. "I was absolutely panicked!"

He was somewhat reassured by the ETs, who according to Fred looked like human beings, except that they wore tight-fitting suits which covered their entire body except for their face. The ETs told Fred that they were, in fact, just like human beings, except that they didn't have all the bacterial infections that most humans have. They also told him that while they had solved many of the social problems that plague humanity, they themselves are intrigued by our sense of individuality, something they lack. Their average height was just over five feet. Otherwise, they were just like humans. Fred reported seeing both men and women aboard the ship.

He asked why he was chosen, and he was told that the choice was made long ago. Fred was then returned to his bedroom. He still remembered snippets of the experience, especially the sensation of going through the closed window. Today he is a successful businessman and author. He has reported no further encounters.[417]

From August 10 to August 13, 1974, a series of sightings hit the northern California towns of Gilroy and San Jose. The mini-wave actually began a few months earlier when a local science teacher and three others used binoculars to observe a strange hovering craft.

Then on August 10 at 11:00 p.m., Mrs. Smith of Gilroy was driving a friend home when they saw a "lighted object" hovering high in the sky in the distance. Suddenly, the object swooped down, hovered over the car, and chased it down the road. Says Smith, "The thing I saw was round, had four large landing gear-like arms coming out of it, evenly spaced all around."

The object was the size of a small house and was flashing colored lights.

Smith pulled up into the driveway of her friend's home, screaming. She had a terrible feeling that the object "was going to take everyone away." Her friends ran out and also observed the object. Says Smith's friend, Mrs. Viktor, "I ran to the street and saw this gigantic round flying machine with four large antennae-type landing gear coming out of it and all these white and red flashing lights ... it was gray metal looking and it was huge. It just sat there in the sky."

After a few moments, it darted away. The witnesses reported their sighting to the local police.

The sighting, however, proved to be only the beginning of a larger experience. One month later, on September 15, it was Mrs. Viktor who was visited by the occupants of the same UFO. She woke up from a sound sleep to find two beings standing next to her. They wore tight-fitting silver suits and had slits for eyes, nose, and mouth. The beings told Viktor to "go up with them."

Viktor found herself escorted through the air into the familiar-looking craft. She was led into a circular room with an emerald-green floor and silver walls covered with instruments. The room was lit by a milky-white light, and Viktor was deeply impressed by the beauty of the scene. Suddenly, she was blinded by a white light and woke up the next morning in her bed (she had been sleeping on the couch.) After investigating the case, Jacques Vallee wrote, "I reached the conclusion that an anomalous event did happen to them and that the sighting was authentic."[418]

Highly-respected southern California parapsychologist Barry Taff reports that he has also uncovered a few abduction cases. In 1974 he worked with a client by the name of Ann who claimed that small figures came into her bedroom and took her into a strange room where she was medically examined. Says Taff, "Her description of the 'funny-looking men' is again very reminiscent of what we now are very used to hearing: 3-4 feet tall, hairless, slim with large inverted pear-shaped heads with no outer ears, no apparent nose except two vertical slits and no lips except for another horizontal slit where our mouths would be positioned."

Ann told Taff that the figures probed her with various instruments and kept repeating not to be afraid and that she wouldn't remember. Ann, however, did remember and without hypnosis. She continued to have encounters with the gray-type ETs, including a mysterious disappearing pregnancy. Taff reports that Ann was badly traumatized by her encounters and suffered emotionally because of them.[419]

The town of Happy Camp lies near the northern border of California. It is a small town centering almost totally around the lumber industry. Interestingly, the area had already produced a number of Bigfoot reports. Throughout late 1975, the town experienced a wave of UFO activity, including a few apparent abductions.

The ordeal began in early September when local police officer Dick McIntyre reported seeing a UFO. He later retracted his report and denied seeing anything. The first verified sighting occurred on September 6, when a mother and daughter observed a disk-shaped craft hovering low over the town. Says the mother, "It was lit all the way around."

Then on October 25, two lumber mill technicians, Stan Gayer (19) and Steve Harris (26), observed two unusually bright star-like objects. The objects moved in darting patterns and, at one point, swooped towards the witnesses. Gayer and Harris left the area but stayed long enough to observe one of the objects landing on the side of nearby Cade Mountain.

Impressed by their sighting, Gayer and Harris returned two days later with another friend. It was late at night as they scanned the same area with flashlights. Suddenly, all three observed a "set of glowing silvery eyes" in the nearby bushes. At the same time, a loud siren-like sound was emitted. The three men retreated in fear down the mountain.

The next day, Gayer and Harris returned with three additional witnesses. Shortly after reaching the same area, all five observed "two silhouettes wearing helmets like a welder and surrounded by a peculiar light." The siren-like noise was also heard again.

Suddenly, the two strange glowing figures approached the group. Three of the witnesses reported strange sensations of pressure, heat or breathlessness. The group retreated in panic and drove down the mountain with the UFO in pursuit.

Five days later, on November 2, three of the witnesses returned again with two more people. They drove to the same area when their truck was suddenly enveloped by a strange fog. At this point, the witnesses became very disoriented and confused.

Some of them recalled the truck stopping and strange figures opening the doors and pulling them out. They observed a large glowing object hovering above the truck. One of the witnesses recalled being lifted up inside the object where she spoke with one of the occupants. She reports that the inside of the object was much larger than it appeared from the outside.

Their next conscious memory is driving down the mountain singing a church song.

Meanwhile, the wave of sightings continued. Writes the principal investigator, Jacques Vallee, "After this major incident, sightings were made throughout the area by various witnesses .... These incidents include other episodes of strange fog with a humanoid shape inside, high-pitched sounds so piercing they hurt the witnesses, and various kinds of spherical or oblong objects flying over the town, sometimes with an Air Force jet in hot pursuit."

Several of the witnesses also experienced bizarre poltergeist-like activity. Writes Vallee, "Coming from an isolated town that does not even have a movie house, this concentration of cases is remarkable."[420]

Another bizarre California UFO abduction cases occurred in November 1975 to two young women, Kathy X. (age 19), and Susan X. (age 20). The incident occurred in northern California. It was around 11:00 p.m. and Kathy was driving. Susan suddenly saw a large globe of white light hovering ahead of them on the left. She pointed it out to Kathy.

Susan became extremely excited and sent a telepathic message to the object to land. Immediately it began to move towards them. Susan pleaded with Kathy to stop the car. However, Kathy reported that the car "slowed down all by itself ... it's like I wasn't even driving the car anymore ... it was like the car knew right where it was gonna go."

As the car came to a halt, Susan jumped out and ran underneath the large glowing object, which now hovered stationary next to the road. Kathy remained in the car, too scared to get out.

At this point, both ladies experienced a period of missing time. Their next memory was of leaving the area. Later, under hypnosis, both ladies recalled being taken onboard the craft and examined.

Susan gives a familiar description of the occupants, "His mouth is just a little place ... it doesn't move. And his ears are real small ... he has no hair. And he has round, large eyes."

During her examination, Kathy reports that one of the beings passed his open hand back and forth over her left leg. She felt a distinct "tingling" sensation. According to Richard Haines Ph.D., who investigated the case, "Kathy had experienced pain in her left knee for many years prior to this event and, soon after the event, it went away for some unknown reason and has not returned to this day."

What makes this case particularly unusual is that both women also reported being taken to an underground cave-like area.

Haines writes that "this particular multiple-witness case is important" because both the witnesses provided "separate and independent corroboration for many of the alleged events both above and underground, before, during, and after the abduction."[421]

In 1974, San Jose resident Clarisa Bernhardt began having "visions" of earthquakes which turned out to be uncannily accurate. After a series of accurate predictions, she soon had her own radio show and announced her predictions publicly.

Then, in 1976, Bernhardt revealed that she had had a series of encounters with extraterrestrials. She believes that she was taken, either physically or non-physically, on more than one occasion from her bedroom and onto a spacecraft "as big as a city block." Bernhardt saw several figures onboard, but was unable to describe them as she could not see what they looked like. "They had on silver-colored uniforms [and] helmets on, so I wasn't able to see the details of their faces. But I did not feel that their heads were out of proportion of their bodies. In other words, they did not present a grotesque appearance."

Bernhardt asked them who they were and they told her to "think of them as Space Brothers." They told her that they came from "several galaxies away." They told her the name of their planet, but Bernhardt says it was "unpronounceable as far as I was concerned."

They explained that they were visiting Earth on a peaceful mission. They were worried about humanity's "primitive emotional characteristics." They warned about the damage from the use of nuclear weapons. They said that they were unable to appear physically until people learned to control their thoughts and actions in a more positive manner.

They told Bernhardt that they were interested in her ability to predict earthquakes and recommended that she warn the scientists of the two biggest earthquakes for that year.

On another occasion, Bernhardt was driving between San Jose and Oakland when she was taken physically from her car and into a craft. As she drove, she felt a strong disorientation and, at the same time, heard a telepathic message, "Don't be afraid."

Seconds later, a "cloud" came over the car, and Bernhardt found that she and her car were inside a large circular room filled with equipment "similar to the panel of an airplane."

The figures told that they had contacted her because she had the power to influence people through her popular radio program. They told her that she "can be of help to them by making others more aware that there are others in this universe besides those of us here on this planet."

After the meeting, they told Bernhardt that she would not remember what happened "for a little while." Suddenly, she felt herself become dizzy. She found herself encased in light and then mist. Her next memory was waking up in her car, thinking she must have momentarily blacked out. She was unable to recognize the area and when she found a street sign, she was shocked to find she was in Oakland. Her last memory was of being in San Jose.

While many of Bernhardt's predictions did come true, some did not. She predicted that starting in March 1978, a ten-year span of seismic events would cause portions of California to fall into the sea. Obviously, the event never took place. However, the theme of warnings of ecological collapse and natural disasters remains a prominent theme in reports of onboard accounts.[422]

An alarming case involving medical evidence took place in mid-July 1997. Revealed by investigator Barry Taff, the case involves a lady named Margie from the Hollywood Hills. Margie was actually Taff's girlfriend at the time of the incident. Margie woke up one morning and told Taff an extraordinary story. She explained to him that in the middle of the night she was levitated off her bed and taken into a strange rounded room where she was laid on a table. She then realized that several "little men" were around her, examining her with various instruments. They began to insert various instruments into her orifices, which she found very painful. She struggled to get away and fell unconscious.

The real shock, however, came in the morning following the incident. Writes Taff, "As soon as Margie got out of bed, my curiosity turned to shock and hers into horror. Around Margie's wrists, ankles, waist, and neck were black-and-blue bands of discoloration, as if she'd been held in tight restraints for some time. Equally disturbing was the fact that Margie was bleeding from her nose, left ear canal, and her uterus, although she was not menstruating."

According to Taff, Margie was devastated by the encounter and never fully recovered.[423]

A surprisingly large number of UFO abductions are reported by young children. While adults also experience abductions, as a general rule, UFO encounters begin in early childhood and continue on into adult life. A typical example is that of Tom X., a computer programmer from northern California. Ever since age thirteen, Tom suffered from severe chronic depression and periodic anxiety attacks. He lived with the symptoms for more than ten years before finally seeking help from a psychologist. By coincidence, the psychologist was none other than Edith Fiore Ph.D., who was quickly becoming an expert on UFO abductions. Upon hearing of her interest, Tom revealed that he had a phobia about UFOs. He guiltily told Fiore that he had an unreasonable fear that "they're out there somewhere and will pick me up ... again."

Tom did have memories of being contacted; however, because of his terror, he had never examined them or brought them to mind. He told Fiore that it was this phobia which caused his anxiety attacks. He called it a "real, absolutely terrified, real spooked, verging on terror sensation." He first recalled having it at age thirteen, after he was taken. That evening, he noticed a mysterious "funny lump" which had appeared inside his nose.

Fiore asked Tom if he would like to be hypnotized to locate the source of his anxiety. Tom agreed, and under hypnosis, was brought back to the 1977 experience at age thirteen that he had refused to look at for so many years. A complex contact scenario emerged in full detail. Tom recalled going out into his backyard when he was suddenly pulled up into the air and into a craft. "I don't know how this is happening. I'm not being supported by them. They're not carrying me physically. I find myself flying through the air all of a sudden. It's exhilarating and frightening all at the same time. It's so strange. And unbelievable .... I'm looking down and seeing the trees below .... I'm being carried up into the ship ... the ship is hovering above."

Tom suddenly found himself "in a room or chamber that is somewhat dimly lit, a reddish orange, quite dim. No harsh lighting." Looking around him, Tom saw four short hooded figures. However, because of his intense fear and confusion, he refused to look at them directly. He only recalled that they were not human and had dark, glittery eyes. "A humanoid appearance ... I found it disagreeable, somewhat frightening, to look at them directly. They don't have eyelids in the same way we do. The eye seems to be covered by a translucent membrane similar to what I've seen on birds ... their ears are not the same as a human ear, maybe more like a crescent-shaped opening. Their features are flatter and less prominent than the human face."

His clothes were quickly removed and he was laid out on a table and examined. "They were prodding and probing and poking. Something was inserted in my penis, and that was distinctly unpleasant, but not painful ... I was subjected to a rectal probe as well. I found that also be unpleasant, but not nearly so unpleasant as the other ... something's being inserted down my throat, and I'm gagging. And again, feeling a probe inside my chest from that .... I'm put into a sitting position in some sort of a chair."

Throughout the experience, Tom experienced extreme terror and anxiety. Because of his reaction, he was unable to gain much information. As he says, "Any attempts they made to communicate with me were really limited to trying to calm me down and keep me under control."

After the examination, Tom was dropped back into a field behind his home. He returned home and was confronted by his mother who wanted to know where he was for the last hour. Tom refused to tell her the truth. "I feel like if I tell her what really happened, she'll accuse me of making up a story and that won't help. I really don't know what to say. She asks me why I went out, and I said I don't know. She's not satisfied with that. I ended up being punished. I felt it was very unfair."

Tom was so traumatized by the event that he pushed it completely out of his mind and told himself that it never happened, that such things *can't* happen. He refused to think about it and never discussed it with anyone.

A few months later, while driving with his family, Tom saw the same craft pacing the family car. Says Tom, "I saw the ship again. I didn't have a clear conscious memory of what had happened before, but I was filled with a sense of dread. You see, a part of me did remember and knew I was not able to avoid it."

Apparently, Tom was right. As he says, "I was taken, along with my brother and sister. My parents were temporarily out of commission, unconscious, while this was going on. We were taken into the ship and there was a physical exam again ... I'm on that table again, being probed. Into my penis again and a rectal probe ... a tracheal probe or esophagus, or both."

Tom wasn't aware of what happened to his brother and sister until they were all returned to the vehicle. Interestingly, they still retained some memory of the event. Says Tom, "At some point on the way back, I compared notes with my brother and sister. She found it much less disagreeable than I did. She was able to exchange information. I was intrigued and envious, and I wondered what was wrong with me. Why couldn't I react like that too?"

As of yet, Tom has reported no further encounters.[424]

On August 30, 1977, nine witnesses spread out over a ten-mile area outside of Healdsburg reported a bright, unidentified craft hovering at treetop level. The main witnesses include the Cray family. They were driving at around 8:30 p.m. when they saw bright lights over the coastal hills. They pulled over to examine the lights. Realizing that they were unusual, they decided to drive closer. As they drove closer, one of the lights left formation and zoomed straight over their car, sending down a powerful beam of light. As Mrs. Cray says, "One hovered above our car about the height of the telephone wires. It had windows." One of children reported seeing a "frog-like" face in one of the windows.

Suddenly, the family became very disoriented. Time seemed to pass too slowly and the object appeared to jump locations as if there was a gap in time. The object darted away, and the family rushed to their destination. The object was still in view when they arrived, and was witnessed by their neighbor. Upon arrival, the entire family displayed physiological effects apparently as a result of their encounter. One of the children began vomiting and was unable to eat for two days. Most of the others experienced headaches, nausea, and insomnia.

When the Crays' sighting ended, another witness in adjacent Alexander Valley reported seeing what was apparently the same object, again hovering at very low altitude. Jacques Vallee, who investigated this case, remains frustrated at the inability of science to solve the UFO mystery. As he writes of this case, "I wish there were a science of things seen at night, and of froglike silhouettes hunting peaceful families on lonely country roads."[425]

Throughout his life, Mark X. of San Francisco had an obsessive interest in UFOs. While his interest was strong, his emotional response to the subject was one of fear. He experienced a series of nightmares about UFOs. In 1988, at age nineteen, suffering from arthritis, he sought the help of a hypnotherapist to ease his pain. While under hypnosis, however, he relived an abduction experience which occurred sometime in 1977, when he was only seven years old. Mark recalled being taken onboard the ship out of his bedroom. "I just go up, and part of the roof just ... I don't know, it's like it's transparent and I go through it ... and then there's a compartment in the bottom of the spaceship that I go up into. And there's two aliens, one on one side of me and one on the other. They put me on a little table ... "

Mark described one the ETs in familiar detail. "His arms are longer than humans' arms are. His fingers are much longer and more bony-looking ... he has real sharp cheeks, they stick out there. He has a real small mouth. It doesn't open. And his nose is just a little mound. And his eyes look like a cat's almost. They're concave .... They're pretty big eyes ... And his head's almost like egg-shaped. I don't see hair."

Mark recalled being medically examined with a strange x-ray-like instrument that revealed his inner organs in full color and detail. He states that a wire-like device was inserted in his penis and sperm was removed. He believes that the ETs also tried to cure him of diabetes, with which he had been recently diagnosed. As he says, "They have a big clamp around the left side of my side, my gut. It's sending pulses, shock waves into my pancreas, for my diabetes. I don't know what it's for, but it tickles sometimes, and every time it sends one of these waves through, my body twitches just a little bit."

The ETs then performed another somewhat familiar procedure. "He helps me off the table, and he walks me to this little chair. There's a round bowl that comes over my head, like you go inside a beauty shop and it dries your hair. And it covers me. I feel this warm feeling over me."

Mark also saw other people being medically examined and operated upon aboard the craft. After the examination, his next memory was being laid down in his bed. It was at that point in his life that his interest and fear in UFOs began. Mark also believes he may have been abducted again at age fifteen, though he was unable to recall any details. He is convinced that the purpose for the contact is the hybridization of humans and ETs.[426]

It is very rare for a witness to obtain a photograph of a UFO. It is almost unheard of for a witness to obtain a photograph of a UFO occupant. However, just this event happened on November 1, 1978, to Reverend Harrison E. Bailey, then an associate pastor of New Salem Mission Baptist church in Pasadena. As a younger man, Bailey had experienced an extensive missing time encounter in his home in Illinois. On this occasion, he was in the bedroom of his Pasadena apartment. Ever since his initial encounter in 1951, Bailey had experienced regular nighttime visitations by short, thin entities with large, bald heads. Bailey was finally put in touch with UFO investigator Ann Druffel who, after investigating his case, suggested that he try to photograph the entities.

Bailey agreed, bought a cheap Polaroid camera, and placed it on his bed table. Then, at midnight on November 1, the familiar entities returned. Bailey quickly snapped a total of eleven pictures of the strange figures inside his bedroom. Incredibly, the pictures confirmed Bailey's story. Says Druffel, "Three of these photographs are extremely provocative. One shows the disembodied face of two entities against a window shade. The other two show diminutive figures of the aliens silhouetted against an open doorway."

The Bailey photographs appear to be valid and have never been proven to be a hoax. They definitely show a strange blurry figure of some kind. Combined with Bailey's sterling reputation, the case remains very strong evidence of extraterrestrial contact.[427]

In October 1978, Malibu resident Robert X. experienced a dramatic missing time encounter involving apparent landing trace evidence. While Robert had always held an interest in UFOs, in 1975 he began having sightings of star-like objects over his home. After three such sightings, he had a much closer encounter. He was lying in bed resting one evening when he heard and felt a low but strong vibration. He attempted to get up and investigate, but discovered that he couldn't move. Says Robert, "I was completely paralyzed and could not open my eyes until the vibration stopped." Afterwards, Robert jumped up to investigate, but found nothing unusual. Then, two days later, he discovered something very unusual. In the middle of his backyard was a "lush, vibrant green seventeen-foot diameter ring of grass about eight inches wide." Robert also noticed that the tip of one of his tall pine trees next to the house was cracked off and hanging down.

Although Robert could only speculate, the whole picture seemed suddenly clear. The ring, the broken branch, the paralysis, and the strange buzzing sound all came together to form a fantastic picture. It was exactly as if a large object had come swooping down out of the sky, clipped off the top of the pine tree and landed in his backyard. It seemed impossible to believe, but there was the physical evidence.

One year later, Robert experienced a repeat performance. He was laying in bed when he suddenly had the distinct feeling of a presence outside his home. Says Robert, "I intended to get up and investigate, then woke up some time later and thought nothing more of it until later that week when a second lush, vibrant green seventeen-foot diameter ring of grass appeared on my back lawn, right next to the first one, which was still there."

Robert was stunned. He realized that he might have had missing time, but has not elected to undergo hypnosis. Since that time, he and his wife have had a number of other sightings. In 1992, they moved to Oregon and have reported no further encounters.[428]

On July 25, 1979, Shari N., a housewife and waitress, was driving home from work in Canoga Park when she experienced a terrifying UFO abduction. Her ordeal began when she saw what she thought was a plane crashing ahead of her. At this point, she experienced a period of missing time and remembered only returning home much later. Under hypnosis, she recalled exiting her car and approaching an extraterrestrial craft which had now landed along the roadside. She entered the craft and found herself inside a rounded room with undescribed beings. She was laid on a table and recalled that a "being probed her shoulder and stomach, inserted something in her leg, and dabbed her eyes." Afterwards, she was returned to her vehicle with no conscious memory of the onboard event.[429]

One week later, on August 4, 1979, Canoga Park was visited by another UFO. An anonymous witness reported seeing a "discoid" object which hovered, then moved and tilted towards her. The object was less than a hundred feet away and the shocked witness could clearly see "two large heads" inside a clear dome atop the UFO. The object then tilted in the opposite direction and took off at high speed towards the west.[430]

Also in 1979, Diane Tai of San Jose had a "dream" that she was taken onboard a UFO. While her family assumed it was just a dream, Tai felt on some level that she had actually had contact and had partial memories of being onboard a craft. The next night on "20/20", Hugh Downs reported, "A UFO was sighted over Cupertino, California, last night" and went on to explain that the object had also been detected on radar at the San Jose Airport.

Tai was stunned. As a child she had many psychic experiences and sometimes felt like she was in contact with aliens. Following the vivid dream and the sighting report, Tai decided to undergo hypnotic regression.

Under hypnosis, she explored the "dream" and discovered that she actually was taken onboard. She recalled waking up because of a strange buzzing noise filling the house. Thinking it was the pool-pump, she went into the backyard where she was struck by a beam of light. As she says, "I feel afraid. I don't know what's happening to me. I'm in this light, and I can't see out of the light. I don't see around me. Now I see okay. There's been a gap somewhere, because now I'm walking in this large ship."

Tai found herself in a strange room with blue lights coming from the ceiling. The air had a sweet smell to it. The aliens looked just like humans and told Tai that she was actually one of them. They explained to her the reason for their visit was to check up on "our children."

Tai saw many other people onboard the ship. The aliens then told her the reason for their visits. Says Tai, "They must keep making contact because certain people, policemen and doctors and healing professionals and psychics, social workers and people who care, those people are drawn to change the negative force that is on a self-destruct cycle ... they want to try to save the planet so we don't destroy it through some ignorance of the others ... they seemed to be concerned about the bombs and lack of love between countries. And so people have to be stronger in order to little by little, raise the vibration of the planet."

The aliens warned her of the power of thought, the importance of eating the rights foods and meditation, the dangers of television and radio waves on the human body, and other topics.

Tai found her encounters not only positive, but highly beneficial. She was delighted to uncover the new information and feels that the experiences she has had have greatly enriched her life.[431]

Another 1979 abduction case was uncovered by David Jacobs Ph.D. Tracy Knapp, a musician, had just turned twenty-one years old. To celebrate, she and her girlfriends decided to drive from Los Angeles to Las Vegas. While en route late at night through the California desert, the young ladies observed a "strange light" swooping down over their car.

At the time, it was not clear whether Knapp and her friends recalled anything other than a sighting and missing time. However, later under hypnosis, a more complex scenario emerged. Knapp recalled that the car was actually lifted up and taken inside the UFO. As she says under hypnosis, "The car's spinning around ... like I'm in a teacup, like I'm spinning, like the car's turning, and I'm grabbing onto the seat and we're screaming ... we're not on the ground .... [It's] like we're being spun up, like we're moving forward and getting spun, and I'm holding on to the car .... [I feel] a force, a pressure. Heavy. Like I'm weak, weighted ... I can't talk. Nothing's being said at that point .... [My friends], they're going limp ... they open the door and I feel like I'm being picked up out of there."

While Jacobs doesn't reveal the details of this particular incident, he does present further cases involving Knapp. About one year earlier (location not given) she experienced an abduction and "fetal extraction procedure." Says Knapp, " ... there's babies ... in these drawers that pull out like a lab or something."[432]

A particularly disturbing close encounter was first investigated by northern California investigator, Marv Taylor, and involves the apparent abduction of an entire family. The episode occurred at 10:30 one evening in mid-July, 1979. The mother, Gloria Hernandez, was driving. Her three children and a friend were passengers.

As they pulled their car out of their driveway, they noticed a star-like light high in the sky. As soon as they started driving, the light swooped down and hovered over their car. Looking up, they saw a circular object at least twenty feet in diameter, sending down a powerful beam of light. When her children started to cry in fear, Hernandez drove away as quickly as possible.

Earlier that evening, two workers at a local steel factory reported that they were outside when a "perfectly round flying saucer" shot down out of the sky and hovered forty feet above them.

Meanwhile, the Hernandez family began to suffer strange after-effects. All of them had strange "lumps" appear on various locations on their bodies. Gloria and one of her daughters also noticed unexplained scoop-marks on their legs. They sought medical attention, but the mysterious lumps disappeared and re-appeared for a period of several months, before finally going away for good. As a final bizarre effect, Hernandez reports that she became extremely psychic following the encounter and was able to predict various events and clairvoyantly determine the whereabouts of her children.[433]

On May 7, 1980, between 9:00 p.m. and 10:00 p.m., an anonymous mother, her two daughters, and their friend were driving through the city of Redding when a "sudden burst of smoke" totally enveloped their vehicle. The smoke appeared almost glowing, and the entire family felt that they were "floating along" inside the cloud. The mother felt as if "time had stopped" and wondered if there had been an atomic explosion.

One of the daughters said she saw a light, at which point the road became very cloudy and bright. She said, "Everything became silent, super-slow, and creepy."

After the disorienting, bizarre episode, the cloud lifted and the family drove home. Immediately, however, they noticed several physiological changes. They all felt extreme fatigue. The mother and one of the daughters had strange puncture-like spots in the same area on their bodies. Another complained of eye irritation. That evening, two of the children had nightmares of threatening men dressed in uniforms. Jacques Vallee, who investigated their case, remains skeptical that it was a spacecraft or abduction, and yet he writes, "I came back from Redding with the opinion that they were not lying, that they had seen something unusual, and that I would probably never know what it was."[434]

In early 1980, Natalie X. of Milpitas was outside her home when she observed a classic flying saucer. But it was an experience on June 26 which really impressed her. On that occasion, she was taken onboard a craft by benevolent "light beings" where she experienced an incredible adventure. She described the ETs as being "very advanced" and very friendly. "I got this overpowering feeling of love and goodness from them. Other beings on the ship sent me peace and love vibrations ... the beings glowed."

Says Natalie, "They took me on a tour of the interior of their ship ... I felt that I should bow to them, but they told me not to. They said that I had once been as they now appeared to me."

The beings explained to Natalie that she had lived with them in a past life. Says Natalie, "I was being activated at this time in this life experience in order to help establish a direct communication link between their planet and earth."

Natalie's adventure continued. "They gave me a demonstration of their powers, which were awesome to say the least. They can make things appear at disappear at will. They also told me to start practicing telepathy, as I will need my previous abilities."

The beings warned her that the Earth was going to experience "coming times of change" and that it was their desire to assist humanity through the transformation.

Natalie was then returned to her bedroom with full conscious memory of the experience.[435]

As we have seen, because they spend a great deal of time outside, patrolling the neighborhood, a large proportion of UFO witnesses are police officers. Charged with protecting citizens from crime, police officers often react in different ways when confronted with a UFO.

An apparent abduction of a police officer occurred on October 30, 1981, in Spring Valley. Reserve Police Officer David Santoro was driving on his beat when, at 10:30 p.m., he was confronted with a sixty-foot, dark, disk-shaped object hovering only fifteen feet above the road directly in front of him. Santoro's car came to an abrupt stop as an "intense luminosity" filled his windshield.

He was shocked to see two small beings suddenly pull him from his patrol car. He is unable to consciously recall what happened next. His next memory began fifteen minutes later when he found himself back in his car. He looked up and saw the disk rising up and hovering. It suddenly sent down a beam of light which moved in circles around his car.

Officer Santoro reacted quickly. As the report on the case reads, "He fired four shots at the craft with his service revolver out the left window and drove home wildly at 90 miles per hour, narrowly missing an accident."

Santoro told his wife what happened. However, the next day, he completely forgot what had happened, and his wife had to remind him. He then examined his car and discovered that the front end was mysteriously polished clean of dirt. Also, all the cassette tapes in the car were garbled and ruined. Finally, he suffered various physiological effects including a persistent headache, abrasions, and soreness on his wrists, ankles, and neck.

Santoro eventually underwent hypnosis and recalled again two small creatures taking him from his car and later putting him back in. He was unable to recall further details.[436]

Also in the summer of 1982, tow-truck driver Mark Grant and his friend, R. H., experienced an apparent missing-time encounter in Topanga Canyon. The two of them had parked their car along the outskirts of the mountains to view the dazzling San Fernando city lights at night. Shortly after they pulled over, they noticed a triangular formation of lights in the sky above them. Says Grant, "About fifteen minutes after we first observed them, they started coming towards us, and they split off in three different directions. The triangular pattern was two on the bottom and one on the top. The one on the top looked like it was going up and away and towards us all at the same time. And the two at the bottom looked like they went straight at us, around our periphery, and at the same time they looked like they were going away too. They kind of disappeared. It was very strange."

Both felt like the lights had been watching them when suddenly they were moving towards them and away from them at the same time. The two of them experienced an apparent period of missing time. They were left badly confused and frightened by the event, and told nobody about it for years. They have no intentions of undergoing hypnosis.[437]

Another dramatic missing-time abduction occurred in 1982 to two men while driving late at night on Interstate 5 in the central valley. It was 2:00 a.m. when the two men spotted a glowing object ahead of them on the road. As they finally approached the object, they realized with a shock that it was not a helicopter or plane as they had previously speculated. One of the witnesses, Keith Boyer, was in the driver's seat. Says Boyer, "The object was pretty indescribable from a distance. The colors and lights seemed rather striking ... it appeared to be some kind of flashing light, something that was hovering over the freeway .... And, as we got closer to it, more and more details became clear. The object was a series of lights, seemingly merging and rotating into each other, with a kind of indefinable mist surrounding the object .... As we continued to zoom towards this object, the light became almost uncomfortably bright, very odd colors, deep rich blues, greens, yellows, reds – a number of them shifting and merging into each other .... It was an odd and terrifying bright object that was scary. And I wanted to get away from it as fast as possible."

At this point, the object landed next to the freeway and sent a beam of light out, which struck the car. The two men became panicky and experienced a period of missing time. Says Boyer, "A beam came out of the object and swept across the field towards us. I remember neither of us wanted to get hit by that beam, but it hit us .... At this point, I don't remember anymore than suddenly realizing that my friend was driving, and I wasn't. The next thing I remember, he was driving."

The two men continued driving down the road in a dazed state, unable to even speak. They refused to discuss the incident for years, and one of the witnesses still refuses to speak of it. Says Boyer, "It was a profoundly disturbing sight because it could not be explained by the brain ... and that was when the shock began. Here was a completely inexplicable object. Disturbing. I mean, distressing! It bothers one ... we were very upset. Both of us were very upset by the sight of the thing."

Boyer has considered undergoing hypnosis, but is afraid of what he might uncover. As he says, "To tell you the truth, I have a horrible feeling that there was more to it, and I really would like to not know about it."[438]

While many people assume that there is no hard evidence in support of UFO reality, the fact is that many cases are on record involving various forms of physical evidence. One of the most compelling kinds of evidence are physiological effects resulting from a close encounter. Medical evidence can literally make or break a case.

A good example is the case of Jozaa Buist. While living in Hawaii with her husband, Buist experienced a series of sightings and an apparent onboard experience. While onboard, she was operated upon by the ETs. After being returned to her bedroom, Buist was left with a scar and pains so severe she had to be hospitalized. Her doctors asked her about the recent surgical scar on her stomach, but Buist told them that she had never had surgery.

Then in 1982, Buist and her husband – who worked in the military – were transferred to San Diego. It was in their new southern California home that Buist had another remarkable encounter.

Early one evening, she was overcome with sleepiness and took a nap on the couch. She woke up at 7:30 because of severe arm pain. Shortly thereafter, she examined it and received an incredible shock. Says Buist, "I stopped dead in my tracks. I am dark complexioned, and this mark on my arm was pure white. It was the mark of a triangle. I measured it, and it was two and one-half inches on all three sides. A line stretched from the top of the triangle, and there was a white dot in the middle."

When Buist's arm pain persisted for three weeks, she finally sought medical attention. Her arm was too swollen to be accurately x-rayed, so the doctor gave her medication and asked her to return in one month for x-rays.

One month later, Buist had her arm x-rayed. The doctor returned baffled, saying that the x-rays were peculiar and he needed to refer the x-rays back to the hospital, and that Buist should come back later.

When Buist returned, she says the doctor was acting strangely and was evasive in his answers to her questions. When Buist cornered him for a diagnosis, the doctor said that there was a foreign object in her arm, a "disk" of some kind that had no logical way of being there. He refused any further comment.

Later Buist had the same arm x-rayed by another doctor. She spoke with the x-ray technician who x-rayed her, and he told her, "I wouldn't touch your arm with a ten-foot pole."

It took six months for the pain to subside. Today, Buist lives with the mystery of the strange object in her arm. As she says, "I could ask the 'persons' who put them there, but who are they? I hoped that more could have been done by naval doctors, but they could only go so far. Civilian doctors sort of shunned me. The marking is still visible to the naked eye. I have told my story over and over again, knowing that these extraterrestrials are real. I did not imagine them." Buist revealed her story in the excellent California-based UFO magazine, titled appropriately, *UFO Magazine*. The magazine, edited by Vicki Cooper, is one of the longest running slick UFO magazines in the United States.[439]

Barbara X. of Sacramento worked in a managerial position for a large company. She was married, had three grown children, and a large home. However, in 1983 her life was turned upside down by panic attacks which rendered her virtually disabled.

In an attempt to cure her problem, she finally sought out psychologist and hypnotherapist Edith Fiore Ph.D. She told Fiore that the panic attacks began following a missing-time UFO sighting. Barbara explained, "I was driving home at night, about 10:40. All of a sudden, I saw a flash of light ... in an instant, twenty minutes had passed. I felt real confused. I started feeling anxious from that point on."

In a matter of months, Barbara found herself hospitalized by anxiety, suffering chest pains, headaches, dizziness, shortness of breath, and more. While in the hospital room, she actually had another sighting. "I was in the hospital, when all of a sudden I woke at 3:00 a.m. and something said, 'UFO.' I looked out and saw a strange streak in the sky. I wasn't sure what it was."

Under hypnosis, Barbara discovered the source of her anxiety and the answer to what happened during the twenty-minutes of missing time. "There's a flash of light. A UFO stops over my car and brings my car to a halt. I am taken out of the car by a light. The light ... pulls me out of the car. I don't want to go. I'm taken aboard a ... a ... ramp. I'm scared. I can't see anything. I'm on a table. I can't move. They keep telling me, 'Don't be afraid. We won't hurt you.' 'I want to leave,' I say. They say, 'Not yet, not yet. You'll be all right. You won't remember.'"

Barbara reports that the ETs used mental telepathy. She was laid out on a table and examined. "They took a skin scraping .... They looked at my bad leg .... They said, 'You had an accident.' And I said, 'Yes.' They said, 'You had your female organs removed.' I said, 'Yes.'" .... They clipped my fingernails and a piece of my hair. They took a blood sample from my finger .... They mainly used the machine ... a big black machine ... they ran it over my body. It didn't touch me, but it was close." The ETs seemed particularly impressed by a peculiar quality of Barbara's skin.

Barbara was also given information. "They said they were exploring and finding out about other people, and because we're such an emotional people .... They're telling me they're from Sirius. They told me not to be afraid. That they do not hurt people."

According to Barbara, the aliens "looked the same as us." She saw three men, dressed in strange tight-fitting gray jumpsuits with a hood. She says that she was treated with kindness and she holds no ill will towards them. After undergoing two regressions, she was cured of panic attacks. As of yet, she has had no further encounters.[440]

In early 1984, Sammy Desmond of Reseda was in his bedroom when he saw a swarm of small lights enter into his room, causing him to pass out. He woke up in the next morning with no other memories of anything unusual. However, a few nights later, he had the same experience. And, two weeks after that, he looked out his window and saw several "four-foot [tall] beings with small visors over their eyes [and] bald pointy-type heads." His next memory was waking up in his bed the next morning.

Under hypnosis, he recalled a complex abduction scenario. Says Desmond, "I was inside a room. It was a small room, all white light-colored and around. There was a table in the middle, and there were wall lights and things all over."

Desmond describes his abductors. "They had white jacket-sort of outfits, sort of like hospital uniforms ... they had flat faces and long heads, bald heads. They had hardly any noses."

Desmond recalled being examined, though there are other portions of the event he was unable to remember. In most respects, Desmond's case is typical of UFO abductions. What's most amazing about his encounter is the fact that it took place in a densely populated suburb.[441]

Many people who experience ET abductions report multiple episodes. Most often, the abductions begin in early childhood and continue periodically throughout life. Starting in 1987, a family living in the outskirts of San Jose report that they have experienced a series of abductions that continue to the present day. Investigated by James J. Hurtak Ph.D., the case involves the entire family and considerable physical evidence.

Most of the details were recalled under hypnotic regression. The main witness, the father of the family, reports that he was taken onboard a craft via a beam of light. Writes Hurtak, "According to both conscious testimony and hypnotic recall, a substantial profile of this case was put together. The contactee indicates that there was medical experimentation done, not only to himself, but to members of his family."

While most of the details of the case are fairly typical, the physical evidence makes it particularly compelling. Large areas of crushed vegetation, broken trees, areas of dead grass, apparent landing indentations in the soil, and even strange marks on the family's horses, all come together to give the case a high level of credibility. The witnesses report that their home has been broken into and UFO evidence taken by unknown persons. The encounters continue to occur.[442]

In 1988, Gloria X. of northern California sought out Edith Fiore PhD. to explore her possible UFO experiences. Recently, she had attended a UFO seminar and was surprised by her reaction. As she says, "I had a really emotional reaction ... I became very emotional."

Gloria kept recalling a dream that she had three years earlier in 1985. She called it a dream, but in fact, she was awake. As she says, "It was so incredibly real, I've never forgotten it. I was in bed with my husband, who was asleep. I thought I was fully awake. I couldn't move. The bed was vibrating. There were several figures around me. They were hideous! Gray. Awful. Eyes that were black holes."

Gloria was especially disturbed by the dream because of an experience she had two weeks earlier. As she says, "Less than two weeks before that dream, I witnessed a UFO and was really shaken."

Gloria told Fiore that she's had nightmares for years about strange beings floating her out of her room, but after the sighting, the "dream," and her overly emotional reaction to the UFO conference, she wondered if she was having actual contact.

Under hypnosis, Gloria recalled that she had been taken onboard. She found herself in a strange room surrounded by gray-skinned bald humanoids. They placed "tubes" into her nose, into her stomach, and her hip. She was unable to move and became afraid. At this point, she observed that among the grays were several human-looking people. "They looked like twins, with blond hair. They looked like football players ... because they were big men. They both looked alike."

Another human-looking figure came up to her and reassured her. "[He was] always on my right, talking to me about my feelings, my thoughts. A very beautiful person. He was human, and he had light brown hair .... I'll never forget those eyes. He seemed familiar."

Following the examination, Gloria was taken into another room where she was given a strange book with symbols to read. To her surprise, she could understand what it said: information about avoiding false belief systems and people's misconception of time. The aliens told her that humans were too warlike and had even tried to fire a missile at their craft. They told her it was their mission to learn about humans and to teach people like her.

Gloria attempted to grab an instrument to take as proof, but it was taken from her, and she was returned to her home. She woke up only with the memory of gray-type aliens standing around her bed.[443]

In early summer of 1988, professional photographer Kim Carlsberg was sitting on the deck of her Malibu home overlooking the Pacific Ocean when she noticed a "particularly bright star" hanging low in the sky. Suddenly "the mystery star shot across the horizon with breathtaking speed and stopped at Point Dume. I was amazed by its velocity! Palos Verdes, where the light had been hovering, is roughly forty miles south of Point Dume, yet the point of light covered that distance in a matter of seconds. I knew I had just observed something literally out-of-this-world! No manmade object could have moved that fast."

Carlsberg wanted to wake up her boyfriend so he could also witness the UFO, but she was too much in awe to look away. At that point, the UFO approached. Says Carlsberg, "As though it responded to my thoughts, the brilliant point of light advanced until it became a luminous sphere some fifty feet in diameter. It ominously hung in the air less than one hundred feet from my window. I couldn't move, I couldn't scream, I couldn't breathe .... The apparent standoff lasted no more than a minute before the sphere departed as quickly as it appeared. It tore away diagonally through the night sky and vanished."

Following the sighting, Carlsberg's life would never be the same. Two weeks later, she experienced a terrifying abduction by gray-type extraterrestrials. After returning home from a late night at work and going to bed, she woke up in the middle of the night to find herself inside a UFO. Writes Carlsberg, "The room I had been shoved into looked like a hospital ward. I couldn't believe my eyes! All through the stark room were rows of operating tables that were only a couple of feet off the ground. They were occupied by unconscious human beings ... my eyes went straight to the creatures who were working on them. They were little naked things with oversized bald heads, big black eyes, and bodies like cheap dolls void of detail, down to the absence of genitalia. The skin was off-white and I thought they looked like anorexic Pillsbury dough boys."

Realizing with horror what was happening, Carlsberg screamed. Evidently, the ETs had not expected her to wake up as she was quickly put back to sleep. Says Carlsberg, "In reaction to my outburst, one of the two taller bald creatures rushed up and slapped me on the back of the neck. I felt myself passing out like I had been anesthetized."

Later during the experience, Carlsberg woke again and immediately became "hysterical." As she says, "I was lying on a cold metal table with one of those nasty creatures skulking in the darkness beside me." She lay there for a few moments, and realized that they had finished doing something to her body. She saw another figure in the doorway, and she cried out for help. The being replied, "Why don't you stop being such a big baby, this will be over enough with soon."

Shortly after this, the experience ended and she woke up in her bedroom. She thought about her sighting a few weeks earlier. As she says, "Both episodes were too bizarre to be mere coincidence; they must be related, and the implications were staggering."

Carlsberg realized she was one of the crazy UFO abductees she had heard vaguely about. Little did she know it was only the beginning. In September 1991, she experienced another dramatic UFO encounter. She had been wondering about her earlier contacts and had decided to see if she could initiate her own encounter. For a few weeks she had been sending out mental requests for another visitation. Then one night, unable to sleep, she had a strong intuitive feeling that she was about to be visited. She felt a strong impulse to get out of bed. To her shock, the living room was "bathed in a faint electric glow." They were here.

Carlsberg stepped outside and received the shock of her life. "A few silent moments passed before a crack of light shot across the water and a rush of wind blew in through the open sliding glass door. Before I could react, a huge, bright metallic disk magically appeared and hovered inches above the patio fence. I fell to the floor and crawled backwards to the nearest corner .... They waited a moment, and I sensed a reassuring message being projected from the craft. We all knew I wasn't ready. The ship disappeared as quickly as it had come. I was so disappointed in myself for losing such an incredible opportunity, but it was still an amazing occurrence. The aliens didn't seem like monsters anymore. Well, not as much. I was deathly afraid of them and yet they came at my request. To me that seemed like an act of love. At least I wanted it to be."

Throughout the early 1990s, Carlsberg experienced numerous nighttime abductions out of her Malibu home. She has since seen different types of ETs including grays and praying mantis types. She had numerous conscious memories of being taken onboard where she was given painful examinations. She reports that the ETs have taken her eggs and created hybrid babies. She was later taken onboard and shown these babies. Carlsberg describes one such encounter: "I'm sitting on the edge of a stool in a dark room filled with incubation boxes. Two figures in white gowns approach me in silence. I call them 'nurses.' They are handing me something so small. I'm afraid to look at it. Oh, my God, I'm so scared. I don't want to see its face." During the encounter, the aliens attempted to get Carlsberg to breast-feed the baby and give it love. They told her, "Love the baby." Carlsberg, however, was torn. "I'm holding it now. It's so frail .... I can't look at its face. I focus on its feet instead. I can't believe they are making me do this. I have to think about something else."

Carlsberg eventually sought out hypnotherapist Yvonne Smith who helped her to recall and process her experiences, most of which involve unpleasant examinations. In one of her encounters, the aliens told her that they claimed to be from Zeta Reticulum.

Overcome with anger, Carlsberg learned how to prevent further abductions by strongly exerting her will-power. Today, she is a profoundly changed person. She describes herself as "a vegetarian, an animal rights activist, and an impassioned environmentalist." As a result of her encounters she is a "hands on healer" and is learning channeling. Her many experiences with ETs are recounted in her profound and poignant autobiographical book, *Beyond My Wildest Dreams*.[444]

Sometime in 1975, teenager Steve Hess was camping with his parents outside Lake Mojave when he saw a thirty-foot brilliant glowing disk hovering in the sky. The sighting was very brief, but Hess was badly traumatized by the sighting, suffering from nightmares for months afterward. Fourteen years later, while camping near the same area, Hess and his wife would experience a bizarre and terrifying UFO encounter involving what appears to be the same ETs.

It occurred over a two-day period, from October 21 and 22, 1989, in the remote Mojave desert. Steve Hess was a supervisor of a large construction company, and his wife Dawn was a stay-at-home mother of three. That weekend, they left their La Mirada home together (the children were left with babysitters) and found a remote campsite in the Mojave desert near Table Top Mountain. Shortly after they set up camp, Steve Hess was shocked to see the same thirty-foot glowing disk he had seen as a child. As soon as he saw it, it disappeared behind a ridge top, but not before he recognized it as the same disk he had seen in 1975, fourteen years earlier.

This marked the beginning of the Hess' traumatic encounter. About an hour later, the couple was stunned to see nine glowing disks in a row above the ridge top. As the objects assumed different formations, Dawn speculated that the military might be responsible. Steve Hess, however, recalled his earlier encounter and knew that they were definitely not military.

As evening fell, the objects suddenly multiplied until there were literally hundreds. According to Steve and Dawn, a mass landing occurred. The couple took refuge in their camper as thousands of three-foot tall, large-eyed creatures surrounded them.

Then followed an event which is familiar to abduction researchers. The couple found themselves put into a trance state while their minds were searched for information. Both were forced to relive numerous emotional events in their lives, as if the ETs wanted to study human emotions. Seldom reported in the UFO literature, it is known among UFO investigators as emotional testing. The two witnesses were put into various hallucinatory scenarios which tested their emotions. The ETs forced Dawn to experience a scenario in which her young son was tortured. Steve was forced to experience a scenario in which he was eaten alive by wild animals.

Following this, the Hesses felt the trailer, with them in it, lifted aboard the craft. Although the scene around them still looked like their campsite, both were convinced that it was illusory and they were actually inside the craft. Their next memory is falling asleep and waking up the next morning. Dawn had a strange scar on her neck, and both were badly traumatized. It was clear to both of them that they had been abducted.

Later, under hypnosis, both recalled being taken onboard through a "tunnel of light." Dawn recalled being laid out on a table and medically examined. A device was placed against her neck and an apparent implant was inserted at the base of her skull.

Steve Hess recalled being taken to a separate room and examined in every orifice of his body. Afterwards, they were returned to their trailer.

Later, the Hesses experienced further encounters. Dawn had an episode involving a bedroom visitation by one of the ETs, during which her face was burned. The event was witnessed by Steve.

The Hesses feel that they are being constantly monitored by the ETs, and although they were terrified and traumatized by their ordeal, they also retain some sense of awe. They also feel that their latest child was conceived as a result in part of the alien's influence. Happily, the child appears to be healthy and normal.[445]

It was a summer vacation in the late 1970s for the Robinson family (pseudonym) as they visited their grandmother's remote cabin deep in Cedar Pines Park, also in the San Bernardino National Forest, just north of San Bernardino. That evening, Mrs. Diane Robinson noticed a "round-like" object with "a lot of bright lights on it," moving in strange patterns. As she says, "We were looking out the window so it was in the distance ... but it was erratic movement, so you could see it moving in the sky. It would hover and then it would just go, shoom, shoom, shoom, shoom! I mean, things, stars don't go all over the place. And helicopters do not move fast and erratically. They don't go quickly from one side to another and then shoot up, and then come down at an angle, and do that in like a faster than sound movement."

Diane's daughter, Kelly, also reports seeing the object "jumping up and down ... just a bright light kind of jumping, you know, back and forth .... We just thought it was a UFO because it was moving in strange patterns. Not like a plane."

Later, Kelly Robinson would have further sightings in the same area, finally culminating in an abduction scenario involving her entire family. Each year, Kelly vacationed at Camp Julian in the Cleveland National Forest outside of San Diego. One night early in 1982, she and her friends were outside at night at the campground when they saw a bright light darting around in the sky. Says Robinson, "A bunch of us saw it. We were just lying down and talking, and all of a sudden we saw it. It was jumping back and forth like aircraft, but going super-fast, going back and forth. The only reason we didn't think it was a plane was because we saw it zigzagging and moving back and forth so fast. They looked like planes, but they were darting in triangular, you know? And we all got scared and went inside. We just basically chickened out and went back to where we had to sleep. We went back and we were all scared. We didn't talk about it."

Kelly reports that she saw the UFOs on more than one occasion, and in the years that followed, she would sometimes see them. The Robinson family had already had a dramatic sighting years earlier. Later, Kelly would experience a full-blown abduction scenario.

One evening in mid-1986, Kelly and her sister Jenny were driving in the suburbs of Encino when they saw a star-like object moving in strange patterns. The object was so obviously strange that Jenny thought that there must be thousands of witnesses. Says Robinson, "[It was] something that didn't move like an airplane. It was just like a light moving in all different directions, and was definitely moving too fast to be an airplane." In the weeks following the incident, she sighted what was apparently the same object on two different occasions over her home in Reseda.

In October of 1987, the younger sister, Kelly, was sleeping in her bedroom in the crowded Reseda suburbs when she woke up to find several "scary-looking" gray-type aliens surrounding her bed. She described them as being very short, having large dark eyes, no hair, and leathery gray skin. They were dressed identically and moved in quick darting movements. They told her, "Don't worry, we won't hurt you."

Suddenly, Kelly found herself in a strange hazy white domed room. The figures were holding her down and asked if they could cut her arm. She refused and screamed at them to take her home. The ETs cut her arm anyway and then told her that they had to do an operation on her brain. Kelly was powerless to stop them, and remembers feeling utter terror. As she says, "I just remember fighting with them, like they were trying to take me away ... they tried to do something with my brain and I was fighting them all the way. They were pulling on me."

Throughout the experience, the figures repeated to her, "We're not going to let you remember. You will not remember any of this."

However, Kelly did remember. Furthermore, she had proof. Says Kelly, "That morning, I had a scratch on my arm and I was really upset about it."

Over the next two months, Kelly experienced three more visitations. On each occasion, strange small balls of light invaded her room, woke her up and rendered her paralyzed. The lights would then descend upon her and drain her mind of information. Kelly said that when the lights came she would "start punching the lights, grabbing at them, and throwing them." At that point, they would enter her brain and a telepathic conversation would ensue between her and the gray-type aliens. Kelly recalls the ETs asking about her job, her church, her work-life, and social activities. Each time, they would tell her that she wouldn't remember anything, and Kelly would furiously reply that she would remember. Amazingly, Kelly was able to consciously recall her experiences without the aid of hypnosis.

This case is very similar to the 1984 case of Sammy Desmond, also in Reseda (see above.) Both involved gray type aliens who would transform into tiny balls of light and invade the mind of the witnesses. The descriptions are so similar, one can't help but wonder if Desmond and Robinson encountered the same alien beings.

In January of 1988, Kelly Robinson experienced one final visitation in her home in Reseda. Shortly after that, her mother, Diane, had an experience that she calls a "dream," but which sounds more like a UFO encounter. The fact that Diane's daughter was also having experiences seems to point to the probability that Diane's dream was actually real. In the "dream" Diane recalled being inside a clean, dome-shaped room – in other words, the typical description of a UFO's interior. Says Diane, "The room was strange. It was not like walls we see. The walls were kind of rounded. It was not a regular room. It was sort of blue, like a pastel."

In the center of the room was a technological contraption shaped like a Christmas tree. The machine contained about twenty cylinders, each of which held a baby. A human-looking lady showed Diane the babies and asked her to hold them and give them love. However, Diane couldn't help but notice that the babies were deformed. Says Diane, "One baby had two heads, which upset me because it was cute, but it had two heads. And another baby had a big head and a little body. And there were Siamese twins in there too."

The lady inside the room attempted to get Diane to hold the babies and nurture them, but Diane refused.

Unknown to Diane, she experienced what UFO investigators call a "baby presentation," a consistent feature of multiple abduction cases. As Diane says, "She wanted me to take one to love ... she said they have everything, but they don't have love." After this experience, the encounters of the Robinson family ceased completely.[446]

The process of becoming aware and accepting that you are an alien abductee can be instantaneous or it may take years. In the case of Melinda Leslie, an office manager from Corona Del Mar, it was the latter. In 1987, Leslie visited Area 51 in the Nevada desert where she had a number of sightings. At the same time, memories began to surface of anomalous experiences in her early childhood, including one episode of missing time.

Two years later in 1989, Leslie woke up to find a series of unexplained bruises and puncture wounds on her ankle. At this time, she realized that something very strange was happening to her. A few months later, while preparing for bed, she experienced two and a half hours of missing time. She spontaneously recalled a portion of the experience. "The first thing that came to my mind was a visual image of three grays that were slightly varied in height ... and they were standing next to my bed and reaching for me."

Leslie wondered if she had really been visited by ETs. Then a few days later, her roommate revealed that she had looked for Melinda that evening and Melinda was not in the house. Then her roommate said, "Melinda, I saw the weirdest thing. I saw this being standing in the doorway. It was real small ... it came up to the handle of the door, and it had this great big over-sized head [and] these big dark eyes that wrapped around."

Then Leslie's roommate's daughter moved in and began having experiences. A short time later, she moved out. Leslie continued to have experiences. One morning she woke to find a bird in her room, although all the windows and doors had been closed.

But it was in July of 1991 when Leslie had one of her most dramatic encounters. It was a warm July evening when Leslie and two friends drove along the remote Angeles Crest Highway. They were going to visit Lancaster where there had been a wave of recent sightings. As they drove, Leslie and her two friends spotted an anomalous light that seemed to be pacing their car. At the same time, the police scanner and a powerful flashlight that they carried both simultaneously malfunctioned.

When the three friends arrived in Lancaster, they discovered it was already 3:00 a.m. They had lost about two hours of time.

Over the next few days, the witnesses spontaneously recalled what had occurred during the period of missing time. All three recalled the car coming to a sudden stop and seeing a gray-type alien standing in the road. All three were removed from the vehicle and taken onboard the UFO. They were each undressed and then examined. At one point they were led to separate rooms.

Leslie was taken into a small room where several ETs surrounded her. A strange device was placed over her head, which rendered her paralyzed. She was then told not to be afraid, and was given what amounted to an exercise in trust. She was put in a standing position and was pushed back and forth by a circle of ETs. Leslie reports that she felt like a punching clown toy, but eventually got over her fear.

Meanwhile, another witness was taken into a room where he was shown how to construct a UFO detector. The device involved two adjacent magnets which created a weak magnetic field. Whenever a stronger magnetic field approached, it would break the connection between the two weaker magnets, thereby indicating the close presence of a UFO.

The third witness was placed in a large chair and a helmet-like device was placed over his head, at which point he was given information which he is unable to consciously recall.

The three witnesses were then brought together. They dressed themselves and were returned to their car with temporary amnesia of the event. In the days that followed, however, the memories of the event automatically returned. After recalling the event consciously, the witnesses still underwent hypnotic regression. While some new details were revealed, the same story emerged. The witnesses recalled seeing what appeared to be a human being dressed in a blue Navy uniform, observing the abduction and examinations from onboard the craft.

Leslie reports that she has experienced numerous other encounters. On one occasion she was shown holographic films of upcoming natural disasters and earth changes. She reports that she was given bizarre emotional testings and was also shown a hybrid baby which the ETs said was her own child. She has also experienced considerable harassment from apparent U.S. military personnel. Leslie's case remains ongoing.[447]

In January 1991, Topanga Canyon resident Susan X. woke up to find herself paralyzed, unable to see or speak. She did, however, sense a presence in the room. "I lay there paralyzed, consumed with fear because I sensed that there was someone else in the room. And I was so fearful or so paralyzed that I could not move. My head was on a pillow to the side, and there was a presence of this figure at the foot of my bed. And I sensed that it was small. I sensed that it was maybe about three or four feet tall."

Susan was shocked at what happened next. "I sensed that a strand of my hair was picked up and cut ... the next thing I felt was that there was something penetrating my vagina. And it was as if this pen that I hold in my hand was merely inserted and then removed. And I could not move. I could not scream. I could not express anything. I lay there simply in fear."

At this point the figure left. Susan reports that it felt as if she were drugged. She compared it to having anesthesia. Susan and other family members later experienced UFO sightings. Susan, herself was transformed by the experience. She has become a vegetarian, an organic gardener, a passionate environmentalist, and has succumbed to a compulsion to save every seed she can find of edible plants. She feels that these changes are due to her earlier UFO experience.[448]

On June 20, 1992, flight attendant and Topanga Canyon resident Sarah Martin (pseudonym) woke up from a very strange dream to find a large unknown object landed outside her bedroom window. Says Martin, "I sat up in bed and looked out my window and there were these bright lights outside ... it was in the field across from my house. And it was a ship. It wasn't humongous; it was just about the size of two or three cars put end to end ... it was all lit up like a Christmas tree ... it was solid. It was a craft."

The object immediately took off and flew out of sight in a split-second. Martin was amazed not only by the sighting, but because moments earlier she was dreaming that she was inside a strange white room, surrounded by strange beings. She began to wonder if she had actually been inside the craft. Says Martin, "I was in a white room with ... things. That's where I have a problem. To be honest with you, I can't remember their faces. I just remember talking to them, and I was in a white room ... and they were talking to me. And this is what they said: 'Why are you so involved in this campaign [for Ross Perot]? Why are you wasting your time? It's going to fall apart, one by one, and whoever wins it doesn't matter because the whole system is going to come down around everybody. And there's going to be a rebellion. And you're not a part of this, so don't get involved.' ... the other thing too is something about an earthquake, a big earthquake."

The next day, the object returned and was observed by Sarah's husband, Roger. He saw a metallic saucer glowing with purple light landed in the field next to their home. After a few minutes, he unaccountably fell asleep.

Over the next three months, the craft continued to land a few days in a row, every couple of weeks, outside the Martin's home. Both felt that the UFO occupants were interested in Sarah because of her unusual pregnancy. She had been pregnant with twins, but one died in utero. She was told that the chances of carrying the remaining fetus to full term were one in five million.

Fortunately, the Martins had a healthy baby boy. They have since moved out of Topanga, partly due to the constant UFO visitations.[449]

On November 20, 1992, two anonymous women were abducted directly from the freeway in Ventura. They were driving northbound in the evening when they both observed a "huge, bright light" descend from the sky straight towards them. Their next recollection was exiting the freeway two and a half hours later.

The ladies sought the assistance of MUFON investigators Mike Evans and Alice Leavy who investigated the case. Later, the ladies underwent hypnosis with Yvonne Smith and recalled a complex abduction scenario involving gray-type aliens and praying mantis-type aliens. Both ladies were separately examined on board the craft. One of them was shown strange star maps. They were then returned with only the memory of the sighting and the missing time.[450]

On March 15, 1994, the TRIAD UFO conference was held in the Coronado Hotel on Coronado Island, just south of San Diego. A few hundred people attended the three-day-long conference.

In the middle of the night on March 15, seven independent attendees reported visitations by gray-type aliens directly into their separate hotel bedrooms. Each of the witnesses has a long history of California UFO encounters, and the case involves considerable physical evidence. No information about this case has yet been published. Because of the large number of witnesses and physical evidence, the case is sure to be ranked high on the scale of importance.[451]

20. The Implant Removal Surgeries

See color section, page 127

On August 19, 1995, one of the most important events in UFO history took place in a small doctor's office in Ventura, California. At 5:00 p.m., the then obscure doctor of podiatric medicine performed three surgeries to remove alleged "alien implants" from the hands and feet of two patients. For those who demand proof before they believe in such things as UFOs, the following case should be very interesting.

The story actually began two months earlier when Ventura physician and private pilot, Roger K. Leir DPM, attended a UFO conference in Houston, where he learned that many people who claim to have abduction experiences believe that they have had foreign objects implanted into their bodies by the extraterrestrials. Leir was stunned. He had a growing interest in UFOs, but this seemed like the "smoking-gun" proof that had been so elusive in the UFO field. He learned that many abductees had actual scars where the implants had been placed, and furthermore, the objects appeared on x-rays as opaque "foreign bodies." To his amazement, he realized that actual conclusive proof of extraterrestrial intervention was just one surgery away.

Leir worked closely with Texas-based researcher Derrel Sims and located two abductees who were willing to undergo surgery to have their implants removed.

On August 19, 1995, at 5:00 p.m., Roger Leir DPM and another physician, "Doctor A.," performed three sets of surgeries, removing three objects from the hands and feet of two witnesses. The surgeries were thoroughly documented and photographed.

One of the patients, Patricia X., had experienced a dramatic abduction while living in Texas. She was the first person to have her implant removed. It was in her big toe. Leir probed into her toe with an instrument when, as Leir recounts in his ground-breaking book, *The Aliens and The Scalpel*: "all at once the sound of a crisp metallic click was heard."

Leir asked the nurse for a Kelley clamp. Says Leir, "I carefully inserted the clamp into the wound, spread the jaws to their maximum, reached in and grasped a solid object."

Leir requested a Number 15 scalpel blade. "With that, I began the careful dissection to free the foreign body from its fatty and fibrous tissue attachments. In just a few moments I announced, 'Here it comes!' and with one final tug, the object came free from the inner confines of the toe."

The doctors stared at the object. Dr. A. said, "What the hell is that?" Leir examined the object visually. "I found myself staring at what appeared to be a T-shaped or triangular-shaped mass that was dark gray in color and slightly shiny. It looked fleshy, not metallic, and was about one-half centimeter long by one-half centimeter wide." Both doctors then attempted to dissect the object with the scalpel, but it was too durable. The implant was photographed and stored for later study. Patricia was prepared for her next surgery, the removal of an implant from her foot.

Leir had removed foreign objects from hundreds of people; however, this was definitely a new experience. His skill allowed him to find the foreign object with little difficulty. He inserted a clamp and "felt the jaws close on something solid." He carefully excised the attaching tissue and "with a gentle upward pressure, I was able to bring the object almost out of the wound."

Says Leir, "The object appeared like a small cantaloupe seed with a few tiny tendrils dragging from its ends. We were amazed to see that this newly acquired specimen was also covered with a smooth, glistening dark gray covering."

The third surgery involved "Paul," an abductee from Louisiana who had a suspected implant in his hand. While there was no entrance wound for the object, it appeared as a solid foreign body on x-rays. Even more incredibly, just before the surgery was to take place, Dr. Roger Leir had a hunch. He placed a Gauss meter over the area of the implant. To everyone's shock, the Gauss meter buzzed, meaning it was detecting an electromagnetic field. To get a clearer reading, the doctors decided to move the patient outside and away from all electromagnetic equipment. They were amazed by the results. Says Dr. Lear, "This damn thing [was] putting out one giant electromagnetic field. [It was] pegging the damn meter!"

The doctors returned the patient to the operating room and performed the surgery. Once the implant was removed, they were again shocked by its appearance. Says Leir, "The little gray object was then placed on the waiting stark white sponge. I was shocked. It looked exactly like the little object that I had removed from Patricia's toe just a few hours earlier. It was shaped like a small cantaloupe seed and appeared to be covered with a dark gray membrane."

Dr. A. again attempted to dissect the object, but was unable to do so. Of course, the objects were later studied extensively, the results of which are published in Dr. Leir's book. The implants appear to be foreign bodies in the truest sense of the word. Suffice it to say that the objects exhibited many highly unusual properties, have not been positive identified, and are continuing to be studied.

Many prominent figures in ufology witnessed the surgeries, which were extremely well documented. Among the witnesses was famed UFO experiencer Whitley Strieber, who later wrote: "To see these surgeries being performed was among the most moving experiences of my life."

Overnight, Roger Leir DPM found himself on the cutting edge of UFO research. He would later remove more implants from other abductees, with equally astonishing results.[452]

On January 2, 1996, Roger Leir DPM and his assistants removed a third "anomalous object" from the left neck-shoulder region of another UFO abductee. The surgery went smoothly and the suspected implant, a "grayish-white ball" was removed. Dr. A. remarked that it looked like a calcifying epitheliomas, or a calcium deposit. However, further analysis of the object proved that this was not the case. Writes Leir, "Such was not the clinical picture presented in this case. In fact it was the exact opposite of what I found in the medical texts. Later analysis of the grayish-white ball would prove this lesion was not a calcifying epithelioma."

The implant was sent to a lab for further study. Dr. Leir now found himself sought after by media outlets across the United States and the world. His life would never be the same. Another set of surgeries were planned to take place in a few months.[453]

On 10:30 a.m. on May 18, Dr. Leir and his associate, Dr. Mitter, performed three separate implant removal surgeries on three different patients. The first surgery involved a lady named "Annie" who had experienced numerous UFO encounters in the past.

The implant was in Annie's leg and had appeared following an abduction experience. X-rays revealed a "small radio-opaque ball" located in the soft tissues just beneath her skin. The surgery went quickly and the implant was removed. Writes Dr. Leir, "Then I heard and felt a little clicking sound. My instrument had touched something solid. There it was – a small round, grayish-white ball that glistened under the powerful surgical light."

Preparations were immediately made for the second surgery. The patient, Doris X., discovered a strange scoop mark near her shin bone following an abduction experience on Coronado Island. X-rays revealed a "small, round, radio-dense shadow in the area."

The surgery was done quickly, and the specimen was placed on a surgical sponge. Writes Leir, "Again, an audible click was heard, and there it was – another small, grayish-white shiny ball."

The third patient, "Don," was diagnosed with a metallic foreign body in his jaw. He also had a long history of extensive UFO encounters. The first step was to examine the object using a flouroscan. Says Dr. Leir, "We quickly moved our eyes to the TV monitor and watched as the tissues of the jaw became visible. Suddenly, there it was ... the small triangular object was visible on the screen."

The surgeons carefully removed the object and surrounding tissue and placed it on a surgical sponge for the preliminary visual analysis. Writes Leir, "I took a surgical blade and began to dissect the soft tissue away from the metal portion. It appeared to be triangular in shape and was definitely metal. Slowly I removed the clinging surrounding tissue until more specific detail could be seen. It was then I noticed it: the metallic portion was covered with the same dark gray, well-organized membrane we had seen covering the metallic specimens we had removed in August of 1995. I couldn't believe my eyes. I picked up the blade again and tried to cut through the membrane. The harder I tried, the more frustrated I became. It would not open, just like the other specimens from the previous year."

The implants were then sent off for study. Because of the enormous costs involved, some of the study was funded by millionaire Robert Bigelow of the Bigelow Foundation.

The studies proved to be highly promising, with the implants showing several unique and inexplicable properties. Not only did one of the implants emit an easily-detectable electromagnetic field, but when the specimens were placed under ultraviolet light, "each one fluoresced, but not all were of the same greenish color. There was a variance of green to pink in color. We did not understand this."

Very expensive metallurgical testing was done, which showed that some of the implants contained as many as eleven different elements in a ratio that is ordinarily found only in meteorites! As Leir writes, "The composition of the objects includes metals whose isotopic ratios are clearly not from Earth. Moreover, the form of these objects is clearly engineered and manufactured with precision rather than being a naturally occurring form."

One of the implants had an iron core and was surrounded by a phosphorus coating. Biological analysis of the surrounding tissues also revealed a lack of inflammatory response or foreign body reactions. Many other puzzling details were found, the full story of which is told in Leir's book. Needless to say, analysis of the implants continues and more surgeries have been planned.

Says Leir, "If these scientifically derived results are not disproven by subsequent analysis, then we can safely conclude that *some individuals with alien abduction histories have artificially manufactured objects in their bodies of a demonstrably extraterrestrial origin.* In short, we now have the "smoking gun" of ufology – the hard, physical, scientific evidence of a continuing alien presence on Earth!"

The implant removal surgeries performed by Dr. Leir and his associates have astonished the scientific community. Prominent UFO researchers are united in their assessment that the implant studies have the potential to yield a major breakthrough in the advancement in solving the UFO mystery.

Leading researcher Budd Hopkins writes, "Dr. Roger Leir has finally and dramatically laid his cards on the table. His carefully documented surgical removal of possible alien implants can no longer be ignored. It may very well turn out to be an event of extraordinary importance."

Highly-respected investigator Raymond Fowler writes, "Dr. Leir is to be praised for his pioneering research into the removal and analysis of suspected alien implants. Only peer review and acceptance separate his findings from being the proverbial *smoking gun* of physical evidence for the abduction phenomenon."

Well-known author and experiencer Whitley Strieber writes, "Sometimes the whole world knows when a historical figure makes his history. As often, though, people whose work is little known make history in the quiet of ordinary life. Dr. Roger Leir is such a historical figure. There will come a time when the extraordinary breakthrough that he has made is noted in every textbook ... the evidence is here ... so overwhelmingly powerful that a sane person cannot easily deny that it is real .... [Leir] proves that there is physical evidence of our encounters, and shows with authority that this evidence cannot be explained in any normal way."[454]

On August 17, 1996, Dr. Roger Leir DPM performed his eighth implant removal surgery in his Ventura office. The results of the surgery were, again, very compelling. Writes Leir, "This procedure was much the same as the other procedures we had performed in 1995. In fact it was so similar that when I saw the object come out of the surgical wound, it literally sent chills running down my spine and made the hair stand straight up on the back of my neck."

The patient, "Pablo," had a metallic foreign body in his thumb with no evidence of any entry wound and no history to explain its presence other than UFO encounters. The implant-removal surgery yielded a familiar-looking object. Writes Leir, "What we removed was almost identical to the little cantaloupe-seed-shaped objects removed in 1995. As a matter of fact it was so similar that I would wager that, if all three were lined up, you could not tell one from the other."[455]

On December 5, 2003, in his office in Ventura, Dr. Roger Leir DPM performed his eleventh implant removal surgery on abductee, "Brenda," who had a suspected implant in her cheek. She had a long history of abductions, but became aware of the implant following dental x-rays. On several occasions, dentists had asked her about the metallic rod in her mouth, six millimeters in length and 1 millimeter in thickness. Brenda, however, had no history of surgery. The object had no right to be there.

Leir and his team had removed several implants already, but were surprised by the unusual nature of this particular one. Not only did the object emit an electromagnetic field of 2.5 milligauss, it also exhibited another strange phenomenon. A Radio Frequency Detector registered emanations ranging from 92.7 to 102.9 megahertz. This was before surgery, while the object was still in Brenda's body.

Another surprise came during the actual surgery. Writes Leir, "If it were not for the fact we had use of a sophisticated and new Flouroscan Unit, we would never have been able to remove the object. The surgeon placed an instrument into the wound and we observed the object, along with the metallic instrument, on a television screen. We all stood dumbfounded as we watched the small metallic object simply turn and dance away from the instrument. For almost an hour a very frustrated patient and surgical team painstakingly sought to grasp this illusive metallic rod. Suddenly, there it was, between the teeth of the instrument, coming to the surface easily, seemingly attached to nothing."

After finally removing the object, the team examined it. Writes Leir, "It is bronze in color and seems to have thickened and beveled ends. It is very lightweight and highly magnetic."

Leir also reports another strange effect. "I noted the stainless steel instrument I had just used to transfer the object had been magnetized. This again is strange because these instruments are made to reduce the possibility of this occurring."[456]

As can be seen, proof of extraterrestrial visitation is now in the public arena. The time for skepticism is over. Now that the existence of UFOs has been essential proven, we can begin to focus our efforts on dealing with the phenomenon and its consequences on humanity.

21. California UFOs Today

See color section, page 128

UFO activity has occurred steadily for more than one hundred years and shows no signs of stopping. Each year brings new reports of sightings, landings, onboard encounters, and more. The last ten years have been as active as ever.

On March 7, 1997, an anonymous Santa Monica resident was outside his home overlooking the Santa Monica Mountains when he observed a helicopter-like object shining down a powerful beam of light. The object, however, was totally silent and was emitting large puffs of smoke. Suddenly, it zoomed upwards to a high altitude. Says the witness, "Within seconds, it was 'parked' next to a star, very far away ... it was as if it was trying to camouflage itself next to that star."

The now star-like object began to emit a rotating red light. Seconds later, it zipped northward at incredible speeds and disappeared. The witness is convinced that it was a genuine UFO.[457]

On August 4, 1998, a highly-visible UFO sighting was reported by numerous residents of Tracy and San Francisco. According to local radio station KCSB, many callers reported their observations of an unidentified blue-white light moving at high speed across the San Francisco Bay area. Witnesses watched as the object separated into two pieces and disappeared moving eastward. The radio station contacted the local meteorological monitoring center and the air traffic control – neither of which had any information or explanation regarding the sighting.

There was also one unconfirmed report of a possible UFO crash. An unidentified resident from Tracy claims to have seen a "round, greenish-blue UFO" plummet to the earth.[458]

In 1998, Steve Thomsen was hiking near his home in Topanga Canyon State Park when he observed a large metallic disk in the clear daylight sky. Having seen UFOs on previous occasions, he always carried a camera with him. He snapped a series of four photographs as the craft appeared to pose for him a few hundred feet away. (See photo section.)

Also in 1998, Michael Davey of Los Angeles was hiking through a remote area in Titus Canyon when he observed a large metallic UFO hovering overhead. He had seen UFOs in the past with his friends, Steve Thomsen and Joe Clower, each of whom had also photographed the objects. Not wanting to be left out, Davey also carried a camera with him on his hikes. On this occasion, he was able to obtain one clear photo of the disk as it hovered in the daylight sky above two radar towers. (See photo section.)[459]

One evening just before midnight in February 1999, a law enforcement officer had a dramatic close-up sighting with a metallic craft outside of San Luis Obispo. Says the witness, Eric Edwards, "I was just about to enter the city limits, when up ahead about 300 yards in front of me and 75 feet above the highway, I observed a huge massive light, lime-green, luminous object drifting/gliding across the highway up to the top of the hill, where it stopped in mid-air. The outer edges of the craft were luminous or fluorescent like neon lights .... This object made no noise .... There were no windows. Its size was half of a baseball field. It moved from south to north and hovered for just around two minutes. Then it started moving a little more north, then headed east, and at literally incredible speed, acceleration was something out of science fiction – no sonic boom, and it was gone."

The witness was deeply impressed by his sighting and desperately wanted answers. As he says, "In my whole life I have never observed anything like this. It was so close to me, not way up in the sky .... I work in law enforcement and I am afraid to tell or relate this for fear of ridicule."

Edwards later found out that there was another witness to his sighting; however, he was unable to obtain verification.[460]

A dramatic and highly credible sighting was reported by two Rialto residents on April 20, 1999. Michael Hawkins (a former Air Force and Lockheed mechanic) and Lia Simmons (an elementary school teacher) were in the spa in their backyard when they observed a disk-shaped craft hovering overhead, darting back and forth over Ontario airport. As they watched, two jetliners approached the object, which emitted a shower of red sparks and instantly accelerated out of sight. Says Hawkins, "I'm familiar with aircraft and this was like nothing I've ever seen. It was one of the strangest events of my life."

Simmons agrees. As she says, "[I] couldn't believe what I was seeing. It startled us. You could plainly see a disc. I said, 'Other people have to be seeing this.'"

It turned out that the National UFO Reporting Center did in fact receive a report that evening of a sighting over the city of Lakewood.[461]

Two months later, in June of 1999, ham radio operator Malcom Uhl and four others were camping in Feather River Canyon outside of Belden when they observed a "large metallic craft 50 feet in length, stationary, bright silver in color and apparently noiseless." The craft zoomed away after a few moments. However, the next day, two gold prospectors were working on their claim in adjacent Rush Creek when they observed what was apparently the same craft.[462]

Another possible UFO-caused power outage occurred on the evening of August 29, 2000. A few minutes after the city of Hidden Valley Lake experienced a widespread and unexplained loss of electrical power, residents of the neighboring city of Clearlake observed a star-like object zooming across the sky. At one point, the object followed a plane, darted in front of it and then accelerated "straight up in the sky." Officials at Pacific Gas and Electric reported that no damage was discovered to any equipment and the power loss remains unexplained.[463]

On September 15, 2000, two witnesses observed an unusual glowing object floating over the Pacific Ocean outside of Berkeley. They used their telescope to observe the object and saw a "black disk ... surrounded by a pulsating orange halo." Both witnesses are professionals and insisted that the object was definitely unconventional.[464]

A recent sighting involving electromagnetic effects occurred on March 9, 2001, to a Simi Valley resident. Says the witness, "I was driving on Route 118 north of Simi Valley at

3:36 a.m. I saw a green fireball/round object about the size of an orange held at arm's length fly over my car and continue in the same direction. I slowed down and lost sight of it. The greenish light around it seemed fuzzy. I experienced a few blown fuses in my car within the next hour."[465]

In November 2001, Santa Clarita resident Tracie Austin-Peters and her husband Jim Peters launched a southern California based public access cable television show focusing on UFOs and the paranormal. Shortly after starting the show, Austin-Peters and her husband experienced a close-up sighting of a massive triangle-shaped craft.

The couple was driving through downtown Studio City. It was 6:45 in the evening of November 13, 2001. They suddenly noticed an object less than a thousand feet above them. Says Austin-Peters, "It was traveling too slow and was at an extremely low altitude .... We rolled down the windows on the car, and lo and behold, totally silent was a black triangular craft that came over the car less than two hundred feet ... we were right under this thing looking up .... I shout out, 'My God, it's a UFO!' And it stopped and hovered over the car. As soon as I said it, the whole thing stopped and hovered. It had white lights running underneath it, cold white lights. And there was an outer framework to this craft. It was black ... it was there for about six seconds, I would say. And then it did this amazing turn that even Steven Spielberg in all honesty would have difficulty trying to recreate. And it just turned and it did this amazing glide, and it went off."

The couple tried to follow the object, but were blocked by a series of red traffic lights.[466]

The Peters' sighting marked the beginning of a wave of black triangle sightings across California. On March 29, 2002, two people were driving along a busy freeway outside of Bakersfield when they and hundreds of others observed a UFO hovering over the freeway. Says one witness, "The craft was diamond-shaped and dark gray color with a red light. It would make very sharp turns that no airplane I have ever seen could have made. It hovered on the northbound side of the freeway, went over a field, and turned very sharply. I thought the object was trying to land. It looked like it was have troubles."

The witnesses also observed a highway patrol officer speeding at an estimated 100 miles per hour in pursuit of the object.[467]

On July 23, 2002 (the same night as a sighting at LAX), numerous reports came from across California, from Los Angeles to as far north as Sequoia National Park. Silverlake resident Jesus Guzman was outside his home at 10:15 p.m. when he observed and videotaped an unidentified string of red lights moving very slowly across the sky. The same objects were observed by three other witnesses from the adjacent city of Hawthorne. Another witness, a security guard based at the tip of Palos Verdes Peninsula also observed the object.

An analysis and computer enhancement of Guzman's video tape revealed that the string of lights was actually one large triangular-shaped object. The entire incident was thoroughly investigated by several MUFON investigators including Ann Druffel, Bill Casey, Ralph McCarron, Bill Hamilton, Steve Murillo, and Georgeanne Cifarelli. It is considered one of most significant and best verified California sightings for that year.[468]

As we have seen, there are definite patterns to UFO sightings. One common pattern that exerts itself is that UFO sightings come in clusters or waves. In other words, if one UFO shows up, the chances are greatly increased that there is or will be another sighting in the same area. Often multiple objects will show up simultaneously.

On September 19, 2002, at 2:30 a.m., a couple from Winnetka was awake in the early morning hours when they observed multiple objects in the sky. Says the main witness, "We saw five objects, three in a row, going downward in the sky ... the objects had flashing lights of different colors. We were able to see them better with binoculars in the eastern San Fernando Valley, and tried to capture them with a digital camera, but the battery died. I am an employee of a public utility and my husband is a welder. We are not usually awake at this hour, but we were preparing to go on vacation."[469]

Another black triangle sighting occurred at 5:20 p.m. on January 1, 2003. At the time of the sighting, the witness was flying in his private plane over San Jose. As he says, "The flying triangles were clearly not flying like planes, nor did they look like any kinds of planes I have ever seen ... this is the first time I have observed anything like this. I have always been extremely skeptical of UFOs ... however these objects were clearly some kind of object I could not identify."[470]

At around 10:30 p.m. on May 7, 2003, four Northridge residents were in their home playing poker when one of them noticed a "very weird thing" moving outside past the window. They rushed outside and saw two more objects. Says the main witness, "There were three green, cigar-shaped flying objects. First they were flying slowly, but then they separated and one flew east, the other two joined it five seconds later and they increased their speed and disappeared into the clouds. That was really scary and creepy!"[471]

On June 6, 2003, a witness with a doctorate education was driving through Camarillo at 5:30 p.m. when he observed a "large, low-flying black chevron-shaped craft moving slowly." At first he assumed it was the stealth bomber, but it appeared to be moving too slowly and was also strangely shaped. Says the witness, "It appeared completely flat on top, unlike the stealth bomber. It flew overhead with no sound." The witness watched the object disappear over the Santa Monica Mountains.[472]

On October 19, 2003, at midday, R. David Anderson was working outside his home in Modesto when he and his daughter observed a veritable fleet of UFOs. The first object approached from the north. Says Anderson, "It was bright, star-like, and it made a loop around the house and hovered above me for about five minutes. I went into the house and got binoculars and went back outside and looked at it ... the UFO appeared to be changing shapes, from a sphere to an elongated form."

Anderson called out his daughter, and together they observed the object split into two separate objects. Suddenly, a "long-shaped" craft appeared between the two objects, and a fourth even larger UFO approached. Says Anderson, "I could see it in detail. It was shaped like a cigar with a triangle on the front of it. On the sides were many rectangular features."

The objects darted across the sky and left. A few hours later, more UFOs showed up. This time, Anderson was ready with a video camera. As he says, "I got the video camera and spotted three UFOs coming from the north and recorded them as they traveled above the house. These UFOs were spherical in shape, bright, and closer, and are the ones in the video. They traveled in unison. About forty minutes later, I also got another shot of a UFO moving above the trees."[473]

At 8:30 p.m., on November 17, 2003, an anonymous gentleman and his daughter were driving through the San Fernando Valley in Burbank when they had a striking sighting. "My daughter and I saw a gold sphere traveling slowly in the southern sky above Los Angeles, similar to a sighting by my wife and me several months ago. It traveled to the southwestern sky in a circular motion for about ten minutes. I tried to get my telescope out, but by the time I got set up, it vanished."[474]

On January 3, 2004, Young Chyren was on the coast of Santa Monica during the afternoon when he observed a metallic disk-like object hovering a few thousand feet above a yacht. The object stayed stationary in the sky, so he quickly grabbed his camera and snapped a photograph. (See photo section.) Because he knew the length of the yacht, he estimated the size of the UFO as being about thirty feet wide. After a few moments, the strange craft darted away.[475]

On January 4, 2004, two residents of Hayward were driving at night when they observed a white egg-shaped object floating in the sky. Says the main witness, "It was about five feet in diameter at its thinnest point and moved north just over us as we drove southbound. Then I saw two more objects about three-fourths that size ... they were also egg-shaped, but gray, not metallic. The white egg shape then changed shape slightly into a smoothened diamond-like shape about 200 feet above me. The two gray craft stopped in mid-air, and the white craft joined them in a delta formation directly over our heads. The white craft then again sped off towards the north, and the two gray craft quickly went straight up and disappeared. The white craft followed us south as we drove off and then sped off."

The witness reports that he snapped several photographs of the objects before they disappeared.[476]

More cases could be listed, but by now the details would only be repetitive. The same types of reports are flooding in from all across California. The conclusion is inescapable: UFOs are real, and they are here to stay.

Epilogue

With an estimated *minimum* of at least 5000 recorded encounters, California remains the nation's top producer of UFO reports.

The entire phenomenon is represented in all its myriad facets including sightings, landings, landing-trace cases, conscious abductions, missing-time abductions, face-to-face encounters, underwater UFOs, contactee accounts, gray-type aliens, human-looking aliens, Praying Mantis-Type aliens, airplane-UFO encounters, angel-hair cases, healings, electromagnetic effects, implants, crashed UFOs ... the list goes on.

California, however, does put its own spin on the phenomenon. For example, the underwater UFO reports: more than a dozen cases are listed, making California a top producer of these types of accounts. With so many underwater UFOs in the same area, one can only speculate on the presence of some kind of underwater base.

Another incredible story is that of Muroc/Edwards. The more than thirty sightings on the public record lend credence to the more fantastic accounts of the Eisenhower-ET meeting, the UFO landings, the storage of alien bodies, and the reverse-engineering of crashed ET craft.

Another bizarre and uniquely Californian phenomenon are the many contactee accounts. While the contactee movement was particularly strong in the 1950s, it never actually ended. Even today, many Californians claim to have continuing contacts with friendly human-looking aliens.

Interestingly, several of the most prominent California investigators have also taken a positive view towards close encounters (i.e.: Richard Boylan Ph.D., Edith Fiore Ph.D., Barbara Lamb MFCC, James Harder Ph.D.). Researcher Yvonne Smith, who has uncovered several harrowing abduction accounts, also claims to have uncovered a case of a man possibly cured of HIV as a result of his encounter. As we have seen, California has also produced a large number of healing accounts.

The research of Roger Leir DPM also deserves special mention because of its potential to change the face of UFO research. Now that there is conclusive hard evidence of UFO reality in the public arena, doors should start to open for more heavily-funded research.

Today, skeptics no longer have the right to disbelieve. The proof is there for anyone with the courage to examine it. One look at *www.Blackvault.com*, the website of Northridge-based researcher David Greenewalde Jr. conclusively proves the government interest in and cover-up of UFO events.

The purpose of this book has been to provide a history and chronology of the extraterrestrial presence in the state of California. However, as any UFO researcher will tell you, only about one person out of a hundred reports their encounter in any official capacity. Of the several hundred people I have interviewed over the past twenty years, less than fifteen have called police, newspapers or any other official agency. The nature of the phenomenon is such that it dissuades many people from running the risks inherent with publicly divulging their encounter. Many witnesses keep their encounters secret even from family members.

Because of this, any statistics showing the actual number of encounters are deflated to the point of being almost meaningless. The actual number of encounters is likely a hundred times greater than the reported number of encounters. It could be significantly more than that.

For that reason, the complete story of UFOs over California may never be told. Fortunately, enough people have stepped forward, and investigators have gathered enough evidence to reveal a fairly accurate assessment of the UFO situation.

Although we have come to the point where we know UFOs are real, what the future brings remains a mystery. One can only speculate.

However, if one examines the evolution of the relationship between UFOs and humanity starting from the 1940s, a definite trend of escalating contact exists. What started with scattered distant sightings has evolved into widespread face-to-face contacts on board apparent ET craft. There is a very real possibility of open, official contact happening sometime in the future. The many recent UFO waves over high population centers points to a publicity campaign on the part of the ETs. In these areas, UFOs are seen by hundreds or thousands of people. They are photographed and filmed. They put on displays for witnesses, and brazenly chase cars down the street, or lead aircraft in a cat and mouse chase. They obviously want to be seen.

We now have conclusive proof of UFO contact. UFOs are here, that much is certain. And if trends continue as they have, the future can only bring more accounts and further dramatic visitations. What this means for humanity will eventually be revealed, perhaps sooner than anyone might expect.

Appendix
Chronology of Unexplained Air Force Blue Book Cases In California
(1947-1969)

Case #36	July 6, 1947	Fairfield-Suisun AFB
Case #50	July 8, 1947	Muroc AFB
Case #69	July 29, 1947	Hamilton Field
Case #208	September 23, 1948	San Pablo
Case #379	May 6, 1949	Livermore
Case #907	March 13, 1951	McClellan AFB
Case #964	September 6, 1951	Claremont
Case #1077	March 24, 1952	Point Conception
Case #1115	April 15, 1952	Santa Cruz
Case #1176	May 1, 1952	George AFB
Case #1194	May 19, 1952	George AFB
Case #1588	July 24, 1952	Travis AFB
Case #16??	July 26, 1952	Williams
Case #1771	August 1, 1952	Lancaster
Case #1920	August 18, 1952	Fairfield
Case #1928	August 19, 1952	Red Bluff
Case #2086	September 14, 1952	Santa Barbara
Case #2128	September 27, 1952	Inyokern
Case #2302	December 28, 1952	Marysville
Case #2326	January 10, 1953	Sonoma
Case #2361	January 28, 1953	Point Mugu
Case #2426	February 20, 1953	Stockton
Case #2686	August 20, 1953	Unknown
Case #2840	December 24, 1953	El Cajon
Case #2844	December 28, 1953	Marysville
Case#2994	May 10, 1954	Elsinore
Case #3140	July 30, 1954	Los Angeles
Case #3222	September 21, 1954	Barstow
Case #3416	February 2, 1955	Miramar NAS
Case #4127	June 6, 1956	Banning
Case #5716	March 14, 1958	Healdsburg
Case #6962	September 10, 1960	Ridgecrest
Case #7133	November 27, 1960	Chula Vista
Case #8548	September 14, 1963	Susanville
Case #9049	August 15, 1964	Yosemite National Park

Endnotes

1. Hynek, 1977, 268-270.
2. NUFORC.
3. Lindemann, 185-186.
4. Jessup, 57-58, 61-62.
5. Blum & Blum, 49.
6. Lorenzen & Lorenzen, 1969, 11-12; Billig, 65.
7. Randles & Estes, 119.
8. Flammonde, 93-95.
9. Clarke & Coleman, 131-151; Flammonde 76-97.
10. Rife, 51-52.
11. Hall, 1999, 6.
12. Hall, 1999, 12.
13. Good, 1998, 29-30; Cerve, 250-252.
14. Lorenzen & Lorenzen, 1969, 19.
15. Good, 1998, 15-17, 446.
16. Good, 1998, 11-13.
17. Lorenzen & Lorenzen, 1969, 22-23.
18. Rogo, 81.
19. Dennett, 1997, 89-92.
20. Dolan, 17; Hall, 1999, 33; Flammonde, 159.
21. Blum & Blum, 77.
22. Hall, 1999, 44.
23. Scully, 191.
24. Hall, 1999, 46.
25. Hall, 1999, 48.
26. Hall, 1999, 50.
27. Hall, 1999, 51.
28. Hall, 1999, 56.
29. Hall, 1999, 52.
30. Hall, 1999, 53.
31. Hall, 1999, 54
32. Hall, 1999, 63
33. Hall, 1999, 69
34. Steiger, 1976, 348.
35. Wilkins, 1954, 80-81.
36. Hall, 1999, 121.
37. Scully, 194.
38. Steiger, 1977, 348.
39. Druffel & Rogo, 150.
40. Scully, 224.
41. Stringfield, 1977, 58.
42. Wilkins, 1954, 138.
43. Druffel & Rogo, 150; Johnson, 50.
44. Scully, 206; Johnson, 51.
45. Scully, 206; Johnson, 51.
46. Scully, 207; Johnson, 52.

47. Scully, 208; Johnson, 52.
48. Johnson, 53.
49. Scully, 214; Johnson, 56.
50. Johnson, 56.
51. Johnson, 56.
52. Scully, 215; Johnson, 56.
53. Johnson, 60.
54. Scully, 223; Johnson, 60.
55. Johnson, 61-62.
56. Johnson, 62.
57. Scully, 225.
58. Dolan, 84, 399.
59. Johnson, 65-66.
60. Wilkins, 131.
61. Druffel & Rogo, 150.
62. Steiger, 1977, 350.
63. Lorenzen & Lorenzen, 1969, 39-40.
64. Steiger, 1977, 350.
65. Dolan, 94.
66. Vallee, 1969, 196-197.
67. Lorenzen & Lorenzen, 1969, 41.
68. Wilkins, 1954, 266.
69. Maccabee, 209.
70. Steiger, 1977, 351.
71. Steiger, 1977, 351.
72. Dolan, 99; Hall, 1988, 241-242.
73. Hynek, 1977, 107-109; Hall, 1999, 167-168; Dolan, 100.
74. Hall, 1999, 172; Ruppelt, 188-189.
75. Dolan, 401.
76. Wilkins, 1954, 267
77. Dolan, 105.
78. Steiger, 1977, 355.
79. Dolan, 402.
80. Wilkins, 1954, 275.
81. Steiger, 1977, 356.
82. Keyhoe, 1955, 218-219; Dolan, 109.
83. Steiger, 1977, 357.
84. Druffel & Rogo, 151.
85. Steiger, 1977, 357.
86. Steiger, 1977, 358.
87. Greer MD, 143-144.
88. Stevens & Roberts, 221.
89. Stevens & Roberts, 221.
90. Steiger, 1977, 359.
91. Stevens & Roberts, 222.
92. Flammonde, 326-327.
93. Lorenzen & Lorenzen, 1969, 39.

94. Lorenzen & Lorenzen, 1969, 50.
95. Steiger, 1977, 359.
96. Stevens & Roberts, 222.
97. Steiger, 1977, 359.
98. Barker, 47.
99. Adamski, 296.
100. Keyhoe, 1973, 40-41; Dolan, 136-137; Lorenzen & Lorenzen, 1962, 178.
101. Barker, 47-48.
102. Wilkins, 1954, 222
103. Wilkins, 1954, 248-286.
104. Wilkins, 1954, 287.
105. Dolan, 137.
106. Steiger, 1977, 360.
107. Good, 1988, 278; Dolan, 136.
108. Dennett, 1997, 111-115.
109. Stevens & Roberts, 226.
110. Wilkins, 1955, 209.
111. Stevens & Roberts, 226.
112. Lorenzen & Lorenzen, 1969, 53; Green, 74; Steiger, 1966, 61.
113. Hall, 1999, 213-215.
114. Dolan, 406.
115. Steiger, 1977, 360.
116. Stevens & Roberts, 227.
117. Druffel & Rogo, 151.
118. Green, 74; Lorenzen & Lorenen, 1969, 61.
119. Wilkins, 1955, 129.
120. Stevens & Roberts, 229.
121. Keyhoe, 1955, 130-132; Good, 282.
122. Vallee, 206; Dolan, 150.
123. Wilkins, 1955, 234.
124. Steiger, 1977, 361.
125. Keyhoe, 1955, 202.
126. Steiger, 1977, 361.
127. Stevens & Roberts, 238.
128. Dolan, 178-179.
129. Steiger, 1977, 362.
130. Stevens & Roberts, 239.
131. Hynek, 1977, 33, 44.
132. Reeve, 86-87.
133. Druffel & Rogo, 152-153.
134. Druffel & Rogo, 149.
135. Haines Ph.D., 66.
136. Thompson, 29-30.
137. Steiger, 1977, 363; Vallee, 253.

138. Stevens & Roberts, 246.
139. Lorenzen & Lorenzen, 1969, 71-72; Dolan, 187.
140. Lorenzen & Lorenzen, 1969, 71.
141. Stevens & Roberts, 248.
142. Stevens & Roberts, 248-249; Steiger & Steiger, 1977, 146.
143. Stevens & Roberts, 249.
144. Stevens & Roberts, 249.
145. Dolan, 194-195; Hall, 1988, 242-244.
146. Rasmussen, Dec 17, 2000.
147. Dolan, 197.
148. Vallee & Vallee, 205.
149. Druffel & Rogo, 152.
150. Hynek, 1977, 44.
151. Druffel & Rogo, 152.
152. Steiger, 1977, 363; Vallee, 270.
153. NUFORC.
154. Fowler, 103.
155. Lorenzen & Lorenzen, 1969, 95.
156. Hynek, 1977, 167-170.
157. Vallee, 279.
158. Druffel & Rogo, 153.
159. Johnson, 10.
160. Johnson, 14-15.
161. Flammonde, 348.
162. Flammonde, 348; Haines Ph.D., 80-81; Hynek, 1977, 92; Dolan, 243; Lorenzen & Lorenzen, 1969, 153-156.
163. Macklin, 172.
164. Greer MD, 263.
165. Macklin, 98-99, 128-129.
166. Vallee, 287.
167. Vallee, 1965, 173.
168. Dolan, 270.
169. Edwards, 1966, 32-33; Dolan, 277; Vallee, 298.
170. Baker, 206-207; Greer MD, 183-188.
171. Clark & Coleman, 230.
172. Dennett, 1997, 127-130.
173. Edwards, 1966, 300-302; Dolan, 286-287.
174. Edwards, 1966, 32-33.
175. Vallee, 1319.
176. Greer MD, 266-267.
177. Vallee, 334-335.
178. Steiger & Whritenour, 68.
179. Steiger & Whritenour, 72-73.
180. Hynek, 1972, 44, 266.
181. Haines, Ph.D., 214.
182. Druffel & Rogo, 152-153.
183. Hynek, 1972, 268
184. Steiger & Whritenour, 99.
185. Dennett, 1997, 191-196.
186. Keyhoe, 1973, 237.

187. Greer MD, 108-111.
188. Keyhoe, 1973, 236.
189. Crystal, 1-4.
190. Dennett, 1997, 169-176.
191. Vallee, 1988, 171-172.
192. Dennett, 1997, 211-214.
193. Flammonde, 441.
194. Blum & Blum, 47.
195. Dennett, 2001, 7-10.
196. Dennett, 1997, 169-176.
197. Druffel & Rogo, 155-157.
198. Hall, 1988, 283.
199. Gutilla, 35.
200. Dennett, 1999, 147-151.
201. Gribble, June 1990, 19-20.
202. Dennett, 1997, 105-110.
203. Druffel, 1978, 15.
204. Druffel & Rogo, 157-158.
205. Dennett, 1997, 19-26.
206. Dennett, 1997, 31-36.
207. Edwards, 9-10.
208. Howard, May 18, 1997.
209. Canlen, Feb. 8, 1990.
210. Dennett, 1997, 47-50.
211. Dennett, 1997, 135-143.
212. Dennett, 1997, 197-205.
213. NUFORC
214. Dennett, 1999, 141-152.
215. Hall, 8-9.
216. Hassel, 9-12.
217. Dennett, 1997, 207-210.
218. Dennett, 1997, 135-143.
219. Dennett, 1997, 57-60.
220. Dennett, 1997, 27-30.
221. Dennett, 1997, 131-140.
222. NUFORC
223. Dennett, 1999, 7; personal files.
224. Dennett, 1997 169-176.
225. Wronge, July 3, 1997.
226. Dennett, 1999, 7-8; personal files.
227. Enterprise, May 27, 1988.
228. Drake, 12.
229. Valaitis, 1.
230. Steinberg, June 21, 1989.
231. Barbour Ph.D., Dec 10, 1988.
232. LA Times, June 20, 1989.
233. Personal files.
234. Grant, Oct 3, 1989.
235. Dennett, 1997, 185-190.
236. Booth, Sep 5, 1993; Canlen, Feb 8, 1990.
237. Bogert, 6.
238. Dennett, 1997, 121-126.
239. Canlen, Feb 8, 1990.
240. Ciborowski, 50-53.
241. Booth, Sep 5, 1993.
242. Dennett, 1997, 197-206.
243. Dennett, 1997, 215-260; Dennett, 1999, 10-41.
244. Steiger & Steiger, 108-109

245. Dennett, 1999, 168-190.
246. Dennett, 1999, 99-100.
247. Spaceage, 36-37.
248. Booth, Sep 5, 1993.
249. McKenzie, 14.
250. Booth, Sep 5, 1993.
251. Dennett, 1999, 117-122.
252. Dennett, 1999, 228-229.
253. Cassidy, Dec 27, 1995.
254. Haines Ph.D., 151-152; personal files.
255. Dennett, 1999, 123-126.
256. NUFORC.
257. NUFORC.
258. Hickox & Miller, Feb. 10, 1995.
259. Jones, 7-8; Wronge, July 3, 1997.
260. Jarvis, Dec. 15, 1994.
261. Girardot, July 4, 1996.
262. Wronge, July 3, 1997.
263. Personal files; Chawkins, Oct 6, 1994.
264. Strieber, 192-193; Leir, 1997, 3-9.
265. Adamski, 10, 13, 17, 23-51, 90-160.
266. Reeve, 226-231.
267. Wilkins, 1955, 30-33.
268. Wilkins, 1955, 35.
269. Olsen, 54-59; Davis, 28-30.
270. Reeve, 109, 302.
271. Beckley, 71-75.
272. Randazzo, 50-62.
273. Clark & Coleman, 228-230; Good, 1988, 276.
274. Randazzo, 40-41.
275. Randazzo, 42-44.
276. Beckley, 1999, 22-23.
277. Keyhoe, 1955, 258; Dolan, 173-174.
278. Beckley, 1992, 15-16.
279. Beckley, 1992, 13-14.
280. Good, 1993, 80-81.
281. Beckley, 1992, 92.
282. Hall, 1999, 57.
283. Wilkins, 1954, 79.
284. Wilkins, 1954, 150.
285. Wilkins, 1955, 237.
286. Haines Ph.D., 279.
287. Dolan, 181.
288. Rogo, 160.
289. Lorenzen & Lorenzen, 1969, 70.
290. Stringfield, 58.
291. Mattingly, 12; Steiger & Whritenour, 67.
292. Lorenzen & Lorenzen, 1968, 52.
293. Lorenzen & Lorenzen, 1968, 53.
294. Dennett, 1999, 164-165.
295. NUFORC.

296. NUFORC.
297. Dennett, 1999, 161-162.
298. Wilkins, 1954, 276.
299. Edwards, 1967, 28.
300. Flammonde, 371-372.
301. www.rense.com/ufo/laxrep.htm.
302. Dennett, *Uncensored UFO Reports*, Vol. I, No. 7, 22.
303. NUFORC.
304. Druffel, *MUFON UFO Journal*, Dec. 2000, #416.
305. NUFORC.
306. Blum & Blum, 76-79; Hall, 58-63; Flammonde, 210-212; Hall, 1999, 58-59; Hynek, 95-98; Ruppelt, 32-34.
307. Scully, 196.
308. Dolan, 119
309. Randles, 1985, 78.
310. Moore, 91-92.
311. Dolan, 149; Good, 1993, 73-75, 275.
312. Wilkins, 1955, 41-42.
313. Steiger & Steiger, 118-119.
314. Greer MD, 379.
315. Greer MD, 233-234.
316. Stringfield, 33.
317. Carlson, *Dispatch*, Feb 24, 2004.
318. Wilkins, 1955, 44.
319. Greer MD, 226-227.
320. Greer MD, 76-77.
321. Greer MD, 95-107.
322. Dolan, 333.
323. Greer MD, 505-506.
324. NUFORC.
325. Steiger & Steiger, 123-124.
326. Bryan, 180.
327. Greer MD, 507.
328. NUFORC.
329. NUFORC.
330. Wilkins, 1954, 268.
331. Cerny, 14.
332. Stringfield, 1978, 32.
333. Johnson, 50-51; Scully, 204-205.
334. Stringfield, 1980, 21.
335. Wilkins, 1954, 268.
336. Stringfield, 1978, 5.
337. Stringfield, 1982, 11-13.
338. Stringfield, 1989, 18-19.
339. Greer MD, 491-504.
340. Greer MD, 388-389.
341. McKenzie, 14.
342. Lorenzen & Lorenzen, 1969, 18.
343. Bowen, 143-144.
344. Adamski, 295-296; Barker, 36-58; Bowen, 146-147.
345. Wilkins, 1955, 147-148.
346. Bowen, 151; Vallee, 251-252.
347. Beckley, 93.
348. Bowen, 178.
349. Bowen, 156-157.
350. Hall, 1999, 253.
351. Vallee, 267.
352. Strieber & Strieber, 30-32.
353. Bowen, 169-174; Good, 1998, 262-265; Hall, 1988, 248-249; Hynek 1977, 210-212.
354. Haines Ph.D., 44-45.
355. Steiger, 1977, 367.
356. Vallee, 298.
357. Vallee, 326.
358. Vallee, 181-193.
359. Strieber & Strieber, 276.
360. Randle & Estes, 286.
361. Randle & Estes, 287.
362. Stringfield, 1977, 140-142.
363. Stringfield, 1977, 143-144.
364. Canlet, Feb 8, 1990.
365. Vallee, 1990, 101-103.
366. Druffel & Rogo, 159.
367. Vallee, 1980, 149-151.
368. NUFORC.
369. Dennett, 1997, 37-46.
370. Dennett, 1997, 79-88.
371. Haines Ph.D., 398-399.
372. Haines Ph.D., 399-403.
373. Dennett, 1997, 79-78.
374. Dennett, 2001, 171-184.
375. Dennett, 1999, 183-200.
376. Fiore Ph.D., 198-201, 212-230.
377. Burt, 291-297.
378. Boylan Ph.D., 67-83.
379. Druffel & Rogo, 15-60.
380. Druffel & Rogo, 36-37.
381. Druffel & Rogo, 79-83.
382. Druffel & Rogo, 166-168.
383. Druffel & Rogo, 168-203.
384. Druffel, 27-28.
385. Druffel, 1978, 16.
386. Dennett, 1997, 9-18.
387. Reiss, 31.
388. Dennett, 1999, 95-101.
389. Dennett, 1997, 145-168.
390. Steiger & Whritenour, 66.
391. Dennett, 2001, 185-197.
392. Hulse, Jan 6, 1994.
393. Vallee, 1988 6-7.
394. Boylan Ph.D., 101-117.
395. Girardot, July 4, 1996.
396. Rogo, 160-182.
397. Bryan, 237-238.
398. Fiore Ph.D., XVIII
399. Hamilton, 3-4.
400. Leir DPM, 45-47.
401. Cannon, 498-548.
402. Fiore Ph.D., 132-145.
403. Fiore Ph.D., 166-197.
404. Dennett, 1996, 36.
405. Steiger & Steiger, 40-41.
406. Dennett, 1996, 122-123.
407. Druffel, 48-50; Dennett, 1996, 108-109.
408. Fiore Ph.D., 89-131.
409. Dennett, 1996, 97.
410. Aronson, 69-76.
411. Dennett, 1996, 49.
412. Druffel, 105-108.
413. Dennett, 2001, 10-15.
414. Lindemann, 167-174, 181, 191.
415. Boylan Ph.D., 95-100.
416. Boylan Ph.D., 85-91.
417. Fiore Ph.D., 295-324.
418. Vallee, 1990, 88-93.
419. Taff, 31-32.
420. Vallee, 1990, 163-170.
421. Haines Ph.D., 394-398.
422. Steiger, 1978, 184-196.
423. Taff, 34.
424. Fiore Ph.D., 67-88.
425. Vallee, 1990, 71-78.
426. Fiore Ph.D., 34-50.
427. Druffel & Rogo, 92-94.
428. Dennett, 1999, 173-175.
429. Hall, 1988, 305.
430. Hall, 1988, 63.
431. Fiore Ph.D., 274-294.
432. Jacobs Ph.D., 1992, 69-71, 118-112.
433. DeVita, Oct 3, 1988.
434. Vallee, 1990, 79-87.
435. Steiger, 1988, 166-167.
436. Haines Ph.D., 169; Canlen, Feb 8, 1990.
437. Dennett, 1999, 3-8.
438. Dennett, 1997, 61-69.
439. Steiger, 1988, 52-56.
440. Fiore Ph.D., 51-66.
441. Druffel & Rogo, 309.
442. Hurtak Ph.D., 24-25.
443. Fiore Ph.D., 146-165.
444. Carlsberg, 31-42, 56-103.
445. Felber, 11-213.
446. Dennett, 1997, 221-256.
447. Dennett, 2001, 242-282.
448. Dennett, 1996, 103-112.
449. Dennett, 1999, 51-68.
450. Hulse, Jan 6, 1994.
451. Personal files.
452. Leir DPM, IX, 63-76, 97.
453. Leir DPM, 76-77.
454. Leir DPM, IX-XIII, 105-123, 151-171, 225.
455. Leir DPM, 143-146, 161-162.
456. Leir DPM, *MUFON UFO Journal*, #429, Jan. 2004.
457. NUFORC.
458. Spaceage, 38; Fitzgerald, Aug. 7, 1998.
459. Personal files.
460. Edwards, Eric, 13.

461. Patton, April 21, 1999.
462. Uhl, 19.
463. Reed, Aug. 30, 2000.
464. Filer, *MUFON UFO Journal*, Nov. 2000, 12.
465. NUFORC.
466. Dennett, *MUFON UFO Journal*, #428, 14-15.
467. Filer, *MUFON UFO Journal*, #410, 14.

468. Druffel, *MUFON UFO Journal*, #416, 3-7.
469. Filer, *MUFON UFO Journal*, #415, 17.
470. Filer, *MUFON UFO Journal*, #418, 15.
471. Filer, *MUFON UFO Journal*, #423, 12.
472. Filer, *MUFON UFO Journal*, #424, 13.

473. Filer, *MUFON UFO Journal*, #428, 12.
474. Filer, *MUFON UFO Journal*, #429, 14-15.
475. www.ufoevidence.org.
476. Filer, *MUFON UFO Journal*, #430, 16.

Sources

Adamski, George. *Inside the Spaceships*. Vista, California: George Adamski Foundation, 1953, 1955.

Aronson, Virginia. *Celestial Healings: Close Encounters That Cure*. New York: Signet Books, 1999.

Baker, Alan. *UFO Sightings*. New York: TV Books, 1997.

Barker, Gray. *They Knew Too Much About Flying Saucers*. New York: University Books, 1956.

Beckley, Timothy Green. *Strange Encounters: Bizarre and Eerie Contact with UFO Occupants*. New Brunswick, New Jersey: Inner Light Publications, 1992.

_____. *UFOs Among the Stars: Close Encounters of the Famous*. New Brunswick, New Jersey: Inner Light Publications, 1997.

Blum, Ralph & Judy Blum. *Beyond Earth: Man's Contact With UFOs*. New York: Bantam Books, 1974.

Bowen, Charles (Editor). *The Humanoids: A Survey of Worldwide Reports of Landings of Unconventional Aerial Objects and Their Occupants*. Chicago, Illinois: Henry Regnery Company, 1969.

Boylan Ph.D., Richard J. & Lee K. Boylan. *Close Extraterrestrial Encounters: Positive Experiences With Mysterious Visitors*. Tigard, Oregon: Wild Flower Press, 1994.

Burt, Harold E. *Flying Saucers 101: Everything You Ever Wanted to Know About Unidentified Flying Objects*. Sunland, California: A UFO Book, UFO Magazine, 2000.

Bryan, C. D. B. *Close Encounters of the Fourth Kind: Alien Abduction, UFOs and the Conference at M.I.T.* New York: Alfred Knopf, 1995.

Clark, Jerome & Loren Coleman. *The Unidentified: Notes Towards Solving the UFO Mystery*. New York: Warner Books, 1975.

Crystal, Ellen. *Silent Invasion: The Shocking Discoveries of a UFO Researcher*. New York: Paragon House, 1991.

Cannon, Dolores. *The Custodians: Beyond Abduction*. Huntsville, Arkansas: Ozark Mountain Publishing, 1999.

Carlsberg, Kim. *Beyond My Wildest Dreams: Diary of a UFO Abductee*. Santa Fe, New Mexico: Bear & Company, Inc., 1995.

Dennett, Preston. *Extraterrestrial Visitations: True Accounts of Contact*. St. Paul, Minnesota: Llewellyn Publications, 2001.

_____. *One In Forty – The UFO Epidemic: True Accounts of Close Encounters with UFOs*. Commack, New York: Kroshka Books, 1997.

_____. *UFO Healings: True Accounts of People Healed By Extraterrestrials*. Mill Spring, North Carolina: Wild Flower Press, 1996.

_____. *UFOs Over Topanga Canyon: Eyewitness Accounts of the California Sightings*. St. Paul, Minnesota: Llewellyn Publications, 1999.

Dolan, Richard M. *UFOs and the National Security State: Chronology of a Cover-up 1941-1973*. Hampton Roads Publishing Company, Inc., 2002.

Druffel, Ann. *How To Defend Yourself Against Alien Abduction*. New York: Three Rivers Press, 1998.

Druffel, Ann & D. Scott Rogo. *The Tujunga Canyon Contacts*. New York: New American Library, 1980, 1988.

Edwards, Frank. *Flying Saucers – Here and Now!* New York: Bantam Books, 1967.

_____. *Flying Saucers – Serious Business*. Secaucus, New Jersey: Citadel Press, 1966.

Felber, Ron. *Searchers: A True Story of Alien Abduction*. New York: St. Martin's Press, 1994.

Fiore Ph.D., Edith. *Encounters: A Psychologist Reveals Case Studies of Abductions by Extraterrestrials*. New York: Doubleday, 1989.

Flammonde, Paris. *UFO Exist!* New York: Ballantine Books, 1976.

Fowler, Raymond. *Casebook of a UFO Investigator*. Englewood Cliffs, New Jersey: Prentice-Hall, Inc., 1981.

Good, Timothy. *Above Top Secret: The Worldwide UFO Cover-Up*. New York: William Morrow & Company, Inc., 1988.

_____. *Alien Base: The Evidence for Extraterrestrial Colonization of Earth*. New York: Avon Books, 1998.

_____. *Alien Contact: Top-Secret UFO Files Revealed*. New York: William Morrow and Company, Inc., 1993.

Green, Gabriel. *Let's Face the Facts About Flying Saucers*. New York: Popular Library, 1967.

Greer MD, Steven M. *Disclosure: Military and Government Witnesses Reveal the Greatest Secrets in History*. Crozet, Virginia: Crossing Point Inc., 2001.

Hall, Michael David. *UFOs: A Century of Sightings*. Lakeville, Minnesota: Galde Press, 1999.

Hall, Richard. *Uninvited Guests: A Documented History of UFO Sightings, Alien Encounters and Coverups*. Santa Fe, New Mexico: Aurora Press, 1988.

Hynek, Dr. J. Allen. *The Hynek UFO Report*. New York: Dell Books, 1977.

_____. *The UFO Experience: A Scientific Inquiry*. New York: Ballantine Books, 1974.

Jacobs Ph.D., David M. *Secret Life: Firsthand Accounts of UFO Abductions.* New York: Simon Schuster, 1992.

Jessup, M. K. *The Case for the UFO.* New York: Citadel Press, 1955.

Johnson, Dewayne, with Kenn Thomas & David Hatcher Childress. *Flying Saucers Over Los Angeles: The UFO Craze of the '50s.* Kempton, Illinois: Adventures Unlimited Press, 1998.

Keyhoe, Major Donald E. (USMC, Ret.) *Aliens From Space: The Real Story of Unidentified Flying Objects.* New York: Doubleday & Company, 1973.

_____. *The Flying Saucer Conspiracy.* New York: Henry Holt and Company, Inc., 1955.

Leir DPM, Roger K. *The Aliens and the Scalpel: Scientific Proof of Extraterrestrial Implants in Humans.* Columbus, South Carolina: Granite Publishing, 1998.

Lindemann, Michael (Editor). *UFOs and The Alien Presence.* Santa Barbara, California: The 2020 Group, 1991.

Lorenzen, Coral. *Flying Saucers: The Startling Evidence of the Invasion from Outer Space.* New York: New American Library, 1962.

Lorenzen, Jim & Coral Lorenzen. *UFOs Over the Americas.* New York: New American Library, 1968.

_____. *UFOs: The Whole Story.* New York: New American Library, 1969.

Maccabee Ph.D., Bruce. *UFO-FBI Connection: The Secret History of Government's Cover-up.* St. Paul, Minnesota: Llewellyn Publications, 2000.

Macklin, Milt. *The Total UFO Story.* New York: Dale Books, 1979.

Randazzo, Joseph. *The Contactees Manuscript.* Studio City, California: UFO Library Ltd., 1993.

Randle, Kevin and Russ Estes. *Faces of the Visitors: An Illustrated Reference to Alien Contact.* New York: Simon and Schuster, 1997.

Randles, Jenny. *Beyond Explanation: Remarkable Accounts of Celebrities Who Have Witnessed the Supernatural.* New York: Bantam Books, 1985.

Reeve, Bryant and Helen. *Flying Saucer Pilgrimage.* Amherst, Wisconsin: Amherst Press, 1957.

Rogo, D. Scott (Editor). *Alien Abductions: True Cases of UFO Kidnappings.* New York: New American Library, 1980.

Rogo, D. Scott. *The Haunted Universe.* New York: New American Library, 1977.

Ruppelt, Edward J. *The Report on Unidentified Object.* New York: Ace Books, 1956.

Scully, Frank. *Behind The Flying Saucers.* New York: Henry Holt & Company, 1950.

Spaceage (The Society for the Preservation of Alien Contact Evidence and Geographic Exploration). *UFO USA: A Traveler's Guide to UFO Sightings, Abduction Sites, Crop Circles and other Unexplained Phenomena.* New York: Hyperion Books, 1999.

Steiger, Brad. *Alien Meetings.* New York: Ace Books, 1978.

_____. *Project Blue Book: The Top Secret UFO Findings Revealed.* New York: Ballantine Books, 1976.

_____. *The UFO Abductors.* New York: Berkley Books, 1988.

_____. *Strangers From the Skies.* London, England: Tandem Publishing Ltd., 1966.

Steiger, Brad and Sherry Hansen Steiger. *The Rainbow Conspiracy.* New York: Windsor Publishing Corp, 1994.

Steiger, Brad and Joan Whritenour. *Flying Saucers Are Hostile.* New York: Award Books, 1967.

_____. *Flying Saucer Invasion – Target: Earth.* New York: Award Books, 1969.

Stevens, Wendelle & August Roberts. *UFO Photographs Around the World: Volume 2.* Tucson, Arizona: UFO Photo Archives, 1985.

Strieber, Whitley & Ann Strieber (Editors). *The Communion Letters.* New York: Harper Collins, 1997.

Strieber, Whitley. *Confirmation: The Hard Evidence of Aliens Among Us.* New York: St. Martin's Press, 1998.

Stringfield, Leonard. *Inside Saucer Post ... 3-0 Blue.* Cincinnati, Ohio: Civilian Research Interplanetary Flying Objects (CRIFO), 1957.

_____. *Retrievals of the Third Kind: A Case Study of Alleged UFOs and Occupants in Military Custody.* 4412 Grove Ave, Cincinnati, Ohio: Leonard Stringfield. 1978.

_____. *Situation Red: The UFO Siege.* New York: Fawcett Crest Books, 1977.

_____. *The UFO Crash/Retrieval Syndrome – Status Report II: New Sources, New Data.* Seguin, Texas: Mutual UFO Network, 1980.

_____. *UFO Crash/Retrievals: Is the Coverup Lid Lifting? – Status Report V.* Cincinnati, Ohio: Leonard Stringfield, 1989.

Thompson, Richard L. *Alien Identities: Ancient Insights into Modern UFO Phenomenon.* San Diego, California: Govardhan Hill Publishing, 1993.

Vallee, Jacques. *Dimensions: A Casebook of Alien Contact.* Chicago, Illinois: Contemporary Books, Inc., 1988

_____. *Passport to Magonia: On UFOs, Folklore and Parallel Worlds.* Chicago, Illinois: Contemporary Books, 1969

Vallee, Jacques & Janine Vallee. *Challenge To Science: The UFO Enigma.* New York: Ballantine Books, 1966.

Wilkins, Harold T. *Flying Saucers on the Attack.* New York: Ace Books, Inc., 1954.

_____. *Flying Saucers Uncensored.* New York: Pyramid Books, 1955.

Magazines, Journals & Newspapers

Barbour Ph.D., Richmond. "Doctor Barbour." *Tribune.* San Diego, California – Dec 10, 1988. (see *UFO Newsclipping Service* [UFONS]; Editor Lucius Farish. Route 1, Box 220; Plumerville, AR 72127. May 1989, #238.)

Bogert, John. "Something's Out There, and It Claims To Have Seen a UFO." *Daily Breeze.* Torrance, California. Jan 15, 1990. (See *UFO Newsclipping Service.* [UFONS] #248, March 1990.)

Booth, D. Wade. "UFOs No Joke To Local Believers: Residents Phone In Mysterious Sightings." *Blade Citizen.* Oceanside, California – Sept. 5, 1993. (See UFONS, Oct. 1993, #291.)

Canlen, Brae. "Maybe What You Saw Was A UFO." *Reader.* San Diego, California – Feb. 8, 1990. (See UFONS, April 1990, #249.)

Carlson, Peter. "Another Book Advances Unlikely Tale of Ike-Met-ET." *Dispatch.* Columbus, Ohio – Feb. 24, 2004. (See UFONS, #416, March 2004.)

Cassidy, Craig. "Close Encounters of a Local Kind: Accountant Keeps X-Files." *Leader.* Oakdale, California – Dec. 27, 1995. (See UFONS, Feb. 1996, #319.)

Cerny, Paul C. "1947 Crashed Saucer Report." *MUFON UFO Journal.* Sequin, Texas: Mutual UFO Network. #156, Feb. 1981.

Chawkins, Steve. "Reports of Strange Phenomena Knock Socks Off County Residents." *News Mirror.* Moorpark, California – Oct. 6, 1994. (See UFONS, Nov. 1994, #304.)

Ciborowski, Anna. "UFO Fleet Hovers Over Desert Marine Base." *UFO Universe.* New York: Charlotte Magazine Corp., June/July 1991, Vol. 1, No. 3.

Davis, Carolyn. "Mohave Desert Fountain of Youth." *Fate.* St Paul, Minnesota: Llewellyn, February 1997.

Dennett, Preston. "The Chatsworth UFO Epidemic." *UFO Universe.* Vol. 2, No. 1, Spring 1992.

_____. "Contactee: Firsthand." *UFO Magazine.* Los Angeles, California: California UFO. Vol. 5, No. 5, Sept.-Oct. 1990.

_____. "Ufology Profile: New Paranormal Talk Show Host." *MUFON UFO Journal.* December 2003, #428.

_____. "UFOs Over Topanga." *Messenger.* Topanga Canyon: Phoenix Rising Inc. Vol. 12, No. 25, Dec. 1988-Jan. 1989.

_____. "Three Tales of Terror." *UFO Universe.* New York: Charlotte Magazine Corp, June/July 1991.

DeVita, Lyla. "They're Heeere! Who Are They?" *Business Times.* San Francisco, California – Oct. 3, 1988. (See UFONS, Nov. 1988, #232.)

Drake, Phil. "Sky is Falling?" *Leader.* Burbank, California. May 28, 1988. (See UFONS, No. 230, Sept. 1988.)

Druffel, Ann. "Black Triangle Investigated in California." *MUFON UFO Journal,* #416, December 2002.

_____. "California Report: Entities and Their Carriages." *MUFON UFO Journal,* #129, August 1978.

Edwards, Eric. "California Sighting Leaves Driver Perplexed." *MUFON UFO Journal,* Nov. 2000, #391.

Edwards, Ron. "Unexplained Naval Encounters." *Unsolved UFO Sightings.* New York: GCR Publishing, Vol. 4, No. 1.

Enterprise, Simi Valley (staff). "Weird-sounding UFO Seen By Two." *Enterprise.* Simi Valley, California – May 27, 1988. (see UFONS, July 1988, #228).

Filer, George A. "Filer's Files: California Disc." *MUFON UFO Journal.* Nov. 2000, #391.

_____. "Filer's Files: California Egg-shaped Objects." Morrison, Colorado: *MUFON UFO Journal* #430. February 2004.

_____. "Filer's Files: California Golden Sphere." Morrison, Colorado: *MUFON UFO Journal* #429. January 2004.

_____. "Filer's Files: Cigar-shaped Objects in California." Morrison, Colorado: *MUFON UFO Journal* #423, July 2003.

_____. "Filer's Files: Flying Triangle in California." Morrison, Colorado: *MUFON UFO Journal* #410, June 2002 & #424, August 2003

_____. "Filer's Files: Objects Reported in California." *MUFON UFO Journal,* #415, November 2002.

_____. "Filer's Files: Triangles In California." *MUFON UFO Journal* #418, February 2003.

_____. "Filer's Files: UFO Video In California." Morrison, Colorado: *MUFON UFO Journal* #428, December 2003.

Fitzgerald, Michael. "Tracy UFO Rumor Hits Web Speed." *Record.* Stockton, California, August 7, 1998 (See UFONS, Oct. 1998, #351: 1.)

Girardot, Frank C. "UFO Movie Independence Day Has Believers Looking Up." *Daily Tribune.* West Covina, California, July 4, 1996.

Grant, Michael. "Michael Grant." *Union.* San Diego, California. Oct. 3, 1989. (See UFONS., Dec. 1989, #245.)

Gribble, Bob. "Looking Back: 1975." *MUFON UFO Journal* #266, June 1990.

Gutilla, Peter. "Contactee: Firsthand." *California UFO*. Los Angeles, California: California UFO, Vol. 2, No. 2, 1987.

Hall, Rich. "Northern California UFO Flurry." *MUFON UFO Journal*. #167, Jan. 1982.

Hamilton, Bill. "Light Show Over Lancaster." *MUFON UFO Journal*. Seguin, Texas: Mutual UFO Network. #286, Feb. 1992.

Hassel Ph.D., William. "Multiple Sightings of Triangular UFOs." *MUFON UFO Journal*. Jan. 1982, #167.

Hickox, Katie and Jeffrey Miller. "Neighbors Encounter Unidentifiable Object." *Orange County Register.* Santa Ana, California – Feb. 10, 1995. (See UFONS, March 1995, #308).

Howard, James S. "UFOs in the Valley." *Bee*. Fresno, California – May 18, 1997. (See UFONS, Aug 1997, #337: 10.)

Hulse, Jane. "UFO Abduction – Survivor's Grim Recollection." *Los Angeles Times*. Los Angeles, California, Jan. 6, 1994. (See also: UFONS, Feb. 1994, #295.)

Hurtak Ph.D., James. "Close Encounters of the Multiple-Abduction Kind." *International UFO Library Magazine*. Studio City, California: UFO Library, Vol. 1, No. 4, 1992.

Jarvis, Michael T. "Sierra Sightings Investigated by UFO Group: Two Saw Something That 'Made No Sound.'" *Review Harold*. Mammoth Lakes, California – Dec. 15, 1994. (See UFONS, Feb. 1995, #307).

Jones, Marie and Laura Miller. "Vista, California Flap." *MUFON UFO Journal*. Seguin, Texas: Mutual UFO Network, April 1995, #324.

Leir, Dr. Roger. "Winter Sightings In Ventura County." *MUFON UFO Journal*. Feb. 1997, #346.

Mattingly, Woods. "MUFON Forum." *MUFON UFO Journal,* Morrison, Colorado: Mutual UFO Network, No. 410, June 2002.

McKenzie, Hal. "Mystery Craft Haunt California Air Bases." *The Missing Link*. Federal Way, Washington: UFO Contact Center International. #122, Vol. 12, November 1992.

Moore, William L. "Ike and the Aliens." *Far Out*. Beverly Hills, California: LFP Inc., Fall 1992, Vol. 1, No. 1.

Olsen, William. "Next Stop ... Giant Rock." *UFO Universe*. New York: Charlotte Magazine Corp, Spring 1992, Vol. 2, No. 1.

Patton, Gregg. "UFO Puts on a Show in Rialto." *Sun*. San Bernardino, California, April 21, 1999.

Rasmussen, Cecilia. "LA Battle Launched a Golden Age of UFOs." *LA Times*. Los Angeles, California – Dec. 17, 2000. (See UFONS, Mar. 2001, #380.)

Reed, Tony. "UFO? HVL Power Outage? An Unusual Sunday Night." *Observer-American*. Clearlake Highlands, California, Aug. 30, 2000.

Reiss, Andy. "Contactee: Firsthand." *California UFO*. Los Angeles, California: California UFO, Jan./Feb. 1987.

Steinberg, Debbie. "Flying Saucers." *Anza Valley Outlook*. Anza, California, June 2, 1989. (See UFONS, July 1989, #240.)

Taff, Barry E. "Close to Home Abductions." *Search Magazine*. Rosholt, Wisconsin: Owl Press. Fall 1991, #188.

Uhl, Malcolm. "California Sighting Similar to One Reported Following Day." *MUFON UFO Journal*. November 2000, #391.

Valaitis, Robin. "Van Driver Reports Sighting UFO in Sky Over Lancaster." *Antelope Valley Press*. Palmdale, California. Aug. 4, 1988. (See UFONS, No. 232, Nov. 1988.)

Wronge, Yomi S. "No Alien Concept." *Breeze*. Costa Mesa, California, July 3, 1997. (See UFONS, Aug. 1997, #337: 6.)

Websites

www.mufon.com (Mutual UFO Network. Hotline: 800-836-2166)
www.nuforc.org (National UFO Reporting Center. Hotline: 206-722-3000)
www.prestondennett.com (Preston Dennett website.)
www.ufoevidence.org (Private UFO Research Organization)
www.rense.com (UFO/paranormal website)

Contact

To contact the author, please email him at prestone@pacbell.net, or write c/o the publisher.